D0742434

THE

BEST

AMERICAN SHORT STORIES

1971

THE

BEST

AMERICAN SHORT STORIES

1971

&

the Yearbook of
the American Short Story

EDITED BY

MARTHA FOLEY

AND

DAVID BURNETT

Houghton Mifflin Company
Boston
1971

FIRST PRINTING C

ISBN: 0-395-12709-2
LIBRARY OF CONGRESS CATALOG CARD NUMBER: 16-11387
PRINTED IN THE UNITED STATES OF AMERICA

"Diesel" by Don Mitchell. First published in *Shenandoah*. Reprinted by permission of Little, Brown and Company from the book *Thumb Tripping* by Don Mitchell. Copyright © 1970 by Don Mitchell.

"The Decline and Fall of Officer Fergerson" by Marion Montgomery. First published in *The Georgia Review*. Copyright © 1966 by Marion Montgomery.

"Magic" by Wright Morris. First published in *The Southern Review*. Copyright © 1970 by Wright Morris.

"The Gift Bearer" by Philip F. O'Connor. First published in *The Southern Review*. Copyright © 1970 by Philip F. O'Connor.

"Requa I" by Tillie Olsen. First published in *The Iowa Review* under the title "Requa." Copyright © 1970 by Tillie Olsen.

"Shirt Talk" by Ivan Prashker. First published in *Harper's* magazine. Copyright © 1970 by Ivan Prashker.

"In Late Youth" by Norman Rush. First published in *Epoch* (Fall, 1970). Copyright © 1970 by Cornell University.

"The Somebody" by Danny Santiago. First published in *Redbook* magazine, February 1970. Copyright © 1970 by Danny Santiago.

"Xavier Fereira's Unfinished Book: Chapter One" by Jonathan Strong. First published in *TriQuarterly*. Copyright © 1970 by *TriQuarterly*.

"The Klausners" by Leonard Tushnet. First published in *Prairie Schooner* (Spring, 1970). Copyright © 1970 by the University of Nebraska Press.

"Bloodflowers" by W. D. Valgardson. First published in *The Tamarack Review*. Copyright © 1970 by W. D. Valgardson.

"The Suitor" by L. Woiwode. First published in *McCall's* magazine, January 1970. Copyright © 1970 by L. Woiwode.

To
Tillie Olsen

Acknowledgments

GRATEFUL ACKNOWLEDGMENT for permission to reprint the stories in this volume is made to the following:

The editors of *Epoch, Esquire, Evergreen Review, Georgia Review, Harper's Magazine, Hudson Review, Iowa Review, McCall's Magazine, New American Review, Northwest Review, Playboy, Prairie Schooner, Redbook, Shenandoah, The Southern Review, Tamarack Review, TriQuarterly, The Yale Review;* and to Russell Banks, Hal Bennett, James Blake, Jack Cady, Robert Canzoneri, Albert Drake, William Eastlake, Beth Harvor, David Madden, Don Mitchell, Marion Montgomery, Wright Morris, Philip F. O'Connor, Tillie Olsen, Ivan Prashker, Norman Rush, Danny Santiago, Jonathan Strong, Leonard Tushnet, W. D. Valgardson, L. Woiwode.

Foreword

SPLENDID SHORT STORIES have appeared this year and there has been a number of interesting developments. One of the latter is the proliferation of the vignette. Long popular in France, the vignette seldom has been seen in America. It is, as the name implies, a literary tendril, a very brief bit of writing. Sometimes it is only a paragraph, sometimes several paragraphs, or it can be even a page or two. Reading a vignette is a little like looking into a window and glimpsing for a moment a person or persons caught in a situation. A better comparison may be that a vignette, when well done, can have the same emotional impact as the haiku. W. S. Merwin is probably the best-known writer of vignettes in this country, and a South American writer of vignettes, Jorge Luis Borges, has stimulated wider interest in the form.

Parodies also have become popular. *The New Yorker* has published a number by such writers as Donald Barthelmé and Roger Angell. *Satire,* published at State College in Oneonta, New York, has delighted in them for some time. It may be that the horror of the present time cannot be faced. One wants to weep but one cannot, and instead finds a sad kind of joy by parodying the work of others.

Reading innumerable stories which either center around dreams or have dreams as an essential part, one might get the impression American writers have been taking their typewriters to bed with them. I wish I had started counting at the beginning of the year the number of such stories, both by well-known writers and newcomers.

It is really a literary phenomenon and I have no explanation for it.

While there have been many novels with homosexual or lesbian characters, comparatively few such stories have appeared in magazines until this year. One of those we liked the most is reprinted here. It is "The Widow, Bereft" by James Blake, which appeared in *Esquire* and is set in a penitentiary.

Tillie Olsen, one of the finest of American storywriters, but whose stories have been much too few, has been one of those authors experimenting with typographical appearance and spacing. Her story "Requa I," from a new magazine, the *Iowa Review,* like quite a few others this year concerns a child who had lost his beloved mother. Perhaps the Women's Liberation movement is having an effect on the viciousness with which "Mom" has been attacked in fiction for many years. Certainly it has done something to that *béte noire* of women, Hugh Hefner. For the first time, a woman has had a story in *Playboy.* That milestone was achieved by Mary McCarthy.

It has always been the contention of this editor that there is no such thing as a "woman's story" or "a man's story." Or a "child's story." A good story can be enjoyed by any literate person. Thus there is no good "black story." Certainly the writing of Richard Wright, James Baldwin, and Eldridge Cleaver has universal appeal. Let's not forget either such black women writers as Zora Neale Hurson, dead much too young, Ann Petry, and others. One of the most original new black authors to appear on the American literary scene is Hal Bennett, author of "Dotson Gerber Resurrected." I hope readers of this anthology will enjoy the humor and fantasy of the story as much as the editors did.

So many superb stories by foreign writers published in American magazines cannot be reprinted in a book with the title "American." Fortunately, Canadian authors can be included and there are some fine ones. It was legally established in a court suit years ago that Canadians are Americans and entitled to that name as much as any citizens of the United States.

Among foreign authors who have appeared in American magazines and whom the editors of this book would gladly reprint if they could are V. S. Pritchett, Sean O'Faolain, Anthony West, Ivy Litvinov, Christina Stead, Nadine Gordimer, Jorge Luis Borges, Dan Jacobson, Samuel Beckett, Sylvia Townsend Warner, Ted Walker, and Doris Lessing.

The bad news has been left until the last. The *Kenyon Review* — one of the most important magazines this country has ever seen or ever will see — is no more. Infuriating as might have been some of its theories of the "new criticism" (in my opinion), the magazine never faltered in its respect for the highest standards in literature, and the short stories it published were usually magnificent.

I am grateful to the editors who have kept this anthology supplied with copies of their magazines, and to their authors for generously granting us reprint rights. The editor of any new magazine is urged to send copies to us.

The editors and staff of Houghton Mifflin are entitled to gratitude for their help. Finally, tribute is paid to the memory of Edward J. O'Brien, who founded this anthology.

Martha Foley
Stonington, Connecticut

Contents

THE BEST AMERICAN SHORT STORIES 1971

RUSSELL BANKS

With Ché in New Hampshire

(FROM NEW AMERICAN REVIEW)

SO HERE I AM, still wandering. All over the face of the earth. Mexico, Central America, South America. Then Africa. Working my way north to the Mediterranean, resting for a season in the Balearic Islands. Then Iberia, all of Gaul, the British Isles. Scandinavia. Then I show up in the Near East, disappearing as suddenly and unexpectedly as I appeared. Reappearing in Moscow. Before I can be interviewed, I have dropped out of sight again, showing up farther east, photographed laughing with political prisoners outside Vladivostok, getting into a taxi in Kyoto, lying on a beach near Melbourne, drinking in a nightclub in Honolulu (a club known for its underworld clientele). Chatting amiably with Indians in Peru. And then I drop out of sight altogether . . .

All this from the file they have on me in Washington. They know that somehow I am dangerous to them, but they are unable to determine in what way I am dangerous, for everything is rumor and suspicion, and I am never seen except when alone or in the cheerful company of harmless peasant-types. My finances are easily explained: I have none. I never own anything that I can't carry with me and can't leave out in the rain, and I am a hitchhiker wherever I go. I accept no money whatsoever from outside sources that might be considered suspicious. Occasionally I find employment for a few weeks at some menial job — as a dockhand in Vera Cruz, a truck-driver in North Africa, a construction worker in Turkey — and occasionally I accept lavish gifts from American women traveling to forget their wrecked lives at home.

Okay, so here I am again, wandering, and everything is different. Except that I am alone. Everything else is different. And then one day, late in spring, I turn up in Crawford, New Hampshire. Home. Alone, as usual. I'm about thirty-five, say. No older. A lot has happened to me in the interim: when I step down from the Boston-to-Montreal bus at McAllister's General Store, I am walking with an evident limp. My left leg, say, doesn't bend at the knee. Everything I own is in the duffle bag I carry, and I own nothing that cannot be left out in the rain. I want it that way . . .

Rerun my getting off the bus. The cumbersome Greyhound turns slowly off Route 28 just north of Pittsfield, where the small, hand-lettered sign points CRAWFORD ½ MI., and then rumbles down into the heart of the valley, past the half dozen, century-old, decaying houses, past Conway's Esso station to McAllister's GULF station and general store, where the bus driver applies the air brakes to his vehicle, which has been coasting since it turned off Route 28, and it hisses to a stop.

The door pops open in front of me, and I pitch my duffle down to the ground and then ease my pain-wracked body down the steps and out the door to where my duffle has landed on the ground . . .

A few old men and Bob McAllister . . . A few old men and Bob McAllister, like turtles, sit in the late-morning sun on the roofless front porch that runs the width of the store building. Two of the old men, one on each side of the screen door, are seated on straight-backed, soda-fountain chairs, which they lean back against the wall. One old man is squatting and scratches on the board floor with a penknife. The others (for there should be more than three) are arrayed in various postures across the porch.

Even though the sun feels warm against my skin, the air is cool, reminding me of the winter that has just ended, the dirty remnants of snow in shady corners between buildings, snow that melted, finally, just last week, and the mushy dirt roads that are beginning to dry out at last. The old men seated on the stagelike platform in front of me stare down at me without embarrassment. This is because they don't recognize me. Through the glass behind their heads I can see the semidarkness of the store's interior and the shape of Alma McAllister's perpetually counting head. She is stationed at the check-out counter, which is actually a kitchen table. Beyond her, I can pick out the shapes of three or four parallel rows of canned foods, the meat locker, and the large refrigeration unit that holds all of McAllister's dairy products, frozen foods, packaged bacon and sausage, eggs, cold drinks, and beer. And farther back in the store, I can make out the dim shapes of hoses, buckets, garden tools, work clothes, fishing rods, and the other miscellaneous items that finish out the store's inventory — Bob McAllister's wild guess at the material needs of his neighbors.

The old men staring at me. They are wondering who the hell I might be. They don't recognize me at all, not yet anyway, although I was able to recognize them as soon as I could see their faces. It is I who have changed, not they, and I have thought of them many times in the last few years, whereas they probably have not once thought of me.

Bob McAllister, of course, is there. And old Henry Davis, he would have to be there too. His sister died back in 1967, I recall as soon as I can see his sun-browned, leathery face, remembering that I learned of the event from a letter my mother wrote to me while I was in Florida waiting to hear from Ché.

The others, now. There is John Alden, who claims he is a direct descendant of the original John and Priscilla Alden. He is. Gaunt, white-maned, and silent, except to speak of the time, and always dressed in a black suit, tobacco-stained white shirt, and black necktie, and continually drawing from his pocket the large gold watch that the Boston & Maine Railroad gave him when he retired back in 1962, drawing it out and checking its time against anybody else's — the radio's, the church's, Bob McAllister's Timex, anybody's who happens to walk into the store.

"What time you got, Henry?"

"I got ten-seventeen, John."

"Check it again, Henry, 'cause I got ten twenty-one."

"Thanks, John, thanks a lot. Hell of a watch you got there. It ain't ever wrong, is it?"

"Not yet it ain't. Not yet."

There are two or three others. There is Bob McAllister, who comes over to the bus as he has done every day for over twenty years and takes the bundle of Boston newspapers from the driver. There is Henry Davis, who plowed the few acres that my father cultivated every year with corn and potatoes and the meadows that were hayed when I was a child — but that was before Henry and his horses got too old and Pa had to go to Concord and buy a Ford tractor to replace Henry. And there is John Alden, who is a direct descendant of John and Priscilla. And there would be Dr. Cotton, too, because it's about five years from now, and Dr. Cotton has retired, no doubt, has left his entire practice to that young Dr. Annis from Laconia, the new fellow from Laconia my mother told me about in her letters . . .

That's four, which is enough. They don't recognize me. Although when Bob McAllister lifts himself down from the porch and crosses between the GULF gasoline pumps to the bus to receive the Boston papers, he stares at me quizzically as he passes, seeming to think that he knows me from some place and time, but he can't remember from where or when, so he merely nods, for courtesy's sake as well as safety's, and strolls by.

I bend down and pick up my duffle, heave it easily to my right shoulder — three years in the jungles of Guatemala have left me with one leg crippled and with deep scars on my face and mind forever. But the years have also toughened me, and my arms and back are as hard as rock maple.

Close-up of the scar on my face. It starts, thin and white, like a scrap of white twine, high up on my left temple, and then runs jaggedly down to my cheekbone, where it broadens and jigs suddenly back and down, eventually disappearing below my ear lobe. Naturally, I am reluctant to talk about how it happened, but anyone who cares to can see that it is the result of a machete blow, and the fact that I am alive at all — however scarred — is a clear indication of what happened to the man with the machete.

The driver closes the door to his bus and releases the air brakes hurriedly, for he is no doubt relieved to be rid of a passenger whose silent intensity had somehow unnerved him right from the moment he left the Park Square Greyhound Bus Terminal in Boston until the moment when the man, without saying a word to anyone, not even to the fat Canadian sitting next to him, finally rose from his seat, which was immediately behind the driver, and stepped down in Crawford. The driver closes the door to his bus, releases the air brakes hurriedly, and the big, slab-sided, silver vehicle pulls away, heads back to Route 28 for Alton Bay and Laconia, and then north to Montreal . . .

The cool, dry air feels wonderful against my face. It's been too long. I've been away from this comforting, life-giving air too long this time. I had forgotten its clarity, the way it handles the light — gently, but with crispness and efficiency. I had forgotten the way a man, if he gets himself up high enough, can see through the air that fills the valley between him and a single tree or chimney or gable which is actually miles away from him, making the man feel like a hawk floating thousands of feet above the earth's surface, looping lazily in a cloudless sky, hour after hour, while tiny creatures huddle in warm, dark niches below and wait in terror for him to grow weary of the hunt and drift away . . .

Leaving Mexico City. As I boarded the Miami-bound jet, I promised myself that if I could make it all the way back home, this time I would not be leaving again. I renew this promise now while walking up the road, moving away from McAllister's store and the silent chorus on the porch, past the three or four houses that sit ponderously on either side of the road north of the bus stop and south of the white Congregational church and the dirt road just beyond the church on the left, the road that leads to the northern, narrow end of the valley. I am limping. I am limping, but while my disabled leg slows me somewhat, it doesn't tire me, and so I think nothing of walking the three and one half miles from McAllister's in the village to my father's house at the north end of the valley. With Ché in Guatemala I have walked from the Izabal Lake to San Agustín Acasaquastlán, crossing the highest peaks in Guatemala, walking, machete in hand, through clotted jungle for twenty days without stopping, walking from sunrise till sunset every day, eating only in the morning before leaving camp and at night just before falling into an exhausted sleep. We never, in three years, set up a fixed camp, and that is why the Guatemalan Army, with their CIA and American army advisers, never caught up with us. We kept on the move constantly, like tiny fish in an enormous, green sea . . .

I know that receding behind me, shrinking smaller and smaller in the distance, there are four old men who are trying to figure out who I am, where I've come from, and why I have come from there to Crawford. They hope to stumble onto the first — who I am — and from that to infer the other two. As soon as one of them, probably Dr. Cotton (he would be the youngest of the four, the one with the most reliable memory), figures out who I am, and then that I have come home to Crawford again, maybe this time for good, as soon as they have discovered that much of my identity, they will try to discover the rest — where I have been and what I have been doing all these years.

"How long's it been since he last took off, Doc? Five, six years?"

"No, no, it's five years, actually. As I recall now, it was back in sixty-seven he took off for parts unknown. Right after he come up from Florida to see his dad, as I recall it, who was all laid up with a heart attack, y' know. *Angina pectoris,* if my memory serves me correctly, was what it was. You remember when ol' Sam took sick, don't you? Paralyzed him almost completely. And the boy, he drove all the way up from Florida soon's he heard his dad was in trouble, even quit his fancy job with this big advertising company down there and everything. Just to make sure his dad was okay. Now that's a son for you. A damn sight better than most of the sons these days, let me tell you. Seems the boy stayed around for a few weeks till his dad got back on his feet, y' know, and then he took off again. Nobody around here knew where he went to, though. Just dropped out of sight . . ."

"How 'bout Boston, Doc? Used to live down in Boston, I heard. You think he went to Boston?"

"Naw, John, we'd a known it if he'd a been in Boston all these years. Word gets out, y' know."

"Wal, Doc, who knows? Maybe this time the boy's come home for good. He sure looks like he's been through hell, though, don't he?"

"Smashed his patella, I'd say, Bob, though I couldn't offer as to how, or how he picked up that scar on his face. It sure does change his looks, though. I'd a hardly recognized him if it wasn't for the fact that I was the one who brought him into the world in the first place."

"I'll tell you, Doc, I'm hoping this time the boy's come home for good, 'cause the family'll be needin' him up there."

"They sure as hell do, Bob. And by gawd, we need him down here, too . . ."

No. Erase that remark. Wipe it out. Doc would never think such a thing, let alone say it, and Bob McAllister hates and distrusts me, I'm sure. Won't even give me credit for a dollar's worth of gasoline.

Be damned if I want to help those people out of their misery. If Doc Cotton ever saw me getting off a bus in Crawford, limping, scarred, back in town again after a mysterious three-year absence (five?), he'd fear for my family's peace of mind, and, panic-stricken, he'd be on the phone, as soon as I was safely out of sight, warning them to be careful . . .

But that's okay. That's okay now, because everything is different. I'm about thirty-five, say. Maybe thirty-six, but no older. I'm about thirty-five, say, and I'm wearing khaki trousers, a white shirt, open at the throat, and high brown work shoes that have steel toes. My hair is cut fairly short, and my face and the backs of my hands are deeply tanned. I look like a construction worker, except for the limp and the scar. And when you are a tall, cold-looking man who looks like a construction worker, except that you limp badly and bear a cruel machete scar across your face, what do people think? They think they're looking at a veteran of guerrilla warfare, that's what they think . . .

Okay. So here's these four old turtles sitting in the sun on McAllister's porch, and the Boston-to-Montreal bus wheezes up, stopping ostensibly to let off the Boston papers as usual, but instead of just the wire-bound packet of Boston *Globes*, *Herald-Travelers*, and *Record-Americans* being pitched out the door, I get off too, first chucking my duffle bag down the steps ahead of me. The bus driver, moving quickly to give me a hand, is sent back to his seat by my giving him a fierce, prideful glare, which silently says to him: *I can make it on my own.* "Okay . . ." he says, almost calling me *Soldier,* but suddenly thinking better of it, sensing somehow that I have fought not for a nation, but for a people, and thus have worn no uniform, have worn only what the people themselves, the peasants, wear . . .

I like the idea of not having a car, of arriving by bus, carrying everything I own in a single duffle bag and owning nothing that can't be left out in the rain. No household goods are carried on *my* back, no sir. Just a duffle, US Army surplus, brought all the way home from the jungles of Guatemala. And inside it — two changes of clothing, a copy (in a waterproof plastic bag) of Régis Debray's *Révolution dans la Révolution?,* which has been as a bible to me. Also in a waterproof plastic bag, the notes for my book (Did I come back to Crawford for this, to write my own book, a book about my experiences with Ché in Guatemala, a book which in actuality would be a theoretical textbook thinly disguised as a memoir and which eventually, it is hoped, would replace the writings of Debray, Guevara, Chairman Mao, and even Lenin?). And the ten essentials: maps (of Belknap County, New Hampshire, obtainable from the National Geological Survey, Washington, D.C. 20540), a good compass, a flashlight, sunglasses, emergency rations (raisins, chickpeas, and powdered eggs), waterproofed matches, a candle for fire starting, a US Army surplus blanket, a pocketknife, and a small first-aid kit. That's it. Everything I own in the world is there. The ten essentials. No, I need to have another: I need one of those small one-man Boy Scout cooking kits. And maybe I should have a gun, just a small handgun. A black, snub-nosed .38, maybe. I would've had trouble, though, with the customs officials in Mexico City — especially since they would've been alerted that I might be coming through and would be carrying something important and dangerous, like secret instructions from Ché to supporters and sympathizers inside the US. Maybe I should leave Mexico from Mérida, crossing overland from Guatemala through the low jungles of the Yucatan in hundred-degree heat, walking all the way, and then suddenly appearing in the line of American tourists checking out of Mérida for Miami. It's when you arrive inside the United States that they check your baggage. They never bother you when you *leave* a place, only when you come back.

Say I picked up the gun *after* I arrived in Miami, picked it up in a pawn shop. Say I managed to lose the agent assigned to follow me, quickly ducked into an obscure little pawn shop in the west end of the city, and purchased a .38 revolver for twenty-seven fifty. Later, at the airport coffee shop, I spot the agent. He's seated three tables from me, pretending to read his paper while waiting, like me, for his plane to New York. He pretends to read, and he watches my every move. I get up from my chair, leave a small tip, walk over to him and say, quietly: "I'm leaving now." Then smile and leave. Probably they would arrest me at some point during my journey, but they would be unable to muster proof that I have been working in Guatemala with Ché for these three — no five — years. They lost me in Mexico City back in '67, and so far as they can say for sure, that is, so far as they can legally prove, I've been in Mexico all that time. At least twice or three times a year, I slip back across the border to make my presence in Mexico known to the officials — I simply let myself be seen conspicuously drunk in a well-known restaurant — and then, taking off at night from a field near Cuernavaca in a small Beechcraft Bonanza piloted by a mercenary, a gunrunner from New Orleans, I return to the jungles of Guatemala. I am valuable to Ché for many reasons, one of which is my American citizenship, and so it is very important that I do not become *persona non grata,* at least not officially. "Conejo," Ché calls to me, using my code name. "Conejo, you are valuable man to me y también a la revolución como soldad, pero también como norteamericano usted es muy importante, y esa noche hay que volver a México y estar borracho en los restaurantes. ¿Comprendes, amigo?"

"Sí, Ché, yo comprendo." We embrace each other manfully, the way Latins will, and I leave with the pilot, slashing through the jungle to his plane, which he has cleverly camouflaged at the edge of a small clearing several miles down the valley from where we have camped . . .

Now, three thousand miles away. I have just disembarked. From a Greyhound bus in Crawford, New Hampshire. I stand next to the idling bus for a few moments, gazing passively at the scene before me, and I become immobilized upon receiving simultaneously the blows of so much that is familiar and so much that subtly has grown strange to me. I remember, upon seeing them, things that I didn't know I had forgotten, and thus I experience everything that comes into my sight as if somehow it were characterized both as brand-new, virginally so, and yet also as clearly, reassuringly, familiar. It would be the way my own face, my very own face, appeared to me when, after having grown a beard and worn it for almost two years, I went into a barber shop and asked to have it shaved off. And because I had to lie back in the chair and look up at the ceiling while the barber first snipped with scissors and then shaved with a razor, I was unable to watch my beard gradually disappearing, with my face concurrently appearing from behind it. And when I was swung back down into a seated position and was allowed to peer at my face for the first time in several years, I was stunned by the familiarity of my own face, and also by the remarkable strangeness of it.

HAL BENNETT

Dotson Gerber Resurrected

(FROM PLAYBOY)

WE SAW THE HEAD of Mr. Dotson Gerber break ground at approximately nine o'clock on a bright Saturday morning in March out near our collard patch, where Poppa had started to dig a well and then filled it in. Of course, none of us knew then that the shock of red hair and part of a head sprouting from the abandoned well belonged to Mr. Dotson Gerber, who'd been missing from his farm since early last fall. We were black folk, and the fact that a white man like Mr. Dotson Gerber was missing from his home was of small importance to us. Unless that white man suddenly started growing from the ground near our collard patch like Mr. Dotson Gerber was doing now for Momma, my sister Millicent and me. We'd come running because of a commotion the chickens had made, thinking that a lynx or a weasel might have got after them. And found Mr. Dotson Gerber's head instead.

"Good Jesus," Millicent said, "I do think I'm going to faint." Millicent had been prone to fainting ever since she'd seen two black men kissing behind some boxes in the factory where she worked. Now she was getting ready to faint again. But Momma snatched her roughly by the apron.

"Girl, you *always* fainting, you don't hardly give other people a chance." And Momma fainted dead away, which left Millicent conscious for the time being and looking very desperate. But she didn't faint and I was glad of that, because I certainly didn't want to be alone with Mr. Dotson Gerber sprouting from the ground. A dozen or so chickens were still raising a ruckus about the unexpected appearance of a white man's head where they were accustomed to pecking for grain. Screeching at the top of her voice, Millicent shooed the chickens away while I tugged Momma into the shade and propped her against the barn. Then we went back to looking at Mr. Dotson Gerber.

I have mentioned the well that Poppa started to dig because it was apparent that Mr. Dotson Gerber had been planted standing up in that hole. Which, of course, explained why his head was growing out first. Although, as I have said, neither Millicent nor I knew then that what we were looking at belonged to Mr. Dotson Gerber. It took Poppa to tell us that.

He came riding on Miss Tricia from the stable, where he'd been saddling her. "Why you children making all that noise out there?" he called from the road. When we didn't answer, he yanked the reins and rode Miss Tricia toward us. "Millicent, was that you I heard hollering? What you all doing out here?" Poppa asked again.

"There's a white man growing from the ground," I said.

Poppa nearly fell off Miss Tricia. "A *what?*"

"A white man. He's growing from that hole where you started to dig the well."

"I *know* I'm going to faint now," Millicent said. And she wrapped her hands around her throat as though to choke herself into unconsciousness. But Poppa and I both ignored her and she was too curious to faint right then. So she stopped choking herself and watched Poppa jump down from Miss Tricia to inspect the head. He walked all around it, poking it from time to time with his shoe.

"That'd be Mr. Dotson Gerber," he finally pronounced.

By this time, Momma had revived and was watching Poppa with the rest of us. "Poppa, how you know that's Mr. Dotson Gerber? Why, he could be any old white man! There's hardly enough of him above ground for anybody to recognize."

"I know it's Mr. Dotson Gerber because I planted him there," Poppa said. He told us how Mr. Gerber had come out to the farm last fall to inspect the well that he was digging, which had been part of Mr. Gerber's job here in Alcanthia County. "He kept calling me Uncle," Poppa said, with some bitterness. "I told him respectfully that my name is Walter Beaufort, or that he could even call me *Mr.* Beaufort, if he'd a mind to. After all, things have changed so much nowadays, I told him I certainly wouldn't think any less of him if he called me Mr. Beaufort. I told him that black people don't appreciate white folks' calling us Uncle any longer. But he just kept on calling me that, so I hit him on the head with my shovel." We all looked at Mr. Dotson Gerber's head; and it was true that there was a wide gash in his skull that could only have been caused by a shovel. "I didn't intend to kill him," Poppa said. "I just wanted to teach him some respect. After all, things *have* changed. But when I found out he was dead, I stood him up in that hole I was digging and covered him up. I never expected to see him growing out of the ground this way."

"Well, that's not the problem now," Millicent said. "The problem now is, what are we going to do with him?"

Momma moved a step closer to Mr. Gerber and cautiously poked him with her toe. "If it weren't for that red hair," she said, "somebody might mistake him for a cabbage."

"He don't look like no cabbage to me," Millicent said. It was clear that she was annoyed because Momma had fainted before she'd had a chance to.

"I didn't say he looked like a cabbage," Momma said. "I said somebody might mistake him for a cabbage."

"He too red to be a cabbage," Millicent said stubbornly. "Anyway, we still ought to do something about him. It just don't look right, a white man growing like this on a colored person's farm. Suppose some white people see it?"

The 9:10 Greyhound to Richmond went by then. Momma and Poppa shaded their eyes to watch it speed down the far road; but Millicent and I were of today's generation and we hardly looked. Although there had been a time when the passing of the Richmond bus was the most exciting event of everybody's day in Burnside. But the years in between had brought many changes. There was electricity now, and television and telephones. Several factories and supermarkets had opened up on the highway, so that farming became far less profitable than working in the factories and spending weekly wages in the glittering markets, where everything that had formerly come from soil was sold now in tin cans and plastic wrappers. Because nobody in Burnside farmed anymore. Like almost everyone else, Momma and Poppa and Millicent all worked in the factories. And Momma bought at the supermarkets, like everyone else. The land around us, given over to weeds, was overgrown now like a graveyard in those first green days of spring.

Momma and Poppa watched the bus until it disappeared. "That Greyhound, she sure do go," Momma said. "It's Saturday now and I bet she's crowded with nigger men going to Richmond for them white hussies on Clay Street."

Millicent grunted. "Let them help themselves," she said bitterly. "After what I seen, a nigger man don't mean a thing to me no more."

"You're right there, sugar," Momma agreed. "A nigger man, he ain't worth a damn."

Millicent curled her lip and she and Momma looked at Poppa and me as though there were something dirty and pathetic about being a black man. I had seen this expression on their faces before — a wan kind of pity mixed with distaste and the sad realization that being a black man is next to being nothing at all. And the black woman is always telling the black man that with her eyes and lips and hips, telling him by the way she moves beside him on the road and underneath him in the bed. *Nigger, oh, I love you, but I know you ain't never going to be as good as a white man.* That's the way Momma and Millicent looked at Poppa and me while they cut us dead right there on the spot. They almost fell over each other, talking about how low and no-good nigger men are. And they weren't just joking; they really meant it. I saw it in their faces and it hurt me to my heart. I just didn't know what to do. I reached out and caught Poppa's arm, that's how hurt I was. He seemed to understand, because he wrapped his arm around me and I could feel some of his strength draining into me. So Momma and Millicent stood there ridiculing us on one side of Mr. Dotson Gerber's head, and Poppa and I stood there on the other.

Then, when Momma and Millicent were all through with their tirade, Poppa said very quietly, "I'm riding in to Dillwyn now. I'm going to turn myself over to the sheriff for killing Mr. Gerber here."

There was a kind of joy in Poppa's voice that I suppose no black woman can ever understand, and Momma and Millicent looked at Poppa as though he had suddenly lost his mind. But I was sixteen years old, which is old enough to be a man if you're black, and I understood why Poppa was so happy about killing that white man. Until now, he'd always had to bury his rich, black male rage in the far corner of some infertile field, lest it do harm to him and to the rest of us as well. But by telling that he'd killed that white man, he would undo all the indignities he had ever suffered in the name of love.

Now Momma looked afraid. "Turn yourself in to the sheriff? What you talking about, Walter Beaufort? What kind of foolishness you talking?" She tried humor to change Poppa's somber mood, laughing in a big hullabaloo. "I bet you been hitting the plum wine again," she said joyously.

But Poppa shook his head. "You always accuse me of that when you want to make light of what I'm saying. But I haven't been near that plum wine, not today. And what I'm saying is plain enough. I've killed a white man and I want somebody to know it."

"*We* know it," Momma said. "Ain't that good enough?"

"I want them to know it," Poppa said. "I want them to know he's dead and I want them to know why he's dead."

"Because he didn't call you Mister?" Momma said. There wasn't a white man in Alcanthia County who didn't call her Auntie, and she started to rage scornfully at the idea of Poppa's rebelling at being called Uncle. "Now, I could see it if you said you were going to hide out for a while, killing that white man and all that—"

But Poppa stopped her with an angry jerk of his hand. "It's not that way at all, Hattie. I don't aim to hide no more. I been hiding too long already—if you understand what I mean. The time's come for me to stop hiding. I'm going to Dillwyn and tell the sheriff what I've done."

Momma jumped straight up in the air. "Walter Beaufort, you gone *crazy* or something? No, I don't understand what you mean. Why didn't you tell the sheriff last year? Why you got to tell him now? Nobody even knows you killed Mr. Gerber. And to give yourself up now, that don't make no sense at all."

"Some things don't never make no sense," Poppa said. He cocked his eye at me. "You coming with me to the sheriff, boy? Somebody's got to ride Miss Tricia back here to home."

I got up onto Miss Tricia with him and we rode off to find the sheriff.

"I think I'm going to faint," I heard Millicent say behind me. But when I looked around, she was still standing there with her mouth hanging open.

As Poppa and I went up the road, Momma's voice followed us like an angry wind. "You see what I mean about *niggers,* Millicent?" Moaning sadly, half happy and afraid at the same time, a kind of turbulent satisfaction marred her voice as she shrieked at Millicent. "You see what I mean about *niggers,* child?"

"That black bitch," Poppa muttered. I don't know whether he knew I heard him or not. He kicked Miss Tricia viciously in the ribs and the mule leaped into a surprised gallop, heading to Dillwyn for Poppa to give himself up to the sheriff. After the way Momma and Millicent had carried on, I didn't see what else he could do.

Even here in Burnside, we had heard that black is beautiful. But I don't think that many of us believed it, because black is ugly and desperate and degraded wherever the white man is sitting on your neck. Still, Millicent and I had worn Afros for a while to show our black pride; but they were too hard to keep clean here in the country, there is so much dust and dirt blowing about. And our kind of hair picks up everything that goes by. Besides, the white people who owned the factories took Afro hairdos as a sign of militancy and threatened to fire everybody who wore one. So everybody went back to getting their hair cut short or straightening it like before.

I was thinking about that as I rode with Poppa to the sheriff's office. I thought about Millicent, too, and the black men she'd seen kissing in the factory. She never would tell who they were, and sometimes I wondered whether it might not have been just a story that she made up to justify her saying that all black men are sissies. At any rate, she complained quite openly that no black man had made love to her since last Halloween, which was almost five months ago, and this probably explained why she was so jumpy and threatening to faint all the time.

As for me, I thought I knew why no black men were interested in Millicent. For one thing, they could go to Richmond and Charlottesville and get white women, now that they had money to spend on the whores there. Also, the black men I'd talked to told me that they didn't find black women so desirable anymore, the way they were dressing and acting and perfuming themselves like white women on television, now that they had money to do so.

So the black men went to Richmond and paid white women, because their own women were trying to act white. And the black women were turning their backs on their own men, because — if Millicent was any example — they thought that black men were sissies. It was all very confusing.

I was old enough to have had myself a woman or two by then. But I was very hung up on Mrs. Palmer and her five daughters; I hope you know what I mean. There was a time when black people said that doing something like that to yourself would make you crazy. Now they said that it would make you turn white. Which was sufficient reason for some black boys to stop. But not me. I actually did it more. But all that happened was that sometimes I felt dizzy and depressed. Sometimes I felt weak. But I never did turn white.

Sheriff Dave Young's office was closed when we got to Dillwyn. Some white men sitting around told us that the sheriff was away to a Christian conference. "He's a deacon in the white Baptist church, you know. He'll be away for the rest of the week." There were some hounds lying around, sleeping in the dust, and one or two of them opened a drowsy eye and looked at Poppa and me without curiosity. The white men looked at us as though we were two hounds who had by some miracle managed to get up onto a mule. That's the way white men are in the South. As for Poppa and me, we looked right through those white men, which is really a very good way of rebelling by pretending that you're looking at nothing. There are other sly ways that we Southern black people have of rebelling — like grinning, or licking our tongue out behind the white man's back, spitting in his water when he's not looking, imitating his way of talking — which is why so many Northern black people think that Southern black people are such natural clowns, when what we're really doing is rebelling. Not as dramatic as a Molotov cocktail or a pipe bomb, but it certainly is satisfying, and a whole lot safer, too. Furthermore, it must be said that we do not hate whites here as black people apparently do in the North. Although we nearly always view them with pity and suspicion, for *they* think that we hate them, as they might very well do if the tables were reversed.

"Uncle, is there any particular reason why you want to see the sheriff?"

"No, sir, no, sir, none at all," Poppa said. He thanked them the way he was supposed to, grinning a little, and rode away.

"Where we going now, Poppa? Back to home?"

He shook his head. "We going to Mr. Dotson Gerber's house up the street yonder. I expect his wife is home. I expect she'd like to know what happened to her husband."

When we got to Mrs. Dotson Gerber's, there was a decrepit old white lady sitting in a rocking chair on her porch and waving a small Confederate flag over the banister, like a child does at a parade. She was the mother of Mr. Dotson Gerber's wife. And while colored people said quite openly that the old lady was touched in the head, white people claimed that she had arthritis; and they said that she waved the Confederate flag to exercise her arm, as though to conceal from black people the fact that any white had ever lost his mind.

She waved the flag and rocked every once in a while, pushing at the banister with spidery legs that ended in two fluffy slippers that had once been white. Her pale-blue eyes were as sharp as a hawk's behind her wire-rimmed glasses; but it was hard to tell whether she was looking into the past or the future, waving and rocking, smiling from time to time.

Poppa got down from Miss Tricia and walked over to the fence. "Good morning, ma'am," he said respectfully. It was dangerous not to be respectful, just in case the old white woman wasn't crazy and really did have arthritis in her arm. She could raise a ruckus for Poppa's disrespecting her that could cause him to wind up on the end of a rope. "I came to see Mrs. Dotson Gerber, ma'am," Poppa said politely, while the old lady rocked and waved the flag outrageously. She might have been saluting Lee's army marching proudly on its way to Appomattox, which was only a few miles away. Her eyes grew large and happy. But she didn't pay any attention at all to Poppa, even when he asked a second and a third time for Mrs. Dotson Gerber. She had arthritis, all right, that old woman. She had arthritis in the brain, that's where she had it.

Just then, Mrs. Dotson Gerber came to the screen door. Drying her hands on a pink apron, she inspected Poppa for a minute, as though trying to figure out whether he was safe or not. "Is that you, Uncle Walter?" She squinted through the screen. "Did you want to talk to me?"

"Yes, ma'am, Mrs. Gerber. I did come to talk to you. I got something to tell you."

"I certainly don't see why you came to my front door," Mrs. Gerber said peevishly, coming out onto the porch. "I *never* receive colored people at my front door, and I'm sure you know that, Uncle Walter. Besides, it bothers my mother's arthritis, people talking all around her." She inspected the crazy old woman, who was waving the Confederate flag and rocking vigorously.

"Well, ma'am . . . I'm sorry I came to your front door. I certainly do know better than that. But I've come to tell you about your husband."

Mrs. Gerber seemed to stop breathing. "My husband?" She dashed from the porch and stood at the fence near Poppa. "You know where my husband is?"

"Yes, ma'am. He's out in my collard patch — where my collard patch used to be."

"What's he doing out there?"

Poppa looked embarrassed. "Hs came to inspect the well I was digging. We got in an argument and I hit him with my shovel."

Mrs. Gerber turned very white, indeed. "You killed him?"

"I'm afraid so, ma'am. I buried him there in the well."

Mrs. Gerber tapped her bottom teeth with her forefinger. She was a sort of pretty white woman and certainly a lot younger than Mr. Dotson Gerber had been. Behind her on the porch, the crazy old woman rocked on, waving the flag at Southern armies that only she could see. "Momma's arthritis isn't too good today," Mrs. Gerber said absently, patting her hair. After a while, she said, "So Dotson is dead. All of us wondered what happened when he didn't come home last year. Knowing him, I was almost certain that he'd gone and got himself killed." But she didn't seem too upset. "Actually, Uncle Walter, you've done me a big favor. Dotson used to treat my poor mother something terrible, laughing at her arthritis all the time." She patted her hair again, although every strand seemed to be perfectly in place. "I suppose you know that I'm to get married again this summer to a very respectable man here in Alcanthia?"

"No, ma'am, I didn't know that."

"Well, I'm surprised," Mrs. Gerber said. "I thought that colored people knew everything. Anyway, he's a very respectable man. Very decent and very intelligent, too, I need not say. We both figured that Dotson was dead after all these months. That's why we decided to get married." She looked at Poppa almost gently. "But I never supposed you'd be the one to kill him, Uncle Walter. Why, you've even been here and done a little work for Dotson and me around the house."

"Yes, ma'am."

"He really must've provoked you, Uncle Walter. What did he do?"

"He kept calling me Uncle. I asked him not to, but he kept on."

"Yes, that sounds like Dotson. He could be mean that way. I suppose you want me to stop calling you Uncle, too?"

"I'd appreciate it if you would, ma'am. I mean, it's an actual fact that I'm not your uncle, so I'd appreciate your not calling me that."

Now Mrs. Gerber nibbled on her thumb. Her mother rocked on and on, waving the flag. "All right, I'll stop calling you Uncle," Mrs. Gerber said, "if you promise not to tell anybody about my husband being buried out there in your collard patch. After all, I'm planning on being married to a very decent man. It would be a big embarrassment to me — and to him, too — if anybody found out about Dotson being buried in a collard patch. As much as he hates collard greens." It was clear from the tone of her voice that the disgrace lay not in Mr. Dotson Gerber's being dead but in his being buried in our collard patch.

"There ain't no collards there now," Poppa said, trying to placate Mrs. Gerber some. "Why, we haven't done any farming for years."

"But collards *were* there," Mrs. Gerber said, almost stomping her foot. "And Dotson couldn't stand collards. I just hope you won't tell anybody else about this, Uncle Walter. I don't know what my fiancé would say if he knew about this. Considering that he's willing to marry me and to put up with Momma's arthritis in the bargain, I certainly wouldn't want him to know about Dotson. Why, I don't know what he'd do if he ever found out about Dotson. You haven't told anybody else, have you?"

"I went to tell the sheriff, but he's out of town until next week."

"You went to tell the sheriff?" She seemed absolutely horrified. "Mr. Beaufort, I know I have no right asking you to think about me and my feelings in all this. But you ought to at least think about your own family. You know what they'll do to you if they find out about this?"

"I know," Poppa said.

"And you don't care?"

"I certainly do care. I don't want to die. I want to live. But I've killed me a white man. That's not something that somebody like me does every day. I think I want folks to know about it."

"But why now?" she cried. "Why didn't you say something before? Before I went out and got myself engaged?"

"It didn't seem important before. Besides, Mr. Gerber was still in the ground then. He ain't in the ground anymore, not exactly."

From time to time, white people had gone past and looked at Poppa and Mrs. Gerber as they talked. "I think you all ought to go around to the back door," Mrs. Gerber said. "My husband-to-be certainly wouldn't like it known that I stood on my own front porch and carried on a conversation with colored people . . ." She turned very red then and took a step or two away, as though she was afraid that Poppa might hit her with a shovel. But Poppa started laughing very gently, the way a man does when he weighs the value of things and finds out that what is important to other people seems absurd to him. And he looked at Mrs. Gerber with a kind of amused pity darkening his eyes, as though he realized now that no white person could ever understand why he wanted him to know about Mr. Dotson Gerber.

"We're going on home," Poppa said. "And don't you worry none about Mr. Gerber, ma'am. We'll take care of him. Your husband-to-be won't ever find out."

"What do you intend to do?" Mrs. Gerber wanted to know.

Poppa's face lit up with a great big grin. Not the kind of tame, painful grin that a black man puts on when he's rebelling. But a large, beautiful grin that showed all of his teeth and gums. "I'm going to plant collard greens around him," Poppa said.

Mrs. Gerber wrinkled her nose in distaste. "Dotson certainly wouldn't like that, if he knew. And you mean *over* him, don't you?"

Now Poppa and I both laughed. We hadn't told her that Mr. Gerber was growing straight up from the ground. And she wouldn't have believed us if we had told her. That's how white people are. "Good-bye, ma'am," Poppa said to Mrs. Gerber. She nodded and went into her house. On the porch, her mother waved the Confederate flag triumphantly. The rocker squeaked like the tread of strident ghosts. We climbed up onto Miss Tricia and rode home.

And we were nearly halfway there before I finally figured out why that old crazy white woman was on Mrs. Gerber's porch. They kept her there instead of buying a doorbell and using electricity. That way, when people talked to her, Mrs. Gerber heard them and came outside to see who it was. Smart. Sometimes I had to give it to white people. They were very smart indeed.

Momma and Millicent were waiting for us when we got home. "Did you tell the sheriff?" Momma said. She looked haggard and very unhappy.

"The sheriff wasn't there," Poppa said. "He won't be home until next week." With Momma and Millicent following us, he rode Miss Tricia out to the collard patch and gave me the reins. "Take her to the stable, boy." But I watched while he knelt and worked the dirt into a mound around Mr. Gerber's head. "There, that ought to do it," Poppa said. "Tomorrow, I'm going to plant me some collard greens here." He stood up happily and wiped his hands on the seat of his overalls.

Momma's mouth dropped open. She ran to Mr. Dotson Gerber's head and tried to stomp it back into the ground. But Poppa stopped her firmly. "You've gone stark crazy!" Momma cried.

Poppa slapped her right in the mouth. She spun around like a top. He slapped her again and sent her spinning the other way. "I don't want no more trouble out of you," Poppa said.

Momma melted against him like warm cheese. "All right, sugar. You won't have no more trouble out of me, sugar."

I rode Miss Tricia down to the stable. Millicent had enough sense to keep her mouth shut for a change, and Momma and Poppa went on up to the house with their arms wrapped around each other. I hadn't seen them together like that for years.

And that is how Poppa started farming again. Helped on by sun and spring rain, Mr. Dotson Gerber and the collards grew rapidly together. It would not be an exaggeration to say that Mr. Gerber's body growing there seemed to fertilize the whole field. Although in no time at all, he was taller than the collards and still growing. Most of his chest and arms was out of the ground by the end of March. And by the middle of April, he had cleared the ground down to his ankles. With his tattered clothes and wild red hair, his large blue eyes wide and staring, he seemed more some kind of monster than a resurrected man. The sun and wind had burned his skin nearly as black as ours. And while there was small chance of anybody seeing him — people in Burnside didn't visit anymore, now that most of them worked in the factories — Poppa still thought it might be a good idea to cover Mr. Gerber up. "You'd better put a sack over his head and some gloves on his hands," he said. Later on, Poppa put a coat and some sunglasses on Mr. Gerber, along with an old straw hat. He propped a stick behind Mr. Gerber and passed another one through the sleeves of Mr. Gerber's coat for him to rest his arms on. He really looked like a scarecrow then, and we stopped worrying about people finding out about him. In truth, however, it must be said that Mr. Gerber made a very poor scarecrow, indeed, because the birds hardly paid any attention to him. It was fortunate for us that birds don't especially like collard greens.

Poppa worked a few hours in the collard patch every night after he came home from the factory. Momma helped him sometimes. Sometimes Millicent and I helped him, too. Then one day, Poppa quit his job at the factory and hitched Miss Tricia to the plow. "You farming again?" Momma asked him. She had been very tame with Poppa since he'd slapped her.

"I'm farming again," Poppa said.

Momma just nodded. "That's very nice, sugar. That's really very nice."

In no time at all, Poppa had planted all the old crops that used to grow on our farm — all kinds of vegetables, wheat, corn. He went to Dillwyn and bought a couple of pigs and a cow. All the neighbors knew what he was doing. But they kept on working at the factories and spending their money at the supermarkets. Until one day, a neighbor woman showed up to buy some collard greens. Poppa sold her a large basketful for a dollar. "I'm just sick to death of store-bought food," she said.

"I know what you mean," Poppa said. "You come back, you hear?" In a little while, other people came to buy tomatoes, string beans, white potatoes, golden corn from the tall green stalks.

Summer droned on. Poppa worked his crops. Word reached us that Mrs. Dotson Gerber had married her decent white man. After school had let out, I had begun to help Poppa full time. Momma finally quit her job at the factory and helped, too. But mostly, she took care of selling and managing the money that we were making. As for Millicent, I spied her one day making love down in the pea patch. And that black man she was with, he certainly was no sissy.

That was all Millicent needed and all a black man needed, too—someplace green and growing to make love in. I never heard Millicent talk about fainting after that, although she did talk about getting married.

Around the end of summer, Sheriff Dave Young came to our farm. "Some of the fellows said you were looking for me," he told Poppa. "But I figured it wasn't really too important, since you never came back."

"It wasn't important, Sheriff."

He bought a watermelon that Poppa let him have very cheap. "You got a good business going here," Sheriff Young said. "Some of the white farmers been talking about doing the same thing."

"It'd be good if they did," Poppa said. The sheriff put his watermelon into his car and drove away.

When fall came and the leaves turned red and gold and brown, Mr. Dotson Gerber turned like all the other growing things and shriveled away to nothing. Poppa seemed very satisfied then, looking over his fields. And I knew how he must have felt, standing there looking at Mr. Dotson Gerber and all the other dead things that would live again next spring.

The Greyhound to Richmond went by and Poppa shielded his eyes to watch. I think that I understood everything about him then and it hurt me so much that I deliberately turned my back. The lesson of that summer seemed a particularly bitter one, because we had done everything and we had done nothing. Mr. Dotson Gerber would certainly be growing in my father's fields every spring forever. And my father, my poor father would always watch and admire the Greyhound to Richmond. The same way that in the deepest and sincerest and blackest part of himself he would always hate himself and believe that God is the greatest white man of all.

"That Greyhound, she sure do run," Poppa said. He sounded very satisfied, indeed. God knew he'd killed a white man. With God knowing, that was knowledge enough. But I was thinking about how it feels to be black and forever afraid. And about the white man, god*damn* him, how he causes everything. Even when He is God. Even when he is dead.

JAMES BLAKE

The Widow, Bereft

(FROM ESQUIRE)

RONNIE HOOKED HIS HANDS around the top bar of the grid in the barred door of the cell. Hanging there, stripped to his shorts against the summer heat of the cell, he watched the changing colors and cloud forms of the riotous Florida sunset.

Cell J-57 was on the top floor of the penitentiary and, though an intervening catwalk ran the length of the range, the windows were open for most of the year and afforded a wide vista: acres of park-like grounds, meticulously pruned and clipped and sheared by convicts who were studying landscape gardening in Vocational Agriculture.

His gaze wandered over the geometrical hedges; regal Washington palms, their fronds like heraldic plumes, raffish leaning coconut palms, formal spruce and cedar. He could see all the way to the high electrified fences, and beyond them, the sudden-death zone with the grass trimmed as close as a golf course. Then the dark mass of pine forest stretching to the horizon.

He had never seen a human figure in that bare expanse between the fences with their guard towers and the dark wall of the piny woods. Often he would imagine one lonely running form, streaking for the shelter of the trees.

He raised his eyes to the evening sky again. "Doug, you got to see this. It's all pink, even the buildings are pink. Looks like the light is coming out of the ground, too. Golden pink. Gold-green and pink."

Northrop said absently, "Too pink. He always uses too much pink."

"No, Douglas, get up, you got to see it. Down near the bottom it's magenta."

"Magenta! What the hell is magenta?"

"It's uh — it's a kind of purple."

"Then say purple."

"Well, it's more — Wow, it's changing to French gray. Like footlights."

"French gray, for Christ's sake." Northrop got up from the bunk where he had been stretched out in his shorts, reading. Dark-haired, deeply tanned, in contrast to the red-haired sunburned Ronnie, he had a movie-handsome face on which a sardonic mind had stamped the permanent cast of discontent. He stood behind Ronnie, resting his chin on the other's hair, curling a long hand around the back of his cell mate's neck.

"French gray, my ass. Just plain old gray-gray."

Ronnie said in tranquil tones, "Okay, it's Oxford gray. Look, now it's — *ouch!*"

From the adjoining cell came the Carolina whine of Newt Barlow. "Northrop? You torturin' that poor Bracken boy agay-un?"

"This poor boy's a phony son of a bitch."

"Well — if yawl gonna beat awn him tonight, do it before lights-out, okay? Ah'd surely like to sleep for a chay-unge."

"Yassuh. Cuhnel, suh." He turned away to lie down in the bunk again and take up his book. "Bracken, stop mooning over the sunset, and make some coffee."

"— Mooning at sunset? You might as well say —"

"Never mind, just dummy up and do as you're told."

Ronnie went to the back of the cell and filled an empty coffee jar with water at the washbowl, dropped the bug in and plugged it into the socket. The "bug" was an immersion heater illicitly made in the prison electric shop from a length of element wire fastened to a piece of asbestos and equipped with a cord and plug.

From the bunk Northrup said, "Put something on the box, why don't you?"

Ronnie looked briefly through the pile of records and put one on the portable phonograph. The familiar opening of *Daphnis and Chloe* filled the cell.

"Oh shit, Ravel. It's too goddamn early for that. Put on some Mozart."

"Mozart, I hate Mozart."

"It figures."

"I think he wrote all that stuff off the top of his head."

"Don't make me get up, Bracken. I'll kill you. Put it on."

Ronnie chose *Nachtmusik* as least offensive. He was handing Northrop coffee in a plastic cup when Artie Dugan stopped outside the cell door. A stocky, muscled Irishman from Jersey City, with the blue-black hair of the Black Irish and, vivid in his tanned face, bright maniacal blue eyes outlined in spiky jet lashes.

Ronnie liked him, liked the way his eyes laughed when his mouth did, though he suspected it might be by design. But it was to Doug that Artie always addressed himself, in a manner that was deferential bordering on sycophantic. He worked hard at being a jazz buff, and Doug played a driving trumpet in the prison combo — he was a celebrity in the joint. Sometimes Ronnie figured Artie's fawning was because of Doug's rich mother and rich wife. But mostly it seemed to be because of the music.

Artie was looking down through the bars at Doug in his bunk. He threw Ronnie a dancing glance — "Whatcha say, doll?" — and returned to Doug. "Jee-zus man, like what kinda long-haired shit you diggin'?"

"That's W. A. Mozart, Artie," Doug said evenly, the studied forbearance in his voice an insult. "Called 'A Little Night Music.' "

"A little goes a long way, man. Why don't you play some sounds, some Basie, man?"

"You buy it, man, I'll play it, man. What are you doing out there after lockup?"

"New gig, man. I'm a surveyor now, on Construction Squad. Number One Trusty, Charlie. Dig my new threads." He turned from side to side, displaying his Trusty uniform, white shirt and white pants with a broad blue stripe running down the sides.

Ronnie said, "You made it, Artie, that's wonderful. I thought you looked different."

"Yeah, man, I'm in the club now."

Northrop said, "Let's resign from the club, Bracken. They're taking in a lot of bounders."

Artie said to Ronnie, "When are you gonna get rid of this square creep?"

"I'm working on it, Artie. Arsenic takes a long time."

"You know where I live, baby. Stay cool, Doug."

"Hang loose, Charlie." When Artie had gone, Northrop let out a long sigh. "God, what a hippydip."

"Artie *is* kind of clanky, but I like him."

"You like him because he comes on with you. You're pussy, Bracken. Beat jailhouse pussy."

"Awww. You're jest a-sayin' that."

From the head of the range came the bellow of the convict range-runner. "Count Time! On the door! Count Time!"

Ever since an escapee had evaded detection by putting a dummy made of bedclothes in his bunk, it was required that the occupants of each cell stand at the door to be counted. Some of the convicts on J-Range, in deference to the new guard, a pink-cheeked ex-Marine, had added a refinement to the procedure. They stood rigidly at attention, staring popeyed into space, and barked out the name and number in what they conceived to be leatherneck style.

Standing at the door, hearing the guard making his way down the range, Ronnie turned toward Doug in the bunk, snarling: "Awright, Northrop, hit the deck! *On* the double! Now hear this! How would you like a taste of the brig, mister? You hear me, North —"

Doug suddenly sprang from the bunk and seized Ronnie about the waist, and while he spluttered protest, half giggling, half in alarm, stood him on his head facing the door, holding him up by the ankles.

When the guard stopped at the door, he was absorbed in painstakingly writing on his clipboard and did not look up as Doug intoned briskly, "Northrop, sir! Five-seven-nine-nine-four!" at the same time letting go of Ronnie's ankles. He collapsed against the door in a thrashing tangle of arms and legs. Struggling to articulate, he gasped out, "Bracken, sir! Five-seven-six-ch-three!"

Startled at the direction from which the voice came, the guard raised his eyes from the board and looked down at Ronnie in mingled distaste and disbelief. He looked up at Northrop.

"What's goin' on hyuh?"

Northrop shrugged, looking down at Ronnie with annoyance. "I don't know what's the matter with him, Boss. If I'd known he was epileptic —"

"What?"

Red-faced, Ronnie struggled to his feet. Shoulders back, he shouted: "Bracken, Boss! Five-seven—"

"Shut up!" the guard hollered. He was glaring at Doug. "One of these days, Northrop —" He passed from view.

Ronnie waited till the guard was out of earshot. "Gee whiz, you did it again. He thinks I'm a lunatic. And ah been tryin' to creep into his heart, the little doll."

"Don't feel bad, he thinks I'm a dope fiend. Well — I hope he's got some mail for me."

"Maybe he'll never give us any mail again."

In a few minutes there was another bellow from the head of the range. "Mail call! Mail call!" And presently the guard Higdon, his face a cold mask of disapproval, stopped outside the door. "Northrop?"

Doug gave his number and received a long envelope. He looked at it and threw it on the bunk. "Parole Board. Jesus." He stared at the envelope.

"Aren't you going to open it?"

"Scared to. I know what it says. A brush-off." He picked up the letter. Ronnie watched him as he read, feeling a growing apprehension in his gut. He watched the dawning delight in Doug's face. — Oh Christ, let me be cool.

Doug looked up from the letter, his face glowing. "Holy smoke, I made it! I *made* it, baby!"

"When do you go?"

He looked at the letter. "— to be employed by — starting date to be — A week. A *week!* Next week, Chicago, wow!" He tossed the letter in the air and fell on his bunk.

"I'm glad, Doug." Hearing it totally hollow as he said it. Ronnie climbed into the upper bunk so that Doug wouldn't see his face.

There was a silence. "Oh, like *that,* huh? You going to mope now, mope around here for my last week?"

"No, Doug, I'll be all right. I promise."

Again the charged, sustained silence. Ronnie slid from the upper bunk and went to the phonograph. He was climbing back up again when the voice of Billie Holiday began: *No fears, no tears/ Remember there's always tomorrow —*

"Bracken, you're a scheming rat."

"Aw, Doug, let it play."

So what if we have to part/ We'll be together again —

"I think I'll just beat the living shit out of you."

Ronnie's head appeared at the edge of the upper bunk. "So every time you hear the tune, you'll think of us. Is that too goddamn much to ask?"

"Okay, okay."

Times when I know you'll be lonely/ Times when I know you'll be sad/ Don't let temptation surround you/ Don't let the blues make you bad —

Later that night, when the lights-out bell had rung, the last guard patrol had been made, and the deep night stillness had settled over the penitentiary, from far off beyond the piny woods came the hoarse urgent call of the air horn on the Seaboard night express westbound for Tampa. Several times it sounded.

In the lower bunk, Doug murmured jubilantly, "Ah heah you, Mistuh Engineer. Talk to me, baby, talk to me."

Ronnie muttered, "You son of a bitch." Then, "Doug?"

"What?" In a tone that said, "No."

"Can I come down there?"

"Not tonight."

"I don't mean for that. I just want to be *with* you."

He groaned. "Oh — all right, come on. But that's *all*, you hear?"

In the following days, Ronnie fought the steadily mounting tension, while Northrop was morose and withdrawn.

One evening Doug said, "I talked to Bud Larrabee today. About moving in here when I go."

Ronnie stared at him. "You got to be kidding. Larrabee's next door to psycho."

"Maybe somebody like you could help him. Nobody ever has."

"But why me? I got trouble just trying to stay with it. I feel sorry for Bud, sure. But —"

"He's heavyweight champ of the joint. Be a good protector."

"Who's going to protect me from Bud?"

"I know you've noticed his build. Quite a body, ain't it?"

Northrop was smiling, a dangerous smiling stranger. Ronnie said, "What's the matter with you? Isn't it bad enough you're leaving, do you have to leave me in a pool of blood?"

"And then, with all the stuff I'll be leaving with you, you'll be a wealthy widow. In demand."

Ronnie's voice was barely audible. "You're like a hyena, Doug. Piss all over something when you leave it."

"Oh? Already got a whiff of that ol' independence, haven't you? Look kid, you better get your mind right. When I go you're up for grabs."

Larrabee . . . Ronnie remembered how hung up he had been at his first sight of Bud. Those unsettling liquid brown eyes that seemed to be constantly beseeching. Like the intense eyes of a deer. Or a dog. Then he had seen Larrabee in a fight in the yard one day and suddenly noticed that throughout the savage brawl, the gentle eyes had never changed. They were frozen forever in mute, mindless pathos.

A couple of days later, Artie stopped outside the cell in the evening, loaded down with belongings.

Ronnie said, "Where are you going, Artie? Running away from home?"

"Movin' to Trusty Range, man. Onward and upward. Next week the warden's daughter!" He looked down at Northrop, lying in his bunk. "Heard about the parole, Doug. Sure glad you made it, man."

Doug sat up. "Why, thank you, Artie. So you're moving to Trusty Range. Fink City. Hmm. Can't beat 'em, join 'em, is that it?"

Artie flinched slightly, but the boyish grin didn't waver. "It's the shortest way out I know of, man."

He looked at Ronnie again, a strangely estimating equivocal stare. "Kinda leaves you out in the open, don't it? What are you gonna do?"

Ronnie shrugged. "I don't know what I'll do, Artie. Maybe commit suttee. You know where I can get a funeral pyre, cheap?"

Artie smiled wryly and inclined his head in an oddly distant formal gesture. "Well — lotsa luck, Bracken. I'll be seeing you before you go, Doug"

Ronnie turned to find Northrup watching him steadily.

"Pretty foxy, aren't you? Why didn't you tell him about Larrabee?"

"I used to wonder about that expression, 'A dog eating glass.' Now I don't have to wonder anymore."

"Getting foxier by the minute. And snottier. See how far you can go, Bracken. I'll let you know when it's too far."

On the day before Doug's leaving, Ronnie spent most of the afternoon walking the Track, the well-worn path around the prison recreation field where so many prisoners had walked with their anxieties.

On one of his rounds he was hailed by Larrabee. Watching him approach, Ronnie remembered Doug's sly allusion to Bud's physique. It was true he moved with feral ease and grace.

Larrabee said, "Did Doug tell you about me movin' up there? I mean — he said it would be all right with you."

"Yeah, Bud. We — talked about it. I guess it ought to work out."

"You like to read a lot, don't you?"

"Well — yes, both Doug and I read quite a bit."

"I was thinkin' — maybe you could help me with that. You know, tell me what you think I oughta read."

"Oh hell, Bud, anybody ought to read what he enjoys."

"No, seriously. I'd appreciate it a lot. If you'd show me."

Walking alone again, aware of having extricated himself too abruptly, he cursed Larrabee and cursed Northrop. From previous experience, he could chart the course of the Larrabee affair. Guide my faltering steps, Bracken, Bud would beseech with those mad hypnotic eyes. Teach me the finer things. Then, one freak scene in the sack, and *pow* for the Great Books.

Anger and bitterness were tonic; he felt better. The afternoon rays of the sun stretched long across the grass; he was alone on the huge field. He walked slowly toward the gate leading into the inner compound of cell blocks and mess hall.

Going through the gate, he heard Doug's trumpet in the combo that played for dinner every night in the mess hall

The band played on a balcony that overhung the entrance to the cavernous room. Ronnie paused under the balcony and decided to sit on the stairs leading to the bandstand. There he could listen without Doug's seeing him. He had found it was often easier to tell his cell partner's mood by listening to him play, rather than by what he said. On the horn he was unable to dissemble.

They were playing "You Don't Know What Love Is." Listening, Ronnie heard loneliness and loss in the music. *There he is, the one I need/ Where does he go, why does he hide?* The song finished, a pause, and the piano man began a slow introduction. Another ballad. Doug was calling all slow tunes. The horn began again: *No fears, no tears/ Remember there's always tomorrow/ So what if we have to part* —

The fog had rolled in from the coast around daybreak, and still hung here and there in isolated patches. Cons called it parole-dust.

Waiting at the gate that led from the inner compound of the prison, Ronnie impatiently watched the hand on the gate clock lurch ahead. It was already eight o'clock, but the guard on the gate refused to pass anyone through until the fog had cleared.

It had to be old man Larkin. Senile old prick. He pressed his face against the bars. "Hey, Mr. Larkin? I'm gonna be late for work, Boss."

Larkin swung quickly on his high stool to locate the threat. A fallen chin, incipient goiter and protuberant eyes gave him the witless alertness of a pigeon. His darting eyes pinned Ronnie. Twitching his sunken lips in dismissal, he aimed an expert jet of tobacco juice at the can beside him, and turned again to stare into the yellow tunnel carved in the fog by the gate searchlight.

"Late for work, shit," he said to the fog. "Yew got your first day's work yet to do, Bracken. Awright, get your ass on out here then."

"Gate!" he called to the man in charge of the mechanism.

With his habitual air of loathing, he watched Ronnie disappear into the mist.

Doug was dressed in a thin gray suit, white shirt and black tie. The change made by the civilian clothing was dismaying. Without the prison uniform, Doug seemed diminished. For two years in the prison band, he had worn the immaculate whites of a Trusty; saturnine good looks deeply tanned against dazzling white, a vivid and dominant figure at the center of Ronnie's existence. Now there remained an uncertain stranger in a flimsy gray suit.

"Wow, man. You look like — like —"

"Ex-con?"

"Naw, man, it ain't a bad suit. You look like the night clerk in a hot-sheets hotel."

"Don't worry about it, Bracken. I'll buy a topcoat in Tampa and cover up this outrage on the plane. Or else freeze my ass in Chicago. I'll miss their lousy Florida sunshine."

"I see you got your axe. You think they'll let you blow?"

"No sweat. I give them a year on parole. After that, I'll be blowing my horn again somewhere."

"Doug — how about — well, how about, you know, the hang-up?"

He forced himself to look at Doug. As he feared, the gray eyes were hard.

"How about discussing something else? Or how about you dummy up?"

"I don't care, man, I got to say it. You kicked the habit while you were locked up. And the shit was available. Why couldn't you —?"

"Did you come all the way out here just to get on my back? You ought to know by now that any promise made in here stops at the gate. I'm going back on the streets, man. It's a new ball game."

"It makes me wish I had something to pray to —"

"*What?* Bracken, for Christ's sake. You better pray to the cat that takes care of half-assed whores. St. Pandarus, I think it is. Pray. Holy Jesus."

A runner approached to say that Doug was wanted in Control Room. They walked slowly along the shiny enameled echoing corridor, halted often by convicts and their good-byes, all of them bawdily instructing Doug as to his first night on the streets. He promised to perform for the honor and glory of alma mater.

Talking to Doug, the convicts slid their eyes over to scrutinize Ronnie, looking for signs of distress.

These cats inhale disaster like it was pot. Take a good look, you motherin' buzzard.

When they were alone again, a shy silence fell between them. "You'll be all right, Bracken. Larrabee will be a good cell partner for you. He'll defend the ranch from the bandits and varmints around here."

"Now if I knew somebody to defend me from Larrabee."

"Don't start again with that, Bracken. You got no idea how remote your troubles are becoming to me. You wanted to move Artie Dugan in, and he'd have moved your ass out. I didn't leave all that stuff with you just to give it to a pinball hustler like Artie. God knows you worked for it. Maybe I should have let it happen. You and Dugan. How about a chorus of 'When Irish Eyes are Smiling'?"

"You know why you did it, Doug. Because you're twisted. So forget it."

They were at Control Room. Other parolees stood around, each surrounded by a group of cons.

"I got to split, Doug. I can't take any more jive from these gossiping jerks."

Doug put out his hand. "Well —" Ronnie stared down at it in confusion. Strangest of all, to be shaking with Doug.

They touched hands. Doug said, "Don't forget, Bracken. Don't forget." Ronnie touched him once more, turned away and did not look back.

At the prison chapel, the other church mice were already at work in the office. He walked quickly past the door of the chaplain's office and went into the empty church. Paused at the piano, sat down, and after some random chords, began "Like Someone in Love." It was damp and chilly in the deserted chapel: the music floated disconsolately up into the rafters. Courting sadness, he went into "I Get Along Without You Very Well." His eyes wet, he crossed the sanctuary to continue his mourning on the organ. Until the chaplain stuck his head in the door, eyebrows raised in his favorite phony attitude, a mixture of consternation and benevolence. This time meaning, Knock it off.

Sinking into a pew behind a post in the chapel balcony, hidden from view, he considered the future. Doug and Larrabee had decided it between them, so he had no choice but to let Larrabee move into the cell as Doug's replacement. Larrabee: unpredictable, volatile, violent. Whatever was done would have to be done with guile and scorpion cunning.

Shortly before lockup, he was lying in the upper bunk in his shorts, trying to read, when Bud came into the cell. He carried a big box of books and a pillowcase stuffed with his gear. Under his arm, a chess set.

Chess? He'll have to kill me first.

"Which bunk, Ronnie?"

"Lemme see, Bud. I'm in this one — "

"I get the lower? Hey, thanks man, beautiful."

"I'm used to this one, so I'll stay here."

"Well, I want you to know I didn't come empty. Can I come up?" An effortless bound and he was sitting on the edge of the upper bunk. "I brought a tube for us. For opening night."

"A whole tube? Baby, I'm witchoo. Break it out."

Larrabee reached into his sock and brought out an amphetamine inhaler. He removed the plastic cap to show the roll of impregnated cotton inside. Two pieces had been sliced off the roll and wrapped in cellophane. He passed one to Ronnie.

"Wow, Bud, that's a bomber, it'll knock me on my ass. Turn on now, or wait till after count?"

"Frig the count. You got any coffee to wash this down?"

"Everything's over the washbowl. You want me to make it?"

"I'll do it. Put something groovy on the box."

Ronnie tried to avoid the records Doug had liked. He chose Andre Previn as suitably noncommittal. Bud heated water in a jar with the homemade immerson heater. When he handed Ronnie his coffee, they exchanged a conspiring smile. A tube of cotton would not only keep them turned on tonight, they could freak out on it for most of the week. Ronnie's spirits lifted a little. He felt the amphetamine taking hold and stoked it with the hot coffee.

Larrabee said, "It's hot as hell in here," and pulled off his T-shirt, then kicked off his pants. He stroked his belly, looking down at his tapering muscled torso. Ronnie watched him.

"How long was Doug in here with you?"

"About two years."

"And how much time left on your bit?"

"Something like two years."

"No reason we can't make it together till you go home, right?"

Ronnie shrugged. "Pretty early to tell, isn't it? Let's do it as it comes. It's hard by the yard, by the inch it's a cinch."

The bright brown eyes regarded Ronnie for a long minute and were abruptly veiled by thick lashes.

Christ, already I'm irritating him. "You got a lot of books, Bud. What are they?"

"Ah, just a lotta shit."

He glowed shyly as he showed his books. Ronnie saw Kahlil Gibran. (Kahlil? Gibran?) *Siddhartha* and the *Bhagavad-Gita*. *Metamorphosis* and *Buddenbrooks*.

"And hey, I got some stuff of mine I'd like you to read. Some poetry. At least it's supposed to be poetry."

"That's great, Bud, I want to see it. After lights-out when the joint is quiet, okay? You don't expect to sleep tonight after that wad you swallowed, do you?"

"Reckon not. You got a night-light?"

"I got a blue one, kid. How does that grab?"

"Groovy."

When lights-out bell sounded, they waited till after the guard had passed on his last patrol, then blacked out the barred door of the cell with a blanket. Ronnie took the night-light from concealment, a Christmas-tree bulb and socket he had stolen from the decorations at the chapel.

He plugged it in. The blue glow showed a shadowy cavern. They went to the back of the cell, where the FM played softly. Bud sat on the toilet, Ronnie on the chair. They swallowed more cotton, drank hot coffee, and rapped in the feverish careening tempo induced by the amphetamine.

Bud described his days as a street kid in Detroit, ending with the night in Palm Beach when he was discovered prowling an oceanfront mansion by the banker who lived there. And killed the banker with one shot. And beat the chair because he was only sixteen. Now he was seven years into "all of it," a life sentence.

The voice was a flat uninflected monotone. Ronnie could see, in the dim blue light, the shadowed hollows where Bud's eyes were, the embers glowing in the depths.

Bud broke off to rummage in his box of books. He handed Ronnie a sheaf of papers. "See what you think of this."

Ronnie read, holding it up to the blue light. Frantically high from the speed, he thought the poetry was banal doggerel, and felt strongly urged to say something definitive about it, something lucid and precise. Gravely, earnestly, he began to outline to Larrabee what was wrong with his verse. Larrabee listened for a while, then rose abruptly to go to the lower bunk and stretch out on it, where he lay smoking in ominous silence.

Apprehensive, Ronnie sat on the edge of the bunk and laid his palm on Bud's hard ridged belly. "Look, Bud, I'm sorry if I came on too strong. I'm wasted behind the shit, dig? But I still tried to tell you honestly what I thought. Why play games, right?"

Larrabee's low voice from the darkness of the bunk was pensive. "And that's what you thought."

The blow hit the side of his head like a hammer. Ronnie saw flashes and livid streaks of light behind his eyes.

"What the hell was *that* for?"

"If I ever hear that snotty superior tone out of you again, Bracken, I ain't gonna stop with one clout. I'm gonna stomp you, dig?"

Ronnie started to rise. "Wait a minute, baby. I didn't do so good in the culture bag. Maybe I'll do better in the sleeping bag. Let's make it."

Daylight found them gray faced and empty eyed. They ate more cotton and drank more coffee. And when the sliding bar was pulled to unlock the cells for breakfast, they went instead to the shower room and stood for a long time without speaking under the warm soothing water.

They had scarcely spoken all night after Larrabee hit him. In silence, save for a few curt commands, Larrabee had methodically blasted him with virtuoso variations on the prison sex canon.

As they were dressing, Ronnie tried again: "Bud, listen man, please don't be salty."

Larrabee smiled. "It's all right, forget it, babe. Now we know what we gotta do. I'll learn to write better and you learn to blow better."

Later in the day, Ronnie slipped away from his job at the chapel and went to the captain's office to consult the convict clerk.

Billy Lane, inmate secretary to the captain, was a thin, intense, waspish queen who ruled the captain's office, and thus much of the penitentiary, with an iron imperious hand. Anyone wanting a cell transfer, a road-camp transfer, or other unspecified accommodations had to go to Billy with the bread in his hand.

Though intimidated by the acid-tongued Lane, Ronnie had established a rapport of sorts with him. Lane played the organ, and Ronnie had arranged for him to make use of the chapel instrument, on which he played earsplitting, window-rattling, inexact

Bach. Their relationship was based on the theory they were both cultured beings marooned in an encampment of Tatar hordes.

"Hey dahling! What brings you to the Gestapo? Oh, let me show you something fabulous. Look what my cool captain managed to dig up. Dope, my dear. Soul-corroding shit corrupting all those clean-limbed convicts. Oh it's a wicked world."

He opened the drawer of the desk to show plastic containers of various pills and capsules, and a quantity of amphetamine inhalers. "Not a minute too soon, either. Your poor old mother was running out of merchandise. Worse than that, she was starting to come down. Here, baby, you're always good to me, take this along."

He handed Ronnie a white plastic inhaler. "Besides, if my man gets his hairy paws on this speed, the orgy won't stop. And we got too many hustles to stay on top of."

He leaned back in the swivel chair and calculated Ronnie. "Now, what's on your mind? I heard the mad Larrabee moved in on you. Is that what's bugging you, baby?"

Ronnie knew that whatever he said would be all over the joint in an hour. There was little choice. "I can't make it with him, Billy. Cat's paranoid. And when he hits you, it knocks your head off."

Billy's nostrils flared and his black eyes flashed theatrically. "You mean that wig-sprung pugilist beat you up?"

Already this harpy is embellishing. "No, no, certainly not. He just banged me up the side of the head, but I'm afraid it won't stop there. I always think I'm masochistic till somebody belts me."

"And you want me to change your cell location."

"I got to go *somewhere,* Billy."

"Mmm. But if you simply transfer to another cell inside the Rock, Bud will find you. And maybe break your jaw. I *know* that one. It's really too bad. Such a wild lay, isn't he?"

"Well — he's diligent."

Billy screamed. "You're too much for your old mother! Listen, I think I got the answer. You have a Trusty card, right? So you're eligible to move out of the Rock. Why not move onto Trusty Range where Polack and I live? In fact I don't know what the hell kept you in that miserable Rock for so long."

"I was with Doug."

"Well, you're going to move out before Larrabee gets back from the gym. We're in a four-man room upstairs and we have a vacancy. I'll move you in with Polack and me."

"You said there were three in the room?"

"Oh. Didn't I tell you? Artie Dugan."

"Artie."

"Don't exactly make you mad, does it, girl? Artie digs you. So you move in and play mother and father. It's a pain in the ass having a bachelor in the pad, he just lies there in the sack listening to Polack and me sexualize. Inhibits me something fierce. I'm sure you can focus his attention elsewhere."

Ronnie went back into the Rock to collect his belongings. In the cell, a freshly laundered sweat suit of Larrabee's lay across the lower bunk. He looked at the books neatly lined up on Bud's bunkside shelf, and felt a twinge of guilt. Doug had told him to help Bud. Now he was running out on the lost and floundering Larrabee.

With the help of a spade runner, he quickly gathered all the things that Doug had left to him — the phonograph and records, the FM, the books, and his collection of pajamas.

Trusty Range was another world from the drab and dingy Rock. The wide hallway immaculate, the floor waxed, two areas with benches for viewing television.

In the big well-lighted four-man room, there were regular beds instead of bunks. Billy was there to help him unpack and show him what bed to take. A chest of drawers between the windows held a large urn with an enormous arrangement of cut flowers.

"You like my flahrs? The spade from the greenhouse brings them to me. Sweet. I think you'll like our little home, darling. We live it up around here."

Inserting a cigarette into a long rhinestoned holder, he sat down on a bed. "Do you know my Polack?"

"I've seen him around and rapped to him a little, but I don't really know him."

"I swear to God it's like being mated to a mandrill. He's got to be the ugliest stud in the world. And the schemingest. But he has one lovable quality, he's free with his bread. Under that armor plate there's a dizzy Polack peasant buying drinks for the house."

"Polack intimidates me. Oh hell, he paralyzes me."

Billy turned to give him a sharply inspecting scrutiny. "Don't ever let Polack see you're afraid of him. He's got a rotten mean mouth. And it wouldn't be good for Artie."

"Artie? I don't get it."

Wanly, he raised manicured eyebrows and fluttered eyelids that were blue from fatigue. The long holder was a baton, the long slender hands gliding and swooping through the air were pale white bats.

"Well, my child — this is maybe a teeny bit sordid — but it's like this. Artie works for Polack. They got a wailing Shylock operation going. You know, cutthroat lending, with a twenty-five-percent clout. Compounded whenever Polack gets the urge to compound."

"What does Artie do?"

"Torpedo. He corrects the cons who don't make their payments. It's tricky work. Artie is very useful to Polack."

"You're trying to tell me something."

"Of course. If Polack thinks you might louse up his main man in a romance, that's not good. So it's up to you, love."

"You got a rusty razor blade? I think I'll slash my wrists."

"Don't be an ass. I'm just giving you the picture." He rose and went to a cupboard. "Come to think of it, the hell with it. I'll make some coffee and we'll turn on some cotton. From the cotton fields of ol' Massa Rexall. Then we can figure better. We might even forget what the problem is."

Shortly after the four-thirty whistle blew, Polack and Artie came in together. Their heads swung from Ronnie to Bill and back.

Brisk and strident, Billy shrieked, "Surprise, surprise! The Easter Bunny was here, Artie baby. He left you a basket. Or do I mean a bag?"

Artie looked down at Ronnie sitting nervously on the edge of the bed. The manic blue eyes danced in their switched-on way, faintly mocking. "Hey baby. Wow." He sat next to Ronnie. "You movin' in, pussycat?"

He nodded. "It would appear."

The blue eyes studied Ronnie. Gradually they turned frosty as Artie's face assumed his borrowed Bogart expression of menace. It was not convincing, the jet lashes that fringed his eyes were incongruous and distracting.

"Larrabee give you a bad night?"

He shrugged. "You know how that goes, Artie. Bud doesn't know what he's doing."

"A bad night," he insisted, watching Ronnie steadily.

"What can I say? Mother told me there would be bad nights. That's the breaks."

He could hear himself sounding stilted, conscious of Polack silhouetted against the barred windows, looking out and listening.

Polack turned to Billy. "What's happening around here?"

"Happening?" He tilted a languid eyebrow. "Ronnie moved in to be with Artie. Everyone should have a hobby, don't you think?"

Polack swung to Artie. "Is that what *you* want, partner?"

Artie didn't look at Polack. He smiled a pale uncertain smile at Ronnie. "Well, yeah man. Like this is my chick. I told you about it. Northrop's old lady."

"Northrop. That musician dude. Went out on parole."

Ronnie watched the clean brown face. The blue eyes that met his were suddenly opaque.

Artie, Artie, oh you weak mother, what happened to Humphrey Bogart?

Polack left the window to stand at the foot of Ronnie's bed. The face grotesque, hypnotic, a megalocephalic head too big even for the big body. Massive mashed nose that seemed to stem from the forehead just under the low hairline, bleak sunken eyes crowding the flattened bridge of the nose. Skin spectral white, cratered with past acne, stretched taut over Slavic cheekbones tapering down to a wide wet sensual mouth.

In a voice between rasp and croak, "Whaddya say, bitch, you figure to take good care of my boy?"

Ronnie tried to look at him and had to give it up. He looked at the floor, knowing his mistake. "I figured the boy for taking care of me, Polack."

Polack stared down at Ronnie's lowered head, and a brief dim smile touched the moist lips. He turned away and said to Billy, "Okay, you brought her in here, remember that. Artie? It's up to you to see that your broad keeps her jaw shut about what goes on in here. You got that?"

"No sweat, partner. She's hip."

"Awright, I'm holding you responsible for your old lady." He regarded Ronnie with a look minutely thawed. "Okay, babe. Use your head. You're not out in the open anymore, you're with Artie. Anybody gives you any shit, tell him. Or tell me, and we'll handle it."

He turned a quizzical glare on Billy. "Awright, don't stand there, bitch. We'll drink to the fortunate couple."

Billy produced glasses and surgical alcohol in orange juice. It was the first lush Ronnie had touched in two years. Maybe I can get blocked, he thought desperately. With Artie's speculating gaze on him, he took a long slug.

Polack and Billy stood at the window, talking in low tones. Ronnie gulped down the rest of the drink feeling it begin to move in him.

"I think I'll catch a shower. Been a hectic day." Stripping to shorts and shower slides, he hung a towel around his neck.

Artie said, "There's a shower robe at the foot of my bed. Take that."

"What for, Artie? I don't need it."

Artie's voice stopped him at the door. "I said put it on, bitch."

The other two turned from their conversation to look impassively at Artie flexing his machismo. Ronnie blinked in dismay, smothering the retort that rose, and put on the white terry-cloth robe.

"That's better. I don't want you showing your ass up and down the hall."

In his head Ronnie heard, "Oh balls, you muscle-bound ox." It came out, "Whatever you think best." He made another try for the door.

"Come over here and sit down."

Artie's voice a murmur with an edge in it. "What's your beef?"

"Nothing, Artie. Nothing at all. Just, I've had a rough week."

"Northrop. You miss Doug, huh?"

He skirted it. "Two years is a long time. It was a habit."

"Look at me when you talk to me."

He laid a heavy arm across Ronnie's shoulder and his hand turned Ronnie's head. The blue eyes locked on his, leisurely perusing, probing. They were darker now, deepened by something Ronnie had never seen before. The robe pushed aside, a hand on his thigh. Pinned by the watchful eyes he felt the hard calloused surface of the moist warm palm against his leg.

The hand curved and grew heavier. "It'll be groovy, pussycat. I thought I lost you when that slick trumpet player moved that goddamn crazy Larrabee in on you. Thought we'd never make it. But you found your old man, didn't you?"

Ronnie heard somebody else with his voice say, "I had to, Artie. But I wanted to."

"That's a smart pussycat. Go take your shower. Oh, wait a minute." He went to a footlocker at the end of his bed. "Here, take this. I want you smellin' sweet." Aphrodisia. "And this goes on your sheets." Talcum powder.

At the early hour, with most of the cons at dinner, Ronnie had the shower room to himself, and stayed for a long time under the water, wishing he would never have to come out.

In the room, Billy rapidly produced a meal from supplies purlioned from the Officers' Dining Room. Ronnie, feeling the buzz from the one drink, decided to continue. He poured from the bottle Billy had left out, and when he turned around with the drink, Artie was watching him. He stared a little longer, as if debating whether to say something, then turned his head to continue talking to Billy.

They had just finished eating when the door burst open and the burly Doc Prescott whirled in. Convict secretary to the head doctor at the prison hospital. He pirouetted to rest beside Polack, on his bed.

"Your frenzied pharmacist is here. How about a drink?"

Polack in one gesture told Billy to serve a drink and indicated to Doc Ronnie's presence.

Doc said, "Oh. Hey, that's Bracken, isn't it? Northrop's old lady. Ex old lady. I bet you're missing your daddy? You move in here?"

Ronnie nodded.

"You know her?" Polack asked.

"Hell, yes. Northrop bought fury pills from me all the time. Those two cats were always stoned out of their skulls."

"Is that right?" A thin gleam of interest in the words. "Okay, friendly pharmacist, what's happening?"

There was a loaded pause. Polack said, "She's okay. I told Artie to keep her trap shut or I'll mash his chops."

"Well then — Your old family quack made a little score today. Dig." He held out a vial for Polack's inspection. In his other hand he flashed a hypo and syringe. Billy stood beside Polack looking down at the display.

"Now that's what I call attractive."

Artie got up and went over. "What kind of shit is it, Doc?"

"The granny of them all, sweetheart. Pentathol." With brisk efficiency, he drew the colorless liquid from the bottle, and after briefly feeling for a good vein, inserted the needle in Polack's arm and pushed the plunger.

Polack froze for an instant, said softly, "Aaaah," and lay back on the bed. Billy offered his thin white arm. As the spike went in he said tensely, "Jack it a little, Doc." The blood rose in the tube, receded, rose again and fell.

"Mmmmh." Billy lay down beside Polack. Artie rolled up his sleeve and held out his big hairy forearm. Then walked like a somnambulist to his bunk and stretched out with a sigh.

The light from the lamp flashed on the works as Doc extended them. Ronnie shook his head. "Thanks, Doc, I'll pass. Hardware spooks me."

"Oh, yeah, I understand," Doc said distantly, as if he had confessed to terminal syphilis. Gazing at Ronnie, he made a studied deliberate routine of saturating gauze with alcohol and wiping the spike. And only then turned back to Polack, laid out on the bed and breathing loudly. He hovered over the recumbent Polack, his gaze brooding, watchful, tender.

"You want to go again, my darlings?" And when they did not move, hit them again, and came over to do the same to Artie. While Ronnie lay in bed trying to read and not to hear anything, the three of them would get the flash, go abruptly on the nod, and soon revive groggily to hold out their arms for another hit.

Eventually, Doc briskly dismantled his equipment, wrapped it in a cloth and put it in his pocket. "Anybody want to come down to our joint for bridge? No. Okay, good night all. Happy embolism." He went out surveying Ronnie.

In a few minutes, they began to stir. Polack sat up and said, "Artie, tell your broad where to go for hot water. I want some coffee."

Ronnie took the pitcher Artie gave him and went into the hallway. It was dark out there. Just outside the door, in the television area, other Trusties who lived on the floor sat on benches before a blasting TV.

Ronnie walked down the long hall to the shower room. He pushed the heavy iron door open into a fog of steam. At one side, naked cons were showering, and at the long sink, several others stood before the mirror, shaving.

The din dwindled to silence as they saw Ronnie. He ran one of the taps, letting the water run over his hand. Ed Jones, a member of the chapel choir that Ronnie directed, was one of those shaving.

"Hey, Ed, what's happening? You still going to do that solo on Sunday?"

Jones surveyed him leisurely before answering. "I don't know, Bracken. I'll have to think about it."

In the silence, the flat hostile tone bounced off the tile floor and walls. Accustomed to hearing only unctuous servility from Jones, Ronnie stood looking down into the sink at the running water, cursing the rising tide of color he could feel in his face. When he had filled the jar, he walked through silence to the door. And when he had closed it behind him, he heard the noise break out redoubled.

Ah so, he said to himself, retracing his steps down the long hall and being careful to look at no one. Ostracism goes with this gig. Not to mention obloquy. I got to ask Billy what gives.

Billy made coffee. Polack grabbed his cup and said to Artie, "Let's dig the TV. Will you take the Pope's chair?"

From against the wall, Artie hoisted a large, ornately carved wing chair upholstered in tapestry cloth. He nodded at Ronnie. "Gimme a hand." They carried the chair into the hall, past the rows of benches where the other cons sat, past those who had brought stools to sit on, and folding chairs.

And placed the big chair before the TV in front of the assembly. There was some muttering and shifting about as Artie and Ronnie, and the high back of the chair blocked the view. Polack, sauntering behind, waited. Then sat down in the big chair, hidden from sight by the wings, lighted a cigarette and crossed his legs. He blew out a fog of smoke that clouded the TV screen.

Artie split down the hall, leaving Ronnie to go back into the room alone. Billy was fiddling with the FM. An orchestra came on, a Prokofiev concerto. He adjusted the volume and lay back on his bed. He winked at Ronnie.

"At last we get some relief from the buffaloes. I hope they got a good long shitty movie to look at."

Ronnie sat on the edge of the bed. "I need some answers, Billy."

"All right, love. Ask a stupid question."

"When I went down to the shower room, I got frost a foot deep."

Billy smiled a feline smile. "Yeah. I used to get it. Still do. You'll get accustomed."

"I will? What is it?"

"Simple. They're all scared shitless of Polack and Artie, so they hate their guts. They know Polack is running the joint, and there ain't a swingin' dick can do a motherin' thing about it."

"So?"

"Oh, come on. Call it hetero-backlash. You won't see them dummying up on Polack or Artie. Once they dig you're definitely Artie's old lady, they'll warm up some. They'll have to."

At lights-out call, Artie came back carrying the chair, followed by Polack. Billy turned on a dim lamp and turned the FM down to a murmur.

Stripping to his shorts, Ronnie crawled under the covers. Stretching, flat on his back, he felt some of the tension abate. Then, remembering, he crawled out and, rolling back the top sheet, he sprinkled talcum powder on the bed, feeling ludicrous.

The dim shape of Artie stood by the bed, wearing the white shower robe.

"Be right back, babe." He returned on a wave of cologne. Sniffing, Ronnie recognized Aphrodisia.

Lo the bridegroom cometh, an eagle on scented wings. He stared at the shadowed ceiling, listening to Artie's movements and the murmur of the FM. A piano was playing "Come Rain Or Come Shine." The music reached out to tell him that Doug was gone. A new ball game . . .

Artie stood at the bedside, with slow deliberation removing his white robe. "You asleep, babe?"

"Coitinly I'm asleep. Something you require — ?"

"I got your require swinging. Brylcreem okay with you?"

"Bryl — whatever you think is right, Mister."

"Crazy. Here you go."

After the initial flurry, Ronnie began to feel that the fervor was contrived, seeming to be somehow linked with the action in the other bed. It was distracting, he listened in spite of himself to the sound at the other end of the room. And thought of the coupling of buzzards. There was a sinister macabre authority in the sounds.

Absently performing, automatically responding, disoriented, he could not keep his mind from wandering.

Could it be second billing that's bugging me, for godsake? Or all these goddamn cross-vibrations hanging me up?

There was a sudden furtive tapping at the iron door of the room. Billy had rigged it shut. Now somebody was making tentative efforts to force it open.

Artie slid swiftly out of bed and into his own. A creaking of springs and muffled curses from the other end of the room. Billy said, low and tight, "You gonna answer that?"

Polack, with calm contempt, "You want him to wake the whole joint?"

Wrapping a towel around his middle, Polack gingerly opened the door. Captain Miller, head of Security, "Dickless Tracy" to the cons, slipped in, his face flushed from emotion or juice or both, his sparse brown hair disheveled.

Polack led him to the windows, where they murmured. The one insistent, agitated, the other with the cadence of command. Once Polack rose to full voice: "I haven't got that much here, good buddy. I'll give you what I got, and more tomorrow, awright?"

A shadow loomed, and Artie slid back into bed with Ronnie. They whispered:

"Are you out of your mind?"

"That lame? He don't bother me."

"Whaddya mean, isn't that — "

"Dummy up and take care of biz, will you?"

Eventually, the caller was maneuvered out the door. Polack returned to bed muttering, "Schmuck, what a schmuck." Low urgent voices from Billy's corner, and finally Polack wearily, "Will you get out of my face, bitch, or do I clout you? I know what I'm doing, he's in my pocket. Lemme sleep, for Chrissake."

In the morning Ronnie was still in bed when Artie went out with Polack. Wearing his hard construction helmet, Artie leaned over the bed to give Ronnie's cheek a perfunctory pat and say brusquely, "Take this and get yourself something today, babe."

When they were gone, he looked at the folded bill. Ten bucks. He lay staring into space as waves of dismay and chagrin washed over him, then slowly drained away, leaving him beached.

On his way to the canteen to buy breakfast, he passed two trusties he knew casually. Approaching, they became suddenly involved in conversation, didn't look at him and seemingly didn't hear his greeting. Stung by the pointed rebuff, he found himself unable to muster a front to enter the crowded lunchroom where the trusties with money hung out. Instead he bought fig bars at the grocery window and walked slowly to work at the chapel.

The hell with them. Moronic slobs. Christ, I got to find a way to cope. Or get used to it. ("Here babe, take this and get yourself something.") Black underwear? Rhinestone jockstrap? I got to turn on or die.

He practiced furiously all morning on the piano and organ. When he returned from lunch, the chaplain called him in. He could see on the chaplain's face that it was Heat. A conclusion strengthened by the throbbing tremolo of reproach in the chaplain's voice.

"Are you in any trouble, Ronald?"

"Not that I know of, chaplain."

"Mr. Darby is here and wants to talk to you. You'll find him in the chapel."

"Yes, sir. Thank you." He went into the toilet and rapidly emptied his pockets into a handkerchief and stashed the bundle under the trash in the wastebasket. Checking his eyes in the mirror, he decided he couldn't risk wearing shades. Just have to keep looking down.

Son of a bitch. Darby, the Assistant Supe. Little Caesar, they called him. Cons claimed he could photostat a rap sheet with his eyeballs alone. And said that he knew everything about everybody, and saved it all for when he needed it. His manner with cons was a wry alert politeness, a deference studded with snares. Alone among the officials he received a grudging respect. And the ultimate accolade: "Con-wise."

Frantically running reels in his head, trying to remember where he might have slipped recently, Ronnie went nervously into the chapel. Darby was sitting in the choir loft inspecting a hymnbook. Short and dapper, crisply groomed, cropped gray hair, and disinterested eyes.

"Hello, Bracken. How are you?" he said.

"Pretty good, thank you, sir."

"Chaplain tells me you're doing a good job with the music program here."

"It's not exactly my bag, sir, but I do the best I can."

"Good, good. Two more years to go, is that right?"

"About that, sir."

"Got a good record so far? No D.R.'s?"

You're asking or telling? He looked at the bridge of Darby's nose briefly and dropped his gaze. There was just so much of the man-to-man, eye-to-eye bit you could hope to sell. With Darby it was important to try to compute it precisely.

"No, sir, I haven't been written up since I've been here. Well, not quite, sir." He was startled to find himself suddenly spitballing. "Once I was gigged for an overdue library book." He smiled primly at the official, sharing a rueful knowledge of the inscrutable ways of minor bureaucrats. Why? I must be losing my mind.

"Is that so? What was the name of the book?"

"Gosh, I don't remember, sir."

"It doesn't matter. I just thought you might have taken a special interest in it, to keep it overtime. Why did you move up on Trusty Range with Polack and his friends?"

"I beg your pardon, sir?"

"Don't give me a routine, Bracken, I'll bury you in Maximum and you'll be rapping to the roaches, chaplain's boy or no. I came over here instead of sending for you. To give you a break. You know my reputation around here, I only get visits from finks. Should I go back to the office and send for you?"

"I — I don't know what to say, Mr. Darby."

"Oh c'mon, Bracken, you can think of something. Like overdue library books. Ever since you've been here you lived in the Rock. Did a good job, kept a good record. Suddenly you jump off the end of the dock. Why?"

Ronnie felt himself losing ground under Darby's steady-rolling pressure. The first bloom of panic popped open inside him and began to grow.

In his throat, his voice: "I lost my cell partner, sir. And I have a Trusty card. So I moved to Trusty Range for a change of scene. Kind of break up this time a little, that's all. There was a vacancy in Polack's room. I wasn't even sure who lived there, sir."

"Well." A sour smile moved one corner of his mouth. "Sounds reasonable." He gazed into the rafters, searching for the rest of the thought. "You got a lot of gain time accumulated, son. I'd hate to see you blow it."

Son! There it was, nitty-gritty. Trying to quell the mounting dread, he caught a breath and plunged. "I hope you won't think I'm lipping off, Mr. Darby. But I'm the one has to build this time, sir. I have to live here. I got a clean record. All of a sudden I get a choice between Maximum Security and Protective Custody. And I haven't done anything."

Darby smiled broadly, shaking his head. "Correction, you haven't done anything *today*. Let's see, you were in the same cell for two years with Northrop, till he left on parole."

Ronnie looked down at his clasped hands, trying to keep them loose.

Let that one go by.

"I just don't get it, Ronald. An inmate with a good job and a perfect record — perfect on the surface at least, we understand that, don't we? Suddenly moves in with a gang of hustlers. Worse than hustlers."

His pulse pounding, waiting to hear the Man drop the Label, Ronnie continued to look gravely at his hands.

Darby sighed a bored sigh and stood up. Leaning against the rail of the choir loft, he reached into the pocket of his crisp short-sleeved white shirt.

"Smoking allowed in here?"

"Not for me, sir."

"I'll give you — what do they call it? Indulgence."

Ronnie took a cigarette from the proffered pack and Darby lighted it for him. "You got a parole hearing pretty soon, haven't you? Well — I thought I'd try. I can't help you if you won't help me. Chaplain says you're a valuable man, Ronald. Says you're the only one he's got who can play the organ."

"Yes, sir."

"You're over your head, Bracken. You could get into some bad shit. So protect yourself. Oh yes. You can tell your new friends about our talk if you want to. But you know how that goes. They'll only wonder how much you're holding back."

He took a few steps and stopped, looking out over the empty pews. Half to himself he said, "From concubine to stooge. Is that up, or down?" He strolled across the sanctuary, not looking back. Across the charged silence, Ronnie barely caught the words: "Keep a good record, Bracken. Be glad you play the organ."

Transfixed, he watched Darby go. Even numb with foreboding, he savored Darby's walk — the dispirited trudge of a man burdened with more than he cares to know, the tireless prowl of one implacably determined to expose and examine the last remaining secret.

Alone in the chapel, he sat stunned, his mind so clogged it was blank. He paced the long aisle, trying to decide what to do, and inevitably he went to the captain's office to see Billy.

"Can you take a break? I got something to tell you, but I think upstairs would be better."

In the room, Billy put some water to boil with an immersion heater. "You look shook, Ronnie. You want to turn on? I got some Dexies."

When they had downed the capsules and were sipping the scalding coffee, Billy reclined on the bed, propping himself on an elbow.

"All right, love. Wail."

"Darby came to see me at the chapel today."

"*He?* Came to *you?* The small Caesar?" Billy sat up to put a cigarette in his long holder. Seemingly absorbed in lighting up, he said, "Let's have all of it."

When Ronnie had finished, Billy sat nibbling the holder. Then, "I knew it. I tried to tell the stubborn bastard. Well." He looked at Ronnie as if seeing him for the first time. "I got to fill you in, my dear. You know Miller has only been captain for a few months. Since Captain Kern collapsed with penis envy or something and had to take sick leave. They didn't figure he'd be out long, so they decided to humor Miller and let him wear the King Hat for a while." He rose and began to pace the floor, waving the gaudy holder. "Miller has political friends, if you can believe that. He also gambles, juices and chases. You couldn't expect Polack to work around him and pass up a hustle like that. He became the understanding Big Brother, The Little Sister of the Poor. Advanced Miller some bread, friendly like. Just enough to bring him back for more. Kept raising the ante, ever so precisely. Sometimes I think he worked it out with a slide rule."

Listening, Ronnie felt like a man descending a sand dune. With every step downward, he slid six on the shifting sand beneath his feet.

"So how much further does Polack intend to ride it?"

"God. I wish I knew. Most of the time I can browbeat him. But now he's got this megalomania thing that he's big time at last. Utterly nutty. Darby has suspected all along that Polack had Dickless Tracy by the scrotum. He's just trying to figure a way to cut Polack's ass in half without splattering merde all over everything. And having it get to the Commissioner in Tallahassee. Every greedy mother in Administration is hustling *something*, and they don't want some square inspector to come in here and shut off the merry-go-round."

Billy stopped pacing and bent to open the cupboard. "Oh, balls. I think we need a stiff belt about now, don't you?"

Drinking the orange juisce and alcohol, he eyed Ronnie carefully over his glass. "All right now, listen closely to your old mother, dahling. This could blow us right across the river into Solitary. We're just a couple of warmhearted hustlers in a world of rape artists, right? So let's sit on this for a while, thee and me. Polack's tantrums bore the shit out of me, anyway. We play it cool and pay attention. Okay, little sister? We'll finish our drinks and go back to work like decent Kelly Girls."

Ronnie gulped the rest of the drink and went to stand looking out the windows. Something in his aspect made Billy swivel his glance to follow him.

At length Billy said, "What's the hang-up, baby? Tell your mother."

Turning from the window, he said, "You got to help me, Billy. or I'm going to crash. I feel like I got to turn on and never turn off again."

There was something that hadn't been there before. Billy inspected him casually, trying to name it.

"Turn me on, Billy baby. I got a right to sing the blues."

"Of course I will, love. I just hope you know what you're doing. What's your pleasure?"

"Cotton, anything, anything to twist my wig. I got to cut the balloon loose and sail for a while. Otherwise I'm going to flip."

Billy kept him supplied with inhalers and pills from the store of confiscated drugs in the captain's office, and Ronnie took off on a journey to the remote interior of himself. During the day, he discharged his routine duties at the chapel automatically, and kept to himself as much as possible. At night he slept very little. When he had performed his connubial routine with Artie, he joined other sleepless convicts around the Trusty Barber Shop. Under the sickly glow of two small naked bulbs, they sat on benches and folding chairs, each man to himself, reading paperbacks. Sometime during the night he would return to the room to lie on the bed, his eyes open, his mind racing, waiting for the day.

On Sunday morning he rose in darkness, having been in bed for less than an hour — he had to play the organ for early Mass. He swallowed some amphetamine, drank hot coffee, and gulped honey from a jar.

A guard answered his ring to unlock the iron door off the Trusties' floor.

It was still dark outside, and the moon was up. The long cell blocks were silent black silhouettes against the sky. He walked slowly through the dappled shadows under the live oaks, tasting the night, solitude, silence. He thought of Doug again. And again, he wished the same old wish.

If he was still here, I could tell him about this when I got back to the cell. The hole inside was getting bigger instead of smaller.

The Catholic priest was already at the chapel, dressing in the vestments of the Mass. He was a ruddy young Irishman of the provincial gentry with a politely disdainful manner, the high color of a wine drinker, and the sleekness of a well-kept horse. Father Aidan considered, and spoke it forth, that Mother Church had abandoned him in a swamp full of cannibals. He loathed Florida and his parish in town, and flew back to Dublin whenever he had the chance. Ronnie would watch from the organ, standing, at the altar, and wonder if the disenchanted Father Aidan had been taking a closer look at the Bride of Christ.

He stopped at his desk to put on a big pair of shades for a barricade, and knocked on the door of the priest's office. Father Aidan looked wasted, Ronnie noted with satisfaction.

In his Irish tenor voice and precise English accent, the priest said, "Ah, here is my cherished organist. I have a couple of suggestions for you." And indicated places in the Mass where he wanted special music.

Beautiful. He's stagestruck again. Probably do Paul Scofield or Brian Aherne this morning. We'll wail.

At the door leading to the sanctuary, he paused to collect himself: Deliberate. Coordinate. Operate. Meticulously he navigated his way across a sea of polished floor under the gaze of those devout convicts who came early to kneel and mutter.

Once he was seated on the organ bench, it was better. The keys of the organ regarded him expectantly and made him eager to play.

Father Aidan made his entrance with the altar boy, and Ronnie gave him austere flourishes and fanfares, then softly improvised behind him as he moved through the Mass, always building toward the climactic Sanctus. When Father Aidan was up in the part, the music had to sustain him and even push his performance a little higher.

Sometimes they got carried away and overblew the gig. One Mass had ended completely off the rails when Father Aidan, after giving Benedictus and Dismissal, had come to the lectern and by some circuitous ploy, launched into a bellowing rendition of "Galway Bay," ending in a florid wild Irish coda. The conservative cons had been stunned and offended.

Now Father Aidan was leading up to the high moment of the Mass, the Sanctus. He raised the chalice high, and the long rays of the morning sun through the tall windows caught the brass cup and struck flame. Ronnie brought up the music crescendo under it, sustained, and stopped.

From here on, it was downhill. He wondered if he had come on too strong with the movie-score music, induced by a sudden vision of Loretta Young as a nun. But no, it was all right — at the end of the Mass, the priest was smiling, nodding his head, bowing slightly toward the organ.

And then, to Ronnie's dismay, Father Aidan blew it again. Advancing to the lectern, he called out, with the false heartiness of an Irish tummler, "And now let us all rise and join in singing 'God Bless America.' "

Ronnie played the introduction too loudly, to express his distaste. The convicts had the words in their songbooks, but there was an unspoken law about patriotic songs, no con in his right mind would sing them. They slouched, they sagged and shuffled, and droned a low grumbling monotone of injury and complaint.

Father Aidan bawled all the louder, making up his own words, and finished with a braying flourish that bounced off the walls. He beamed fatuously down at the organ. Ronnie, walled up behind his big shades, told the lower half of his face to smile: And there he goes, folks, the Singing Priest. From Vatican to Vegas, overnight.

The short winter of northern Florida was coming to an end Wandering in the isolation of an amphetamine dream, Ronnie was suddenly surprised and gratified one morning to notice the redbud trees in clouds of blossom. With the longer days, he was able to delay returning to the room until dark. He spent the time between the end of his workday and the twilight reading on a small porch at the rear of the chapel. Or wandered the prison grounds, mourning for Doug, unable to heal the pain of his loss.

The warmer weather also brought the return of Yard Night, when the huge banks of lights on the prison recreation field were turned on for a weekly sporting event. On the first of these nights, there was a program of bouts by the boxing squad.

Virtually the entire prison population came out for the show. Some to visit with friends they could not otherwise see, most of them to enjoy the darkness and the night air as a change from the grinding bleakness of daylight existence.

Polack and Billy, Artie and Ronnie, dressed in immaculate, freshly starched whites, went into the Rock to see the fights. Ronnie cringed at the entrance Polack insisted upon making, a promenade before the stands packed with cons, before taking seats on the topmost level, where nobody would be behind Polack. There were cracks, and some random booing, as they climbed up. The prelims were already in progress. The windup was a bout between Bud Larrabee and a highly touted newcomer to the joint.

Ronnie saw Bud by the ring, jogging back and forth and shadow-boxing. Bud took off his robe and in his trunks came up into the stand where they were sitting. In his tentative diffident way he nodded to all of them. "Hey, whatcha say? Got some visiting wheels here tonight, huh?"

Polack said, "You gonna flatten this mother for me tonight, partner? I got a lotta bread riding on your handsome ass."

"My ass ain't where it's at. Partner. You shouldn't gamble, it rots your teeth."

He turned his head suddenly to catch Ronnie unaware, pinning him with the unsettling fixed brown stare. "Evening, Bracken, how you been? How's everything in Fink City?"

Ronnie was thankful for the shades he wore. "Good to see you, Bud. You going to take this cat?"

"I'm gonna make you a present of his ears." He turned and made his way back to ringside. He knocked out his opponent in the first round, and after the fight Polack kept them waiting while he rapped to Larrabee.

Walking back to Trusty quarters, Ronnie heard Billy say, "What did Larrabee want?"

"Bread. I let him have it. He earned it."

"You *gave* it to him?"

"Are you nuts? I loaned it to him. His brother sends him money every week, he's good for it."

Next day, one of the chapel clerks, with an indefinable air of emphasis, told Ronnie somebody wanted to see him outside. On the steps of the chapel he was surprised to see Black Daddy — the wheeling-dealing hyper-hip spade who was ramrod of the Negro convicts in the Black Rock. His air of power, his enameled sophistication and his mocking oblique way of rapping had always rendered Ronnie near speechless the few times they had talked.

"Black Daddy. Hey man, what's happening? You're early, church ain't till Sunday."

A shadow that might have been a smile flitted over the impassive jet-black shiny face, the big lips barely moving. "Say, Bracken. Ain't nuthin' shakin'. Got a minute?"

"For the King of Africa? Command me."

The guttural chuckle was more formal response than mirth. They walked around to the side of the chapel and sat on the grass behind some shrubbery. Black Daddy handed him a box and Ronnie opened it to find a gold wristwatch.

Startled, he gaped at the spade chieftain, an electric surmise on his face.

With a sardonic grimace Black Daddy said, "Naw man, cool it, it's from Larrabee. He knows I got gate passage. Asked me to bring it to you."

"From *Bud?* What the hell for?"

"Hey man, I just brought it, that's all. I don't know nothin'."

"I — Jesus. I don't know what to say. You puttin' me on a hummer? I don't know what to think."

"You hear anything from Doug?"

"No man, don't expect to. You know how that is. When they go, they're gone."

"That was a blowin' cat. I miss that horn."

"*You* miss it."

"Listen, Bracken. Larrabee's my main man. Only white stud besides Doug I ever rapped to. He's a brother."

Ronnie tried to find a clue in the impenetrable sculptured black face. "What key is that in, Black Daddy?"

"Splivy broad, ain'tcha. I liked Doug. I dig Larrabee. I dig the way *you* blow sometimes. Sometimes. Otherwise — "

"Awright man, sorry. What's the story?"

"Larrabee's pissed, he's fixin' to rumble with Polack. And your half-hip stud."

"Rumble about what?"

"The shylockin', for one. Lotta cats are pissed, but now they got Larrabee in front of 'em. And when he goes, he don't feel nothin'."

"Is that all he's hacked about?"

"You're kiddin'. If I had a broad moved out while I was away from the cell, and stripped it, I'd ventilate her snatch with an ice pick."

"Wait a minute, Black Daddy, that's not all of it, he — "

"I give a shit, man. I'm just doin' this for Bud. If you wanna keep that toy stud of yours in shape to take care of biz, you better tout him off."

"Hey man, I feel like you, this rumble shit is a drag. Nobody wins."

"Okay, just tell your old man to stay out of the Rock. I don't wanna see my boy mess up his hands. They make a lotta bread for me."

"I got no eyes for that hassle, Black Daddy. And I don't think Artie goes into the Rock all that much, anyway."

"Sheet. What joint are you in? He's a collector, right? Him and Polack hit that joint at daylight, most mornings. Move in on the cats before they're awake. Make the bar-man pull the bar, go in the cat's cell, waste him, and split. You got yourself a *man,* babe. *Real* high-roller." The lips curled in a massive sneer.

Ronnie looked at the ground, the desolation inside him deepening. "Dig. Tell Bud — if he cares — I fouled up and I'm payin'."

A snort of derision. "The hell you think that gold block is for? Jeez if you were my — ah nuts, I got to split."

His contempt lingered in the air. Ronnie looked at the costly watch, tried it on, took it off and put it back in the box.

He walked over to the captain's office and showed it to Billy.

"Rolex! Jesus Christ, girl, what did you have to do for *that?*"

"Bud sent it."

"Larrabee? *Larrabee* sent it?" He folded his arms and stared into space. Ronnie was startled to see him throw his head back and burst into wild barking laughter. When he paused, his eyes wet, he looked at Ronnie and burst again into redoubled hilarity.

"Oh, Christ," he murmured. "Oh Jesus Mary and Joe. My perishing ass."

"Billy. Gimme a break. What's so goddamn funny?"

"He — he — Larrabee borrowed the bread from Polack. From Artie, you might as well say."

They stared at one another. Ronnie murmured, "He set them up for a burn. Black Daddy said — "

"He's inviting Artie to try and collect." Billy was smiling, a look of rueful admiration. "You said what about Black Daddy?"

"What? Oh nothing. What am I going to do with this ridiculous watch?"

"You're not going to wear it? You ain't got a hair in your ass — "

Ronnie shook his head. "Uh-uh, madame. You don't agitate me into nuttin'. You're trying to stir up some shit for laughs."

"Who, me? *Larrabee,* you mean. When I think of how I have

low-rated that boy. He's crazy? Some lunatic. The son of a bitch turns it on and off like a faucet."

"Crazy? No. Bud isn't crazy. The demon that goes everywhere Bud goes is crazy."

"So what are you going to do with the bauble?"

Ronnie looked at the white box. "The impulse is to bury it with my other bones. But Larrabee's playing games. So I think I better send it back. Besides, it may be hot."

That evening Polack and Artie came in looking grim. Ronnie was lying on the bed reading a magazine. Artie sat down by him. "Where is it?"

"Where's what?"

"Larrabee gave you a gold Rolex. Where is it?"

"I, uh — sent it back."

"Where is it?"

"I told you, Artie, I sent it back."

Polack came over. "Forget all that, forget it." To Ronnie, "What's with you and Larrabee?"

"Nothing, Polack. He's hot at me, so he's trying to put me in the middle, that's all."

Artie said, "You sure you sent it back?"

"I told you, partner, *forget* it. We got more to think about. I got some muscle lined up. We go in there tomorrow."

"Into the *Rock?*"

"You know any other way to get that wise punk?"

Artie got up to walk. "Christ, Polack. He's got half the Rock with him."

"He thinks he has. They'll fold when it comes down to it."

"Jeez, I don't know. That cat's out of his skull."

The deep-set eyes measured Artie. "If you're chicken I better know it now."

Artie swung around, bristling. "Wait a minute, Polack, I ain't chicken but I ain't crazy either."

Billy had been sitting there immobile and silent, his head down. "He's right, Polack. Go in there now is stone bugs."

"Keep your jaw shut or I'll wire it shut." To Artie, "Either we're in business or we ain't. I'm not lettin' that punchy athlete back me down. So make up your mind."

Artie chewed his lips. "I'm with you, but — "

"Awright. Tomorrow early."

Billy said, "I truly hope you know what you're doing."

Polack wheeled, pointing, livid. "I told you *once!*"

"Okay, okay." Grimacing in distaste, he got up. "I have to work tonight. I'm way behind. If you'll excuse me."

That night, instead of the routine perfunctory sex, Artie stayed for most of the night with Ronnie, lying silent in his arms between the surges of bleak troubled sex. For the first time in a long time Ronnie was stirred by his nearness and held him close, his face pressed into the thick lustrous black hair.

It was not yet daylight when somebody tried to force the door of the room open, and failing, rapped violently. Artie slid into his own bed. The pounding grew in volume, till Billy got out of bed and deftly removed the spike holding the door shut.

One of the night guards pushed it open. "Majewski?" He stepped further into the room. Louder: *"Majewski?"*

Polack raised his head from the pillow and growled, "*What?* What do you want, Peters?"

"Pack your shit, Polack. You're going to the road. Be at Control Room in half an hour."

Polack leaped naked from bed. "*What?* What the hell are you talking about?"

Peters retreated to the door. "Control Room, half an hour, Polack."

Billy sat huddled on his bed, seemingly locked in. Artie got up to stand aimlessly in the middle of the room, as Polack, muttering curses, stumbled into his clothes. The brass tang of panic thickened the air.

"I'll get that shitbird Miller on the phone. Somebody's ass is gonna burn for this." He banged out of the room.

Artie started to put his clothes on.

Billy said, "Better stay out of it, Artie."

"Hell, you mean stay out of it. I'm goin' down there."

"*Artie.* Go back to bed. I'm telling you, baby, this is sticky shit." Billy had finished dressing and was at the door. "For once use your pretty head. Get back in your rack." He gave Ronnie a tight tired smile. *"Sauve qui peut, chéri.* I'll try to rescue the groceries. Looks like happy Armageddon."

He went out. In a few minutes the door burst open again and Polack came in, two guards along with him. One, the burly Lieutenant Johnson, said, "Awright, Polack, quit stallin'. Get your stuff and let's ramble. The bus is waiting."

The formidable face was clogged, incandescent with fury. He threw the contents of his footlocker into a cardboard box.

Artie hovered anxiously. "What happened, Polack, did you get him?"

"Bastard won't answer. It's a shanghai job. I'll be back, partner. Just hold the fort." He hoisted the box on his shoulder and left with the two guards.

Artie opened the cupboard and took a long drink of alcohol from the bottle. He sat on Ronnie's bed. "Jesus. Miller blew it."

Ronnie, at a loss, curved his hand around the big hairy forearm. "Hang loose, Artie. Better his ass than yours, right?"

He jerked his arm away. "Aw, *man!*" And began to pace the floor again.

Billy slipped in. He raised his eyebrows at Ronnie, exhaling a long breath. "Hoo-eee, baby. Groovy moving day. Lions in the street."

Artie grabbed him by the arm. His voice shrill, "What the goddamn hell is going on?"

Billy spread his long pale hands, shrugging his thin shoulders. "Caesar finally nailed Polack. Simple as that. They put him on a bus for Deep Lake."

They gaped at him and repeated, "Deep Lake!"

Billy nodded, a mordant smile touching his lips. "Siberia. *Sic transit gloria.*"

Artie said, "What the hell is that?"

"Gloria vomited on the subway. You want some coffee, Ronnie?"

"Coffee. I need a pill. Everything's moving too fast."

"As to that, I saved the groceries, anyway. Now all we got to sweat is getting shipped across the river."

Ronnie said, "I still don't know what happened."

"It's shit-simple, babe. Darby shipped Polack before daylight so he couldn't reach Miller. Before Miller got here, dig? And he sent him to Deep Lake, dig?"

"In the middle of the goddamn Everglades," Artie said. "Higgins is Boss there. A murderin' redneck bastard."

"You get the picture. In a couple of weeks or so we'll hear that Polack escaped."

Ronnie said, "You mean they'll *let* him escape?"

"I mean that in a couple of weeks or maybe sooner, Polack is going to be belly down in the swamps with the ants munching his eyeballs. I guess you *could* call it a bust-out. Poor bastard."

Artie sat on his bed, his elbows on his knees, face in hands, staring at the floor. His dark tan was sallow. "What happens now?"

Lips pursed, Billy considered him. "Us poor kids, you mean? Hmmm. Speak low, walk slow, love Jesus."

Ronnie went about his duties at the chapel, anxiously wondering what Darby's next move would be. He passed him on the grounds one day. Darby had nodded cordially, with the familiar smile that seemed to be secretly amused, perfectly devised to disconcert those with guilty knowledge. But that was all.

Avoiding Billy and Artie as much as possible, he delayed returning to the room in the evenings until just before Count Time. And usually when he got there, he found the two of them deep in conversation.

And to further puzzle and discomfit him, convicts who had been giving him frost suddenly began to greet him ostentatiously, or to seek him out when he was eating in the canteen.

I liked these creeps better the other way, he thought. They act like I personally turned Polack up. The idea hooked in his mind . . . Turned Polack up . . . He stared blankly as his thoughts raced, circling the sudden suspicion. Something like fear moved in him . . .

The sex scene with Artie became a source of acute uneasiness now, with Billy lying alone in his bed, listening. It improved some when Billy eventually began spending the first part of the night away from the room, with the stay-up cons around the barber shop.

One night when they were alone in the room and in bed, Artie startled and shocked Ronnie by presenting himself, making it clear that he wanted Ronnie to assume the aggressive male role.

Stunned and baffled, he concurred, his mind in a turmoil, his body operating automatically and seemingly without direction. On the ensuing night, the reversal of roles became the permanent arrangement.

He spent much of the day dreading the coming night — in a daze of conjecture, trying to figure what had happened. It was not uncommon in the joint, it even had a name — FlipFlop — but it was the first time in Ronnie's experience. He forced himself to function, in a riot of confusion and ambivalence.

He had been tempted to confide his dismay to Billy — but increasingly, for the first part of the evening between Count Time and lights-out, Artie and Billy were together, to the pointed exclusion of Ronnie. The relationship between Billy and him grew steadily cooler, Billy's manner one of careful distant politeness.

One day during lunch hour, Artie came into the chapel office. "Can I see you for a minute?"

Ronnie took him into the empty church and they sat in a pew. Artie's manner was portentous — grave, and subdued. Blue-eyed sincerity, Ronnie thought, nagged by the remembrance of the bed scene the night before, of Artie's unnerving and shameful turnabout.

"I don't know exactly how to say this, Ronnie."

Ronnie regarded him in silence, calmly waiting, feeling the strange and new poise that stemmed from his domination of Artie in the sack.

In the daylight Artie seemed the same as always. "It's like this, Ronnie. We ain't squares. We're both hip intelligent people, right?"

Ronnie nodded. "Both hip, yes."

"Well — " Then in a rush, "See, Billy and I got eyes for each other and I wanna — we wanna — "

Remote, he watched the dialogue unfold as in a predictable movie. "I think that's wonderful, Artie. I think that's beautiful. I love you both."

"You're not — you don't mind."

The boyish eyes so troubled, so blue. So true-blue. "Mind, Artie? Well, yeah, how could I not? But what kind of a prick would I be?"

"Jesus, thanks a lot, Bracken. You're beautiful, you're too much." He got up, blushing, and shook Ronnie's hand warmly.

Artie gone, he sat for a while, speculating, bemused by the charade. In some tribal way, he had failed. Falling among jackals, he had sought acceptance by accepting jackal rules, jackal manners. And all along they had known he was not a true jackal, and would have to go. His chest was stuffed with what felt like a gusher of wild insane giggles ready to erupt. (Were they sobs?) And a squalid sense of pique at having been rejected and jilted.

"Jilted." He tried it aloud, and decided not to repeat it for fear of hysteria. Or whatever it was, lying there in ambush. Later it would be funny. Now, somehow, it was not.

He took a pill, and sat waiting for it to hit. Then he went to see Billy.

"Artie told you." The brassiness was absent, the hard black eyes were wide, almost demure. "We couldn't help it, love, believe me."

"I think it's charming."

"You really do? You really don't mind, baby?"

"What's to mind? It was an arrangement, Artie and me. Only thing is, what do I do now? I got to move, you know that."

"Yes, I think that's wise, love, but I hate to see you go."

"I hate to go, love. But find me a place to move, okay?"

"Of course." Billy took out a chart and studied it for a moment. "Jesus, baby, I don't know what I can do, though. There's no vacancy on Trusty Range. Before all this goddamn heat, I could move them around like dominoes. But now I got to watch myself." He studied the chart again at length, and looked up at Ronnie, eyes wide.

"This is absolutely nutty. The only vacancy there is, is in the Rock: J-fifty-seven."

Ronnie searched the smooth, concerned, slightly pained face raised to him. "What kinda stupid jive is that? The cell I came *out* of? Larrabee's still in there, isn't he?"

Billy nodded. "He's in there alone. Everybody that moves in, he muscles out."

"What are you trying to do to me?"

A note of the familiar arrogance and asperity was heard. "Listen, baby, you asked me for a move, and that's what I'm giving you. I told you I have to watch it now. You want to go back in the Rock or don't you? Are you scared of a numb-numb like Larrabee?"

Ronnie let the smile come on slow, delaying the shaft. "Why shouldn't I be? Artie is."

Billy said icily, "I think we can agree that it's not quite the same thing. Do you want it or don't you?"

"Oh, shit. All right, run it."

Bud was in his shorts, lying on his belly in the lower bunk, when Ronnie opened the door of the cell just before lockup. Behind him were two spades, on loan from Black Daddy, to carry the phonograph, records, FM, and the books.

Larrabee looked around startled, and jumped to his bare feet. "Hell's goin' on? You on safari?"

"I got moved, Bud. They assigned me here. If you say no, I'll go down and get another assignment. If I can."

The liquid brown eyes were fixed on him, and again he had the sensation of immersion, sinking.

Larrabee scratched his shaven head. "I'll level with you, Bracken, I don't dig it worth a shit. But Doug was my friend, and when he left he asked me to look out for you. He said you'd be a pain in the ass, and I got to go along with that."

He began to remove the books and clothing that littered the upper bunk. "It might be kind of dull for you here. After you bein' with the Billy Lane Circus and all."

He turned and transfixed Ronnie with the hypnotic gelid gaze. "I got some new poetry I want you to read."

A week later, Ronnie lay stretched out on the grass at the side of the chapel. Screened by some shrubbery, he was stripped to his shorts, letting the hot Florida sun soothe him, ease his tension.

Billy suddenly appeared around the bushes, and dropped to the grass beside him. "So peaceful here. Mind if I join you?" He pulled off his shirt and lay down on the blanket. There was a silence.

"Pretty sly, Bracken. You really sold me a blind mule, didn't you?"

"I don't understand, babe."

"Oh god. I'm beginning to see how you do it. *Artie,* I'm talking about. All-Boy Artie."

"You may have bought it. I didn't sell it."

"Uh-huh. The way you do the suffering victim. It's too much."

"Just living is suffering, Billy."

"All right, okay, but don't bleed on me. How is it with the mad Larrabee?"

"I found out he isn't mad. Just maddening. You know what it

is? He's simple. Intolerably, deviously simple. Anyway, I'm on probation. I'm studying Poetry Appreciation. Well . . . at least, nobody *else* is bugging me. The wife of the centaur, whoopee."

Billy lighted a cigarette. In the bright sunlight, there was a sudden flash of gold at his wrist. Ronnie sat up and lowered his shades to look.

"Isn't that the Rolex? That started all the hassle?"

Billy regarded the watch fondly. "The only thing that hasn't turned to shit for me."

"Do you mind if I ask you — ?"

"Not at all. I did a favor for a friend."

"For Larrabee."

"I think you could say Bud's a friend of mine."

"Devoted, it would seem. Such handsome payment. A difficult favor."

"Difficult, no. Peculiar, maybe." A trace of testiness in his sigh. "He was looking for a cell partner who understood poetry."

"Ah. And you delivered this — rarity."

"In a way. In a way."

The sun beat down. They lay motionless and silent.

"You turned Polack up, didn't you?" Ronnie asked.

Billy didn't answer right away. When he did, he sounded tired. "You know what a rumble like that would have done? Locked everything up, tight." He propped himself on his elbow and looked down at the recumbent Ronnie. "And you, little flower, and I would now be across the river. In that birdcage with the rest of the parakeets." He lay back and raised his thin arms, stretching luxuriantly. "This is nicer, don't you agree?"

"Expediency." It was a murmur, bemused. "I wish I knew how to do that."

"Oh Bracken, c'mon. *You?* You with the laminated motives? All I can say is, I hope *I* never have you for a victim."

JACK CADY

I Take Care of Things

(FROM THE YALE REVIEW)

IT WAS LATE beyond the usual time of the sirens. I sat on the driver's side of the cruiser waiting for Frank to quit heaving. Our light was flashing a circular beacon into the blackness of the surrounding trees. We were just inside the park. The light made a changing red glow in the trees and pulled darkness behind it like a vacuum. The trees were moving in a light wind and spitting a few leaves. The light ticked, rotating. My hands were tense. There had been a wreck. Two kids on a motorcycle had missed a curve at speed. One was a girl. She had been thrown against a guy wire. They must have rapped into the curve at sixty-plus. It had been a big bike.

Fire equipment was parked fifty yards down the road. A fireman in a yellow slicker leaned hard on the straight stream nozzles that could whip the hose like snapping steel cable if it got loose. The water hit the pavement and bounced into a spray of red from the emergency lights.

Between us and the fire truck another fireman came from behind some trees. His face seemed paler in the flash of red than in the darkness. He steadied himself against a tree. Then he stepped onto the road. I eased back in the seat and watched. Pretty soon we could go.

Frank was getting quiet. He sat with the car door open and his feet in the road. He raised his head like he was testing himself. Then he wiped his mouth with his shirt sleeve. He touched his hand to his shirt front and dropped his hand fast. He had pulled the boy out from the broken frame of the motorcycle.

"I will," I told him. I reached to unbutton the shirt which had a lot of blood on front. The blood was cold and slick. It is always a strange feeling. I opened the buttons down to his belt. He pulled the tail out of his pants and got the rest. He jerked the shirt off and balled it up, throwing it on the floor in back.

"Your badge," I told him.

"Screw the badge," he said, "and you, too." His voice was close to hysteria. He got out of the wet undershirt by pulling up and holding it away from his face. His hair was pushed around. He was getting bald toward the front. The thin side hair tangled and stood up. His brows were heavy and looked messed. Probably they looked like that because his eyes were wild. He was only thirty-three or -four, but he looked like a crazy man of sixty.

"I'll get the badge," I told him.

"And the rest of the world."

"Everybody, huh."

"Them, too. Leave me alone."

He is older than I am by a couple of years. In some ways he is younger because he never learns. At least his feelings never learn. I saw him break up once before. Cops are wrong to break up.

"Be back," I told him, and climbed from the car. The ambulance was being loaded. They were about finished. I walked to the back of the ambulance. The guys were not careful.

The driver was an old man, very tall if he would straighten up, but he was stooped. His gray hair was streaked red and black in the lights. His helper was a kid. The kid looked wrong. Almost like a head. He looked high.

"You ready?" Their job was bad. You could tell about the body. Across the bridge of her nose there was a scrape that was nearly bloodless.

The driver looked at me. He was about to close the door. "Nearly ready. You want to check it?"

"No need."

"No need to hurry either," the kid said, and grinned. He was tall like the driver. His hair was too long. It was black and was slicked against his head. His hands were manicured. A homosexual maybe, or something different. All kinds of perversion hang around death. Up close you could tell he was high. He giggled.

"You like it." I watched him. He stopped giggling. His eyes looked all right except that they were excited. He was not high on drugs.

"No," he said. His voice was trying to go low and serious. He could not quite get it down there.

"Sure he does," the driver said. He was old and looked old. Ambulance guys working a big city are usually losers. Paid by the shift. Sleep in.

"Come over here," I told him. We walked away from the ambulance and toward the cruiser. About midway I stopped. There was no reason to let him see Frank.

"Make an inventory?"

"Didn't you?" He looked indignant. I gave him a leaf of paper from my book because the forms were in the car. He began scribbling, using the back of the book. They had custody of a couple of watches, a billfold and a few bucks currency. "He doesn't steal," the old man said, "and I don't need to." He was hot. It was my job.

"He ride in back?" I pointed to the kid.

"Sometimes. He don't always ride with me."

"With live ones?"

"I ride with the live ones. He don't go with me all the time. I don't know what he does with other guys." He knew trouble, that old man. He signed the paper and gave it to me. There was a kicked look in his eyes. He wanted to say something and either did not know how or did not know what.

"Sorry about the list," I told him. He turned and walked back to the ambulance. The helper climbed in the riding side and they pulled away. Before they were around the curve the old man secured his light.

It was about wrapped up. The firemen had pressure off the hose. I was going to ask them to shoot under our car but it was too late. Instead, I walked to where the girl had hit. A human has a lot of blood. The pavement was clean under the lights. Beside the road the gravel was gone. It had been washed back into the grass. The roadside was slick with mud. Grass was beaten down and washed out in one big area. There is a lot of pressure on those hoses. Later on, the park crews would come around and sod. Maybe they would not even know why the grass was washed out. Mabye they would bitch. It was clean. A good job.

I waved to the nearest fireman and went back to the car. When I climbed in Frank looked better. He was still not good but he seemed to have some control. He was sitting straight, not slumped over. His arms were muscular but his chest was kind of bony and thin. His chest was heaving. It looked like a contradiction after seeing his arms.

"I'm sorry," he said. He looked straight ahead.

"Sorry is for kids," I told him. "I'll take you home. They don't need for you to check in naked."

"Taking a chance."

"Can't you tell the difference? Taking no chance. The shift's out in an hour anyway." I drove to the edge of our sector before calling in to report the scene clear. Then I took us out of service. It was past four-thirty Thursday morning. A loose time. Even if I was seen I could explain.

"Coffee," I told Frank. I pulled beyond an all-night restaurant and walked back. The counter man was sitting and reading a magazine. I have known him for a couple of years. He can guess things, the way guys can sometimes when they are used to being alone. He looked up when I walked in.

"Hi, Burns," he said. "You had a bad one." He stood up and poured coffee in two paper cups. He did it slow. Rheumatism.

"Bad enough." I leaned on the counter. The walk-boards in back of the counter looked greasy and slick.

"I heard the noise." He is not a nosy guy. He was just asking if I needed anything besides coffee.

"Make it black," I told him. "You ought to wipe this counter." I had leaned in a spot of mustard or some kind of slop. The counter was cracked linoleum, dark green where it was not peeling.

He passed me the coffee. "What a crappy job," he said. By the time I was through the doorway he was reading the magazine again.

Frank spilled some of the coffee in his lap. It scalded and he sat still. Probably it helped steady him. Then he started drinking the coffee and that helped more. A pretty fair cop, Frank. But wrong-headed. ~~He relates.~~ Takes it personal. When he first saw that body I know he thought of his daughter. She is thirteen and healthy and does not ride on motorcycles. He thinks muddled. He gets one thing on his mind and it means something else. ~~At first I thought it was~~ morals. He would lose his temper. I've seen him beat a pusher into the hospital and the guy was only dealing in pot. It is not morals. He relates.

"I got something to tell you," he said. His voice still sounded lousy. There was a tremble like someone who was crying.

"I probably don't want to hear." I drank off the rest of my coffee and pulled away. It was true. I did not want to hear because he gave me an uneasy feeling. Something he had done had made no sense. Fooling around.

When we got to the scene we had checked the kids out fast. I went to run traffic by and chase the ghouls off. When they did not leave I put our spotlight on the girl and that got rid of some of them. Frank had been in the bushes freeing the boy's body. The ambulance guys could have done that.

"I got to tell you," he said.

"Save it."

"Now." The more he talked the worse his voice got.

We rode for a while. It was less dark. Not light really. It was the way it looks just before you get the first far-off suggestion of dawn. Frank leaned forward like he was completely exhausted.

"Listen," he said, "put yourself in my place."

"There ain't no amount of money."

His voice got on a low monotone. Probably he figured to control it that way.

"I looked at the boy," he said, "and you went out to the road. Then I went and looked at the girl. Clean cut. Surgical."

"Forget it."

"I got mad. Cars backed up. People walking off to puke and then coming back for another look. Just a little girl."

"Everything dead looks little." I looked at him because I was hearing something. His hands were out of control. His eyes were wild again. His mouth hung open. He was panting like a dog. That was what I was hearing. A dog pant. His control was gone and suddenly, right there, I hated him. It was a strange feeling.

I hated him for not controling his emotions.

"Get it over," I told him. I could not remember hating anyone like that before.

"Went back to the boy. Big hump of stuff in the bushes. Part human and part iron. Wedged into the bushes getting madder. That girl. Hating. Crying. Started to swear. Felt for a pulse."

"Found one, didn't you?"

He turned to me, shocked out of his panting. I had him cut from under. "Yes, light pulse."

"Thanks." I looked out at the street. We were near his house. "So you got mad and turned the whole mess upside down like you were pulling out a body. That what you wanted to tell me?" I was ahead of him. It wrecked his climax.

"His back was broken. It twisted and then there wasn't any more pulse." He was gasping so hard he could hardly breathe. He could not say anything more. I drove. It was only a couple of blocks.

Death. You work with it. Sometimes it's dirty like when a drunk goes out in an alley. Sometimes it's painful. Old people with heart attacks. Automobile injuries that bleed them white and cold before you can get it stopped. Gas. Fire. Drowning.

I pulled up to his house. He did not move.

"You want me to decide," I told him. "You want me to make it right by doing something. Make up your mind for you." I hated him.

"You know what it is."

"Well, the hell with you. Get the coroner's report."

"You know the word. You know what it is."

"Sure, the word is that it's five-thirty in the morning and I need sleep." I turned to him. "Okay, give me your gun."

He passed it over like he was glad. He was actually breathing better. I dropped the gun between the seat and the door on my side. "Get out," I told him. He got out like he did not understand. I reached over and slammed the door.

"Get some sleep," I told him. I shoved it in gear and got away before he could answer. The gun was beside the seat. He could not shoot himself. Instead, he was going to have to stand in the growing light without a shirt. The whole world chases itself in an eighty-mile-an-hour frenzy. He could match his mind to that along with whatever he called a conscience. He could walk to the nearest precinct or he could damned well go in the house to his wife, take a shower, and go to bed.

There was the beginning traffic. Milkmen and other route guys. I felt better than I had for an hour. Leaving Frank like that was a help. It had been uncomfortable when I hated him.

ROBERT CANZONERI

Barbed Wire

(FROM THE SOUTHERN REVIEW)

"AN UNCLE would be the merest of appendages if there were something to be appended to." The boy read the sentence aloud to his mother from the letter he was holding. "Is that supposed to make sense?" he demanded.

"Your Uncle Royce never seemed to consider it important to make sense," his mother said.

The boy thought about it for a few minutes. He was sixteen and his face was fat and freckled. He was confident of becoming almost as good a journalist as his father would have been if he had lived. He was impatient of school, and he wanted to make a real start — perhaps the same one his father had made. Big words did not bother him. "I'm going anyway," he said.

"Well," his mother said doubtfully. "It's where you're from."

The boy had been two years old when his father was killed and his mother took him north to her home. Aunt Janey had visited them, but her husband, Uncle Royce, he could not envision at all.

Royce did not want the boy to come. He felt as if his life over the past several years had been composed of trying to get around aging men who planted themselves unaccountably in his path and said to him with eyes deliberately alight and faces expectant, "I believe in living." He was certain the boy would be like that — eyes alight and face expectant. Off and on all summer Royce lay awake nights hoping the boy wouldn't come.

It was a hot dry day in August when the boy arrived on the bus from Indiana. There had been a long drought, and now pasture grass was brown, dust was thick on everything, and cow ponds were nothing but crusted hoofprints down to the base of their dams, where there was just about mud enough for a sharecropper's pig-pen. That was Royce's description in his weekly paper. The boy got off the bus and felt sweat pop out all over him. He was sore from sitting so long and his seat was creased from the wrinkles in his pants.

Aunt Janey looked just the same except smaller. Now he had to lean down to let her kiss him, and he could see to the roots of her fine hair which used to float out against the light like a halo. She was his father's sister.

The newspaper office had an old brick front. The boy searched among the black-shaded gold letters on the window for his father's name — left perhaps because of laziness or perhaps out of sentiment or perhaps as a tribute to his great contribution to the world of journalism — but although the lettering was very old, no trace of his father's name was visible:

THE SENTINEL

Lucius County's Oldest, Largest, Fastest Growing
and Only Newspaper
Royce Weatherly, Editor and Publisher

FOR SALE:

Typewriters, Office Supplies
The Whole Damn Paper including the Editor,
a few Books of doubtful value,
Pens, Pencils, new or used Paper

PRINTING

The *Sentinel* was not really for sale. When Royce had been approached about selling out — only twice in twenty-seven years — he had responded, "Every man has his price. Mine's just fifty cents higher than your highest offer." It was not because he was the third Weatherly to own the paper, nor was it because underneath his cynical exterior he was either sentimental about the newspaper or devoted to the community. It was rather, as Royce had written editorially, that he had

been around just enough to know that nowhere — not anywhere available to man — is there a truly better place to live, are there truly better people, is there possible a more meaningful existence than right here in Lucius County.

No wonder the human race is trying to blow itself off this unstrung yo-yo we call Earth.

It was also because Royce could say what he damn pleased. " 'At's just old Royce," they'd say. "He's a caution though, ain't he?"

Once a minister had dropped by to enlist Royce on the side of the Lord. "Mr. Weatherly, you take some unpopular stands. But I wonder," he said, "if you wouldn't have more effect if you attacked specific local evils."

Royce broke in before he could name any. "Right, Preacher. I was just about to concoct an editorial on people who come around telling everybody else what to do."

The preacher blinked his eyes a couple of times and then said, "I feel it's my duty to indicate the Lord's will."

Royce had been sitting in a swivel chair with his green eyeshade on and his sleeves pulled up with garters, not altogether because it made him look quaint but because it shaded his eyes and saved his cuffs; now he stood up. "Preacher," he said, "you can't imagine what an infinitesimally minute fraction of an utterly casual goddamn I give what you feel."

If the boy had been old enough to remember such things, he might have noticed that Uncle Royce looked like a good clean stick of stovewood. As it was, he only noticed that his uncle was short and compact — straight up and down — with hard skin a few shades lighter than the red clay banks through which the country roads cut.

"Well, boy?" Royce said to him. They were standing by Royce's old rolltop desk in the newspaper office. The boy saw an ancient typewriter that looked like an upright piano, spikes with haystacks of paper on them, pencils.

"Is this where my father worked?" The high school newspaper office was neater and had newer equipment, but here there was the smell of the real thing and the boy breathed it the way he imagined a sailor would salt air after being long inland.

Royce sat in his swivel chair and put on his green eyeshade. "I reckon by now you've had pretty much of your boyhood. Played hooky so you could go to the ole swimmin' hole, where you shucked your clothes and dived in off the bank. Played baseball. You've gone fishing with overalls on and a rag around a sore toe, using a bent pin and worms to pull up old boots near a NO FISHING sign."

The boy shook his head. "I got my lifesaving badge in Scouts this summer. Is this where he worked?"

"You haven't done all those things? Then you can't live in the newspaper world." Royce paused. "That's where your father worked. In the newspaper world. He hung around here to do it, but this desk and the typewriter and pencils — those things weren't real. He believed what he read in the paper."

"Didn't he write it himself?" The boy was watching Uncle Royce closely. He was not sure he understood.

"Sure. Some of it. Even thought he was thinking it up." Royce reached into a pigeonhole and took out a half pint of whisky, unscrewed the cap and took what looked like a long drink, though the level seemed to be unchanged when he put the bottle back.

"Could you show me some of the things he wrote?"

Royce shook his head. "Could if I hadn't had to rewrite everything, I suppose. Couldn't pick them out, now."

The boy wandered around the big room and stopped at a table where ads had been cut out and were pasted onto another sheet of the newspaper. "What was it like?" he asked. He was trying to imagine into this office his father of the snapshot, the tall man with the smiling open mouth and the eyes cut aside. "I mean, I know how newspapers work, and how to write a story, and all that." He had written Uncle Royce that he was assistant editor of the school paper. "But what was it like here, back then?"

"Same old thing all the time," Royce said. "You're looking at it. Same old ads and the same old stories every week. Just paste it up out of an old copy, any date. When it's spring, you run in a cartoon of an editor trying to get finished at his desk because his rod and reel's right there waiting for him. Newspaper spring. Nothing to do with life. Down here you could go fishing almost any day of December or January — any time. I don't fish, myself."

"My father fished, didn't he?"

"Of course. And hunted and talked about baseball. Certainly. John Q. Public with the little mustache in a country that hates hair on the face. Uncle Sam with a white beard. Churches with little scrolls by them saying to go worship. Sure he did. He got married in the Society Pages and had you in the Birth Announcements and died as a contribution to the Obituary Column."

The boy looked at him. His mother had said he didn't make sense. She hadn't said that he would talk this way. "He was my father," the boy said.

"I never contracted with anybody," Royce replied, "to pretty up your old man to suit you and your mother and your Aunt Janey." He walked to the front window and looked out at the dusty street in the blinding sun.

The boy sat down carefully. He did not want his voice to shake. "That's just your opinion of him," he said.

Royce didn't move. "I can't spit anybody's spit but mine."

The boy and Aunt Janey had lunch together. She gave him a saucer of cold peach cobbler for dessert, and she talked while he ate.

"Of course your father was my younger brother, and when he married your mother he hadn't even finished his education — college, I mean — and he needed a job, so Royce had him helping on the paper. Oh, I reckon that was five or six years before you came along."

"Uncle Royce didn't like him, did he?" the boy said.

"Well," Aunt Janey said. Her face was smooth and she looked as if she had been kept in a glass case. The boy wondered how she had lived all these years with Uncle Royce. "Well," she said again, "of course he liked him, but you know how brother-in-laws are."

"I'm beginning to," the boy said.

"Well," she said, "soon as I've had my nap we'll go over and see where y'all used to live."

The house was small and white, set on tall brick foundations so that the bare ground beneath it looked cool. A rusty swing set was in the side yard. The lawn was withered, and the fig trees in the back looked limp.

"You used to crawl under the house," Aunt Janey said, "and your mother would have to go get you."

The boy could remember nothing about the house. Where were those first two years of his life? The house seemed as much an absurd concoction as did Uncle Royce's account of his father.

"We went by the house," Aunt Janey said when Royce came in.

Royce didn't respond. He stopped in the middle of the living room floor and looked directly at the boy. The boy looked back at him. He did not like Uncle Royce, and he was sure that his father hadn't liked Uncle Royce.

"I guess there's one more place you want to go," Royce said.

The boy was startled. He had not wanted to mention it — he wasn't sure it was at all the thing to do. "Yes, there is," he said finally.

"There's plenty of daylight left," Royce said.

Royce drove slowly with the windows open, and the hot air swirled up dust around their feet. They didn't speak for a long time, until once when they were driving alongside a field of brown-leafed cotton, with wads of white showing already.

"Cotton," the boy said, to show he was not totally ignorant.

"Old man Peeples' place," Royce said. "Nice white house, you see there now. But old man Peeples planted cotton and stayed broke all through the depression and rayon and nylon and all those other things, and wore the land right down to the nub. So the county agent rebuilt his soil, and then some scientists figured out — somewhere else, not on old man Peeples' place — how to make a cotton shirt you can throw in the washing machine and take it out and wear it, and with that and the government old man Peeples has got some money at last. Downtown the other day he was bragging about his wisdom. Said he'd always told 'em a feller ought to stick with cotton. Them fellers they send out from the schools tried to tell him to plant something else, but he knowed better." After a moment Royce added, "Spent seventy-odd years broke. If he'd died at any normal retirement age, he wouldn't have had money for a coffin."

The boy shifted in his seat. Uncle Royce was probably getting at something, but he didn't know what. "Money's not everything," he said.

"True," Royce said. "There's all those blissful years of chopping cotton."

It seemed to the boy that the route they took was as devious as Uncle Royce's mind. After leaving the blacktop, they drove on three gravel roads and two dirt roads, with dust rolling up behind them so that the boy wondered if from an airplane it looked like a dirty jet trail. Finally they stopped at the edge of a field of brown sage grass.

"We can get there quicker by wading through," Royce said. The boy wondered what wading through was quicker than, but he did not ask. The sage came up to Royce's chest, but he plowed right on. In the distance was a solid wall of trees and before it pasture land lay flat like the front yard of a house.

"You wouldn't know about such things," Royce said, "but my mother used to cut swatches of sage grass like this and make her own brooms. She'd bind the stems into a handle. Swept everything in sight, but she wasn't much better off for it." His head and shoulders moved above the dry sage as if floating, hardly bobbing at all. The boy could imagine that that was all there was to him, a talking bust. "She believed that because she did her duty and was thrifty and kept a clean house, happiness was supposed to descend upon her like a dove. She was a bitter woman, always wondering why the Lord let her suffer. But she hung on 'til she died in her late seventies of a failure of the kidneys."

The boy was scarcely hearing. Heat radiated from the sky and the tall grass and the ground, and the sun was just low enough to be in his eyes. Uncle Royce's head was suspended on a bright brown haze, the voice continuing as if to no one, like the sound of bees.

"Watch out here for the fence," Royce said. The sage thinned slightly, and then they were in a narrow bare strip alongside a barbed-wire fence. Royce put his foot on the middle wire and pulled up the top one with his hand. "Crawl through," he said.

The boy wondered, but could not bring himself to ask, if this were *the* fence. He hesitated a moment. He would have preferred stepping over the top strand, anyway. He was tall enough; he would have to press it down only a couple of inches. But he stooped and went through and then held the wire for Uncle Royce.

"Nope," Royce said when he straightened up. "This is not the one. We've got to walk on over to the fence by the woods."

The pasture was dull yellow with bitterweeds; dust drifted from the flowers and puffed from the ground with every step the boy took. By the time they reached the other side of the pasture, Royce's shirt was wet and gray, clinging to his shoulders and to his undershirt. The boy's sight was blurred with sweat and his eyes and his face stung.

Royce put a hand on a post and said, "It was this fence. It wasn't a day like today, though. It was late in November, during a frosty spell." He looked down along the fence as though he might point out something, but then he said, "Let's get in the shade of a tree and cool off some."

This time the boy held the strands of wire apart to let his uncle go first. Royce bent over and was astraddle the middle strand when a voice shouted, "Hold on there!" from so nearby that Royce straightened and jabbed his back on the upper wire. The wire beneath him sprang up, too, and barbs scraped his thigh.

"Goddamn it," Royce said. He couldn't move either way.

"My foot slipped," the boy said. "I'm sorry." He was watching an old man in overalls approach from the woods with a long heavy stick, but he looked down and, as Royce removed the barbs from his trousers, pushed the wire down carefully with his foot. Then he worked a barb loose from the wet shirt back; it left a small metallic hole in the cloth which looked as if it ought to be made to bleed.

"Hold on there!" the old man shouted again.

"Hold on yourself!" Royce shouted back. He stood up beside the fence, his face dark red and running with sweat.

"This here's my land," the old man said, coming up to them. "Who is it?"

Royce wiped his face with his sleeve, violently. "Royce Weatherly," he said. "And this is my nephew."

The old man peered closely into Royce's face and said, as if the name had not just been told him, "Royce Weatherly, ain't it. Just didn't recognize the boy." He looked at the boy. "You don't live around here, I reckon."

"In Indiana," the boy said.

The old man looked at him, studied his face, saying, "Well, it's hot, ain't it?"

"Yes," the boy said, "it is."

The old man kept looking at him. "It's your daddy was killed out here four-five year ago, ain't it?"

"Fourteen years ago," the boy said.

The old man nodded. His face was coarse and brown; there were deep wrinkles at his eyes and beside his mouth. "I knew your daddy. He used to come hunting out here. Lots of squirrels before folks begun shooting them out of season. I figured maybe before I realized who it was that y'all was fixing to shoot a few."

Royce was trying to rub the sore place on his back. "With our bare hands," he said.

The old man nodded. "That's so," he said, but about what the boy could not be sure. "But your daddy and me used to talk now and then. He was a real smart man. Used to explain to me all about how to hunt scientific. Big man." He was looking at the boy. "You remember him?"

The boy shook his head.

"Worked for the newspaper, you know. Royce's here. He used to explain to me how a feller goes about it, starting out a piece in such and such a way, and all."

The boy wanted to quote, "Who, what, where . . ." but Royce spoke first.

"I could tell you in four minutes and you could talk about it the rest of your life," Royce said.

"Not me," the old man said. He was still looking at the boy. "It takes a smart man like your daddy for that. Educated, and all. Had some of them degrees, too."

"Ninety-eight and six-tenths," Royce said.

The old man nodded. "That's so. From some universities around over the country. Could of been called doctor in the phone book, I recollect he told me once, except folks would have thought he was a medical or a vetinary." The old man moved along the fence a little way. "You come to see where your daddy died?"

The boy nodded, although now the old man was not looking at him.

"Well, it was right along at this section, right here. He come out alone without even a fice dog or anybody, and he was bent on getting in the woods before good daylight, and he forgot the rules of safety-first. Used to tell 'em to me, I bet fifty times."

The old man paused, taking his stick in both hands like a shotgun, to demonstrate. "Well," he said after a moment of thought, "I never seen him that many times. But he used to open the breech — he told me you never put a shell in 'til you're in the woods is a rule of safety-first. And then he'd put on the safety catch anyway and slide the gun real careful under the fence flat on the ground. And then he'd come over the fence himself and pick up his gun all safe and sound."

The old man straightened, still looking at the boy. The sun was still well above the tree tops and the boy felt as though his head would burst. "You come here to learn about your daddy now you've got to be a right smart sized boy yourself, ain't you?"

The boy nodded. For a moment he had a feeling of hot resentment, almost believing that Uncle Royce had planted the old man here — perhaps had invented him altogether.

"Well," the old man said. "That day he just forgot all them rules of safety-first he was so proud of. Pride goeth before a fall, it says in the Good Book, but that don't make it no easier, does it. Had a shell in the breech and the safety catch off and was putting the shotgun thorough the fence butt first when it went off in his face." The old man shook his head for a long time. "I never heard the shot. I was still in the barn. They come and got me, seeing as it was my place it was on."

The boy looked at the ground where his father must have fallen. The blood would have soaked in, been diluted with rain, washed down through the earth, filtered itself to water long ago. Grown up in bitterweeds. Popped out as sweat.

"I told 'em then," the old man said, "that he was as fine a man as ever I come acrost." He turned to Royce. "It's good cotton weather but hard on the cattle. Tell 'em" — he meant, Royce knew, the newspaper readers — "the signs is plow deep and plant shallow, come spring. My daddy knew about such things the way his daddy knew about newspaper writing and all."

It was not until the old man was gone that Royce and the boy realized they were standing on different sides of the fence.

"You want to come on over and find some shade, or go on back home?" Royce said.

The boy looked at the fence. "Is this really the place?"

"Close enough," Royce said. "It's hard to tell one post from another."

The boy stood a moment, not satisfied but unable to say why. Finally, without speaking, he held the fence and Royce carefully came through.

They walked in silence across half the pasture before the boy stopped and looked back at the woods and the fence. "Was that the way it was?" he asked.

Royce took in a deep breath and let it out in a long sigh. "Who knows? You wouldn't remember about slop buckets any more than about sage brooms, but it used to be that everybody had a bucket in the kitchen to drop all the leftover food in, and when it got full you'd take it out and empty it in the pig trough, where it belonged."

The boy looked at him sharply. "And?" he said.

"It was just undigested scraps of stuff, all thrown together. And that's what I think of when I have to stand and listen to people like that old man talk. I feel like he's emptying the slop bucket in my face."

The boy didn't move. He found that he was breathing heavily through his mouth and could faintly taste the bitterweeds. "And you're saying my father was like that."

"Who knows how it was that morning?" Royce had never said it before, but it came as if he had written it as an editorial and memorized it. "Was he careless, or was it that he didn't care? Maybe he didn't have anybody to talk to but the barbed-wire fence, and the fence wouldn't put up with it and shot him with his own gun. Or maybe he got across to the fence what he couldn't say to any human being and it helped him pull the trigger, because it was himself and not the fence that had to stop the talk and couldn't do it any other way. Or maybe," Royce went on, wishing the boy would interrupt, would stop him, had stopped him before he got started, even, "or maybe it was the gun itself, talking back, showing him finally how to compress all banality into a single unanswerable sound and be done with it."

He stopped and the boy stood there flushed and sweating for a long time before they continued walking toward the car.

Royce didn't look at the boy when they got out of the car at home. He stretched and looked up. The red was going out of the sky, and everything seemed to focus directly overhead in a clear blue. "As easy as filling a slop bucket," Royce said, "and the pigs don't know the difference. But if you think that's what you want, you're welcome."

The boy realized after a moment that Uncle Royce was talking about the newspaper, and that earlier in the day that was what he would have wanted. Now he was not at all sure. Now he knew a little better who his father had been and what had happened; he had seen where and he had been told more about when. But without the why, what was the story? Was it merely an obituary? He did not know why, not only about his father, but about Uncle Royce, about himself. "I better get on through school," he said tentatively.

They crossed the yard and Royce paused with his hand on the screen. "Well," he said, "that's as good as anything, I reckon. If you just don't swallow too much."

ALBERT DRAKE

The Chicken Which Became a Rat

(FROM THE NORTHWEST REVIEW)

"HE AIN'T *eating* THE EGGS," Uncle Boswick said. His voice carried that same amazed indignation as when he had asked my father, "Yer *paid* for the window?" or when he had reported to me, "He did it with the *sam-yer-eye*." His world had its own practical logic of survival; these were acts which left him confounded. "The Jap ain't eating the eggs and he won't sell them."

"What's he plan to do?" I asked.

"No plans." Uncle Boswick shook the beads of dew from his slacks, and pointed his whangee cane across the tall grass which stretched from our house to the Jap's tarpaper shack: within the wire I could imagine the gaunt, long-necked hens eyeing each other suspiciously. "Nothing — the chickens are getting wild, the eggs are piling up, the garden's full of weeds — I don't get it."

And then, after picking out the grass kernels which jutted from his perforated two-tone shoes, Uncle Boswick was off to the USO club. To build the boys' morale.

I was surprised that his attitude toward the Jap had changed from hatred to amazed indignation. The Jap had disappointed him. Eggs were rationed and Uncle Boswick saw the Jap's reluctance to sell his not as a foreign plot but rather as evidence of the humorless intensity of a backward race: Uncle Boswick would know how to make money here, somehow, if the Jap would only work *with* him.

What surprised me most was the change in the Jap's property:

weeds choked the garden, the corn stalks were stunted and brown, the chicken coop was a box of rusty wire, a small concentration camp. If Uncle Boswick was baffled, how could I be expected to understand? But it seemed that after V-E Day the Jap had given up, as if he knew the Allies would win, and now the land was reverting to the desolation it had been a year ago—a wasteland beyond the city's limits, marshy in winter, baked hard in summer. It now resembled the useless landscape of before last spring, when one night the Jap had infiltrated our neighborhood. He had sneaked in without noise or luggage, and the next morning, when I peeked through the gun-slot of Venetian blinds, he was on the flatlands, bent to his hoe, against the rising sun.

It was the third year of the war.

His blade flashed like a bayonet into American soil. Silhouetted against the sun which spilled red across the tips of furrows, his insect shape reminded me of something I had seen or read — something thin, creepy, and utterly evil.

Then I recalled the source. On the coffee table was the current *Liberty*: on the cover Hitler assumed the body of a jackass, his hoofs kicking Europe; beside him Mussolini was a baboon, dangling mindlessly from a stripped, war-wrecked tree; and in the upper-right corner Tojo was a furry, menacing spider whose web, like the land around our Jap, was stained blood-red.

The pavement ended at our house, and home-front defenses honeycombed the neighborhood's perimeter. The day after the sneak attack on Pearl Harbor we had marched into this wasteland and each boy had dug a foxhole, a hiding place against the bombing raids which seemed imminent. The only bombs to fall were random fire-balloons which fizzled out in the wet forests west of Portland; but as weeks turned to months and to years, all our young muscle was directed at the war effort. We dug a gridwork of slit trenches, pillboxes, and tunnels, and for armament we had stacks of dirt clods, stones, bags of smoke dust, apples drilled to accept a firecracker, and of course our BB guns. Uncle Boswick had often said that we could expect a Presidential E flag.

Into these trenches we crawled — Piggy, Slats, Mike, The MacGregor, and myself — soot streaked across our faces, like commandos in movies; and we moved out, sinking low until the last observation post, where smooth throwing rocks and solid dirt clods were piled. For we were children of war, and had been taught to hate.

"I can smell him," The MacGregor said.

I crawled to the rim and partly turned, one eye on the Jap and the other on The MacGregor, who braced a foot against the dirt wall, his arm cocked. When I raised my finger he fired a distance round. It sailed across the broken landscape and dropped so far behind the Jap did not pause in his stroke.

"Correct elevation," I whispered.

The MacGregor sent off another stone, which arced white against the blue, until, falling, it became a black speck lost in the weeds. Still the enemy hoed on.

I realized that if The MacGregor, our strongest gunner, couldn't make the distance, none of us could. But I whispered, "Harrassment rounds," and raised two fingers, which meant to fire at will.

Our hate spun five clods upward, where they teetered against the sky, to fall in uneven arcs on the dull ground. The Jap, untouched, continued his insidious ground work, chopping treacherously at this piece of the United States, knocking crystals of dew from the weeds as he enlarged his claim.

Over our heads a whistle pierced the sky.

The black speck seemed to travel forever in its swift, guided flight, diminishing until it reached an invisible peak; with a flash of white, the gesture of a wingtip, it peeled off, screaming earthward, to crash through the window of the Jap's shanty. The enemy jumped, dropped his hoe, and ran, flapping his wings like a chicken attempting flight.

We cheered, and as I turned to see who our supporting artillery might be, a volley of laughter strafed the field. At the edge of the pavement Uncle Boswick flipped a heavy stone from hand to hand; he looked more than ever like the posters of Uncle Sam.

It was toward the Jap that he pointed: I WANT YOU.

I could not understand why my father, when he learned of our victory, carefully folded the evening paper, hitched up his pants, and strode down the street, off the pavement, and across the field.

He was gone a long time, and dinner was halfway through before he returned. In fact, Uncle Boswick was well into seconds, his mouth so full he could barely exclaim: "Yer *paid* for the window?"

"But why?" I asked. Was he a traitor? Aiding the enemy. I almost believed this in spite of the signs on our front door glass: WE BOUGHT OUR QUOTA. WE HAVE A BOY IN THE NAVY; the blue cloth with the gold star. V FOR VICTORY . . .

"Because your uncle broke it," he said, spreading white margarine on his bread, digging into the Relief gravy over cereal-laden hamburger. "And because what that Jap does on that gawd-forsaken land is none of your business."

Now I could not believe it. I felt sick, confused, as shattered as the Jap's window. I looked to Uncle Boswick, but he was smiling as he snubbed out his cigarette — smoked as usual to the middle. Another wasteful habit which aggravated my mother.

"Just leave him alone," my father said quietly, always chewing. "Stay away from his place."

Uncle Boswick could not tolerate the sight of my father calmly eating supper, asking us to leave the Jap alone. 'But he's the ENEMY!" he shouted, fists clenched on the table.

"How do you know?" my father asked.

"Well . . . he's a gawdamn Jap, ain't he?"

"There," I said, jumping up, pointing to the wall. "There." On the kitchen wall were two pages my mother had torn from *Life* magazine: *How to Tell Japs from the Chinese.* The photos had an overlay to show that Chinese have long, fine-boned faces, parchment-yellow complexion, and never have rosy cheeks; Japs have squat faces with the nose a flat blob, earthy-yellow complexion, and sometimes rosy cheeks. I read: *An often sounder clue is facial expression, shaped by cultural, not anthropological factors. Chinese wear rational calm of tolerant realists. Japs, like General Tojo, show humorless intensity of ruthless mystics.* The other page showed tall Chinese brothers and short Japanese admirals — our allies and our enemies.

"He looked just like the short Japanese admirals, and . . ."

"Did he have rosy cheeks?" my father asked, smiling.

"Yes," I said, although I really wasn't sure. I hadn't been able to see my enemy's face.

"I don't like that Jap any better than you do," my father said, looking at me, Uncle Boswick, my mother. "But he's had a rough row to hoe." As he cleaned his plate with a final slice of bread, he repeated the story the Jap had told him: there had been a large farm near Gresham, where the fields sloped off toward the sun, and where seeds would not stay in the ground — in spring the strawberries grew big as a boy's fist, and in fall the corn was so large and tender that a single ear would make a meal. My father told the story in the dreamy, tragic tone of a man who has not owned anything himself — saying that in only two more years the farm would have been paid off, but after Pearl Harbor it was confiscated by the government and sold at auction, and the Jap — a Nisei, who had been born on the farm, and was therefore an American citizen — had spent the past two and a half years in an internment camp near Pendleton. Now released, he had no family, no farm, no money. "So I think you — everybody — ought to lay off him."

"Whadda think the Nips're doing to our boys?" Uncle Boswick shouted. "Wake Island, Bataan, the Death March. And don't forget Pearl Harbor: those jokers didn't pay us for any broken windows there. I wish . . ."

My mother got up and began to clear the table. No doubt she was thinking of Grant on the U.S.S. *Plymouth,* now a month out of Hawaii. My father rolled Bugler into tan, wheat-straw paper, touched his tongue to the edge and flattened the ends. He always enjoyed one of Uncle Boswick's real cigarettes after dinner, but he would not ask; nor was one offered tonight.

The last thing I heard as I got up and went to sit on the front porch was Uncle Boswick finishing his sentence: ". . . I could get my licks in."

Uncle Boswick was our hero. The declaration of war was being read over a million radio speakers when Uncle Boswick's foot missed a tailgate at Fort Ord; he lay screaming in pain as Roosevelt's voice called for unlimited sacrifices from our fighting men. The truck had been barely moving, but something had happened to Uncle Boswick's back. He was given a medical discharge and a fifty-per-cent disability pension, which meant he did not need to work even if he could. In the confusion of that December the papers officially honoring him as the first casualty of the war were lost in channels, but Uncle Boswick got the pension, a Purple Heart, and freedom from rationing: he had unlimited supplies at the airbase PX. It was unfortunate, my mother often said, that the PX did not stock eggs and meat, but only cigarettes and liquor.

With my father it was different: he was 4-F.

At times I felt that he was letting us down by not being in uniform. Oh sure, building Liberty Ships was pretty important work, but I could not get too excited about it — not even on those days when we would go to Swan Island for a launching, when after the speeches and free lunch he would show us the whirly crane he drove, a tiny cab sitting a hundred feet high on delicate girder legs. But seeing it sail down the tracks, with a bulkhead dangling from the long cables, just wasn't the same as seeing those thin, censored V-letters that The MacGregor's father sent from North Africa.

So I could not understand why he had paid for the Jap's window. Although we were not so poor as we had been before the war, there was no money to spend foolishly. Oh, perhaps I had a vague idea why my father had paid off: because he believed that every man should own a piece of ground and a house, and that all others should respect the limits of ownership — even if it was a house no better than ours, where the wind whipped through the ivy-covered latticework which was its foundation.

As I looked through dusk across the field I could see the Jap, his hoe flashing in the dim light. The sight made me furious. How were we to leave him alone? He was the Enemy: newspapers, magazines, our teachers, had taught us to hate him. And we learned well to hate. Oh, how we hated him — deeply, intensely. He was the grinning monkey-pilot who gleefully leaned into his gunsight to machine-gun parachutists. He was the spidery Nip who saved bullets by using his bayonet on the wounded. We knew too well of his exquisite tortures — bamboo splinters ignited under toenails, fingernails removed by pliers, the eyelid lifted off by the knife's thin whisper.

These thoughts were bothering me when Uncle Boswick came out to sit on the porch. "What I'd like to know is how he got *released*. With a war on."

"Maybe he escaped," I suggested.

"He's up to something," Uncle Boswick whispered. "Keep your eye on him, kid. That slant-eyed devil is a spy or a saboteur."

Our eyes were on him all right. Every day after breakfast Piggy, Slats, Mike, The MacGregor, and I gathered in the farthest observation post. We pushed Uncle Boswick's binoculars over the rim of the hole until the lenses were full of yellow skin — earthy yellow, I was sure. We harassed the Jap with random shots. We saluted him with raised middle fingers and screamed *banzai,* and asked how the hell Tojo was.

But the Jap refused to notice us, and anyway, we saw nothing suspicious. Just the hoe striking the ground and weeds flung from the tiny green shoots which were beginning to appear. This went on for a week, and suddenly the eighth day was summer. By ten o'clock it was seventy, the flatlands shimmered, and the Jap, slashing with his hoe or carrying buckets of water, looked like a movie mirage.

The OP was an oven. When Piggy refused to drink the brackish canteen water, he went home. Then Mike remembered the bandoliers of ice in his mother's refrigerator. Soon only The MacGregor and myself sweated in the hole, pouring water over our heads, swearing, hating the Jap for keeping us there.

And at noon, when the sun was straight up, erasing any shade, we went swimming.

But the war, glorious and dreadful, near and distant, continued to touch us in many ways. Every day my mother scanned the paper fearfully:

TODAY'S
ARMY-NAVY
CASUALTY LIST
Washington — Following are the
latest casualties in the military
services, including next of kin.
ARMY-NAVY DEAD

Her finger would tremble through the list to where Grant's last name, first name, rank, might be; then the newspaper would collapse in her folded hands and she would cry or pray or both. Sometimes, in the afternoon when the house was empty, I would burst in from play to find her at the writing desk, sobbing over a stack of tissue-thin V-letters; they were all postmarked *San Francisco, Censor's Office,* and she was wondering, no doubt, where in the wide Pacific her oldest boy might be.

Elsewhere, Captain America turned bullets off his shield, the

Green Lantern sought truth, and even the Submariner turned to the side of good: another ring of filthy rotten Nazi spies and saboteurs was broken. The Axis shed their animal skins in defeat. In our comics we fought the war, and in the papers we read of its progress: June 6th was D-Day; during that month V-1 bombs, a terrible undreamed of weapon, began to fall on England; the Marianas Campaign pushed ahead. The pleasant summer advanced, and so did our boys: troops landed at Saipan, and during July the big drive began through Normandy; Guam and Paris were liberated in August.

At home the war controlled us. Our battles were fought every day: we could buy comic books, but few fireworks and no bubblegum. The BB's for our guns turned to lead. The currency of conversation was ration discs and coupon books. In our driveway my father's 1934 Terraplane sat without tires, graded by the C sticker on its windshield. Now he drove only the sedan, a 1930 Hudson; it was an immense, magnificent car, dark and square; and when he placed an ironing board across the jump seats he was able to haul nine people every day to the shipyard. However essential this was to the war effort, he could not get the red and white B sticker changed to the coveted grade A — so the coupe rested on its rims and the sedan eased around town at 35 mph on ancient patched rubber and there was not enough extra gas that summer to even go to the beach.

But we fought on: we flattened tons of tin cans for tanks and salvaged kitchen fat for munitions and bundled high stacks of newspapers and magazines for who knows what. We bought a twenty-five-cent savings stamp a week, and when the book was full it became a war bond. On walks and walls we chalked our beliefs — *Hitler is a Heel* — and assertions of evolution — *Tojo is a Monkey's Uncle.* We said prayers, pledged allegiance, saluted the flag; and a thousand times our razored hate cheered John Wayne's single-handed assault against the Japs on Friday nights.

One bright morning, when even the haze of war could not hide the sun, I came from behind the humped, tireless coupe in the driveway and suddenly noticed the marshland had become a profuse garden. The corn was a screen, thick as any bamboo grove, and below the tomatoes glowed red: tiny suns of nippon. Bayonets of onion greens stabbed upward; potatoes, peppers, lettuce, carrots camouflaged the ground. Even the tarpaper shack seemed to stand a little straighter in the chaos of flowers, and its shutters and front door were painted bright yellow.

Sneaking through the foliage was the Jap: he was building tripods, small tent skeletons, for the beans.

Behind me Uncle Boswick came out, stretched, and surveyed the changed, technicolor landscape. He sported a new Panama hat and two-tone perforated shoes, and I guessed that he was on his way to the USO club, although it was pretty early.

"Poppies," he said. "And not the kind the Legion sells."

I admired Uncle Boswick — I would never have thought of *opium* — and so I said yes, when he asked me to reconnoiter the area and to get some fresh vegetables, to be sent to his friends in Washington, D.C., for analysis. In spite of my father's order that the Jap be left alone, I wanted to get in the fight. Our fight. The rest of the day was spent with the Gang mapping out a plan of action. It was only after the details were settled that Slats mentioned it didn't get dark until nine, his bedtime. Our hoots and jeers at Slats were suddenly silenced when we realized that there wasn't one of us could stay out that late.

Therefore, at nine, as the sun fell beyond the muted, blacked-out neon of Portland, I crawled from my bedroom window and slipped into the high grass. In the near darkness I groped along the trench work, and at the farthest OP I began to inch toward that garden on my stomach, a hunting knife clenched between my teeth. Near my face the *chiirrruup* of crickets was deafening, and at every shift of my body the gas-mask bag slipped noisily; I paused to look back, and through the summer mists I saw the dull yellow cracks around black-out curtains in our front room, far away.

Crickets chirped nearby, an echo of bullfrogs farther out in the marsh, and along Johnson Creek the Galloping Goose cried into the night. A veil of wind blew a pungent, acrid green and then I saw the oiled, metallic sides of vegetables: cucumbers lay like small surface mines, aimed in every direction.

I waited, staring into the blackness at the tarpaper shack. Then the knife blade slipped across prickly stalks and three large specimens were in the bag. I crouched among the corrugated sides of squash, knife slashing, and moved quickly into the bayonets of green onions. Beyond were tomato plants, the hard black balls swimming in metallic greenness. Among the wide, sharp leaves of corn I was shielded, and it was not until the fourth ear had been split from its stalk that I felt a pang of fear. In the terror of silence leaf rasped on leaf. The knife was in my hand when I stood to stare into the silent, black night.

Not three plants away the Jap waited, arms folded, hat tipped to conceal his inscrutable face.

Even as I jumped I knew it must be a scarecrow — but I threw the knife overhand and flung away the gas-mask bag and ran across the misty, deep grass, the uneven ground falling away under my racing feet. Only when I was again in bed, rubbing my legs to stop their trembling, did I realize that the Jap had my knife — that he was now *armed.*

I slept with this fear and in a dream I heard voices at the back steps: *well they are lovely* and *let me pay* and *I may keep the bag?* I heard the screen door open and my mother say *Thankew* — it was a trick, no doubt — but then the door slammed shut and a figure passed outside my window. It shuffled under that same loose, flowing shirt and broad hat I had seen last night — but again *I could not see any feature of the face.*

"Well, you're awake," my mother said. She was running water into a dishpan at the sink, and on the table, the gas-mask bag spilled out vegetables like a horn of plenty. "The Jap man *gave* us these," she said. "He wouldn't take any money, but I asked him to bring us some every week and I said I'd pay him a quarter — does that sound fair? He said he wants to buy some chickens."

Once a week until November the Jap came with a bag of produce, to accept my mother's money (as if there was no war on!) and to pass so close beneath the window that he must have felt the glow of my hatred.

He never did return my knife, either.

In what seemed the middle of summer, school began again.

No matter that Paris and Guam and Palau had been liberated, or that bombs were falling on Manila, Luzon, and Okinawa, we marched into dull classrooms, carrying new notebooks already marked A.A.F.: we were all destined to become pilots, wearing white scarfs, chamois helmets, and leather jackets with the Flying Tiger patch on the back, like Errol Flynn. School for us was the twice-weekly war communique film, where in the fluttering light we saw Patton tanks smash hedgerows, and bombs tumble like eggs toward the ultimate explosion. We squirmed with excitement as infantry charged across beaches strewn with dead and debris, as a flame-thrower sucked burning Japanese from caves, ending their ruthless mysticism. When the narrator's voice and the marching music ground to a halt and the projector stopped and the olive-drab blinds were raised, the boys would turn to look at one another and even Ellie Chombrake, the skinniest kid in the class, wore a sense of purpose on his face. The war was a common bond, holding us together; we all knew our role in this struggle for freedom.

Besides Christmas, only two things happened that school year.

One night in December, shortly before vacation, I was doing homework when I heard shouting in the field: it was The MacGregor.

From my front porch I heard him shouting crazily at the Jap and there was a distant crash of glass. I ran across the field, leaping trenches, until I saw the blurred outline of The MacGregor lobbing rock after rock at the tarpaper shanty; through the dark mist came the report of splintering boards. He was screaming and falling forward with every rock he threw, and I waited a minute before placing a hand on his shoulder. The face that turned was distorted into a crazy mask, and I stepped back, but not quickly enough — his throwing fist, clutching a rock, came from the night to smash into my face.

It was my father who helped us both home, and when he returned from The MacGregor's house, to hold an ice pack against my bleeding cheek, he told us that Mr. MacGregor had been killed in what the newspapers celebrated as the Battle of the Bulge — where General McAuliffe said "nuts" to the Nazis. The telegram from the War Department assured Mrs. MacGregor that her husband had died a Hero.

My cheek no longer hurt: I felt good, and I wanted to shake The MacGregor's hand. But it was too late that night, my father said, and for the rest of the week The MacGregor's desk at school was empty, and by Saturday the mother and son had moved to Seattle, leaving a dark, lifeless house.

The next week, as if to replace our loss, Piggy's uncle sent home a large, olive-drab box from the Pacific. Piggy was certain it was a Christmas present for him but Gussie, his aunt, who was staying for the duration, said the box contained souvenirs, and that she had been instructed *not* to open it until Jed came home.

And within five minutes she had a crowbar against the lid, splintering wood; inside lay three long, dark rifles, a pistol wrapped in tan, oil-slick paper, and two Jap officer swords. Everything was coated with a thick rancid grease, but the guns were beautiful and the swords were works of art: they had scabbards crafted with inlaid wood and pearl, into which the delicate blade whispered. Gussie, who no doubt expected silks, hammered the lid back and from then on the basement door was kept locked.

But for us, knowing those weapons were there, the war seemed much closer.

School was a huge wheel, grinding toward spring. Its monotonous progress was interrupted only by the excitement of paper drives and tin-can collections, practice blackouts and marches to the basement, which was now called the Air Raid Shelter. Here we huddled until the all-clear bell, discussing how we would fight the war when called, even though we could not see how it would last another eight years: the newspaper maps showed wide arrows, and by April the Americans and Russians were shaking hands in a defeated Berlin, while most of Europe was occupied by our boys. Although the Japanese were using kamikazes and Baka Bombs, Iwo Jima and Okinawa had been captured and it was only a matter of time before we would invade Japan itself.

Our winter had been mild and the spring rains turned the ground an energetic green. The trenches were hip-high in water, but from my bedroom window I watched the Jap at work seeding and hoeing. I wondered what he thought — surely he knew now that his country was defeated. A hundred short Japanese admirals were no match for one tall John Wayne marine. Why had he come here? What did he want? What was he working so hard for? No matter if he should again transform that wasteland into a blooming paradise, the whole neighborhood blotted him out with hate. Yet he foolishly worked on: feet bare, pants rolled to the knee, he dashed along the furrows in a lurching, forward-slanting crouch under the wide straw hat. When he was not working the land, he was building the chicken coop. He had scrounged fragments of wood and wire; and the coop, a temporary, tottering structure, made the tarpaper shack seem a palace. Apparently he had sold enough vegetables the previous summer, because one morning the fenced area was filled with small puffs of yellow, like frantic flowers. His dream was coming true, and I wanted to cross that field to make sure he understood that this could only happen in America — this was free enterprise, democracy.

The Jap had his chicks, V-E Day was celebrated, my dad was talking about the new car he would buy when this war was over, the neighborhood grew green, and school would soon end. It was into this spirit of optimism that Piggy's uncle returned.

If I had not seen him in uniform for a fleeting minute, as he walked from the car to the house that first day, I would not have believed that he had been in battle: all day, every day, he sat on the front porch in a rocking chair, wearing faded bib overalls and a brown shirt, and bearing no visible wound. He was a strange man with small, dull eyes, and skin which became red without tanning; when he spoke his voice faded through short sentences, and he refused to talk about the war, even to Uncle Boswick.

"All he wants," said Uncle Boswick, "is to get back to that Alabama dirt farm, and sit."

"That's okay," my father said. "A man ought to own a bit of land."

"Gussie, now she's cut from a different bolt," Uncle Boswick said, winking. "I know her pretty well. She likes it here — plenty of ocean and forests and no niggers. Bet you five dollars she don't leave with him."

"Oh, now," my mother said, but her protest was weak for she had the gossip about Gussie straight from Piggy's mother: how Gussie had worked at Oregon Shipyard for two weeks after Jed had been shipped overseas. She had been back only for launchings, when the company gave out free beer and food, and we were told that any Saturday night she could be found along Harbor Drive, where ships on the Willamette tied up. Gussie, my mother said, was "wild" and "needed a baby to keep her home." Now that Jed was back she was sure that Gussie would "straighten out." Uncle Boswick, who seemed to know an awful lot about Gussie, said he wasn't so sure.

But rain or shine Jed remained in his rocking chair on the front porch, surveying the neighborhood with dull eyes. His uniform remained in the closet, and Piggy reported that Jed had gone into the basement only once to check the heavy box of souvenirs.

So we were surprised to see Gussie with the big samurai sword.

That late June sun was already an explosion of fire, burning life from the grass, but Piggy, Slats, Mike, and I worked in the trenches anyway; we felt needed, for after V-E Day the war focused on the Pacific, our ocean. We repaired trench walls where the rains had worn them away, and filled sandbags, piled our rocks, and sometimes lobbed an occasional missile at the Jap's chicken coop — but halfheartedly, for now that we knew Tojo was finished our Jap seemed more like a docile intruder: unwanted, but harmless. Uncle Boswick had even taken to crossing the field two or three times a week, to "interrogate" the Jap about when the hens would start laying. For eggs were still rationed.

I trained Uncle Boswick's binoculars on the Jap's shack, then slowly swept them across the chicken coop, the vast garden — for I wanted to see my enemy's face, to see if in these last days of the war that face could maintain its humorless intensity — when at my elbow Slats said: "What's that noise?"

All I heard was Gussie's radio. Whenever she was sunbathing her radio blared hot hillbilly music into the quiet neighborhood. But today she was not sunbathing. When I swung the binoculars past our house to Piggy's back yard, I saw Gussie in the far corner wearing tiny shorts and halter.

The noise that Slats heard was the blackberry vines being chopped, and what Gussie was using was the big Jap sword.

She was working, and I recalled what my mother had said about Gussie "straightening out" with Jed home. It was the first time I had ever seen her do work of any kind. Like Uncle Boswick, she did not need to work.

We charged from the trench, knowing that long wooden box of war souvenirs was lying open in an unlocked basement. But Piggy said: "If we wait for Jed, *he'll* show them to us."

Under the hot sun we waited while on that porch Jed rocked, his eyes focused on something above the rooftops, and in the far corner of the yard the sword flashed like a mirror. We waited, wondering how many American boys' heads that long blade had lopped off. We shuddered, for the courageous blood spilled on Bataan, Corregidor, Wake Island, and for the blade each time that Gussie hit a rock. Through the binoculars I watched Jed's face, dull and impassive, and finally I saw the lips tighten slowly, pulling his eyes narrow. Suddenly the field of vision was filled with his striped bib overalls. I lowered the glasses to see Jed stand up; he spit once over the porch rail, scratched his seat, and started down the steps as we charged from the trench.

Jed walked slowly past the basement door, down the driveway, and was blotted from sight by our house. We were halfway to the road when Jed reappeared, to take the sword from Gussie.

Later I was unsure exactly what I saw — we were still a good distance away, and it happened very fast. She had the sword raised overhead in both hands, to assault the tenacious blackberry vines, when Jed stepped from behind and grabbed the blade. The surprise of his movement sent her spinning off balance, and she fell among the daggers of the vines. We heard her cry once — a single, abrupt noise — and saw the blade flash, an arc of sunlight across our eyes, forever impressed. An irregular, stunned line of boys watched in horror as Jed came from behind the trees and the obstructing house; he lurched toward that cool dark basement.

We retreated to the trench, where I exchanged one nervous glance with Piggy: Gussie lay in the vines, pumping her blood out, and beyond that dark, recessed doorway Jed had the guns. We gripped the lip of turf, not even pretending to arm ourselves with throwing stones, until we heard the thin siren droning from Loaner's Corner, an insect in the hot afternoon; and at the same instant a muffled explosion churned up from that basement, growing like a cloud to envelop the neighborhood.

A few minutes after Uncle Boswick jumped the fence which separated Piggy's yard from mine, the police car rocked to the curb. As the officers moved up the driveway, guns thrust into the yard's calm, we raced to the road and saw Uncle Boswick point to that far corner. Blood smudged his shirt, and his eyes slanted against tears — at the time, it was my impression that he had cut himself coming over the fence.

And before the policemen came back from viewing Gussie's slim, decapitated body, and before Uncle Boswick chased us into the street, we gathered at the small, dirt-spattered basement window: Jed was sitting in the corner, propped against the dirt wall by the Jap rifle. The big toe of his right foot was hooked into the trigger guard; the barrel pointed into the darkness where half his head was missing. Behind him a fan-shaped stain drew flies.

The deaths were not mentioned that evening at supper, a meal eaten in silence; but later on the front steps, Uncle Boswick announced, as if I did not already know: "He did it with the *sam-yer-eye* sword. Can you believe that? Ahhhh, she was a beautiful girl." He went on, in a voice charged with amazed indignation, to tell how he had seen the blade flash once across the sun from the chaise longue in our back yard; he thought it was a dream. From that moment his world was one of missing pieces, of edges that never did quite meet, and when I asked him again what *really* had happened all he could say was: "He did it with the *sam-yer-eye*."

But that was not what I wanted to know.

Nor did the Jap make any sense to him. A few days after the deaths Uncle Boswick crossed that wasteland to "interrogate" the Jap, and when he returned his voice was charged with amazed fury. "The hens are finally laying, but *he ain't eating the eggs*. The Jap ain't eating the eggs and he won't sell them. I'm telling you the whole world's gone nuts."

After Uncle Boswick left for the USO club, I got out his binoculars and my plane spotter's manual — for four years I had been searching the skies for a Zero or Mitsubitsi bomber. From the blue skies I lowered the glasses to focus on the Jap's shack, and for the first time I noticed that the profusion of flowers had shrunk back into the mud. The shack leaned to its own shadow; a yellowed newspaper fluttered from the window broken long ago by The MacGregor's stone. I shifted to the garden out back, and saw corn burned by the sun fold into stiff stalks, diminishing like candle wax.

The glasses focused on the slanting assemblage of wood and wire, and although the nests were concealed I could see the clumps of dirty white which flashed from corners: the hens had begun to lay their eggs in any depression. I slowly swung the glasses across the Jap's property — scanning every inch of peeling paint, broken glass, and browned foliage — but I saw no sign of the Jap. The chickens milled about the dusty arena, without food or water, eyeing one another suspiciously. The eggs began to pile up, dropped from the starving, wiry hens, and I knew this was another fiendish, exquisite Eastern torture. I pictured the Jap hiding in a corner of the shack, drunk on sake, giggling his sharp-toothed, rat-faced fanaticism.

The eggs piled up, delicate and white, and every day Uncle Boswick crossed that wasteland to beg, plead, argue the Jap into selling him some eggs. I would watch Uncle Boswick cross the field and stand by the bottom step of the porch; I could see his mouth moving, hands flying — *but I never saw the Jap.* Only a shadow across the broken window, a faint movement which might have been the curtain blowing. On any day during the past year he would have been running on short admiral legs across the tilled soil, a water bucket in each hand, or he would have been leaning on his shovel, or kneeling over seeds, as if in prayer. Now he did not come out of the tarpaper shack, not even to feed the chickens.

It was not until two weeks later, when the heat of summer shifted into August, that Uncle Boswick was able to learn *why* the Jap refused to part with his eggs.

Uncle Boswick was trying to talk my mother into going across that field to plead with the Jap. "You've got to go — the egg route is all sewn up, I've got the customers. We've got to make some money soon, before this war is over. Gawd knows every businessman has lined *his* nest: the junkyards selling gas stamps and tires from wrecks at black-market prices, the gas stations, the meat markets — they're getting rich!"

We had never had any money, and he was trying to appeal to her only fear: poverty. But apparently she feared the Jap even more, for she would not go — not even when he told her what he had learned.

"Do you know *why* he won't do anything with them?" Uncle Boswick asked. "He bought the chickens so he could have some eggs — and now he tells me he can't eat the eggs of hens he knows *personally*. That he has fed with his own hands. *Hens he knows personally!*"

For Uncle Boswick this was the ultimate puzzle, and he abandoned his attempt to collaborate with the enemy. Other afternoons would be spent in the chaise longue, warming his war wounds against the sun, clipping moneymaking advertisements from magazines.

But I continued to watch the drama of torture with a strange fascination: every morning I went to the foxhole and focused binoculars on the chicken coop, where lean hens milled, eyeing each other suspiciously. Their high wiry bodies bobbed and crowded as they rotated in an endless circle under the blazing sun. I saw those near the fence stretch through the wire, their hysterical beaks reaching for any green leaf.

One day toward noon, just as I was about to return home for lunch, I saw a hen squat in the dust and when it rose, the quizzical eye aimed at the sun, its dusty, hoarse clucking was suddenly strangled. The hen's head darted like a wedge; the sharp beak smashed the shell, and the hen began to devour her own egg.

From the side another hen kicked high into the air, wings flapping, mad with the smell of food. A cloud of feathers exploded over the oily yolk as the two fought — others jumped in, and mass hysteria spread like the rising dust cloud. I watched with excited horror, for I had been waiting for something like this — the dust, torn feathers, the savage choked cries. From behind the wire a gas cloud rose, and the smell of rotten eggs drifted on the wind, an ominous yellow cloud which would stain every house, touch every life.

Fifteen minutes later, when the air was fairly clear, I could see that every egg had been pecked open.

Again the tide rotated wing to wing, hungry for food, space, the freedom of flight. They pressed together tightly, accelerating in a small circle within the confines of the wire until motion became a brown blur. Their movement held no hope for escape, but the smell of food had driven them mad and this was a kind of direct action — in desperation their yellow feet raced across the baked earth, the head at the end of the arched neck in pursuit of something. I waited, watching with that same sense of excited horror I had known the day Jed walked off the porch and the morning the Jap had first appeared on our horizon.

Then, near the wire, one stumbled with exhaustion. Her wings fanned the dust, but before she could rise the beak of her neighbor slashed out. She struggled, her chalky *cluuuuk* filled with urgency and alarm, but from the circle's momentum a dozen hens peeled off and were on her, necks extended, beaks chopping at her eyes.

When two of the attackers drew back, their dusty feathers were speckled with blood. Through binoculars I could see the stained hens lift their wings, crane their necks at a difficult angle to drink off the beads of blood. Behind them the circle began to disintegrate, and the smell of blood carried to my foxhole as hens surrounded to attack the attackers.

Originally there were perhaps thirty chickens, and the next day when I returned there were half that number. On the third day their were ten, and then five walked among the debris of feathers and bones. These five had grown heavy, nourished by the fallen, and they waddled grotesque and wary. One stayed in each corner of the coop, and one paced a small circle in the center.

Later there were only two left, and these had been changed until they looked more like buzzards — their necks were plucked bare, and what lower feathers remained had turned black from the blood and dust. Seen through the binoculars the birds looked arrogant, fierce, and utterly mad. Their feet were claws and their heads like hatchets, topped by the blood-filled comb. Each preened and arched in her space, proud that she had survived. I wondered whether inside the shack the Jap was giggling or filled with revulsion — after all, these were hens he had known personally.

And suddenly the war was over.

On our small street people spilled from houses, cheering and shouting, touching one another. My mother, after saying a prayer to God, even smoked a cigarette in her excitement, and there was cold beer on the table. The cloud of war had lifted. Relief and happiness passed through our house like a seismic wave.

From the radio came the official details: *At twelve-oh-one the Great Artiste dropped the second bomb . . . a pillar of purple fire, ten thousand feet high, shot skyward with enormous speed, moving to become a mushroom-shaped cloud which eventually attained a height of sixty thousand feet . . . officials estimate that the blast caused extensive damage . . .*

The war had ended. In that room I sensed a curious mixture of gladness and despair, as if we were suddenly released from what had held us together. I could not remember a time before Pearl Harbor, I could only recall a world at war, and all my energy for four years had been consumed by the war effort — I'd spent hundreds of hours digging the home defenses, scanning the sky for enemy aircraft, watching war communique films at school. I had collected tons of waste paper, tin cans, old cooking fat. I had grown Victory gardens, stayed up nights watching for tire thieves, helped my mother to keep the OPA Consumer's Pledge.

"Jesus." Uncle Boswick heard the news and his hand reached for another cold beer.

My father had his bank book out, and was searching the columns with a scowl. The war had killed the Depression, moving him into the only prosperity he'd ever known. He wet the pencil tip against his tongue and began to figure on an old envelope, moving into peace halfheartedly.

I walked to the street's edge and looked both ways, as if I might see that cresting mushroom cloud, or be touched by its gigantic shadow. For the war *had* touched us all: I thought of The MacGregor, Gussie, and Jed — in the dark enigma of that basement, that stained wall, I later realized we had viewed every casualty.

And in the field where we had labored hard and well, grass already grew in our trenches.

Perhaps because the Jap was no longer my enemy, but more likely because I was curious of the face I had never seen, I walked slowly through the yielding high grass toward the leaning tarpaper shack. Against the broken window the old newspaper floated, the type erased by sun and wind. Closer, I saw that the shutters threatened to fall from rusty hinges, and that their bright yellow paint had now curdled into rivulets. My knock was timid, and unanswered, but the door was ajar and I could see through the single room to the back yard.

The house was empty. Any furniture the Jap might have had was gone, and so was he. There was not even the smell of soy sauce, nor the odor of yellow; not even a grain of rice captured in the floor's parallel cracks remained as evidence. I stood in the tiny room, where dust motes drifted like dandelion fuzz across the sun's scorching shafts, and I wondered where he had gone. I wanted him to see my triumph — we had won, Japan was conquered. Also, I wanted to see his face — just once, up close, to see if he wasn't an exact copy of the grinning monkey the magazines had shown us. Where was he? Had he committed hari-kari in the garden?

The only evidence that the empty room had been lived in recently were the newspapers covering one wall. Bold headlines jumped from the yellow paper; the print faded into blurred words, columns of statistics, tracing the war's progress — down to the two-day-old newpaper taped at a crazy angle in the corner, its ink still firm.

Under the low ceiling the August heat collected; thick blue flies hummed furiously in the hot air, and as I walked out the back door it occurred to me that the Jap's departure would *really* baffle Uncle Boswick.

The garden was leveled; except for the small, open dirt mound, a row of scabs where the corn had been, all traces of the Jap's industry were sucked into the baked earth. A few loose feathers drifted across the space where last year cucumbers had lain in profusion, like surface mines, and the night air had been green with the metallic darkness of hard, fist-sized tomatoes. The feathers drifted from the rotting pile within the chicken coop, mute testimony to the destruction. The ground within the wire was perforated with the puck marks of claws, littered with bleached, dry bones. From inside the shed came a brittle noise, and I wondered if there could be a survivor — I had imagined those last two hens fighting by moonlight until each had driven a slashing, crescent beak into the other. The noise — a chewing, tearing sound — continued, and I searched the baked earth for a handful of grass, to throw over the wire fence.

As the grass drifted down, each blade flashing like a knife, the burlap cover at the small doorway moved. Then the single remaining chicken emerged. She dashed across the enclosure on thick legs to where the blades were still falling; cautiously, she sniffed at my offering but did not touch it — she had acquired a taste for blood.

The angular, massive head turned and behind deep folds her fierce eyes were fixed on me; with a crouching run she accelerated, to crash heavily into the wire. Her thick, short neck absorbed the impact, and she moved back, grunting, to try again. Her rush had carried the terrific odor of fowl, blood, dung, dust; and with this stink in my nose I now saw that she had lost all of her feathers and the skin was a silky black, broken only by the white scars. Grown short and fat, the crescent beak hooked like a primitive tooth, she had metamorphosed into a kind of rat.

Of the flock, this was the Victor.

WILLIAM EASTLAKE

The Dancing Boy

(FROM EVERGREEN REVIEW)

WE WERE STAYING at the Minzeh so I met my connection at the Emsallah off rue de Mexique. We crossed over to the Mahtura Shasti, then down the Ingleterra to the Grand Socco and the Kasbah. For a connection, the connection was silent. Like most street boys of Tangier he spoke five languages and he was silent now in all of them. How did he know I was not the police? How did he know I was not Beethoven? Beethoven was an easy foreign name for him to remember because there was a street named Beethoven in Tangier, another Bach, another Wagner. Not that the Tangierites are particularly music conscious, because they have another street named Cervantes, and another rue La Fontaine, and a rue Ernest Hemingway. All this because very recently Tangier was an international city, an international port without customs duty. It prospered wildly under mysterious plots, fraud money, sealed bodies carried through the Medina in the light of day, and princes of the blood living under a nom de Hashish. But a few years ago Tangier received its liberty from Spain and is no longer a place for the strange — or is it?

Abdullah continued silent. We had a drink at the Tout Va Bien on the Petit Socco, mint tea — tea was all you could get. They had a law, a Muslim law, that covered not only the Kasbah, but all the Medina from the rue d'Italie to the rue de Portugal — no liquor.

From a slot through the buildings you could see way down past the Gare de Tanger to the bay where none of the great ships came anymore. The world has abandoned Morocco. Everyone stays at home now. The English used to come. The French came, everyone had come to Tangier somewhere between the ages of nineteen and twenty-six, then they went home and married their neighbor and lived happily ever after, but they had the memory. I do not know where all of the young people of the world go now between the ages of nineteen and twenty-six.

From the Tout Va Bien you could see the Cimetière Musulman which looked grim and, when none of the djellabaed traffic was in the way, you could see out through the rue de la Kasbah all the way to the Tombeaux Phoeniciens, which was interesting.

"What do you want from me?" the connection said.

"Nothing you do not volunteer," I said. "I am not a journalist. No facts. No lies. I am a writer."

"Ambiances," Abdullah said. "Ambiances," giving it the French pronunciation. "Would you be interested in my genius?"

"Your what?"

"The Tangier police believe I have a genius."

I did not want to push him or even guide him. This never obtains what I truly want. I must nurture him, tolerate him, accept him, but not push him.

"Would you like some more tea?" I said.

"About the police — Yes, I'll have more tea. About the police, even when they wanted to become business partners I was so frightened I began to shake. An Arab street boy is supposed to be tough, sly, sophisticated, fearless, but the police always make me shake. Kif, or hashish, sells for twenty-one dollars a kilo in Tangier and one hundred dollars in Paris. It is very simple, a simple business transaction, but I begin to shake. The police want the boys of Morocco to be successful, particularly the children of Tangier. The police know I am a failure, but they will not accept this."

Abdullah took his tea. Abdullah As-Salem As-Sabah sniffed for the mint, then tasted it. The tea of the Kasbah is rank with sugar, so much so that when the tea of the Kasbah cools it crystallizes.

"The police of the Kasbah will not give up," Abdullah said. "Perhaps I could forge documents, become a contrabandista, a con man, a blockade runner, a bigamist, a sodomist, a spy, a dipsomaniac, a kleptomaniac, or a nymphomaniac."

"You have to be a woman to be that," I said.

Abdullah sipped his tea before it crystallized. "I use many words that I do not know what they mean," Abdullah said. "To impress myself, but that one I know. Yes, the police want me to become a woman."

"Do you want to explain that?"

"I won't have to," Abdullah said. "I will show you. Come with me tonight to the Dancing Boy."

Albert Decker came up now. He sat down at our table and it began to rain. He ordered tea and the rain began to dilute it, but we sat there until the waiter rolled down the awning with the bright red and green sign, TOUT VA BIEN. Albert Decker had a thin blond beard. He looked like a Russian painter from Omsk, but he was an English poet from Sudsbury. He was one of the few English poets between nineteen and twenty-six who still got to Morocco.

"How are things going, Abdullah As-Salem As-Sabah?" Albert Decker said.

"Tout va bien," Abdullah said.

"Have the police found anything for you yet?"

"Pas encore."

"They will," Albert Decker said. "They're determined sons of bitches. Can I read you something that I wrote in jail?"

"No," Abdullah As-Salem As-Sabah said.

"The police arrest us," Albert Decker said, "out of an act of faith. No suspicion, no evidence, pure faith. Jail is really the only place you can write poetry. You can't write poetry in the cafés as my grandfather did in the Paris of the twenties. The sights here are too distracting. Who can write poetry while being watched by a camel? Who can compete with a whirling dervish? A houri? And a cobalt sky? I bet they never had a cobalt sky above the Rotonde in the twenties. Paris is gray," he said. "That's why we go to jail in Morocco. The police are accommodating. We don't have a Deux Magots, but we have a jail. Can I read you something? A jail with food, lodging, bed, and breakfast all in. Dancing if you tip the warden a few shillings."

"Don't boast," Abdullah said. "Everybody's been in jail."

"I suppose so," Albert Decker said. "Can I read you something?"

The waiter rolled up the awning. The rain had ceased. Abdullah looked up at the Moroccan sky. "No," he said.

"I understand," Albert Decker said. "I don't suppose the police have found anything for you yet, Abdullah As-Salem As-Sabah. Well I don't suppose they really care. They don't give a farthing really what happens to us poor beggars. I thought I'd have another go at the Muse. You interested, Abby?"

"No," Abdullah said.

"Well," Albert Decker said, rising, "I'll bug off."

No one seemed to object. Not wanting to leave without solicitations to stay, Albert Decker sat down again. He wanted to quit when he was ahead. Albert Decker leaned over toward me above the tea.

"I met Abdullah when he robbed me on the beach. I hitchhiked through Spain with two seventeen-year-old Scottish girls I met in France. I tried to sell them here in Tangier but the girls sold me. The Arabs wanted my clothes too, stripped me naked here in the Plaza getting them, came to about twenty-three dirhams. Not bad, but it was a Bond Street suit, sentimental value, badly worn, the only way to have them. Arabs realize that. Good holes. Clever beggars. So I put on my bathing suit, strolled down the Kasbah to the beach, and slept there. Someone stole my bathing trunks with three pounds ten shillings. Abdullah here waked me, naked there under that cobalt sky, asked me what I wanted. Pants. He got some for me and a policeman came up and demanded his cut. 'We can't have anything illegal going on in Tangier,' the policeman said. 'Honesty is the best policy. The police are your friends.' " Albert Decker felt he was ahead now and got up to leave. "The police will find something for you, Abdullah."

Abdullah As-Salem As-Sabah watched him go. "He is a foreigner," Abdullah said. "Everything to him is comic. He only sees the comic. He does not see the tragic because he does not want to. Tomorrow he can get on the boat and leave the country. He is not a victim. He has a passport. No one can do anything to him because he has a passport. So Morocco is a joke. Everything is a joke. With me it cannot be funny. I am getting older, past fifteen."

"Fifteen is not old," I said.

"Fifteen is old for Morocco," Abdullah said. "You are born old in Morocco. All the boys in the Kasbah are old. They speak five languages."

"From the University of Despair," I said.

Abdullah toyed with his spoon. "You were recommended to me by B," Abdullah said. "You do not behave like B."

"How did B behave?"

"Like a person," Abdullah said. "Will you be free tonight?"

"Not tonight," I said, "but soon."

"But soon," Abdullah said, standing up.

I dropped a pile of dirhams on the table knowing Abdullah would distribute it. "Soon," I said, waving myself away.

"But soon," Abdullah As-Salem As-Sabah said, watching me go.

"Was there anything interesting in the Kasbah?" Martha said from her easel on the veranda of the Squiggle Hotel. We called it the Squiggle because this is the way the sign looked in Arabic.

"The boy that B recommended," I said, "has some genius, but I haven't discovered what yet. When I get back from Fez I will see him again. He seems to know his way around. Did you get anything done?"

"I've been trying to draw those Arabs over there at El Khedive, but they move."

"Send a boy over with ten dirhams asking them not to move," I said. "Are you sure you don't want to go to Fez?"

"Not Fez," Martha said. "I'm still under the weather."

"I could stay and we could see the Phoenician Tombs."

"No, you'd better see Fez," Martha said. "The Phoenician Tombs can wait. I will walk downhill to the station with you and take a Petit Taxi back."

We went down to the train through the Kasbah. In going down to the train or the boat or the buses from the main town in Tangier, it is difficult to avoid the Kasbah without going around where it is extremely steep. There is a wildfire grapevine in the Kasbah and, by the time we got down to the Gare Tanger-Fez, there was Abdullah waiting. He did not show up in the waiting room, but outside in the train section where you pay one dirham to get in, almost nothing, but enough to keep the poor out. I had called a Petit Taxi for Martha, bought my ticket, and got into the train station. There was Abdullah.

"I thought you might want someone to show you Fez."

"Not Fez," I said.

"But you said last night — "

"I mean I can't afford to take you to Fez." Which was the truth, but a blunder. The American is forced into a role in Morocco. Whether he likes the role or not, it is forced on him. In all the poverty of Morocco, the American is a rich man; whether he is a poor American student, a writer, a painter, he is still a rich man in Morocco. His clothing alone is worth the national budget, and when you say you cannot afford a guide to Fez, it is not the truth even though it is true.

The train was late, but that is not true for Morocco either. It was supposed to leave at 8:22 A.M., what everyone in Morocco knows to mean some time in the morning. It was still some time in the morning.

We sat on the wooden bench and watched dry, dim, blue Spain across the Straits.

"Like everyone in Morocco," Abdullah As-Salem As-Sabah said, "I want to go to America, but that is absolutely impossible, so we say we want to go somewhere else. That is impossible too, but it is not crazy. Morocco is the poorest country in the world, but only those of us who speak many languages can even dream about going. The rest are resigned. Do you realize that a passport costs two thousand dollars? I have an American friend who was offered two thousand for his passport in Marrakesh. John Siebel from Topeka, Kansas. Do you know him?"

"No."

"Right now I would settle for one dollar — six dirhams — to see my dying mother in Ceuta."

"Here is seven dirhams," I said, counting it out. "The extra dirham is a tip for your mother."

"No one believes the dying mother in Ceuta story," Abdullah said, "so I believe it is not lying. I would not lie to you. So the dying mother in Ceuta story is a way around lying. In our small acquaintanceship you would resent it if I asked you directly for five dirhams for hunger."

"As long as you don't ask me for two thousand dollars for a passport," I said.

"If I do not find something soon — some way out soon," Abdullah said, gazing solemnly at the cobalt Straits, "I will end up at the Dancing Boy."

"It's not that bad."

"It is unspeakably bad for me," Abdullah said. "Unbearably bad bad bad bad. Just thinking about it is bad."

"How about another five dirhams?" I said.

"No," Abdullah said. "I had planned on five. That is all I need for today."

"When I saw you," I said, "I had planned on giving you ten."

"Thank you, no," Abdullah As-Salem As-Sabah said. "I can only take so much, only the fee, no more than that. To perform the small functions of guiding you for the money is bad enough. When there is only money, something dies. It is dead. There is no longer life. It is dead."

The train was threatening now to leave.

"When you get back," Abdullah called after me as I made my way to the train, "I will take you to the Dancing Boy."

"All right," I said.

"You will not believe it," Abdullah called after me.

The train to Fez passed lonely camels posing on landscaped horizons for the *National Geographic* magazine. It also passed date palms, eucalyptus, and swamps. You do not believe there are swamps on the deserts, but there is a great swamp between Tangier and Rabat. Only the wide, padded foot of the camel can negotiate it, and only the camel tried. The railroad goes around, close to the edge, but around.

I changed trains at Sidi Cassim, got off the train at Fez in a big rain, went with an Arab who knew his way around to the Hotel Plicae, and began my tour of Fez when the rain stopped. Two days later I was back in Tangier and Abdullah As-Salem As-Sabah was waiting. How did he know I was arriving on the 10:45? The 10:45 never arrived at 10:45 before, and he did not even know the day I was coming back, but he was there. I do not believe in any form of telepathy, extrasensory perception, but I believe in the Arab.

Abdullah As-Salem As-Sabah was solicitous about my trip to Fez, said he had seen Martha who was well, and the children were a picture of health — "roses in their cheeks."

"But we have no children."

"If you had they would have roses in their cheeks." Abdullah As-Salem As-Sabah was in fine fettle.

I gave Abdullah a gold coin.

"The Café Tout Va Bien tonight," Abdullah shouted.

"The Café Tout Va Bien tonight," I called back as the Grand Taxi spun off.

At the Tout Va Bien that night Abdullah As-Salem As-Sabah was doleful.

"We don't have to go to the Dancing Boy," I said.

"I must show you my fate," Abdullah said.

"Speaking of fate, when are you going to take Martha and me to the Phoenician Tombs?"

"You would not like them," Abdullah said. "They would bore you." Abdullah looked up. "Do you think your Martha would enjoy the Roman Stadium?"

"I'm sure she would love it," I said. "When was the Roman Stadium built?"

"Last year," Abdullah said. "The nicest view in Morocco," he said, "is another country."

Albert Decker came up now.

"Did you get a passport? Did you find the two thousand dollars? The ten million dirhams? Or did you get a job? There are only three jobs in Morocco," Albert Decker said. "The king in Rabat, the mechanic in Tangier, and the dancing boy. Somebody's already got the mechanic job and the king won't be shot for another seven months yet."

"No, I haven't got the passport or the job, but why do you push me?"

"Because you're a genius," Albert Decker said. He looked at Abdullah now. "Why, when a man has as much talent as you do, I can't understand why — "

"Because the dancing boy," Abdullah As-Salem As-Sabah said, "is dressed like a woman — treated like a woman. You know?"

"But you're in Morocco. We're in Morocco. Right?"

A boy tried to sell us the Gibraltar paper. The wind blew the cloth of the Tout Va Bien over our heads.

"But a man into a woman, even in Morocco — " Abdullah stared at the paper as though to see some news of this, but blankly. The boy turned away with the paper.

"There must be another job," I said.

"No," Abdullah said.

We reached the Dancing Boy by going down all the streets that are on no map. The streets of the Medina are on no map and the inner redoubt of the Kasbah is even unknown to those that dwell there, the people who live near the Dancing Boy. You cannot say it is eleven blocks from the Tout Va Bien because you coast down slippery slits, wind back onto yourself, spiral up and over low rooftops, taste the vileness of sewers and the sweet breath of lurking assassins. The Kasbah is not a city, the road to the Dancing Boy not a street anyone knew, but the whole labyrinth is more like trenches in some war in which the soldiers wear roses in their hats and scream at each other.

Now we were at the Dancing Boy. The music sounded low-keyed, religious, and obscene. You entered into a high nimbus cloud of hashish. The players were in a corner on a raised divan so they seemed to be hugging a mountain above the rising cloud below. Hashish smells bittersweet, a kind of green, musky tang, mesmerizing and sweet. Coming through the cloud were the vendors of small boys and girls. They also sold Chiclets and yo-yos. One of the vendors had a goat under his elbow.

We sat down in the cloud next to some Sudanese on holiday from Khartoum and three lost-looking pilgrims from Lebanon who smelled of asp.

Decker demanded service by pinching a waiter. The waiter turned out to be God, but he brought us tea anyway. He was a great black man with an enormous white beard. The sail-white djellabah he wore bunched up like a dress. He wore thin gold glasses on his wide purple-black face.

"There's no reason God can't be a black," Albert Decker said. "They're getting all their rights now. This is the kind of place, the kind of cloud, where we would expect to find God."

Abdullah As-Salem As-Sabah was silent, smoking a hashish pipe, but with stateliness, like the great savage who knows where the action is. Abdullah passed me the pipe as though to another voyager. We seemed no longer in Tangier now. We were in the aftercabin of a ship that was lost without a trace. The ship swung gently at anchor. We sat staring at each other over the pipe. You could hear the *click click click* of something, and a slow grinding screech of something distant, and below that might have been a hawser. Decker moved his hand. His diamonds did not sparkle, they had only a dull greasy sheen this evening in the porthole spot. Out of the sweet dim mist, the sweet bitter soft mist to the left of the Arab orchestra and out on the cloud, danced the dancing boy, dressed like a girl.

The Arab orchestra twanged him or her or it on bravely, twanged on and then reversed itself, and then you realized that's how Arab music goes. The music turns upon itself, swings upward in ever-tightening circles, and then abruptly it is somewhere else, part of the vortex carrying the dancing boy, lifting him and turning him in his gossamer Arabess and Arabesque costume so that he appeared at times only a twirling whirr, something seen off the bowsprit in a cloud, only the cloud was hashish, only the storm was real and violent, only the long tambourines, the thumping drums, the lyre, the lute, the ungodly high screams to Allah and the dancing boy, undreamt of and real.

"Why anyone, why a man would be afraid — "

"Because it's a woman and I am a man."

"Still," Albert Decker mused through the music, the smoke, the dervish. "Still, it's an Arab culture. They do these things."

"This dancing boy, el Estafa, is going to Mecca next week," Abdullah said. "So that is why they are hiring me."

Soon the spinning boy would be in Mecca. The turning boy in a cloud would be replaced by the one at my side.

We were out of the place, out of the cloud now, and sitting in some alley slit, outside someplace, and someone speaking French with some Riff thrown in. Then Albert Decker moved.

"Well," Albert Decker said, "a boy goes to Mecca and our Abdullah gets a job."

"Or gets killed," I said.

"I don't have anything," Abdullah said. "Not even an enemy."

"I have to go home," I said.

On the balcony of the Squiggle Hotel, Martha said, "We must go to Abdullah's opening."

"I don't think so," I said.

"Then we will leave for Marrakesh without seeing Abdullah again?"

"Yes. That is the way he would want it," I said.

But I did see Abdullah again. I saw Abdullah again very dead.

Dead.

That's the way it is in Morocco. They die young.

They speak five languages and they die still children.

From hard stuff. A broken needle. The enemy.

Some people don't want to be women. Some do. Some don't.

A broken needle . . .

Some don't.

The dancing boy, Abdullah As-Salem As-Sabah was dead.

You would have thought, anyone would think, that the best thing to do is *not* get yourself born in Morocco, not in Tangier, the Medina, the Kasbah. Not get involved with those that do. If you do, forget it. Exactly.

But I can still hear that music, still smell, feel, touch, see Morocco, Tangier, the Medina, the Kasbah, the dancing boy. I guess I always will.

BETH HARVOR

Pain Was My Portion

(FROM THE HUDSON REVIEW)

THEY ATE THEIR PICNICS as they sat shored up against the graveyard wall — on the living side — with a view down into a far field where there were cows. Even from that distance they could see how the cow's fly-warding tails kept swinging with the languid regularity of bellropes, while much closer they could feel, warm and cracked at their backs, the sun-warmed cemetery wall.

Ralph's wife, Gladdie, always held her head high. It came, Ralph said, from an Edwardian childhood of too many blouses with high dog-collared collars, all in starched and unyielding cotton. Ralph had a theory about clothing styles changing the physiognomy of whole generations. "No receding chins in that era," He would say. And he liked to point out to Gladdie how her hair was always seeking its Edwardian beginnings — how no matter how tightly and classically she wound it up on top of her head in the mornings, it still, as the day wore on, worked itself out from its mooring of pins and became more Gibson Girlish. His own hair was in a silver brush cut, his eyes were military-looking (they looked toughly into a secret distance), his clothes were in restrained colors, except for the one light touch of powder-blue sneakers. In fact, most people hadn't even thought they were Americans when they had first come. Not by the way they dressed or talked. They weren't like the ones who came up with their loud plaids with voices to match. The Fraziers, when they wore plaids, wore dark plaids that looked as if they had been steeped in pots of tea, and their specialty-shop sweaters looked as if they had been cut from hairy peat bogs and had dull pewter buttons on them. And they were not wild pleasure seekers either; they did research, their own project, supplying information from the gravestones of the Kingston cemetery to the Hampton Historical Society, which, in an earlier summer, they had helped to found.

Their place of research was very windy and dry. The trees were too big. What had begun as shelter had ended as deprivation, and the graveyard lay like the environmental equivalent of a pale and over-protected child. It seemed as if the wind never stopped moving in the tops of the big trees — a wind that made the leaves fly-cast their spotted shadows across forgotten mounds and faded grass. But the Fraziers had been gradually changing all that. Even after heavy rains had pelted the graves with leaves ("Like walking in wet corn flakes," Gladdie said), they were sometimes to be seen there, in milky plastic raincoats, gathering more evidence to help in the reconstruction of the history of the early community, kneeling to their researches like supplicants, tenderly feeling along the fronts of stones through crude pockmarks and embossed granite-colored moss to find clues to names and dates. "A kind of braille in reverse," Gladdie called the incised letters. And on fine days they sometimes did charcoal rubbings. There was one verse that Gladdie particularly loved, one that she had made rubbings of for the kitchens of all her Boston friends:

PAIN WAS MY PORTION
PHYSIC WAS MY FOOD
CHRIST WAS MY PHYSICIAN
WHICH DID ME NO GOOD

They marveled at the anger and the humor of it. "Anger turned to humor," Ralph said, "by the alchemy of rhyme."

The early graves belonged mainly to United Empire Loyalist dead. That great exodus had long since reversed itself and gone back the way it came; now there was only the most irregular travel from south to north — made up of big loud prodigal sons who came to "Canader for the summah, Florider for the wintah," and who lived in places like Boston and Springfield in between; or there were the tourists who came up to the northeast coast of the continent for a quick change of country and a slightly cooler climate; or there were the draft dodgers and deserters whom the Fraziers didn't like to think about. They didn't approve of the war their government was fighting *either,* but they didn't think that dodging the draft should be necessary in a country that had universal suffrage. *"Universal suffrage?"* someone had cried, and when someone else had pointed out to them — and it was a Canadian who had pointed it out — that a boy could be shipped back home, neatly tucked in his coffin and wrapped in flags, long before he was ever old enough to vote, they had to agree; and when someone else, another Canadian (the Canadians were getting just as argumentative as the people back home) pointed out that the Loyalists had *also* been draft dodgers, the Fraziers had to agree again, but still *emotionally* they preferred those draft dodgers of the past, who had left their Georgian legacies along all the richest river valleys. A Canadian neighbor they had once been fond of made the mistake of saying that as a raison d'être for not fighting in a war, the Fraziers preferred king to conscience. In self-defense the Fraziers decided that this man had become bitter and cynical. And so they continued annually to resolve their difficulties by trying to live, for the summer months of every year, not only in another country, but in another century of another country. Their summer house was an early Loyalist one which they had got cheaply and restored expensively — though simply. Ralph would occasionally remark that it cost a lot to live such a simple life — as he scoured the countryside for early maple and butternut cabinets to use as fronts for electric dishwashers and hi-fi equipment. In fact, the twentieth century ran through the house in hidden veins of pipes and wires, not talked about, but *there,* like a crude word for a functional thing. On the surface though, everything was "period." They had found a Boston store that carried black-and-brown gingham wallpapers and fabrics of early prints. They had found early glass for the windows and early brick for the stairs, so that even if they suffered from astigmatism as they looked out at the brilliant mornings, even if they felt as if the stairs would crumble beneath them as they ran down into the brilliant mornings, they could still assure themselves that the reproduction they lived in was a faithful one.

Marian was their only child and had been born late in their marriage. She was a sad-necked girl with long, weakly gold hair and poor eyesight. Gladdie didn't like glasses (she was a tyrant for the natural) and she would frequently lift the glasses from the face of her pale helpless-eyed Botticelli daughter and advise her to go to her room and practice her eye exercises. When the eye exercises didn't seem to make an improvement, she thought of various compromises — having the glasses attached to black velvet reins, or to a chain of braided human hair so that they could hang down on the front of the bosom (*"What bosom?"* Marian had asked) and be swung up to the eyes in times of emergency. Marian, who still had a small guilty residue of respect for the opinion of her peers, carried the glasses in the pocket of her jeans. Gladdie didn't care about Marian's peers. Or their opinions. The ones in Boston were too fast; the ones in Hampton were too dull. In fact, what connection these empty-eyed teen-agers had with their salty keen-eyed grandparents, Gladdie simply could not see. In two generations — and in some cases, one — all the naturalness had been drained from these people; she could not imagine any robust haystack sex preceding the large annual yield of illegitimate babies; instead, she thought of the girls lying obedient and dull as cows in the backs of cars, their white thighs flopped open, their eyes looking up at nothing, even at the height of the act, chewing gum. Chewing cuds! (When Ralph listened to Gladdie lamenting the passing of robust haystack sex, he kept his mouth shut. A gentleman never tells, he thought, giving that old saw a new, piquant, and strangely opposite meaning, for only he was in the unfortunate position of knowing that Gladdie's sexuality was locked back in the eighteenth century — like her taste.) And the clothes they wore! Gladdie went on. She had seen them at the Saturday night dance wearing rhinestone imitations of the Queen of England's necklaces (and the Queen of England's taste was certainly nothing to stand up and cheer about) and dresses made from maroon taffeta with a large grain in it like plywood. Their teeth had potato eyes in them from what she imagined to be a constant diet of root beer and lime rickey — that is, the ones who *had* their teeth, for it was their collective ambition (and probably, Gladdie thought, the only ambition they had ever had) to have all their teeth pulled out by the time that they were twenty. She averted her eyes from them in embarrassment and pain — she loved "character" and "naturalness" — and she tried to make Marian see how wrong they would be as friends. "But what about the kids in Boston?" Marian had asked. "*They're* natural." And she thought of the kids of Boston, the girls without make-up and wearing long hair and faded pants. Or else they wore short calico dresses, demure, high necked, smocked. Gladdie saw red when she thought of those cocoa, blue and slate-colored dresses that were made of calico patterns appropriated from the eighteenth and nineteenth centuries and cut off at thigh length. They reminded her, she said, of Georgian houses cut down into ranch style. And this was how she won all the arguments. With her perfect taste and her feeling for the authentic. "And the kids in Boston have no *character*," Gladdie told Marian. "They have poor posture and no ambition." And so Marian, who also had poor posture and no ambition, went everywhere with her parents: to timeless afternoon teas with two old sisters who lived in a high old house at the helm of a large loose garden, to the sour parlors of people too proud to go to nursing homes, to endless mornings on the sunken verandahs of the town characters, for long country drives hunting down Canadiana, on picnics, and to the graveyard near Kingston.

Marian's memories of the graveyard were both peaceful and bizarre. Most of her childhood seemed to have been spent there among its moss-mottled stones and she could remember strange (strange because so casual) meals eaten at a large family gravestone made in the shape of a table, accommodating at least six people above ground and what appeared to be a whole dynasty below. She seemed to remember ham sandwiches being carefully divided out over IN LOVING MEMORY OF, and milk spilled on dark eroded stone, and the careful recording of how long the people had lived, how long outwitted a cruel fate, not just the pathetically meager years only, but often the more generous months and days as well. But then with Marian memory often lacked the quality of an accurate recording of events, and seemed sometimes to be imagination in retrospect.

But as the years passed by, the Fraziers spent less time in the Kingston graveyard. Their passion for Loyalist statistics gradually became sated, they became preoccupied with the restoration of their house, and they often had long visits from American friends.

The summer Marian was fourteen, Esther Abrams came to visit. None of the Fraziers had ever met her before she came, but they felt as if they had known her for years, for she was the sister of one of their oldest friends, Helen Helpmann. They had got a letter from Helen early in July asking if it would be all right if she and Esther arrived the following week. Esther was sick, Helen wrote, so they were taking the plane rather than the train for reasons of comfort. Also to save time: for Helen also wrote that the doctor had given Esther four — at the most, five — more months to live. The Fraziers rose to the challenge of this disheartening news, terribly aware of its irony. They had wanted for years to meet Esther, and now at last their wish was going to be granted, and they would all meet, only to know that they would never meet again. It had the boomerang quality, the malevolent charity with which wishes are granted in fairy tales, and Gladdie lamented for Esther, for Esther's husband, for Helen, for themselves, as she cheered up the room at the top of the stairs. She rounded up the brightest colored cushions from the other bedrooms and unpacked the red and white quilt made by the Ladies' Aid. She took down "Pain Was My Portion." She took down a Currier & Ives engraving called *The Farewell* and put a Dufy poster in its place. She imagined the kinds of flowers she would pick, not the heavy-scented creamy ones like peonies and roses, but molecular peppery ones — Queen Anne's lace, caraway, lupines — and vigorous ones — tiger lilies, devil's paintbrushes — all gathered into gay improbable bouquets. She took Marian aside and explained about the cancer, that it was incurable, that Esther Abrams herself knew that she was going to die.

"We will try to make it a very happy visit, dear, and I want you to know the facts about it so you don't start talking about cancer or dying or anything like that."

And then, propelled by her own kind of tense bustle, she was off to the clothesline with a pan of washing. Marian came down the steps after her, and stood watching.

"Where is it, Mother?"

"Where's what?"

"The cancer."

Gladdie pegged the last sheet to the line, then rolled the pulley out. It was one of her limitations that she frequently found the truth to be in bad taste. "There is nothing they can do," she said, hoping *that* would do.

"But *where* is it?"

"Last year she had a breast removed," Gladdie said in a far-off voice. "They thought they had got it all out, but they hadn't."

Marian continued to stand there, waiting.

The sheets, filled with wind, moved in solemn columns.

"There's nothing more to *tell,*" Gladdie said sharply. "Go to your room now, and tidy it up."

Much as they may have felt prepared for Esther, the Fraziers were all surprised by her. She seemed so incredibly alive, and for a woman who had only four months to live, she seemed very sure of herself. And she had big breasts. Marian was cross with herself when she realized how much this surprised her. Surely she hadn't expected her to come with one half of her bosom limp and flat like a war amputee with his empty flat sleeve tucked into his pocket. How stupid can you be! she thought sternly to herself. Still, she found herself keeping her eyes carefully averted from Esther Abrams' breasts, and even from her face.

"Dear, *try* to be a little more *natural,*" her mother said to her one afternoon, giving her a fiercely reassuring smile.

"Yes, Mother," Marian said, sighing heavily, walking up the stairs — Yes mother, yesmother, yesmother, yesmother.

She did soon become more relaxed, though. It was Esther who did it. She put them all at their ease, all of them, even Marian. "She's remarkable!" Gladdie and Helen were constantly reminding each other, in their new, low, charged voices, even when they could see Esther through the kitchen window far off in the field picking wildflowers, even when they knew she was faraway at the beach, they spoke in their new low voices. They would do anything not to be her, anything. Bestow any praise, renounce any pleasure. They spent their days conspiring diversions: trips, picnics, bonfires, charades. And Esther tried not to be one of those tiresome invalids who never needs anything done for her. She allowed herself to need almost everything, the hot toddies at night, the warm pine baths in the late afternoon, the wild batik of Gladdie's made up into an amusing dressing gown, the impulsive flights into town to see the grade-B movies that they snorted over like demented teen-agers, the back rubs, the rests after lunch. And Gladdie put a great deal of love and care into the meals. Breakfast was made to be Edwardian-ample with omelets and bread dipped into eggnog and fried, with Scottish marmalades, English jams, Oriental and South American teas. Sometimes they let breakfast go on for hours. They told a lot of stories and laughed a lot and were afraid of silences. Every breakfast was distinguished by the desperate gaiety of the *Titanic* going down. It was as if they were trying to pretend they could control time, but in the end, thought Marian, anxious to go swimming, they only wasted it.

Marian came to idolize Esther. "Esther down yet?" was the first thing she would say when she came down to breakfast in the mornings, and "Where's Esther?" when she came in from swimming in the afternoon — "Esther in?" Gladdie and Helen both noticed how Marian adored Esther. And one day when Gladdie was puttering in her room, Marian came by. She was on her way to the neighbors to get some eggs. She needed money from her mother, got it, then hesitated a moment. Gladdie was wearing a sensible black bathing suit, but she was one of those fortunate people on whom the sensible looks classic.

"What is it?" she asked her daughter. Marian had been looking pale lately, she thought.

"I was wondering."

"What is it? What were you wondering?"

"Something about Esther."

Gladdie listened for a moment, in the direction of downstairs, with her eyes.

"Are they all out?"

Marian nodded.

"Well?"

"I was wondering what kind of padding she puts in it — I mean in the other half of her brassiere."

Gladdie looked shocked. Looking shocked was a ploy she had occasionally used with children. All parents do, she imagined. Nice people don't ask such things, her look said.

"Oh well," said Marian, defeated, "I just wondered . . ." And she went down the hall and slowly descended the stairs in a series of sad little hops.

"Marian." Her mother's voice, behind and above her. Her mother was standing on the landing. Her high blades of cheekbones looked polished — she must have been creaming her face. She towered there at the stair top, an icon in a channel swimmer's bathing suit. And, "She has a kind of foam-rubber pad built into her brassiere," she said quickly, like a child saying something she's been dared to. And at that moment the broad handsome planes of her face fragmented, buckled up, became the terrible terrain of fear, of terror. She jerked her face away from Marian so that her own daughter would not see the shame of her fear, and went quickly down the hallway to her room.

Marian fitted the money into her pocket and just before she stepped out into the sun, she cupped her hands under her own small breasts. Then she deftly darted her blouse into her shorts and started off for the next farm. Lately she had begun to wake up at night, needing to use the toilet. She didn't try to discover why (too much cocoa? too few blankets?) and so prevent its recurrence; she only stumbled, bewildered but dutiful, downstairs to the bathroom, then upstairs again and at once back to sleep. One night, though, she made the mistake of trying to orient the sky to the night (is it near morning? she wondered) and she made her way through wicker mounds to one of the sunporch windows. It had turned cold for summer and although the hills around the house were dark, the sky was not very dark, it was medium blue. But cold. And speckled with stars. Everyone's asleep, she thought, the living and the dying. Those words "the living and the dying" came to her without warning and they filled her with such immediate and spontaneous terror that her only thought then was to get upstairs as fast as she could, and she fled to the stairway. And all the way up it was as if a powerful hand was clutching for her ankle, filling her legs with tremors so that thrills of terror ran down them, so that they seemed to have no more consistency than running water, like legs in dreams. At last she got to her room, got the door closed tight behind her, stood leaning hard against it, everything roaring and pounding inside her. "Ideas rose up in crowds," she thought, remembering a line from a book in her father's study. And that quickly turned into "ideas rose up in shrouds." She had always been able to terrorize herself by rhyme. And she had kept the light on till morning that night; it wasn't till the sun rose and began to fill her room with pallid early life that she had finally fallen asleep.

A few days before Esther and Helen were due to leave, Gladdie got saddled with some kind of committee meeting at her house, and she suggested that the two of them go off for a drive and take Marian along as their guide. "Esther looks tired," Gladdie said in a low voice to Helen. Esther, coming down the stairs in a dark wool skirt and a blue sweater, did not look especially tired, but there was, among the others, almost a ritual of anticipating exhaustion on her behalf. Marian ran up to her room for her cardigan, and when she came down again the three of them set off on the northbound road out of Hampton. Sussex, "the dairy center of the Maritimes" according to the map, did not particularly entice them, and soon after they left Hampton they turned left and took the road down the Kingston Peninsula. Marian suggested they visit the old Merritt-Wetmore house, now restored, and once the home of one of the first Loyalist families in the district. Tea was served there too, Marian said. It had started to rain. They decided to go to the Merritt-Wetmore house. The black car moved under a roof of dripping leaves and came, beaded with black rain, out into the open near Kingston.

They found the house and looked around and had their tea. When they came back to the car, there was a long glaring underbelly to the navy sky — did it mean more rain or did it mean clearing? It had turned cold, it seemed like a day in October. They got into the car and started out toward Hampton.

"What church is that?"

"The Kingston Anglican church. We can turn left here, if you'd like to see it."

Helen turned left and they soon swung in beside it. Their thighs felt stuck together, their legs stiff. They got out. It was curious, Marian thought, she had not been down here since last year, and now the church looked dilapidated, blotched with rain. The paint had mostly worn off, what was left was flaky silver, and the stained-glass windows, so gaudy from the inside, only looked black from the outside, and a little rough, like black water the wind had lightly blown over.

They went inside. In there it smelled of the sweet damp of an old and closed building. It had some hideous bits all right (the Victorian windows donated in advance by wealthy parishioners in memory of themselves, for instance), but on the whole it was a beautiful building. "Preserved in a state of original sin through lack of funds for modernization," was what Ralph always said about it, adding that he would contribute only to its upkeep, but never to its renovation. He had even composed a small prayer that contained the words, "Preserve us, O Lord, from marbled arborite and chrome." Marian quoted this, and the two women smiled. They came outside, blinking in the strange after-rain light.

Marian led them into the churchyard and showed them the tombstone with the angel smoking a pipe, and the lovely sentimental ones with weeping willows, and the ones with shapely limp hands laid over roses. Then there were the six little Elizabeths all in a row, all daughters of one of the early ministers of the church. It was a rather terrifying case of stubborn optimism, Marian explained. He had named his first daughter Elizabeth and when she had died as an infant, the second-born child had been named after her, and so on right through the sixth birth and death. A man who had refused to be intimidated by omens, and who had lost. That was how Ralph had put it, anyway. And at the end of the row was the father's own grave and the grave of his wife who, after such an orgy of tragedy, had also died young. Marian took them to the knoll where the tombstone in the shape of a table was, and she pointed out to them the four table legs made in the shape of burial urns. Then she led them down into the lower reaches where she found and read aloud the inscription beginning "Pain was my portion." After a little searching she was also able to locate the grave of the Wetmore who had built the house they had visited earlier in the afternoon.

"Well! And where all did you go?" Ralph asked as they sat down to supper that night. Helen said that they had gone down the peninsula and had visited the Merritt-Wetmore house. And she immediately launched into a discussion of the house and its chairs: Hitchcock, thumb-back, Acadien. Marian was waiting for a chance to add that they had also visited the Kingston church, and was just on the point of saying so when it suddenly struck her: she shouldn't have taken Esther there! Oh God, don't let Helen tell Mother, was all Marian could think, all through the meal, please God, please God, please.

And that night she watched them, kneeling to her low bedroom window. She was wearing one of her mother's long satin nightgowns — this one had insets of beige lace and a beige lace butterfly appliquéd on it close to the ankle. Not for her the baby-doll pajamas of her peers. And down below her, down in the garden, down by the pond where the singing of the frogs was like beeps from outer space, the two women, Gladdie and Helen, walked, their arms linked, murmuring like doves in their houndstooth checked slacks. She wondered what they were saying, but all the same she was grateful that she didn't have to know.

The day that Esther and Helen left was one of tense ebullience. Ralph and Gladdie had anticipated, they felt, all the emotional snags, and with a loving cunning circumvented them all. They had got presents for both but the presents had been hidden in the car to be saved for the airport — for the last ten minutes before takeoff. They presented Helen with hers first: a buxom velvet box. "Oh, you shouldn't have — " she had already started to say, before opening it, and when she did undo the clasp, expecting, as she later said, "a diamond necklace at the very least," a jack-in-the-box green monster leaped out, causing all the grownups to shriek and roar till tears streamed down their faces. It was Esther who in the end got the necklace — a nice silver one, simple and tasteful (but that's what people say about gravestones, Gladdie thought, struck with horror) — for they had decided against liquor or perfume since both so obviously lacked permanence, and the necklace was given Esther in an immense cardboard carton. She had to go through what appeared to be a year's supply of newspapers to reach it at the bottom and this caused more hilarity, and a general need for drinks. "Thy word is a lamp unto my feet," Ralph said ringingly, when his wife, according to plan, expressed a desire for drink, and he pulled a thermos up from the picnic basket, and some paper cups. "The man who thinks of everything," he said, handing the cups around. He even gave one to Marian. "Learn now, pay later," he said, although "Fly now, die later," was the horrible counterslogan which hovered immediately unbidden in his mind. The drink was quite weak, concocted to get them over the worst, but not of a strength to start crying jags.

Esther did not die in four months after all, or in five. After she had got back to Seattle she was put on a new drug which for a while seemed to hold her disease stable — for a while she even seemed to improve, but toward the end of winter whatever hold the new drug had had weakened, and she was put into the hospital. Her husband and Helen and Helen's husband spent many hours of every day there with her, for her condition was now so serious that there were no visitors' restrictions. The room seemed to Helen like a starched white apron seen through a thick lens; white light hitting so much white linen and bouncing off and welling around so many glass and chromium fittings. The only human thing about it was the smell of dying, not quite hidden under the stepped-up smell of ointment and flowers. And Esther was like a child in her johnny shirt — sickness and institutions had brought out the waif in her — and yet not like a child at all, but like a figurehead, a woman at the prow of her pain. It was only in the movement of the legs that the pain showed, her legs were restless in the bed, always bending and straightening and bending again, forever moving in the small sea of her bed, as if through the agency of her legs she was trying to dissipate her pain. And so up there, in the top of the hospital, in Esther's glass and chromium shrine, the level in the intravenous bottle kept dropping like the level of sand in an hourglass — even that, even the intravenation which was supposed to prolong her life, reminding them, with every drop, how her life was running out.

That summer the Fraziers went to Hampton as usual. While they were there, early in July, a letter came from Seattle. Gladdie opened it, then went immediately into the back garden to find Ralph.

"Ralph!" she called in an urgent disintegrating voice. "Ralph!" He turned and saw her face, her eyes like flags of pain. "Esther?" She nodded and he came to her and took her in his arms. After a little while they went in to make themselves tea, then carried the lukewarm cups, shaking in their saucers, out to the garden. They cried as they drank. Even when you expected it, it was still terrible.

"Poor Marian, I hope she doesn't take it too hard."

"Where is she?"

"Gone into town. To the store."

"Well, maybe you'd better go to meet her; that way she'll know something's up."

But Marian, turning into the long laneway from the main road saw only that her mother was coming to meet her. She didn't know that something was up. She waved to Gladdie. Gladdie raised her arm in a stiff salute, then let it fall abruptly to her side.

"I think I remembered everything!" Marian called.

Gladdie came up to Marian and took her free arm and without saying anything began to walk with her.

"Something's wrong," Marian said, after a few minutes.

"We got a letter from Helen. Esther's . . . gone."

Marian didn't cry after all. All afternoon her parents kept plying themselves with tea, kept reaching over and clasping hands, kept looking, Marian thought, like thunderstruck spaniels. Finally she took a walk to the field and took a book with her. And for a long time she sat up on the field hill, stubble piercing her bum, trying to remember what Esther looked like. But she could call forth no clear image of Esther. The shock of a sudden visual image hadn't jelled; maybe she'd looked at Esther too steadily instead of being surprised into remembering her. There were so many other things she *could* remember. She could remember how on the first day Esther had come and they were showing her her room, how off and on all that afternoon wide bands of dark had been moving down across the hills whenever clouds crossed the sun. And while they'd been showing it to her, Esther's room was suddenly steeped in dark. Then everyone had started to talk at once, a bad sign, always, and then, after what had seemed forever — ten seconds? fifteen? — the sun had come out again, and the lacelike flowers seemed made of sun and fire, and the red and white quilt from the Ladies' Aid shone out with its ritual backwoods geometry. "What a marvelous room," Esther had said, taking it all in. And then Marian remembered how sometimes when she had been younger and they had been doing research at the Kingston graveyard (her father, her mother, herself) how sometimes there would have been a new death, a fresh grave, and they would never work near it, wanting to keep their distance from it, with its harsh green raffia square of fake grass on it, not color coordinated to the real grass but looking like a scatter rug on the great tawny dried-up floor of the cemetery.

Supper that night was late. It was a convalescents' supper — more tea of course, and cold leftovers from the fridge. Every man for himself. Gladdie was feeling very upset about Marian's lack of sorrow. She remembered what Helen had told her about Marian taking her and Esther to the Kingston cemetery and dragging them over every inch of consecrated ground. An exhaustive guided tour of the dead. And a strange business, too. The phrase "psychiatric help" had been mentioned between them, rather tentatively at the time. Now Gladdie looked at her daughter with shrewd anxiety.

Marian helped with the supper dishes, then said she was going upstairs to bed. It was late to be finishing dishes, after ten. "I seem to have lost all sense of time," Gladdie said, leaning into her husband's embrace. He kept patting her on the back. As if losing all sense of time was some sort of achievement. Marian, making no comment, and no comment was disapproval enough, climbed the stairs. Through the open window she could hear how the eleven- and twelve-year-olds were singing down on the beach. They were singing "Red Sails in the Sunset," dragging the words so slowly over the melody that the melody was lost almost entirely. In another year or two they would be able to go to the Saturday night dances and dance to it. "Red Sails in the Sunset" was what was always played for the final dance of the night. "A dirge in three-quarter time," was what Ralph usually called it, trying to make Marian feel better about not being one of the crowd. Walking along the upstairs hall, Marian could hear the singing quite clearly, all the way up from the beach.

Gladdie soon detached herself from Ralph and went up the stairs. "Marian?" she said, outside her door. "Okay if I come in for a minute?" Oh, it was hard raising daughters. Hard.

"Sure."

Marian was sitting on her bed, unbuttoning her blouse. What a closed expression her face has! Gladdie thought, alarmed.

"Marian."

"Yes, Mother?"

"Esther was very fond of you."

Like a vulture for grief, her mother seemed to her now, with her bright prominent eyes fixed on her in a hard assessing way.

"Yes, I know."

But Marian couldn't cry. Gladdie stood in the doorway a little longer, then it became awkward, her being there, and neither of them saying anything. "Good night, then." But I am disappointed in you, her eyes said.

"Good night, Mum."

After Gladdie had left, Marian folded her blouse and shorts and put them on a chair. Then she leaned over and unhooked her brassiere, a precious extra thing to put on and take off (since last month). As its straps slid down her arms, she suddenly felt the most intense burning pain in her throat. She lay down, pulled the sheet up to her armpits, then lay still as a statue on the catafalque of her bed. The moonlight drained her arms of tan. And her long, burning, painful column of neck kept separating her stony head from her anguished heart.

DAVID MADDEN

No Trace

(FROM THE SOUTHERN REVIEW)

GASPING FOR AIR, his legs weak from the climb up the stairs, Ernest stopped outside the room, surprised to find the door wide open, almost sorry he had made it before the police. An upsurge of nausea, a wave of suffocation forced him to suck violently for breath as he stepped into Gordon's room — his *own* two decades before.

Tinted psychedelic emerald, the room looked like a hippie pad posing for a *Life* photograph, but the monotonous electronic frenzy he heard was the seventeen-year locusts, chewing spring leaves outside. He wondered whether the sleeping pills had so dazed him that he had stumbled into the wrong room. No, now, as every time in his own college years when he had entered this room, what struck him first was the light falling through the leaded, green-stained window glass. As the light steeped him in the ambience of the early forties, it simultaneously illuminated the artifacts of the present. Though groggy from the pills, he experienced, intermittently, moments of startling clarity when he saw each object separately.

Empty-beer-can pyramids.

James Dean, stark poster photograph.

Records leaning in orange crate.

Life-size redhead girl, banjo blocking her vagina, lurid color.

Rolltop desk, swivel chair, typewriter.

Poster photograph of a teen-age hero he didn't recognize.

Large corn-flakes carton.

Ernest recognized nothing, except the encyclopedias, as Gordon's.

Debris left behind when Gordon's roommate ran away. Even so, knowing Gordon, Ernest had expected the cleanest room in DeLozier Hall, vacant except for suitcases sitting in a neat row, awaiting the end-of-ceremonies dash to the car. He shut the door quietly, listening to an automatic lock catch, as if concealing not just the few possible incriminating objects he had come to discover, but the entire spectacle of a room startlingly overpopulated with objects, exhibits, that might bear witness, like archeological unearthings, to the life lived there.

He glanced into the closet. Gordon's suitcases did not have the look of imminent departure. Clothes hung, hangers crammed tightly together, on the rack above. The odor emanating from the closet convulsed him slightly, making him shut his eyes, see Gordon raise his arm, the sleeve of his gown slip down, revealing his white arm, the grenade in his hand. Shaking his head to shatter the image, Ernest opened his eyes, but saw swift images of young men in academic regalia rising from the ground in the front rows, staggering around, stunned, blinded by blood, shrapnel, burning shreds of skin and cloth. Green leaves falling. The force of the concussion spraying locusts that stuck to the clothes of the parents. Old men crawling on their hands and knees in brilliant sunlight at the back of the platform.

Turning abruptly from the closet, Ernest moved aimlessly about the room, distracted by objects that moved toward him. He had to hurry before someone discovered the cot downstairs empty, before police came to lock up Gordon's room. The green light drew him to the window where the babel of locusts was louder. Through the antique glass, he saw, as if underwater, the broken folding chairs below, parodying postures into which the explosion had thrown the audience. The last of the curiosity seekers, turning away, trampling locusts, left three policemen alone among knocked-over chairs.

I AM ANONYMOUS/HELP ME. Nailed, buttons encrusted the window frame. SUPPORT MENTAL HEALTH OR I'LL KILL YOU. SNOOPY FOR PRESIDENT. As he turned away, chalked, smudged lettering among the buttons drew him back: DOCTOR SPOCK IS AN ABORTIONIST. After his roommate ran away, why hadn't Gordon erased that? Jerking his head away from the button again, Ernest saw a ball-point pen sticking up in the desk top. On a piece of paper, the title "The Theme of Self-Hatred in the Works of — " the rest obscured by a blue circular, a message scrawled in lipstick across it: *Gordy baby, let me hold some bread for this cause. My old lady is sending me a check next week. The Carter.* The circular pleaded for money for the Civil Liberties Union. Ernest shoved it aside, but "The Theme of Self-Hatred in the Works of — " broke off anyway. Gordon's blue scrapbook, green in the light, startled him. Turning away, Ernest noticed *Revolution in the Revolution?, A Tolkien Reader, Boy Scout Handbook* in a bookcase.

As he stepped toward the closet, something crunching harshly underfoot made him jump back. Among peanut shells, brown streaks in the green light. Gordon tracking in smashed guts of locusts. Fresh streaks, green juices of leaves acid-turned to slime. He lifted one foot, trying to look at the sole of his shoe, lost balance, staggered backward, let himself drop on the edge of a cot. If investigators compared the stains — using his handkerchief, he wiped the soles. Dying and dead locusts, *The Alumni Bulletin* had reported, had littered the campus paths for weeks. Everywhere, the racket of their devouring machinery, the reek of their putrefaction when they fell, gorged. Sniffing his lapels, he inhaled the stench of locusts and sweat, saw flecks of — he shut his eyes, raked breath into his lungs, lay back on the cot.

Even as he tried to resist the resurgent power of the sleeping pills, Ernest felt his exhausted mind and body sink into sleep. When sirens woke him, he thought for a moment he still lay on the bare mattress in the room downstairs, listening to the siren of that last ambulance. The injured, being carried away on stretchers, passed by him again: the president, five seniors, several faculty members, a famous writer of the thirties scheduled for an honorary degree, a trustee, a parent of one of the graduates. The Dean of Men had hustled Ernest into a vacated room, and sent to his house nearby for sleeping pills. Sinking into sleep, seeing the grenade go off again and again until the explosions became tiny, receding, mute puffs of smoke, Ernest had suddenly imagined Lydia's face when he would have to telephone her about Gordon, and the urgency of being prepared for the police had made him sit up in the bed. The hall was empty, everyone seemed to be outside, and he had sneaked up the narrow back stairway to Gordon's room.

Wondering which cot was Gordon's, which his roommate's, and why *both* had recently been slept in, Ernest sat up and looked along the wooden frame for the cigarette burns he had deliberately made the day before his own commencement when he and his roommate were packing for home. As he leaned across the cot, looking for the burn, his hand grazed a stiff yellow spot on the sheet. The top sheet stuck to the bottom sheet. An intuition of his son's climatic moment in an erotic dream the night before — the effort to keep from crying choked him. "I advocate — " Leaping away from the cot, he stopped, reeling, looked up at a road sign that hung over the door: DRIVE SLOWLY, WE LOVE OUR KIDS. Somewhere an unprotected street. What's-his-name's fault. *His* junk cluttered the room.

Wondering what the suitcases would reveal, Ernest stepped into the closet. Expecting them to be packed, he jerked up on them and jolted himself, they were so light. He opened them anyway. Crumbs of dirt, curls of lint. Gordon's clothes, that Lydia had helped him select, or sent him as a birthday or Easter presents, hung in the closet, pressed. Fetid clothes Gordon's roommate — Carter, yes Carter — had left behind dangled from hooks, looking more like costumes. A theatrical black leather jacket, faded denim pants, a wide black belt, ruby studs, a jade velvet cape, and, on the floor, boots and sandals. In a dark corner leaned the hooded golf clubs Ernest had handed down to Gordon, suspecting he would never lift them from the bag. "You don't like to hunt," he had blurted out one evening. "You don't like to fish. You don't get excited about football. Isn't there *some*thing we could do together?" "We could just sit and talk." They had ended up watching "The Ed Sullivan Show."

Ernest's hand, paddling fishlike among the clothes in the dim closet, snagged on a pin that fastened a price tag to one of the suits he had bought Gordon for Christmas. Though he knew from Lydia that no girl came regularly on weekends from Melbourne's sister college to visit Gordon, surely he had had some occasion to wear the suit. Stacked on the shelf above: shirts, the cellophane packaging unbroken. His fingers inside one of the cowboy boots, Ernest stroked leather that was still flesh soft. Imagining Lydia's hysteria at the sight of Gordon, he saw a mortician handling Gordon's body, sorting, arranging pieces, saw not Gordon's, but the body of one of his clients on view, remembering how awed he had been by the miracle of skill that had put the man back together only three days after the factory explosion. Ernest stroked a damp polo shirt, unevenly stained pale green in the wash, sniffed it, realizing that Carter's body could not have left an odor that lasting. Now he understood what had disturbed him about Gordon's clothes, showing, informal and ragged, under the skirt of the black gown, at the sleeves, at the neck, as he sat on the platform, waiting to deliver the valedictory address.

Gripping the iron pipe that held the hangers, shoved tightly together, his body swinging forward as his knees sagged, Ernest let the grenade explode again. Gentle, almost delicate, Gordon suddenly raises his voice above the nerve-wearying shrill of the seventeen-year locusts that encrust the barks of the trees, a voice that had been too soft to be heard except by the men on the platform whose voices expressed shock — at *what* Ernest still did not know — and as that voice screams, a high-pitched nasal screech like brass, "I advocate a total revolution!" Gordon's left arm raises a grenade, holds it out before him, eclipsing his still-open mouth, and in his right hand, held down stiff at his side, the pin glitters on his fingers. Frightened, rearing back, as Ernest himself does, in their seats, many people try to laugh the grenade off as a bold but imprudent rhetorical gesture.

Tasting again Gordon's blood on his mouth, Ernest thrust his face between smothering wool coats, retched again, vomited at last.

A key thrust into the lock, the door opened.

"You sure this is the one?"

"Don't it look like it?"

"What's that smell?"

"Lock it back and give the marshal the key."

"This'll lock automatically, won't it?"

"Just push in on that gismo."

The voices and the lock catching roused Ernest from a stupor of convulsion.

As he tried to suck air into his lungs, gluey bands of vomit strangled him, lack of oxygen smothered him. Staggering backward out of the closet, he stood in the middle of the room, swaying. Avoiding Gordon's, he lowered himself carefully onto the edge of Carter's cot by the closet. He craved air but the stained-glass window, the only window in this corner room, wouldn't open, a disadvantage that came with the privilege of having the room with the magnificent light. The first time he had seen the room since his graduation — he and Lydia had brought Gordon down to begin his freshman year — he had had to heave breath up from dry lungs to tell Gordon about the window. Early in the nineteenth century when DeLozier Hall was the entire school — and already one of the finest boys' colleges in the midwest — this corner room and the two adjacent comprised the chapel. From the fire that destroyed DeLozier Hall in 1938, three years before Ernest himself arrived as a freshman, only this window was saved. Except for the other chapel windows, DeLozier had been restored, brick by brick, exactly as it was originally. "First chance you get, go look in the cemetery at the grave of the only victim of the fire — nobody knows who it was, so the remains were never claimed. Probably somebody just passing through." He had deliberately saved that to leave Gordon with something interesting to think about. From the edge of the cot, he saw the bright eruption of vomit on Gordon's clothes.

The chapel steeple chimed four o'clock. The racket of the locusts' mandibles penetrated the room as if carried in through the green light. Photosynthesis. Chlorophyll. The D+ in biology that wrecked his average.

Rising, he took out his handkerchief and went into the closet. When the handkerchief was sopping wet, he dropped it into a large beer carton, tasting again the foaming beer at his lips, tingling beads on his tongue in the hot tent on the lawn as the ceremonies were beginning. He had reached the green just as the procession was forming. "You've been accepted by Harvard grad school." Gordon had looked at him without a glimmer of recognition — Ernest had assumed that the shrilling of the locusts had drowned out his voice — then led his classmates toward the platform. Ernest was standing on a dirty tee shirt. He finished the job with that, leaving a corner to wipe his hands on, then he dropped it, also, into the carton.

He sat on the edge of the cot again, afraid to lie back on the mattress, to sink into the gulley Carter had made over the four years and fall asleep. He only leaned back, propped on one arm. Having collected himself, he would make a thorough search, to prepare himself for whatever the police would find, tag, then show him for final identification. An exhibit of shocks. The police might even hold him responsible somehow — delinquently ignorant of his son's habits, associates. They might even find something that would bring in the FBI — membership in some radical organization. What was *not* possible in a year like this? He had to arm himself against interrogation. "What sort of boy was your son?" "Typical, average, normal boy in every way. Ask my wife." But how many times had he read that in newspaper accounts of monstrous crimes? What did it mean anymore to be normal?

Glancing around the room, on the verge of an unsettling realization, Ernest saw a picture of Lydia leaning on Carter's rolltop desk. Even in shadow, the enlarged snapshot he had taken himself was radiant. A lucid April sunburst in the budding trees behind her bleached her green dress white, made her blond hair look almost platinum. Clowning, she had kicked out one foot, upraising and spreading her arms, and when her mouth finished yelling "Spring!" he had snapped her dimpled smile. On the campus of Melbourne's sister college, Briarheath, locusts riddled those same trees, twenty years taller, forty miles from where he sat, while Lydia languished in bed alone — a mysterious disease, a lingering illness. Then the shunned realization came, made him stand up as though he were an intruder. On this cot, or perhaps the one across the room, he had made love to Lydia — that spring, the first and only time before their marriage. In August, she had discovered that she was pregnant. Gordon had never for a moment given them cause to regret that inducement to marriage. But Lydia's cautionary approach to sexual relations had made Gordon an only child.

Glancing around the room again, he hoped to discover a picture of himself. Seeing none, he sat down again. Under his thumb, he felt a rough texture on the wooden frame of the cot. The cigarette burn he had made himself in 1945. Then *this* had been Gordon's cot. Of course. By his desk. Flinging back the sheets, Ernest found nothing.

He crossed the room to Carter's cot where a dime-store reproduction of a famous painting of Jesus hung on the wall. Jerking hard to unstick the sheets, he lay bare Carter's bed. Twisted white sweat socks at the bottom. He shook them out. Much too large for Gordon. But Carter, then Gordon, had worn them with Carter's cowboy boots. Gordon had been sleeping in Carter's bed. Pressing one knee against the edge of the cot, Ernest leaned over and pushed his palms against the wall to examine closely what it was that had disturbed him about the painting. Tiny holes like acne scars in Jesus' upturned face. Ernest looked up. Ragged, feathered darts hung like bats from the ceiling. Someone had printed in Gothic script on the bottom white border: *J. C. Blows.* Using his fingernails, Ernest scraped at the edge of the tape, pulled carefully, but white wall paint chipped off, exposing the wallpaper design that dated back to his own life in the room. He stopped, aware that he had only started his search, that if he took this painting, he might be inclined to take other things. His intention, he stressed again to himself, was only to investigate, to be forewarned, not to search and destroy. But already he had the beer carton containing Carter's, or Gordon's, tee shirt and his own handkerchief to dispose of. He let the picture hang, one edge curling over, obscuring the lettering.

Backing into the center of the room, one leg painfully asleep, Ernest looked at a life-sized girl stuck to the wall with masking tape, holding a banjo over her vagina, the neck of it between her breasts, tip of her tongue touching one of the tuning knobs. His eyes on a sticker stuck to the pane, he went to the window again: *Fruit of the loom. 100% virgin cotton.* More buttons forced him to read: WAR IS GOOD BUSINESS, INVEST YOUR SON. How would the police separate Carter's from Gordon's things? FLOWER POWER. He would simply tell them that Carter had left this junk behind when he bolted. But Gordon's failure to discard some of it, at least the most offensive items, bewildered Ernest. One thing appeared clear: living daily since January among Carter's possessions, Gordon had worn Carter's clothes, slept in Carter's bed.

From the ceiling above the four corners of the room hung the blank faces of four amplifiers, dark mouths gaping. Big Brother is listening. *1984.* Late Show. Science fiction bored Ernest. Squatting, he flipped through records leaning in a Sunkist orange crate: *Miles Davis/The Grateful Dead/Leadbelly/The Beatles,* their picture red X-ed out/*Mantovani/The Mamas and The Papas/The Lovin' Spoonful.* He was wasting time — Carter's records couldn't be used against Gordon. But then he found Glenn Miller's "In the Mood" and "Moonlight Serenade," a 78 rpm collector's item he had given Gordon. "Soothing background music for test-cramming time." *Tom Paxton/The Mothers of Invention/1812 Overture* (Gordon's?)/*The Electronic Era/Joan Baez/Charlie Parker/Bartók.*

Rising, he saw a poster he had not glimpsed before, stuck to the wall with a bowie knife, curled inward at its four corners: a color photograph of a real banana rising like a finger out of the middle of a cartoon fist.

Over the rolltop desk hung a guitar, its mouth crammed full of wilted roses. The vomit taste in his own mouth made Ernest retch. Hoping Carter had left some whisky behind, he quickly searched the rolltop desk, finding a Jack Daniels bottle in one of the cubbyholes. Had Gordon taken the last swallow himself this morning just before stepping out of this room?

Finding a single cigarette in a twisted package, Ernest lit it, quickly snuffed it in a hubcap used as an ashtray. The smell of fresh smoke would make the police suspicious. Recent daily activity had left Carter's desk a shambles. Across the room, Gordon's desk was merely a surface, strewn with junk. The Royal portable typewriter he had given Gordon for Christmas his freshman year sat on Carter's desk, the capital lock key set.

Among the papers on Carter's desk, Ernest searched for Gordon's notes for his speech. Ernest had been awed by the way Gordon prepared his senior project in high school — very carefully, starting with an outline, going through three versions, using cards, dividers, producing a forty-page research paper on Wordsworth. Lydia had said, "Why, Ernest, he's been that way since junior high, worrying about college." On Carter's desk, Ernest found the beginnings of papers on Dryden, *The Iliad, Huckleberry Finn.* While he had always felt contentment in Gordon's perfect social behavior and exemplary academic conduct and achievements, sustained from grammar school right on through college, Ernest had sometimes felt, but quickly dismissed, a certain dismay. In her presence, Ernest agreed with Lydia's objections to Gordon's desire to major in English, but alone with him, he had told Gordon, "Satisfy yourself first of all." But he couldn't tell Gordon that he had pretended to agree with his mother to prevent her from exaggerating her suspicion that their marriage had kept him from switching to English himself after he got his B.S. in Business Administration. Each time she brought up the subject, Ernest wondered for weeks what his life would have been like had he become an English professor. As he hastily surveyed the contents of the desk, he felt the absence of the papers Gordon had written that had earned A's, helping to qualify him, as the student with the highest honors, to give the valedictory address.

Handling chewed pencils made Ernest sense the taste of lead and wood on his own tongue. He noticed a corn-flakes box but was distracted by a ball-point pen that only great force could have thrust so firmly into the oak desk. The buffalo side of a worn nickel leaned against a bright Kennedy half dollar. Somewhere under this floor lay a buffalo nickel he had lost himself through a crack. Perhaps Gordon or Carter had found it. He unfolded a letter. It thanked Carter for his two-hundred-dollar contribution to a legal defense fund for students who had gone without permission to Cuba. Pulling another letter out of a pigeonhole, he discovered a bright gold piece resembling a medal. Trojan contraceptive. His own brand before Lydia became bedridden. Impression of it still on his wallet — no, that was the *old* wallet he had carried as a senior. The letter thanked Carter for his inquiry about summer work with an organization sponsored by SNCC. In another pigeonhole, he found a letter outlining Carter's duties during a summer voter campaign in Mississippi. "As for the friend you mention, we don't believe it would be in our best interests to attempt to persuade him to join our work. If persuasion is desirable, who is more strategically situated than you, his own roommate?" Marginal scrawl in pencil: "This is the *man* talking, baby!"

As he rifled through the numerous letters, folded hastily and slipped or stuffed into pigeonholes, Ernest felt he was getting an overview of liberal and left-wing activities, mostly student-oriented, over the past five years, for Carter's associations began in high school. He lifted his elbow off Gordon's scrapbook — birthday present from Lydia — and flipped through it. Newpaper photo of students at a rally, red ink enringing a blurred head, a raised fist. Half full: clippings of Carter's activities. AP photo: Carter, bearded, burning his draft card. But no creep — handsome, hair and smile like Errol Flynn in *The Sea Hawk.* Looking around at the poster photograph he hadn't recognized when he came in, Ernest saw Carter, wearing a Gestapo bill cap, a monocle, an opera cape, black tights, Zorro boots, carrying a riding crop. When Ernest first noticed the ads — "Blow Yourself Up" — he had thought it a good deal at $2.99. Had Gordon given the scrapbook to Carter, or had he cut and pasted the items himself?

Ernest shoved the scrapbook aside and reached for a letter. "Gordy, This is just to tell you to save your tears over King. We all wept over JFK our senior year in high school, and we haven't seen straight since. King just wasn't where the action's at. Okay, so I told you different a few months ago! How come you're always light years behind *me?* Catch up! Make the leap! I'm dumping all these creeps that try to play a rigged game. Look at Robert! I think I'm beginning to understand Oswald and Speck and Whitman. They're the *real* individuals! They work alone while we run together like zebras. But, on the other hand, maybe the same cat did *all* those jobs. And maybe Carter knows who. Sleep on *that* one, Gordy, baby." Los Angeles, April 5. Suddenly, the first day back from Christmas vacation, Carter had impulsively walked out of this room. "See America first! Then the world!" That much Gordon had told them when Ernest and Lydia telephoned at Easter, made uneasy by his terse letter informing them that he was remaining on campus to "watch the locusts emerge from their seventeen-year buried infancy into appalling one-week adulthood," adding parenthetically, that he had to finish his honors project. Marriage to Lydia had prevented Ernest's desire, like Carter's, to see the world. Not "prevented." Postponed perhaps. A vice president of a large insurance company might hope to make such a dream come true — if only after he retired. Deep in a pigeonhole, Ernest found a snapshot of Gordon, costumed for a part in *Tom Sawyer* — one of the kids who saunter by in the whitewashing scene. False freckles. He had forgotten. On the back, tabs of fuzzy black paper — ripped out of the scrapbook.

Mixed in with Carter's were Lydia's letters. "Gordon, Precious, You promised — " Feverish eyes. Bed rashes. Blue Cross. Solitude. Solitaire. "Sleep, Lydia." Finding none of his own letters, Ernest remembered writing last week from his office, and the sense of solitude on the fifteenth floor, where he had seemed the only person stirring, came back momentarily. Perhaps in some drawer or secret compartment all his letters to Gordon (few though they had been) and perhaps other little mementos — his sharpshooter's medal and the Korean coin that he had given Gordon, relics of his three years in the service, and matchbooks from the motels where he and Gordon had stayed on occasional weekend trips — were stored. Surely, somewhere in the room, he would turn up a picture of himself. He had always known that Gordon preferred his mother, but had he conscientiously excluded his father from his life, eliminating all trace? No, he shouldn't jump to conclusions. He had yet to gather and analyze all the evidence. Thinking in those terms about what he was doing, Ernest realized that not only was he going to destroy evidence to protect Gordon's memory as much as possible and shield Lydia, he was now deliberately searching for fragments of a new Gordon, hoping to know and understand him, each discovery destroying the old Gordon who would now always remain a stranger.

But he didn't have time to move so slowly, like a slow-motion movie. Turning quickly in Carter's swivel chair, Ernest bent over the large corn-flakes box, brimful of papers that had been dropped, perhaps tossed, into it. Gordon's themes, including his honors thesis in a stiff black binder: "Anguish, Spiritual and Physical, in Gerard Manley Hopkins' Poetry. Approved by: Alfred Hansen, Thorne Halpert [who had come to Melbourne in Ernest's own freshman years], Richard Kelp, John Morton." In red pencil at the bottom, haphazard scrawls, as if they were four different afterthoughts: "*Dis*approved by: Jason Carter, Gordon Foster, Lydia Foster, Gerard Manley Hopkins." Up the left margin, in lead pencil: "Piss on *all* of you!" Ernest saw Gordon burning the box in the community dump on the edge of the village.

Ernest stepped over to Gordon's desk, seeking some sort of prospective, some evidence of Gordon's life before he moved over to the rolltop desk and mingled his own things with Carter's. The gray steel drawers were empty. Not just empty. Clean. Wiped clean with a rag — a swipe in the middle drawer had dried in a soapy pattern of broken beads of moisture. Ernest saw there an image: a clean table that made him feel the presence behind him of another table where Gordon, now in pieces, lay. Under dirty clothes slung aside lay stacks of books and old newspapers, whose headlines of war, riot, murder, assassinations, negotiations seemed oddly remote in this room. The portable tape recorder Ernest had given Gordon last fall to help him through his senior year. He pressed the LISTEN button. Nothing. He pressed the REWIND.

LISTEN. ". . . defy analysis. But let's examine this passage from Aristotle's *De Interpretatione*: 'In the case of that which is or which has taken place, propositions, whether positive or negative, must be true or false.' " "What did he say?" Someone whispering. "I didn't catch it." (Gordon's voice) "Again, in the case of a pair of contraries — contradictories, that is . . ." The professor's voice slipped into a fizzing silence. "I'm recording your speech, son," he had written to Gordon last week, "so your mother can hear it." But Ernest had forgotten his tape recorder.

The headline of a newspaper announced Charlie Whitman's sniper slaying of twelve people from the observation tower of the university administration building in Austin, Texas. But that was two summers past. Melbourne had no summer school. Folded, as though mailed. Had Carter sent it to Gordon from — Where *was* Carter from? Had Gordon received it at home?

A front-page news photo showed a Buddhist monk burning on a Saigon street corner. Ernest's sneer faded in bewilderment as he saw that the caption identified an American woman burning on the steps of the Pentagon. Smudged pencil across the flames: *The mother of us all.* Children bereft, left to a father, perhaps no father even. Ernest tried to remember the name of one of his clients, an English professor, who had shot himself a week after the assassination of Martin Luther King. No note. Any connection? His wife showed Ernest the Student Guide to Courses — one anonymous, thus sexless, student's evaluation might have been a contributing factor: "This has got to be the most boring human being on the face of the earth." Since then, Ernest had tried to make his own presentations at company meetings more entertaining. Lately, many cases of middle-aged men who had mysteriously committed suicide hovered on the periphery of Ernest's consciousness. It struck him now that in every case, he had forgotten most of the "sensible" explanations, leaving nothing but mystery. Wondering whether those men had seen something in the eyes of their children, even their wives, that Ernest himself had been blind to, he shuddered but did not shake off a sudden clenching of muscles in his shoulders. "When the cause of death is legally ruled as suicide," he had often written, "the company is relieved of its obligations to — " Did Gordon *know* the grenade would explode? Or did he borrow it, perhaps steal it from a museum, and then did it, like the locusts, seventeen years dormant, suddenly come alive? Ernest had always been lukewarm about gun controls, but now he would insist on a thorough investigation to determine where Gordon purchased the grenade. Dealer in war surplus? Could they prove he meant it to go off? "When the cause of death is legally ruled — " Horrified that he was thinking so reflexively like an insurance executive, Ernest slammed his fist into his groin, and staggered back into the bed Gordon had abandoned.

His eyes half opened, he saw his cigarette burn again on the wooden frame beside his hand. He recalled Gordon's vivid letter home the first week of his freshman year: "My roommate turns my stomach by the way he dresses, talks, acts, eats, sleeps." Ernest had thought that a boy so different from Gordon would be good for him, so his efforts, made at Lydia's fretful urgings, to have Carter replaced, or to have Gordon moved, were slapdash. He very much wanted his son to go through Melbourne in his old room. Books on Gordon's desk at the foot of the cot caught his attention. Some dating from junior high, these were all Gordon's, including the Great Books, with their marvelous Syntopicon. As the swelling pain in his groin subsided, Ernest stood up, hovered over the books.

A frayed copy of *Winnie the Pooh* startled him. "To Ernest, Christmas, 1928. All my love, Grandmother." The year he learned to write, Gordon had printed his own name in green crayon across the top of the next page. As Ernest leafed through the book, nostalgia eased his nerves. Penciled onto Winnie the Pooh was a gigantic penis extending across the page to Christopher Robin, who was bending over a daisy. "Damn you, Carter!" Ernest slammed it down — a pillar of books slurred, tumbled onto the floor. He stood still, staring into the green light, trying to detect the voices of people who might have heard in the rooms below. Ernest heard only the locusts in the light. A newspaper that had fallen leaned and sagged like a tent: Whitman's face looked up from the floor, two teeth in his high school graduation smile blacked out, a pencil-drawn tongue flopping out of his mouth. His name was scratched out and YOU AND ME, BABY was lettered in. Ernest kicked at the newspaper, twisted his heel into Whitman's face, and the paper rose up around his ankles like a yellowed flower, soot dappled.

Ernest backed into the swivel chair, turned, rested his head in his hands on the rolltop desk, and breathed in fits and starts. He wanted to throw the hubcap ashtray through the stained-glass window and feel the spring air rush in upon his face and fill and stretch his lungs. Cigarillo butts, scorched Robert Burns bands, cigarette butts. Marijuana? He sniffed, but realized he couldn't recognize it if it *were*.

Was there nothing in the room but pale emanations of Carter's gradual transformation of Gordon? Closing his eyes, trying to conjure up Gordon's face, he saw, clearly, only Carter's smile, like a weapon, in the draft-card burning photograph. *Wanting* to understand Gordon, he had only a shrill scream of defiance, an explosion, and this littered room with which to begin. He imagined the mortician, fitting pieces together, an arm on a drainboard behind him. And when he was finished, what would he have accomplished? In the explosion, Gordon had vacated his body, and now the pieces had stopped moving, but the objects in his room twitched when Ernest touched them. Taking a deep breath, he inhaled the stench of spit and tobacco. He shoved the hubcap aside, and stood up.

Bending his head sideways, mashing his ear against his shoulder, Ernest read the titles of books crammed into cinderblock and pineboard shelves between Carter's cot and the window: *120 Days of Sodom,* the Marquis de Sade/*Autobiography of Malcolm X*/*The Postman Always Rings Twice,* James M. Cain/*Mein Kampf* — He caught himself reading titles and authors aloud in a stupor. Silently, his lips still moving, he read: *Boy Scout Handbook.* Though he had never been a scout, Ernest had agreed with Lydia that, like a fraternity, it would be good for Gordon in future life. *Freedom Now,* Max Reiner/*Nausea,* Jean-Paul Sartre/*Atlas Shrugged,* Ayn Rand/*The Scarlet Letter.* Heritage, leather-bound edition he had given Gordon for his sixteenth birthday. He had broken in the new Volkswagen, a surprise graduation present, driving it down. Late for the ceremonies, he had parked it illegally behind DeLozier Hall so it would be there when he and Gordon brought the suitcases and his other belongings down. *Castro's Cause,* Harvey Kreyborg/*Notes from Underground,* Dostoyevsky/*Lady Chatterly's Lover,* Ernest's own copy. Had Gordon sneaked it out of the house? Slumping to his knees, he squinted at titles he had been unable to make out: Carter had cynically shelved Ernest's own copy of *Profiles in Courage,* passed on to Gordon, next to *Oswald Resurrected* by Eugene Federogh.

There was a book with a library number on its spine. He would have to return that. The Gordon he had known would have done so before commencement. Afraid the police might come in suddenly and catch him there, Ernest rose to his feet. Glancing through several passages, highlighted with a yellow Magic-Marker, he realized that he was reading about "anguish, spiritual and physical, in Gerard Manley Hopkins' poetry." He rooted through the corn-flakes box again, took out Gordon's honors thesis. Flipping through the pages, he discovered a passage that duplicated, verbatim, a marked passage in the book. No footnote reference. The bibliography failed to cite the book that he held in his hand and now let drop along with the honors thesis into the beer carton onto Carter's fouled tee shirt and Ernest's handkerchief.

Why had he cheated? He never had before. Or had he plagiarized *all* those papers, from junior high on up to this one? No, surely, this time only. Ernest himself had felt the pressure in his senior year, and most of the boys in his fraternity had cheated when they really *had* to. Now he felt compelled to search thoroughly, examine everything carefully. The police had no right to invade a dead boy's privacy and plunge his invalid mother into grief.

In Carter's desk drawers, Ernest searched more systematically among letters and notes, still expecting to discover an early draft of Gordon's unfinished speech; perhaps it would be full of clues. He might even find the bill of sale for the grenade. Across the naked belly of a girl ripped from a magazine was written: "Gordy —" Carter had even renamed, rechristened Gordon. "Jeff and Conley and I are holding a peace vigil in the cold rain tonight, all night. Bring us a fresh jar of water at midnight. And leave your goddamn middle-class mottos in the room. Love, Carter."

A letter from Fort Jackson, South Carolina, April 20, 1968. "Dear Gordon, I am being shipped to Vietnam. I will never see you again. I have not forgotten what you said to me that night in our room across the Dark Gulf between our cots. As always, Carter." Without knowing what Carter meant, Ernest knew that gulf himself. He had tried to bridge it, touch Scott, his own roommate, whose lassitude about life's possibilities often provoked Ernest to wall-pounding rage. He had finally persuaded Scott to take a trip west with him right after graduation. Scott's nonchalant withdrawal at the last minute was so dispiriting that Ernest had accepted his father's offer of a summer internship with the insurance company as a claims adjustor.

A 1967 letter described in detail the march on the Pentagon. "What are you doing down there, you little fink? You should be up here with the rest of us. My brothers have been beaten by the cops. I'm not against the use of napalm in *some* instances. Just don't let me get my hands on any of it when those pig sonofabitches come swinging their sticks at us. We're rising up all over the world, baby — or didn't you know it, with your nose in Chaucer's tales? Melbourne is about due to be hit so you'd better decide whose side you're on. I heard about this one campus demonstration where somebody set fire to this old fogey's lifelong research on some obscure hang-up of his. I can think of a few at Melbourne that need shaking up." Ernest was shocked, then surprised at himself for being shocked. He wondered how Gordon had felt.

As Ernest pulled a postcard out of a pigeonhole, a white capsule rolled out into his hand. For a common cold, or LSD? He stifled an impulse to swallow it. By chance escape what chance might reveal. He flipped the capsule against the inside of the corn-flakes box and it popped like a cap pistol. Comic postcard — outhouse, hillbillies — mailed from Alabama, December 12, 1966. "Gordy, baby, Wish you were here. You sure as hell ain't all *there!* Love, till death do us part, Carter." In several letters, Carter fervently attempted to persuade Gordon to abandon his "middle-class Puritan Upforcing" and embrace the cause of world brotherhood, which itself embraced all other great causes of "our time." But even through the serious ones ran a trace of self-mockery. He found Carter's draft notice, his *own* name crossed out, Gordon's typed in. Across the body of the form letter, dated January 1, 1968, was printed in Gothic script: *Non Servium.*

As Ernest reached for a bunch of postcards, he realized that he was eager not only to discover more about Gordon, but to assemble into some shape the fragments of Carter's life. A series of postcards with cryptic, taunting messages traced Carter's trail over the landscape of America, from early January to the middle of March, 1968. From Carmel, California, a view of a tower and cypress trees: "Violence is the sire of all the world's values." Ernest remembered the card Gordon had sent him from Washington, D. C., when he was in junior high: "Dear Dad, Our class went to see Congress but they were closed. Our teacher got mad. She dragged us all to the Smithsonian and showed us Lindbergh's airplane. It was called *The Spirit of St. Louis.* I didn't think it looked so hot. Mrs. Landis said she saved the headlines when she was in high school. Did you? Your son, Gordon."

Ernest found a night letter from Lynn, Massachusetts. "Dear Gordon, Remembering that Jason spoke of you so often and so fondly, his father and I felt certain that you would not want to learn through the newspapers that our dear son has been reported missing in action. While no one can really approve in his heart of this war, Jason has always been the sort of boy who believed in dying for his convictions. We know that you will miss him. He loved you as though you were his own brother. Affectionate regards, Grace and Harold Carter." June 1, 1968, three days ago.

Trembling, Ernest sought more letters from Carter. One from boot camp summed up, in wild, impassioned prose, Carter's opinions on Civil Rights, the war, and "the American Dream that's turned into a nightmare." In another, "God is dead and buried on LBJ's ranch" dispensed with religion and politics, "inseparable." May 4, 1968. "Dear Gordy, We are in the jungle now, on a search and destroy mission. You have to admire some of these platoon leaders. I must admit I enjoy watching them act out their roles as all-American tough guys. They have a kind of style, anyway. In here you don't have time to analyze your thoughts. But I just thought a word or two written at the scene of battle might bring you the smell of smoke." Ernest sniffed the letter, uncertain whether the faint smell came from the paper.

He pulled a wadded letter out of a pigeonhole where someone had stuffed it. As he unwadded the note, vicious ball-point pen markings wove a mesh over the words: "Gordon, I'm moving in with Conley. Pack my things and set them in the hall. I don't even want to *enter* that room again. What you said last night made me sick. I've lived with you for three and a half years because I was always convinced that I could save your soul. But after last night, I know it's hopeless. Carter." Across the "Dark Gulf" between their beds, what could *Gordon* have said to shock Carter? Had

Gordon persuaded him to stay after all? Or was it the next day that Carter had "impulsively" run away? Ernest searched quickly through the rest of the papers, hoping no answer existed, but knowing that if one did and he failed to find it, the police wouldn't fail.

"Gordy, baby, Everything you read is lies! I've been in the field three weeks now. My whole life's search ends here, in this burning village, where I'm taking time to write to you. Listen, baby, this is life! This is what it's all about. In the past weeks I've personally set fire to thirty-seven huts belonging to Viet Cong sympathizers. Don't listen to those sons-of-bitches who whine and gripe and piss and moan about this war. This is a *just* war. We're on the right side, man, the *right* side. This place has opened my eyes and heart, baby. With the bullets and the blood all around, you see things clearer. Words! To hell with words! All these beady-eyed little bastards understand is *bullets,* and a knife now and then. These bastards killed my buddy, a black boy by the name of Bird. The greatest guy that ever lived. Well, there's ten Viet Cong that ain't alive today because of what they did to my buddy, and there'll be another hundred less Viet Cong if I can persuade them to send me out after I'm due to be pulled back. Yesterday, I found a Viet Cong in a hut with his goddamn wife and kids. I turned the flame thrower on the sons-of-bitches and when the hut burned down, I pissed on the hot ashes. I'm telling you all this to open your eyes, mister. This is the way it really is. Join your ass up, get over here where you belong. Forget everything I ever said to you or wrote to you before. I have seen the light. The future of the world will be decided right here. And I will fight until the last Viet Cong is dead. Always, your friend, Carter." May 21, 1968, two weeks ago.

Trying to feel as Gordon had felt reading this letter, feeling nothing, Ernest remembered Gordon's response to a different piece of information some kid in grammar school dealt him when he was eleven. Having informed Gordon that Santa Claus was a lie, he added the observation that nobody ever knows who his real father and mother are. Just as Ernest stepped into the house from the office, Gordon had asked: "Are you my real father?" In the living room where colored lights glazed on the tree, Lydia was weeping. It took two months to rid Gordon of the fantasy that he had been adopted. Or had he simply stopped interrogating them? But how did a man know *any*thing? Did that professor ever suspect that one day in print he would be labeled "the most boring man on the face of the earth"? Did Carter ever sense he would end up killing men in Vietnam? Did Gordon ever suspect that on his graduation day —

Now the day began to make sense. After Carter's letter from Vietnam, reversing everything he had preached to Gordon, Gordon had let his studies slide, and then the plagiarism had just happened, the way things will, because how could he really care anymore? Then did the night letter from Carter's mother shock him into pulling the grenade pin? Was "I advocate a total revolution!" Gordon's *own* climax to the attitude expressed in Carter's Vietnam letter? Or did the *old* Carter finally speak through Gordon's mouth? These possibilities made sense, but Ernest felt nothing.

His foot kicked a metal wastebasket under Carter's desk. Squatting he pulled it out, and, sitting again in the swivel chair, began to unwad several letters. "Dear Dad —" The rest blank. "Dear Dad —" Blank. "Dear Dad —" Blank. "Dear Father —" Blank. "Dear Dad —" Blank.

Ernest swung around in Carter's chair, rocked once, got to his feet, stood in the middle of the room, his hands dangling in front of him, the leaded moldings of the window cast black wavy lines over his suit, the green light stained his hands, his heart beat so fast he became aware that he was panting. Like a dog. His throat felt dry, his tongue swollen, eyes burning from reading in the oblique light. Dark spots of sweat on the floor. "Gordon. Gordon. Gordon."

Whatever Gordon had said in his valedictory address, Ernest knew that certain things in this room would give the public the wrong image of his son. Or perhaps — he faced it — the right image. Wrong or right, it would incite the disease in Lydia's body to riot and she would burn. He rolled the desk top down and began stuffing things into the beer carton. When it was full, he emptied the contents of the corn-flakes box onto the desk, throwing only the honors thesis back into it. When he jerked the bowie knife out of the wall, the banana poster fell. He scraped at the clotting vomit on the clothes hanging in the closet, and wiped the blade on the sole of his shoe. Then he filled the corn-flakes box with letters and other incriminating objects.

He opened the door and looked out. The hall was dim and deserted. The surviving seniors had gone home, though some must have lingered behind with wounded classmates, teachers, parents. The police would still be occupied with traffic. The back staircase was dark. He stacked the beer carton on top of the corn-flakes box, lifted both in his arms, and started to back out the door. But under the rolltop desk in a bed of lint lay a piece of paper that, even wadded up, resembled a telegram. Setting the boxes down, the cardboard already dark brown where he had pressed his forehead, Ernest got on his knees and reached under the desk. Without rising, he unwadded the paper. URGENT YOU RENEW SUBSCRIPTION TO TIME AT STUDENT RATE. STOP. WORLD NEWS AT YOUR FINGERTIPS. STOP. Mock telegram technique, special reply pencil enclosed.

The boxes were heavier as Ernest lifted them again and backed out the door, almost certain that the grenade had not been a rhetorical flourish. Bracing the boxes against the wall, lifting his knee under them, Ernest quickly reached out, pulled at the door knob. When the door slammed, locked, startling him, he grabbed the boxes as they almost tipped over into the stairwell.

He had to descend very slowly. The narrow staircase curved twice before it reached the basement. His shoulder slid along the wall as he went down, carefully, step by step. The bottom of the box cut into his palms, sweat tickled his spine, and his thighs chafed each other as sweat dried on his flesh. He saw nothing until he reached the basement where twilight coming through the window of the door revealed the furnace. As he fumbled for the knob, already the devouring locuts jangled in his ears like a single note quivering relentlessly on a violin.

Locusts had dropped from the ivy onto the black hood of the Volkswagen, parked up tight against the building. He opened the trunk, set the boxes inside, closed the lid, locked it.

As he got in behind the wheel, a glimpse of the cemetery behind the dormitory made him recall the grave that had so awed him during his freshman year. From where he sat, turning the ignition key, the larger tombs of the historic dead obscured the small white stone, but he had not forgotten the epitaph: HERE LIES AN UNIDENTIFIED VICTIM OF THE FIRE THAT RAZED DELOZIER HALL, MAY 16, 1938. Since all the Melbourne students had been accounted for, he (or perhaps she) must have been a visitor.

Pulling off the highway, he drove along a dirt trail, new grass sprouting between the wheel ruts. Here, as visible evidence testified, Melbourne students brought the girls who came down from Briarheath. Parked, he let dusk turn to dark.

Then he left the woods, lights dimmed until he got onto the highway. On the outskirts of the town, looking at this distance like a village erected in one of those elaborate electric train sets, he turned onto a cinder road and stopped at a gate, got out, lifted the latch, drove through, then went back and closed the gate.

Headlights off, he eased over the soft, sooty dirt road, the rough bushes on each side a soft gray blur, into the main lot, where the faculty and other townspeople dumped junk and garbage.

The smell made him aware of the taste at the back of his mouth, the stench of burning rubber and plastic and dead animals made his headache pound more fiercely, his left eyelid beat like a pulse.

He unlocked the trunk, lifted out the corn-flakes box, and stumbled in the dark over tin cans and broken tools and springs and tires, set the box down, then went back and got the other box.

The boxes weren't far enough into the dump. He dragged them, one with each hand, backward, up and over the rough terrain, stumbling, cutting his hand on rusty cans and nails in charred wood, thinking of tetanus, of Lydia without him.

Standing up, he sucked in the night air, feeling a dewy freshness mingled with the acrid smoke and fumes. He reached into his pocket for his lighter. His thumb began to hurt as he failed repeatedly to make the flint catch.

A bright beam shot out over the dump, another several yards beside it, then another — powerful flashlights — and as he crouched to avoid the lights, rifle fire shattered the silence over the dump. Reaching out, grabbing the cardboard flaps to keep his balance, Ernest squatted beside his boxes.

"Get that son-of-a-bitch, doc!"

Twisting his neck around, Ernest saw the beam swing and dip through oily smoke coiling out of the debris and stop on a rat, crouched on a fire-blackened icebox door. It started to run. But the slick porcelain allowed its feet no traction.

DON MITCHELL

Diesel

(FROM SHENANDOAH)

THE SHE-TRUCK cleared her throat passing Gary and Chay on the ramp, coughed into a lower gear and braked to the shoulder. Her lights blinked warmly against the dark and Gary whooped, jogging after her. As they reached the truck, her giant driver jumped to the road to feign examining his tires — sure sign that hitchhikers were welcome.

"Thanks a lot," said Gary, breathing hard. And Chay now on his right. "You heading north?"

"I do believe, fifty more miles tonight. Seattle tomorrow," he grinned. "Now get in that cab before the man catches me." Gary boosted Chay to the door, threw the sleeping bag to her, then swung himself up into the compartment. The driver plopped into his seat and eased into first gear.

This bouncing cab was new — two years at the most — roomy and cheery above the road with glossy pinups taped to the ceiling and dash. Bolted to the hump of motor between the two seats were a cartridge tape deck and a box of tapes; the stereo speakers were hung on either side of the cab. "I'm Diesel," the driver introduced himself. "Diesel Stewart, produce hauler." Tipping his hat, he flashed a silver badge engraved with the words, "Produce Hauler."

Gary introduced Chay and himself while Diesel worked through a dozen gears on the expressway to the Golden Gate Bridge. But he had to cut back to first at the tollbooths. By night, the gold was spread across the bridge with yellow lights spaced through the wandering fog. Gary felt the bridge shudder beneath the truck's rumbling, then the firm rock of Marin.

"Is that your real name — Diesel?" Chay shouted above the motor.

"Right." He grinned. "Diesel's the name. My daddy saw he got a boy for a kid. He told my ma, 'That boy'll drive a truck when he's big. Just like his pa, he will. So we'd best name him Diesel.' I believe he picked right, too."

Gary nodded, amiably. "We're going to a commune," he shouted. "Morningstar Ranch. It's pretty near Sebastopol."

"What's that?"

"Near Sebastopol," he repeated, louder than before. Diesel could project his voice above the roar of his engine. But Gary and Chay had to shout, inflecting each word as if it were urgent. This truck, Gary saw from the start, was a woman; now she screamed over her passengers to separate them from each other.

"Take you into Sebastopol." Diesel nodded. "They got a load of fruit for me there. But they don't start work until six. I believe I'll take it easy, maybe hit a couple truck stops for coffee. Unless you're in a hurry?"

"No hurry." Gary shook his head. Diesel lit a cigarette, a Lucky Strike, and the orange glow bathed his face when he dragged. Big head on his massive frame, tough features discontented with loneliness. He was wearing a cowboy shirt with snaps for buttons, open at the top where the hair welled from his chest. A strong man, and the cigarette lighting made him look retarded — or maybe Gary just wished him big and stupid. On the dash, Diesel's alarm clock said quarter past one.

"You own this rig?" asked Chay, trying to show she knew the slang. Sitting crosslegged against the canvas door to the bunk, she had the commanding view of the highway. And glancing sideways at her, Gary could see the yellow swatch of panties tight against her crotch — which meant Diesel could see, too. Immodesty, naiveté that made Chay exciting: he couldn't hassle her about it. Still, he knew, chicks got raped for being less provocative.

"I do believe I will," answered Diesel, "come October. Used to haul for a company. Two-man sleepers, relay runs. But the money's in this, if you get work year-round. And I like to be my own boss.

Good trucker on his own'll match any two-man sleeper. You keep rolling, you'll take 'em all."

"You drive nights usually?" Chay asked, talking directly into his ear.

"Well, miss, you never ask a trucker when he drives." Diesel chuckled, threw his cigarette out the window. "Because they're always driving. But that's against the law" — he winked — "so they can't tell you."

"Oh?" She smiled back. "Why do you do that?"

"Retire faster." He shrugged. "And when you're trucking it gets into your blood. Can't hardly stop for meals. But I believe I'll stop. When I'm thirty-five, when I have enough dough. Build me a little house there on Lake Mendota — ever heard of that? — Lake Mendota, Wisconsin. I bought the land last year. Give me seven more years in this baby, just set here shifting gears, I'll be all set."

"Far out." Chay nodded. "The way you look at it. But don't you ever sleep?"

"Course I sleep. A man needs his rest, else he'll run down like any machine. Most I ever went was twenty-two days. Back when I was young. Now, two weeks and I've had it. Drive her two weeks and I sack out for three days. Three, four days, then I'm back on the road. But you take some guys, I believe they'll drive a whole month. Drive a month and sleep a week. Not me. I believe I need more rest."

"Right." Gary approved his restraint, incredulous. "What do you take, Dexedrine?"

"Pretty much now. Used to like bennies, but I believe they're like whisky. Dex is smooth, just like vitamins. Look here." He reached under the scalloped flap of his shirt pocket, produced a plastic pillbox. "See these? Sixty grains apiece."

"Jesus." Gary whistled. "Sixty grains! I never heard of that. Jesus, they're little footballs."

"They're my vitamins, all right. Used to be one of these would get me from New York to Frisco and back, twice. But I got used to 'em. Now I believe I'd just about make it once, boosting on the way."

"Sounds pretty heavy," said Chay. "What do you boost with?"

He brought out another pillbox full of smaller capsules in two sizes. "These long ones are ten-grain Dex. The shorties are five-grain Methedrine. The Meth's good to wake right up with. But it don't last too long."

"Oh, wow!" Chay was saying that more and more lately, and it bothered Gary. "Wow! How long you been going for now?"

"Let me see," he said, shifting gears. "Tuesday, Thursday — I believe it's eight days."

"Wow!" Chay said again. "Dig it, Gary: eight whole days! In eight days we've hardly done a thing — and you've probably been all over! In eight days — wow! How often do you boost?"

"Depends which ones I'm taking." Diesel grinned again, evidently delighted with Chay's interest. "For the Dexies, twice a day. Matter of fact, I believe it's time now. Like to join me?"

"Wow! You said twelve hours, right?"

"I believe yours'll run longer, unless you're used to it."

"How's that Meth?" suggested Gary.

"Six, seven hours. I believe they're stronger than the Dexies, but they run shorter. Let you down rough, too."

"Then let's all take Dex," proposed Chay. "So we'll be doing the same thing."

"Help yourself." Diesel handed her the pillbox. "I believe you'll find a thermos under your seat, Gary." Gary found the thermos and poured a cup of coffee which they passed around, each popping his cap with a swig of it. It tasted terrible.

Eating dope was always heavy for Gary: the act of swallowing was irrevocable. Hours from now, he'd have to keep handling his head, working out his trip from within it. If he got scared, if he freaked, he could not shuck the drug. It was impossible to pass out or fall asleep. And he knew he could bum himself just waiting to get off, thinking these thoughts. But he always thought them.

"How long before you get off?" asked Chay.

"What?"

"Before I'll feel the Dex."

"Oh. Twenty minutes. I believe they're timed; they hit you nice and even. Cigarette, Gary?"

"Thanks." He took a Lucky Strike and sweetened his mouth with it, barely inhaling, trying to frame his mind for the coming rush. Not, please, to pit himself against the drug; rather to use it, to move with it. But Jesus! Here was the Diesel living on speed, and never hassling such questions. Never even posing them. Probably a trainable, figured Gary, able to do one trip and one only — like shifting gears, controlling his baby. Smarter people had to ask questions about their dope. And they learned more, yes, and it had to make a difference.

"Want music?" suggested Diesel. "Anything you like, pick it out. I believe I'll sell that stereo soon. For a TV. They got movies on TV now. Be real nice to watch up here at night. You find a tape?"

Chay had strewn the tapes across the motor casing, finding nothing she liked. "Whatever you want," she told him.

"Well, I believe you'd like that Patsy Cline there. That woman can sing a song." He punched the cartridge into the player and Patsy's voice flooded the cab. "I'll bet she does some other things right, too."

The stereo was trained on Diesel's seat, so the speaker next to Gary's right ear blasted at full volume. He first ducked out of range, then squirmed to sit sideways against the door, beneath the speaker. She was, he decided, less woman than Diesel's truck; Patsy's human voice was nothing to the hoarse whine of the motor.

"You always pick up hitchhikers?" Chay asked Diesel.

"Nope. But I try not to pass up the little ladies. I hate to make 'em walk."

"Well, thanks."

"You're plumb welcome." He grinned back at her. "The girls are fine with the Diesel. So's one guy hitching, fine with me. But two guys, three guys up here and they get a mind to rolling me. I learned the hard way, too. Couple guys one night pulled a knife for my wallet. I slugged 'em through that window with my right arm, driving the whole time with my left. Bet they'll never try that again."

They sat quiet for ten minutes, watching Marin County asleep around them. Mount Tamalpais up on the left, Patsy Cline overhead and suddenly Chay blinked, shook her head from side to side. "Oh, wow! I'm getting it! Already, I'm *getting* it!"

Diesel gave her a queer look, chuckling. "I believe it beats me," he told Gary, because Chay wasn't listening, "what you kids see in these here vitamins. I been taking these for years, you know? To keep awake driving. Because my daddy fell asleep behind the wheel once. Jackknifed his rig, and he laid nine weeks in the hospital. Came out skinny as a rail with stitches all over here." Diesel traced the scars on his own chest. "And he handed me a bottle of bennies. I'd been driving six months, and he gave me these bennies. 'Boy,' he says to me, 'you take these if you're driving a truck. Don't you never fall asleep.' "

Gary nodded.

"But these crazy kids," he continued. "What are they, hippies? All this long hair and dressed like fools to take the same damn vitamins. I believe it beats me."

"Wow, I'm flashing on the white lines down there! Bip! Blip! Bip! Blip! Wow!"

"I see what you mean," Gary yelled back at Diesel. "Hey, Chay?" He grabbed an ankle and she looked at him, like a stranger. "Chay? Take it easy, Chay. You get it all at once?"

"Wow, I think — no, you get off all at once — but it hangs with you! I mean, it gets behind you and throws you forward!" She demonstrated with her arms how she was thrown forward.

Gary watched, realizing now that he'd never done speed with her; best to plan on a communication gap. He hoped not. But he'd have to wait to get off, then play it by ear. He knew that the way acid brought people together, speed could throw them apart. Into their own dimensions. "This doesn't faze you, does it?" he shouted to Diesel. "I mean, you don't feel any different."

"Not much. Like I say" — he pointed to Chay — "I can't understand this business. I'm wide awake, I feel that. Sometimes I get jumpy. Like a kangaroo. Feels like I got to bounce her over the traffic. You got nothing yet?"

"Nothing. Maybe I — "

"Maybe you got the Meth instead. That takes longer to work. But it's a fine vitamin when it does, boy. You'll wake right up."

"Shit. I bet that's just what I did." With Chay a white line herself now, bipping and blipping beneath the truck, Gary stopped wanting to get into her trip. His hands were full with his own head, trying to steady for a Meth flash. He swigged more of the stale coffee, maybe getting off a bit. What the hell was he doing here? he wondered. Damn speed, such a private dope.

A week, eight days they had spent in Berkeley with Davey. Chay was tired of the hitching — of sleeping out and eating less, of gas station johns and never any privacy — so Gary had agreed to a break. Davey received them with an open icebox, hot showers and opium-cured grass. That first night they sat rapping into the morning, trying to explain what had gone down on the trip to L.A. What amazed Gary was finding how little was credible anymore: the duller rides he'd forgotten, and the fantastic ones he disbelieved. Impossible to accept, in a living room, his own stories from the road — impossible that such freaks had existed, had affected him. Only standing on an asphalt ramp with the cars racing past — each car a possible experience, if it stopped — there he could believe what this thumb tripping was about. That people should be crazy, and share it. That they should see how far they could go together, wherever, just to see. He was onto some new ideals, farther fetched than his old ones.

But Chay had tired of the hitching. She'd slept for two days, then followed Davey to his classes all week; well, she was his friend in the first place. Restless, Gary'd copped eighty purple tabs — syndicate acid, but righteous enough — and spent the week dealing in the Haight. One of the nobodies drifting down the street, forever whispering, "Acid, two dollars?" in strange ears, sleeping in dark pads littered with needles and geezers. He cleared fifteen dollars, but it wasn't the money that mattered. Just to know he'd done that, to know it for future reference.

"Wow! I just flashed on that mirror out there!"

On Tuesday he'd cleaned his hands of it, unloading the last twenty at wholesale price. To a new nobody who'd take his place, someone else who'd look back, after making it in straight life, on the time he'd dealt acid. Back in Berkeley Gary patched it up with Chay, got out front about the fight they almost had. At a Chinese restaurant, with fortune cookies for each other: "Be careful in love," "Happiness will come when you apply yourself."

"Wow, I'm really flashing on that mirror!"

"My convex?"

"Wow, yes! Convex? It goes in a circle, I can see — we're all in it, and everything outside's in it — far out! Gary? Aren't you even off yet?"

"Not yet." He decided not to tell her about the Meth. "Give me time, I'll catch up to you."

"I do believe we'll stop up the road for some coffee," announced

Diesel. "In Novato. I believe I could eat through a hamburger, too. You like a hamburger, Gary?"

"Sure. Good idea." Tuesday, and then Wednesday he'd taken her to Golden Gate Park. That was yesterday — no, today before midnight. He wanted it to be yesterday. Walking through the park they'd stumbled onto a free concert, with rock bands they'd never heard of. After listening awhile and smoking with the natives, they wandered all the way to the ocean. Mile after mile of such flowers, such trees; it grew dark. A beautiful park, this, and they would have stayed longer except for the noise.

Stoned people giggling or crying, Chay heard, in the bushes, so they climbed in to find a couple tripping. On acid, the cat's face ashen white while his chick worked this thing from her thighs. Dripping fetus she aborted herself, or miscarried, or something but it was right there, dripping out beneath her awful eyes and she mouthed, "Heavy, heavy." Chay had asked, could she help? Somehow. "Heavy." And the cat, panicked, told them to get lost. So they did. The north coast, he told her; they would go north to be happy again. To think what it meant, and to stop thinking what it meant, and to be, eventually, happy again.

And all Chay had said was, "Ooo, Gary. That's how it is here, right on. Let's go." But he thought: maybe his purple tabs. They could be making that trip behind his acid, two dollars Jesus. Any such bummer and he had to split, had to run far away. Nothing on the road was that sick. So at one A.M. they got back on the asphalt ramps, at one-thirty into this truck. And at two-fifteen he sat ducking from Patsy Cline, hearing the truck-woman groan beneath him and waiting to flash behind Methedrine. Heavy trips, lately. Too heavy.

"Wow! Now I'm flashing on these calendar girls! That redhead — see her, Gary? Far out!"

"I do believe she's my favorite," agreed Diesel. The glossy chick held a fat breast in each hand, propping them up and grinning proudly.

"Gary, think — if I had boobs like that? Far out!"

"She shoots up on hormones," he said drily.

"So what?" She giggled, hysterical. Diesel told her to calm down and pick a new tape; Patsy was just finishing. She picked Roger Miller.

Then it began to hit Gary, first in his ears where the new music throbbed: the words grew longer, stretched until he could think whole sentences in the space of single notes. Mental energy warping time to the steady bounce of Diesel's cab, off and running, a fine drug, running behind clean speed. He resolved to say nothing stupid, not one stupid word. Then the full rush came.

Outside a breeze came up, chilly, and it began to snow gently. When the flakes came thicker, he watched them melt dry on the road. For a time he could choose not to see the snow, but it grew richer, heavier than his will. No. He mustn't believe that, that would bum him for sure. He made the snow slack off, peter out, drift away.

Pink neon lights from Mike's Novato Truckstop danced up the road, miles before Diesel hit the airbrakes and turned into the parking lot. After he did, though, it took an age of low-gear hassling to park; Diesel found a slot in the second row of trucks and patiently backed into it. When he killed the motor, the quiet was frightening.

"I believe I can handle *two* hamburgers," said Diesel, opening his door. "Let's go see." They jumped down from the cab and walked together past truck after truck, steel and rubber shaped into sensual machines, walking toward the lighted restaurant and store. Must be going on three A.M., Gary guessed, moonless night past truck after truck. It took a long time, and they might have been walking fast; but finally Diesel reached the glass door, swung it open for his guests and steered them into a booth.

The restaurant was bright inside, paneled in knotty pine, and its booths, covered in orange plastic, were slashed here and there to spill gray tufts of stuffing. Half a dozen truckers looked up from early breakfasts to nod hello. Gary met all their eyes. They were slashing the plastic over there—he could hear it—their sheer weight ripping clean holes in the fabric.

"Well, good *morning,* Diesel!" A dyed-blond waitress came over, at thirty-five smiling like everybody's mother. "I had a feeling, I says to Sammy, 'I bet the Diesel's coming through tonight.' I says, 'It's been two weeks, so he'll be here.' And sure enough!"

"You call this a truck stop, Candy?" Diesel grinned back. "I believe you're running a cemetery. You got thirty men out there sleeping in their cabs! Where's the music? I want to *hear* that jukebox.

And you got so much air conditioning, you trying to freeze us? Look at this" — he pointed to Chay — "I brought my new girl friend to meet you, and you got her shivering! Her teeth are chattering, see that?"

"N-no." Chay giggled. "I al-always do this. You know what I mean? I-it doesn't f-feel cold, it just looks it."

"Honey." Candy laughed back. "I know just what the Diesel's been feeding you, too. Him and his damn vitamins! Well, Diesel? Were you planning to introduce me?"

"Just coming to that." He chuckled. "This here's Chay. And that's Gary next to her. I believe she's Gary's girl, really. They were hitchhiking out of Frisco."

"Well, you got a good ride, then." Candy winked at Gary. "The Diesel's got no brains, no manners, no nothing. But he can drive a truck and he'll treat you right. What're you having, Diesel?"

He ordered four hamburgers — two for himself, one apiece for his guests — two coffees, and a milkshake for Chay. "To fatten you up." He laughed, and she trotted off giggling to find the ladies' room. Diesel pulled a pocketful of change from his gray pants, pushed two quarters into the jukebox and punched a dozen buttons, asked Gary what kind of smokes he liked and bought him Pall Malls, more Luckies for himself. Gary's head buzzed, he wanted to sing but couldn't, not here. In the truck he could sing, head and body screaming together and no one heard. But in here it only buzzed, and the echoes were deafening. Across the room a driver put his fork down; he could hear it distinctly, fine tuning vibrations. Christ. Diesel came back with the cigarettes, lit up Gary and then himself, letting the smoke billow from his wide nostrils. "I believe I got something to ask you," he said after a couple of drags.

"Oh?" Gary tore his head down from the walls, back from across the room. "Oh, a question?"

"Gary, you're a man." Gary hated to hear that, he was a little boy after all. "Gary, would you get mad at a man if he spoke outright? I mean, if he didn't beat all around the bush?"

His head buzzed louder. Not, please, a serious conversation. "What?"

Diesel dragged again, exhaling all at once to say, "Gary, I believe I like your girl. I'd like to sleep with her." The words got all mixed with the smoke.

Fuck it, thought Gary, in a wave of coherence. All the debts were out to Diesel. First the ride, then the speed, now hamburgers and cigarettes — all for this. He wasn't up for hassling, and least of all for this hassle. Not over Chay, not tonight. Not trying to rein in his head while it raced around the room meeting glances, intruding on lonely breakfasts. He had to get control of his head, had to brake down the speed.

"Don't you worry about getting her pregnant, if that's on your mind. Ain't no girl gets pregnant from the Diesel. I got my ducts tied. Four years back. And I believe I can prove it, too. Last year a bitch from Detroit hauled me into court, tried to blame her kid on me. I got the doc that fixed me, I put him right up on that stand. I believe he told that dame a few things. Because I decided way back, no one saddles the Diesel with no kid. Don't you worry about that."

"It's not that." Gary shook his head deliberately, trying to slow this scene by blurring it. A good reason, he had to think up a reason that the Diesel would accept. Brains vs. well, brawn. And he had the mental energy, he just had to channel it. Something good, now. "I'll tell you what it is," he said, at length but satisfied. "She's having her period. You know, her period? And you see how small she is? It hurts her when she's having her period. I wouldn't go in myself, not for a couple days. She has cramps all the time."

Candy brought the burgers, teased Diesel about getting old and flabby. When she left, he shook a rich laugh from his belly and leaned across the table. "Boy, let me tell you something my daddy taught me. He used to say, 'It's one pisspoor injun wouldn't try to win a bloody battle!' " He laughed again, guffawed, straightening up as Chay appeared across the room. "Well, you think about it," he whispered. "I believe I'd make it worth — let's see — twenty bucks to you? Well, here's Chay back — now we can eat."

Chay slipped into the booth. "Wow, wow! I keep flashing on all these mirrors! The one in the john's all cracked and spooky. Mmmm — suck this milkshake, Gary! It comes oozing up the straw, right on, right into your mouth!"

Gary looked into the wide pupils of Chay, whom he now had to protect somehow. Her eyes danced with their own energy, independent of Diesel's caps and Gary's moods. Chay was silly, yes, but for the moment it seemed a silliness worth meeting halfway. So he sipped on her straw and told her it was far out. But a pisspoor injun, a piss, poor — the snow started falling again, softly, because he wanted to freeze.

Chay couldn't manage her hamburger behind the Dex, so Diesel ate it for her and smoked another cigarette. Then he made Candy open the store to sell him a shirt. He stripped the old shirt off his back and threw it in the trash, putting on a new one exactly like it. No time to do laundry on the road, he explained. Got to keep rolling.

Wandering back through the snow and trucks to Diesel's rig, Gary wondered how the big man could think of sex behind this orgasm of speed. Not to mention handling it with *her* — Chay wasn't a third his size. But then he remembered they were doing different drugs. His chemical climaxing, hours of stretched seconds shivering his mind and groin — they weren't into that trip. The others weren't into Methedrine, weren't feeling the wasted sound of it, with body shudders: Meth. They were behind Dex; now there was a cowboy-sounding drug. Texas Dexas, or Dex Dexas from Texas; Gary flashed, swinging himself up into the cab again. The banality crept into his head from everywhere.

Diesel turned the key in his steady woman, shoved the stick into first gear. Down the rows of broads and bitches he worked her, out onto the highway. Chay sat Indian-style — injun-style — on the hump of motor, all shivergiggles while Diesel showed her how the shift went through fourteen positions. She put her hand over his on the stick, worked through the gearbox with him; Gary felt his mouth go dry, sticky dry beneath his tongue, Methedrine, jaw clamping shut as the muscles in his cheeks tightened.

On the highway, gathering speed, Diesel explained his tachometer and interlock to her. Chay, silly Chay, knowing nothing and trusting so much — damn her. And his trip to protect her, with his brains — lies — not brawn. Not to get his head busted, please. But damn Chay, she ought to know when a lonely, horny stranger was making a pass. She had to know that much, so what was she doing? Running through the gears with him, Jesus, shivergiggling: "Oh, wow!" What was she doing, testing him? Testing if he'd defend her, hold her legs together against strangers? Or did she want it? Maybe she wanted it: wanted Diesel's thick, sterile stick in her own box, shifting gears.

Flashing this way with his mouth tight, his mind racing down the empty highway, Gary realized how much things had changed. He had liked Chay when they started down the coast. Liked her, and that made it plausible that he might like others. People with free generosity, unaffected people who'd let him flow with the waves and highways. And he'd tried, he knew he had tried, to accept whatever came along. Whatever and whoever. Asking no questions to bum no trips to bring no one down; they brought him down instead.

But Jesus, that cunt groaning behind the acid, bleeding with that, that kid — there he had to pull out. Had to get the hell out and decide what it meant. Implications of freedom and flowing, like when it led to *that,* well, then what? He saw it all again now, freaked into it, "Heavy, heavy," "Get lost, man." And awful eyes. He freaked behind it, utterly freaked, understanding why he didn't like anyone anymore. Not the boring many he'd forgotten, not the weird crazy few he remembered, not even Chay so much, and barely himself. Because no one could trust his head, his trip to another. As once he'd thought he could. Generosity whored for the giver's egos was never free or flowing, and Gary was tired of paying for it. The snow fell thicker around him, began to accumulate.

"What time is it?" asked Chay.

"Quarter to four. Sun'll be up soon," said Diesel. "I believe I like it dark."

"Wow, but we'll see it all happen! The whole sunrise — far out! Thanks, Diesel. Thanks for all this!" She gestured expansively, as if Diesel had offered to haul the sun over the horizon. On his truck. Some flash, that. "Gary?" She turned to him. "Wow, Gary! You're sure off now, aren't you? You're somewhere else!"

Gary smiled, tight lipped, at her. "Right on, I'm off. Look, there's snow all over here. But everything *is* the snow! *Snow* — little white flakes, see them?" She didn't.

"What'd he say?" Diesel asked her, laughing at him.

"I sure don't know." Chay giggled back. "He's really far out. I'm sort of caught up with it now, leveled off."

"Right." Diesel nodded. "They're timed, like I said. Real smooth. I believe you'll stay like this until supper, too. Supper tomorrow. You want more music?"

"Sure." She shut her eyes and plunged her hand into the pile of tapes. "Johnny Cash?"

"Fine." He pushed the cartridge into the machine and the rich, bass voice poured out from the speakers. A song about truckers, dodging scales and fixing their logbooks, going to make it home tonight. Gary squirmed out of range again. His rib cage ached: his seat was bolted to the floor, not spring-mounted like Diesel's to cut the cab's jerking. But Gary decided to use his closer contact, mentally stripping the she-truck naked. Steel rhythm in her vast rubber thighs, moving, greasy, and the whole mechanical bitch unaware of his pain and quaking.

Which must be, he flashed, how Diesel saw her. Hand on that stick, his finger in her lubricated box. Truck-driving a man's job because it was sexual aggression. And what could he see, having mastered this truck woman, in Chay? How could he squeeze into human flesh on that bunk, built as it was onto his truck? She'd be offended, she'd respond with whining and grind her gears. How could he think it? Gary couldn't himself, not anymore. He was wasting the drug on these bitter flashes, he was wasting everything.

But they were going to Morningstar, he made himself remember, trying to work his head into a better place. Hip commune which he'd heard was making it: one of the few places where gentle people were surviving, growing. It would be better there with Chay. They'd smoke in the sunshine, shake off the city's paranoia and start over. Get their heads together and start over. A week, hell, two weeks they could stay, helping others build makeshift houses and eating vegetables, emptying their heads. If the dawn would just come.

"I believe I could use some fresh coffee," said Diesel, when Johnny Cash had finished. They were rolling into Santa Rosa. "Take in this next truck stop, we will."

Gary stared at the Diesel, watched him drive. He and his truck were perfect for each other. More together than Gary dreamed of getting with Chay, or anyone else. He wanted to touch her now, but couldn't find her through the blizzard. And orgasmic Meth was sapping his strength, efficient chemical masturbation. No, he vowed, not masturbation. He would dedicate it to the she-truck. Crazy whim, but he'd do it: because Diesel wanted Chay, he would take the Diesel's woman. And he'd do it with her, actually do it, by act of dedication. Jesus, he was spaced! No matter. She wouldn't find *his* ducts tied.

The truck stop in Santa Rosa was smaller than the one in Novato, or looked it because fewer trucks were parked in the lot. Diesel pulled into the darkest corner, where the asphalt was cracked like dry clay, and ordered Gary to go in for the coffees. He said it twice before Gary heard.

"What?" His mind was still in fourteenth gear. "Sorry." He shrugged. "I'm in no condition. I got this snow all over me." Besides, he couldn't leave them alone together. Couldn't.

"Aw, for — "

"I'll go in," Chay offered quickly. "I want to use the john, anyway. Maybe they'll have a mirror like the last one — far out!" And she was over Gary, out the door before Diesel could object.

Diesel lit another cigarette, slowly. "Hey, boy, what's the matter with you? I don't believe you'd trust a man for two minutes."

Gary was just picking up on the silence now, absence of churning in the mechanical thighs beneath him. Had he quieted her? With that orgasm. Had he even had one? Then, dimly, he sensed the confrontation had begun in earnest. And that it was his move. He started mumbling.

"What's that, boy? Speak up!"

"Uh." He pulled it into focus, showed a semblance of control. "Not under the circumstances. Oh, fuck. I mean, you already said — "

"Look. When she comes back with them coffees I'm giving you twenty bucks to go to the john, buy yourself a hamburger. I'm just going to ask her for it, see? If she says no, I won't touch her. Honest. And I believe I'm a man of my word. Let the girl decide for herself, is what the Diesel says."

"Sorry, man, she's not for sale. And I'm not a pimp." Gary's head was killing him. Too much hassle to straighten it out for this showdown, to keep it level when it wanted to fly, race, indulge in fantastics. But somehow here he was, and calling himself no pimp. Jesus.

"Easy does it, boy. Nobody called you no pimp. I just thought you could use the money, right? I believe you *could* use it, couldn't you?"

"That's not where it's at." He shook his head. His jaw wanted to clamp shut; whenever he forced it open, words came spilling out. Except for this time — unable to say where it was at, it hung open, mute.

"What if I told you something? What if she was playing with my balls down here? When you were staring out the window with that vitamin working, she was trying to get at my balls!"

Oh Jesus, fuck, not that. Not Chay, he knew her better. Did he? he wondered. "Listen, I don't believe you."

"Tell you something else," Diesel pressed on, unconcerned with what Gary chose to believe. "I say it's not her period. And I believe you know it."

"It is so her period!" Eager to defend his lies, always he had energy for that. But what had she done, told him? "I should know if it's her goddamn period."

"I believe you're lying," he drawled, blowing smoke. "Like my daddy taught me. 'Boy,' he says, 'you can always tell bloodcunt from the eyes.' Now her eyes ain't bloodshot. They ain't even a little dull. They're bright and sparkly, so she's not having no period."

Gary had to freak again now, behind that word. "Bloodcunt." Diesel shouldn't have said that, it brought everything back: "Heavy, heavy." "Get lost, man." He freaked behind the whole night, this whole freaking night. "Jesus. Look. I *know* this for a fact." Injun, piss, po — defend the lie, cover that lie! "I don't care what her eyes are doing, I *know* this!" Poor, piss.

"Ha! Know what, boy? I believe this'd be worth your while. I seen you don't trust me, and you don't trust that girl neither. But you're thinking about marrying her, aren't you? Well, you'd better find out if you can trust her. Like I say, I'll pay you twenty bucks *and* I'll get you the answer. I do believe that's a bargain, boy."

"I don't care," Gary said, ridiculously soft this time, "if she sleeps around." Bloodcunt, his mind was going and he couldn't talk much longer. The snow was drifting around his waist; he had to climb up, out of it.

"If you don't care" — Diesel chuckled — "I believe you'd let me ask her for it. How about that?"

Jesus Christ, checkmate logic from this truck driver. This trainable, he'd thought once. And now should he explain the "New Morality"? Whatever that meant. Poor. Fuck with anyone but not you, buster, because I say so? Piss. Or perhaps to define their relationship? Which went through more changes than he could keep up with. Bloodcunt. Tonight it looked like Chay the Hippie Chick, seen, through Meth snow, by Gary the Think-Tripper. Well, Ego-Tripper. But it had been more than that, once, and might be again. If they could just cool it until dawn, until Morningstar. So not you, buster. Piss. How to explain that? Poor, liar. He was defending her virtue, damn it, her right to selective fornication. From herself. Injunpiss. Of course he didn't trust her.

"I believe you're short on answers, boy."

"No, wait." Bloodcunt! "There's an answer." There had to be one, because he was right. Injunpiss. He had to be right. "She's hitching with me, now. It's our trip, see? And she doesn't expect me to" — cunt, cuntpiss — "to just let someone else" — injuncunt — "take her." Jesus, trying to think behind this freaking. "Jesus. If she wanted me to split, she'd say so."

"I believe I'd call that playing with my balls saying something, boy. I ain't seen that in a while, either. But all right." He shrugged. "Have it your way." Mercy, pity for the freaking Gary. "Because I can get laid all up and down this road. Anytime I want it. That's a fact, boy. But I believe I could've done you a favor tonight."

"Yeah, well, thanks for trying," Gary mumbled in cold, spreading relief. His head was exhausted, skull muscles strained to the freaking limit; now he could perhaps relax them, loose the balloon of his mind to float skyward. Higher than the snowbanks.

He heard a tap on the door and opened it for Chay. She handed in the coffees, then hoisted herself up over Gary to sit on the motor hump, next to Diesel. And what about that business, baby? he thought. That balls business. But he made himself relax, he wouldn't ask her here. No fights here, please. Diesel must have lied to him. Must have. And if he hadn't — if it was the truth — then it wasn't his Chay that had done it. That had goosed the Diesel. It was the drug, it wasn't really her. Piss, poor, he flashed: the drugs revealed people's true selves, and they were accountable. Completely accountable, right on. So the Diesel had lied, the

Diesel must have lied to him. Glancing over, he saw her hands were in her lap. No hankypanky here. Diesel had lied. At least they evened up, the lies. That shit about her period, pisspoor. The lies balanced each other, canceled out, but his mind refused to relax. He didn't trust her.

"There's no mirrors," announced Chay, "in the john here. None at all."

"That's a shame, honey. But thanks for the coffee. Say, how about one little kiss? For your driver, just one little kiss? Then we'll get back on the road."

"Well — "

"I sure do like you, Chay. I believe I never met a girl like you."

"Just one, all right."

Injunpiss, fuck a truck, Diesel's kiss was taking forever. He wouldn't let her go. New blizzards swept over Gary, and he swallowed hard the muddy coffee. Coming in his pants, was he? Three of them, he told himself, three in this room above the motor — but he was miles from the two of them. He hadn't left them alone, but they'd managed it anyway. And *he* hadn't kissed her that way in weeks.

But she was out of his arms now. He heard her on his left, somewhere, offering backrubs. Great pacifiers, those backrubs, he approved. And lots of us need pacification, right on. Sublimate the old libido — but no, "No, thanks." He shrugged. "Give one to Diesel there, he could use it." Because his seat's up there on springs, he needs one. Gary heard him going, "Ooooh, aaaah Down there. Yes." Well, fine, just fine. He was better than these backrubs. Better than people who gave him rides, better than people who didn't and better than Chay, who stopped cars with her legs, not her thumb. Cars and trucks.

Diesel started shifting gears again, made his mechanical woman groan toward the highway. And Gary's body sang: he was safe. Private solos, ditties for the truckbitch. He knew Chay and Diesel were mechanical, too — only they chose to deny it. Behind this Meth, in this blizzard he could see they were mechanical first, and human only when they felt pain, only freaking and dying. He was better than that.

They rumbled west toward Sebastopol now, running hard from the grays of dawn behind them. Gary watched the light grow in the convex mirror while Diesel moved faster and faster, through countless gears, working to preserve the night. Gary stopped singing to the truckbitch: he knew she couldn't hear him, she was preoccupied. Diesel's hand kept working that stick in her box, and if he could do it for seven more years . . .

The dawn caught them, though. In Sebastopol, when Diesel asked a sleepy gasman where this Morningstar place was.

"The damn hippie farm?" He cocked his head and spat on the pumps.

"I believe that's right. Just tell me where it is."

"Three miles to the fork, left and then two miles. You see a big cross on your left, that's the place. What're you going there for?"

But the Diesel shifted more gears, he couldn't wait to answer while the gray, then purple, then pink streaked across the sky from behind. The warmth melted Gary's snow into colors and he saw scenery again, farms and forests. Five thirty-three: official end to this abortive, sterile, but so sensual night. And they had gained the north coast, Gary could celebrate that, and Chay still with him. Well, next to him — a fair enough place to start, again. It would be better at Morningstar. He'd eat vegetables with her, broccoli and asparagus.

His coming crash first panicked Gary as Diesel swung left at the promised fork. On the motor hump Chay was laughing with the light and arranging Diesel's tapes in the box. She had it: control. Her body synced up with her head, and she'd keep them together all day. Whereas he'd squandered his drug on a half dozen ego trips, bummers, to save her from a danger she wouldn't believe. If he even told her. An hour, maybe less he had before crashing. "Look," he would say to her, "Chay, I got the Meth, it was awful." Then down, down into exhausted depression that had to come, and then tormented sleep. And he hadn't deserved it completely. A long night behind chemical, emotional power, not his fault.

Brakes squealing in the crisp morning, the she-truck quaked to a standstill. Gary shrugged: she had never noticed him. Diesel pointed up the scraggly hill. "I do believe that's it, that cross there. Is it a church?"

"No." Chay laughed. "They just have that, but it's Morningstar. Thanks a lot, Diesel. It's been a great night."

"Right, thanks," murmured Gary.

"You're plumb welcome." The Diesel grinned back. "Plumb welcome. How about one little good-bye kiss from the lady?" Piss kiss. And then a handshake. "So long. I do believe I'll get loaded now, head up to Seattle."

"Have a nice life," said Gary, jumping to the road. He caught Chay's legs, lowered her to himself and slammed the door. Diesel pulled off over the hill.

"Wow! Wow, that's over!" Chay told him. "You won't believe this, Gary, but I think he wanted to make me! I mean he got really forward."

"Oh? Strange. Well, he's gone. Well."

Morningstar lived by the sun, which was over the horizon by the time they climbed the trail. Up top, they found wooden shelters with bronze, naked hippies coming out of them, coming into the orange morning. Gary, Chay gently stripped each other to join them; and Gary, weary, downshifted, finding on the way down even he was mechanical.

MARION MONTGOMERY

The Decline and Fall of Officer Fergerson

(FROM THE GEORGIA REVIEW)

THE CHIEF OF POLICE, of course, knew from the beginning that Officer Fergerson would not last, but there was the pressure. Fergerson was unstable and vague, as anyone who watched him a day or two could tell, but there was the pressure and the chief could do nothing but put him on. Fergerson was in town, apparently, because his brother-in-law had settled there. His brother-in-law had come to manage the new clock-parts factory that the mayor had arranged to get located at the city limits. The factory brought five hundred jobs with it and an annual payroll of two and a half million dollars. The mayor was assured therefore of reelection, and Fergerson therefore was assured of a position as police officer in spite of the chief's misgivings. He could have gotten a place in the factory itself (the chief thought). But, whether because he did not get along that well with his brother-in-law or because by holding a job outside the plant he could maintain a semblance of independence or because there was a company rule against his holding a position — whatever the reason — he did not go into the new factory. The chief surveyed the inexorable series of events leading up to the appointment, and then gave Fergerson a post.

That Fergerson would not stay, the chief knew very well. He had energy, but he spent it in casual curiosity, and so he did not make the citizens aware of his presence as guardian and friend. There was also a puzzled seriousness about him, as if he were looking for something but not sure exactly what that something was. He was, in short, a bit peculiar so far as the chief and the other officers could tell. He did not join in the talk and speculation at the station house. After a month and a half he had no friend on the force, though he was not unfriendly. He did his work, apparently with a minimum of interest in the work itself, and appeared restless and puzzled in a way that could not be accounted for by saying that he was new to the job.

That was why, trapped as he was, the chief put Officer Fergerson on the morning shift at Star Center. The whole town was bursting at its seams, including Star Center, but that suburb was the quietest and the least trouble, particularly in the morning when children were in school and most parents were housecleaning or at their offices downtown. So the chief assigned Officer Fergerson a Harley-Davidson to strengthen his presence and gave him strict instructions about the routine of traffic direction at the intersection where the five streets came together and then sat back helplessly to see how long Fergerson would last.

So Officer Fergerson — thirty, curious, restless — had as his duty the presiding over a metamorphosis. After two awkward days, he got control of the Harley-Davidson. Then he patrolled Star Center, née Five Points, from seven-thirty in the morning until four-thirty in the afternoon, with thirty minutes off for lunch, usually at one o'clock just after the lunch traffic had cleared and just before the school children came in droves. In the late summer when there were no school children he sometimes had lunch at one-thirty. And always, or at least with only memorable exceptions, he had his lunch at the antiseptically bright and chromed drugstore. After lunch he sometimes chose a pocketbook from the rainbow sweep of them along the neatly paneled magazine and pocketbook section and leafed through it while he finished a second cup of coffee. It was a privilege he shared with the anonymous herd of sixth and seventh graders who stormed the drugstore with their nickels just after school was out. But Officer Fergerson leafed through his book with more of the reserve and careful dignity of the older students who took over the drugstore while on family errands, who were themselves replaced by an older group of less reserved, more practiced sophisticates of the early evening.

Officer Fergerson, in addition to being concerned for the order and safety of the impregnable youth, was equally concerned, or rather more concerned, with the decadent old. Those original settlers, fast thinning, were more ignorantly or deliberately opposed to the community's new identity and therefore endangered themselves and others, whereas the young generally only annoyed. There had been, originally, a small grocery, run by a Mrs. Smith, next to the drugstore. It was extremely small and its contents limited. But Mrs. Smith provided in-season vegetables and fruits at convenient prices and kept a supply of respectable staples which appealed to the housewives of the surrounding, loosely settled blocks. Sometimes the vegetables she got were actually from the gardens of some of those housewives, and as often as not when the Negro maids left Mrs. Smith's with dinner's vegetables, they also carried back to their mistresses the name of the housewife who had grown them. Of course, as often as not neighbors shared vegetables directly across back fences, which was no inconvenience to Mrs. Smith since she still maintained herself in comfort sufficient to her needs in spite of such neighborliness. Mrs. Smith's store was still one of the establishments, but its limited space and contents made it inconspicuous in the face of the new High-V store across the way. Mrs. Smith, one of the early pioneers, capitulated. She sold her business to a small, nondescript Mr. Harrison, and lived in secluded comfort two blocks from the Center in a house built by her grandfather. Mr. Harrison, though not a dynamic businessman, at least knew how to survive in competition with the High-V. He hired a young Negro boy, provided him a bicycle with a large wire basket bracketed to wheel and handlebars, opened charge accounts for the timid or lazy or traditionalist — all those not inclined to bustle into the air-conditioned and enormous supermarket whose sign with its tremendous V practically cast a shadow across Smith's Grocery. Mr. Harrison kept the old name, of course, for though he was of the new forces in the community, he was too well aware of the surviving pioneers and their importance to his business not to take advantage of the tradition. Those ladies who could not bring themselves to learn to drive, once the automobile was definitely established, were forced to call Smith's Grocery unless they planned a weekly expedition with the aid of husbands or sons or daughters-in-law who would sometimes bring them to the huge store on Thursdays or Fridays for the weekend specials. And those middle-aged ladies, now turning elderly, who had learned to drive in self-defense, were as likely as not to stop at Smith's Grocery on Mondays and Tuesdays.

These drove nearly always in the mornings, and therefore were Officer Fergerson's concern. He used the new Harley-Davidson, complete with radio receiver and transmitter, to cruise the heart of the expanding Star Center and adjacent blocks with fear and trembling his first week, later with resignation, later still with something of despondent affection for those elderly drivers. But in the first weeks he was cautious, observant, and often frustrated. The ladies drove a variety of automobiles, all of them more or less outmoded. There was, in particular, Mrs. Johnson. Mrs. Johnson, six blocks from the Center, still drove the 1937 Oldsmobile her husband had left her. There were old Packards, antique and sound. And there were of course Fords. But it was the 1937 Oldsmobile that first became a problem for Officer Fergerson. The danger was not, of course, the old cars themselves but the ladies driving them. They had grown up with the automobile, and so, unlike the young conservative students from downtown or the young conservative high school children of the Star Center area, they were old conservatives. That is to say, where the young knew and believed only in laned driving at extreme speeds, the old knew principally that traffic moved in two directions, that the car in the lead had property rights to its half of the road, and that whatever maneuver was convenient (necessary) at the instant was one's to make. Therefore Mrs. Johnson swung her Oldsmobile close to the center line when she prepared to turn right, swung close to the curb when she prepared to turn left. She always made a sign, always put her hand out the window in a gesture which said with drawing room courtesy and nonchalance, "I am about to turn. Would you please . . ." Fortunately, there were few of the younger drivers abroad at midmorning when Mrs. Johnson made her excursions to Smith's Grocery. And those who were in the area were careful enough to keep their distance, not through courtesy but through that instinct for survival which has so mysteriously grown with the complication of physical living. The young wives who bought the noon and evening groceries at about ten o'clock in the morning (and at the High-V store) were not in a rush since the vacuuming was done, the house straight, the children out with the maid or down for a midmorning nap. So they gathered leisurely in slacks and shorts for a Coke and to choose languidly whatever husband and fathers would rush home to eat at twelve or twelve-thirty or at six in the evening. So these were usually safe from Mrs. Johnson and her fellows because none was really in a hurry, and should Mrs. Johnson swing wide into the facing traffic to park awkwardly over a parking line in front of the Town Tower gift shop or Smith's Grocery, the momentary confusion was not a dangerous one. It provided such wives, in fact, with a tale to bear to or withhold from their husbands, depending upon whether the husband was likely to make jokes about women drivers (when a woman puts her hand out the window you can be sure of one thing — the window is down) or whether they registered more sympathetic indignation (My God, when will the legislature come to its senses and refuse such people driving permits).

So Officer Fergerson's first duty on the force was to preside over the metamorphosis and to assure as far as possible that the process of change proceeded smoothly and painlessly. He cruised the streets, nodding to Mrs. Johnson and the other ladies, tipping his hat in an old gesture he came to feel rather than to practice consciously. He sometimes, at first, followed the old pioneers at a safe distance so that they would sense his presence or hear his Harley-Davidson and be warned, for they did not ever use rearview mirrors. It was tedious, exasperating, because like washing dishes, the chore had always to be done again tomorrow. But he did not lose his temper. Occasionally he opened up his siren and flagged down through traffic which came off the Macon Highway and through the Center too fast. Occasionally he warned a late student, driving hard to make his nine o'clock class at the University downtown. But Mrs. Johnson and the pioneers seemed exempt, or so the shopping younger wives reported to their husbands, who, in due time, reported to the city attorney with whom some lunched, who in turn passed word on to the chief of police, who one morning pulled up beside Officer Fergerson's Harley-Davidson at the traffic light and asked him to get in.

Officer Fergerson cut his engine, kicked down the stand, and got in beside the chief.

"Fergerson," said the chief, "so far you've been doing a damn good job out here. The kids get along swell with you. You handle traffic well in the afternoon when they're going home. That's fine. But I keep getting complaints about careless drivers, old people it appears, women in particular. There're more of them out here, you know. Anyway, I've been getting complaints. We'd better clamp down a little. No use endangering everybody by letting some of these old biddies loose who are still used to driving wagons."

"Yes, sir," said Officer Fergerson.

"In particular there is a woman who drives an Olds — '36 or '37. She's caused some bent fenders this past month and she's going to cause something worse sooner or later. You'd better ticket her I think."

"I'll watch for her," said Fergerson. Then he got out of the chief's car and went back to his motorcycle. The chief waved his hand and drove off as the light blinked from warning to green. Officer Fergerson went to the drugstore and had a cup of coffee, wondering exactly how he would approach Mrs. Johnson or any of the other pioneers. But there was no way except to stop her. He looked at the clock and then, reluctantly, went out and cranked up his motorcycle and cruised toward the oak-lined drive from which Mrs. Johnson issued each morning between ten-fifteen and ten-thirty. When she came out, he followed her respectfully, waiting. At the second corner she swung out into the path of an approaching taxi cab and turned smoothly to the right without slowing from her steady twenty miles an hour. He didn't blow his siren. He pulled up beside her, careful to keep a safe distance, and called to her.

"Lady, would you please pull over to the curb a minute?"

She smiled and nodded. It took her half a block to slow down and stop. Officer Fergerson was embarrassed by his motorcycle. He wished there were some way to make the incident inconspicuous. He had no doubt it would arouse indignation among Mrs. Johnson's friends should one happen by. But when he came up to her door she was not embarrassed in the least.

"Well, officer," she said. "I must admit that you young people are very prompt. It was barely fifteen minutes ago that I called in."

"Beg pardon?" he said.

"About John Hardt. Poor man. But he does suffer terribly, and he's so lonely, what with being there in the house all this time since

Miss Lucy died and neither of his children so much as sending him a Christmas card. You can't blame him. But it is dangerous, and I thought it best to call."

"I'm afraid I don't understand."

"Didn't they tell you? Well, John's insisting he's going to drive that old car of his again. You know what happened last year."

"I wasn't . . ."

"Diabetes, you know. Selima — his cook — Selima called me this morning. She's supposed to call his son George in Atlanta about such things, but he couldn't get here in time, so she called me, naturally."

Officer Fergerson's radio began to squawk and he excused himself to answer it. It was about Mr. Hardt. He made a note of the address and went back to Mrs. Johnson.

"Anyway, last year he passed out driving it. He'd just got past Five Points intersection, I mean Star Center — I'm so used to the other name, you know, and I forget sometimes. He ran into a telephone pole. It didn't hurt him — the wreck — but Dr. Thompson had a time with him. He hadn't been taking his insulin and he'd been down to the grocery to get some chocolate, against Dr. Thompson's orders. They had to tow the car home, and his son came over and almost fired Selima because she let him go and because she hadn't made sure he was taking his insulin shots, which really wasn't her fault. Dr. Thompson had quite a time bringing him around again, and the Chief of Police absolutely forbade him to drive anymore. I really didn't like to do this, but I felt it was simply for his own good. That's why I called."

"Yes ma'am," said Officer Fergerson. "I just got the call and I'll go talk to him."

"Poor thing," she said.

"Mrs. Johnson," said Officer Fergerson. "I . . . I really stopped you to ask you to be a little more careful."

"Why Officer," she said, smiling and flipping her fingers at him daintily. "Of course I'm careful. I've been driving twenty-five years, and I'm too anxious about all the careless driving I see not to be careful. Of course I'm careful. Good morning," she said pleasantly. "And you call on me if I can be of any help. I've talked to him of course, but I think it might be better if you did. Together we may be able to accomplish something."

Officer Fergerson stood back tipping his hat as she drove off. He cranked his motorcycle and followed since he had to cross Star Center anyway to get to Mr. Hardt's house. Two blocks later, as Mrs. Johnson approached the High-V and Smith's Grocery, she pulled out across the center line and then cut sharply into a vacant parking space. Officer Fergerson did not stop.

He remembered the house. He had noticed it from the first because, unlike its neighbors, it had retired from the struggle between the old Five Points and the new Star Center, though he did not at first learn that the house had begun its decline with the death of Miss Lucy. What seemed obvious was that it had been retired from the world by a passive neglect rather than by a defiant withdrawal such as Mrs. Smith's had finally been. It was a wooden, story-and-a-half building, the half story housed by a steep slope of the roof. There was a wide porch on the front and on one side, with a waist-high banister. The front yard was shaded by three huge pecan trees, so there was not much grass on the hard soil — some patches of green moss, a few runners of Bermuda grass which boys moving through the neighborhood with lawn mowers sometimes cut for a quarter instead of their usual fifty cents. The hedges around the porch they apparently did not trim, for these were so grown up that Officer Fergerson could hardly see the banister until he was walking up the three wooden steps at the end of the eroding brick walk. The side yards were a jungle. A wisteria vine at the side porch, out of control, covered one whole side of a pecan tree and was gathered in such thick loops along the roof of the side porch itself that the light scarcely got through onto the big rocker sitting there. Between the hedges and the porch, weeds had grown thickly except for a thin path that water from the roof had kept clear. He noticed scraps of paper blown against the hedge from the street litter, and behind the hedge at the corner was a tin can already rusty.

He knocked on the door and waited. Then he knocked again. Finally he heard a screen door slam at the back of the house, and a Negro woman emerged into the gloom of the hall coming hurriedly to the front door.

"Thank goodness," she said. "I been hoping and hoping you'd come, because I can't do a thing with him and he's out in the back right now pouring water in that old Ford." She held the door open. "You come right through here. I'll show you."

He followed her through the dim hallway toward the rear. When they got to the back screen, Selima stood there with Officer Fergerson looking over his shoulder.

"There he is," she said.

Mr. Hardt had set the water bucket down in front of the old Ford, which had its hood raised high in the air like a bird waiting for a worm, and was walking toward a small house in the back yard. He stopped under a tree at one corner of the little house and picked up something.

"He's worried 'bout that house," Selima said. "Won't nobody rent it because it cost too much. November jest whistles through it like a dead corn field. He made it about five years ago, but it ain't no good, and now it's troubling his mind . . . more than any chocolate. Poor old man." She held her apron as if drying her hands to show her compassion, shaking her head slightly.

Officer Fergerson went out the back door and down the steep back steps toward the old man. Mr. Hardt, he could see from a distance, had a thick stubble of beard, or rather neglected whiskers. He had on an old suit and a dress shirt, but he wore no tie. His hat, frayed at the brim, had a careful crease down its crown. He was looking at what he had picked up under the tree.

"Mr. Hardt?" said Officer Fergerson.

"You know what this is, Mr. . . ."

"Fergerson."

"Mr. Fergerson? Bet you never saw one." He handed him the chestnut.

"A chestnut, I think."

"Chinese chestnut. This is the only tree in the state. My son planted it here ten years ago — with the Department of Agriculture," he explained. "I was just remembering when we used to ride north of here in the fall and gather American chestnuts in big sacks."

"Yes, sir."

"A long time ago," he said. "Well, you didn't come to talk about

Chinese and American chestnuts, did you, Mr. Fergerson? Shall we go around front where we can be comfortable?"

"Thank you, sir. But I have to get back to my job. I was asked to come by and speak to you about . . ."

"My car. Yes, I know. Selima has been getting impatient. It's really too bad I can't fire her. You see, the difficulty is that I don't pay her and so I can't run her off. Well, what about the car, Mr. Fergerson?"

"My instructions are to warn you that you aren't supposed to drive."

"I have been warned, Mr. Fergerson. I haven't driven."

"Yes, sir."

They walked back to the car. "I was putting in water. I thought it a good way to keep down rust in the radiator, don't you think so?"

"Well, sir, I think it might be better if you drained it good."

"I suppose so."

"I'd be glad to do it for you."

"But don't I need to run the motor some to keep up the battery?"

Then Mr. Hardt turned suddenly upon Officer Fergerson.

"Suppose, Mr. Fergerson," he said, "suppose you were seventy-five, as I am. Suppose you had been a contractor, taught agriculture, raised a family, lost a good wife, been left alone sick and dependent with orders to give up whatever gave you the last pleasure so that you could live two or three years longer, sitting on the front porch, rocking, bored to death but forbidden to die by doctor's orders and a son's and daughter's long-distance solicitude. Don't you think you might enjoy driving down two blocks to get a bar of chocolate and driving back to eat it?" The old man's eyes were challenging, the dignity and reserve which had shone through the worn suit and unshaven face routed now by loneliness. "What would you do?"

"Well, sir, I think I'd remember what might happen to some of the school kids on their way home."

"I see."

"You really ought not to drive, Mr. Hardt. You wouldn't be safe and neither would other folks."

"I haven't driven, Officer, not since last year. But it is terribly difficult." He smiled. "I shall try extremely hard, Mr. Fergerson. But if I should break over, why then of course you'd be perfectly justified in taking my license, wouldn't you?"

"I hope you won't, Mr. Hardt. Suppose . . . suppose if you need anything, you have Selima call and I'll be glad to bring . . ."

"Chocolate, Mr. Fergerson?" Mr. Hardt's smile was mischievous. "What else would I need? I have my son's house here — you know I signed it over to him long ago. I have a devoted maid. She is religious about my welfare because she is independent and can afford to be. Her money comes by mail. She could be keeping rabbits as well and with the same concern. And I have pocket money from that apartment upstairs — student couple. What else would I need?"

"Anyway, Mr. Hardt, I hope you won't try to drive this car."

"Mr. Fergerson, you may be able to help me. Perhaps you know someone who needs an apartment. This little house you see here is empty. You might tell them about it."

"Yes sir," he said, and then awkwardly, "I'll have to be going now, but if you need me . . ."

"Good morning, Mr. Fergerson," said the old man, smiling.

Officer Fergerson didn't go back through the house. He followed the drive around, noticing the litter of cans and bottle caps, no doubt thrown there by the itinerant couples, or dropped accidentally by Selima, until the litter was considerable. He felt as helpless and unsatisfied as he had from his interview with Mrs. Johnson earlier. Both had been friendly and impervious. So that he knew that he had really accomplished nothing, that tomorrow morning Mrs. Johnson would swerve out in front of approaching traffic to park her Oldsmobile in front of the bleak front of Smith's Grocery or the sleek, narrow-bricked, pine-trimmed gift shop. And tomorrow or this afternoon, or even before he got back to the intersection at Star Center to direct noon traffic, Mr. Hardt might be driving out of the overgrown back yard into the path of whatever truck or car might happen along. Or perhaps he would faint with his foot on the accelerator, as he had done last year. Officer Fergerson felt irritated and helpless.

It was a week later that Mr. Hardt decided to drive out to Smith's Grocery. Selima had called in, and Officer Fergerson took the order over his radio and drove quickly toward the old house. He got there just as Mr. Hardt choked the Ford down in the drive at the side of the house. He approached the car nervously. Mr. Hardt was smiling at him from behind the wheel.

"Well, Mr. Fergerson. I think you got here a little too soon, don't you? Five minutes more and you could have had my license. But here I am still on my place — on my son's place rather."

"You're not going to drive out, are you, Mr. Hardt?"

"How can I?" said Mr. Hardt, still smiling, a little sheepish. "You've caught me. I'm a naughty boy. Now Selima will write my son and you will be tisking me."

"Mr. Hardt, why don't you sell the car? Wouldn't that be better?"

"Sell it? Then what could I do to occupy myself, Mr. Fergerson? You see, so long as it sits here in the yard I can say to myself, shall I defy Selima — it has really become a game, hasn't it — and drive downtown? It gives me some hope, you see. If I can't fire her, she can't make me not drive. And if I might drive out for chocolate, that keeps Dr. Thompson engaged, too. And now the police force is concerned enough to send an officer twice. You see, it is a game. You people are trying to keep me alive and I'm trying to die naturally."

"It's not exactly dying naturally to drive in front of a truck, Mr. Hardt."

"But I haven't. I haven't. You see, I'm a good driver really. Do you know what I was going to do? I was going down to buy a whole box of milk chocolate. Tell me, Mr. Fergerson, have you had a bar of candy this past week?"

"No, sir, but . . ."

"But you don't eat them. Because you can have them, and I want to eat them because I can't. I think it is the same sort of devil in us both, don't you?"

The talk was strange to Officer Fergerson, and he began to suspect the old man's mind was giving way.

"Suppose you try to eat one this afternoon. Just suppose. Listen, here's a dime. You buy one this afternoon. And tell me whether you enjoy it or not. You don't have diabetes, do you?"

"No, sir."

"Suppose you try it. If you will promise to do that, I will promise not to drive out. But you must come back tomorrow to see me."

"All right. If you will promise to leave this here," he said, indicating the Ford by leaning back from the running board.

"Here's the dime, then."

"Let me get it myself."

"No, I insist. This dime."

So he took the dime and, somewhat bewildered, left the old man. He was conscious of the coin as he was not conscious of the change in his other pocket. Carefully, he had put the dime in his watch pocket, separate and weightless. But its presence was so constant that it might as well have been hot and heavy. For a while he hid up the street, having circled the block, to make sure the old man did not try to drive out after all. Then he felt guilty about that. He began to wonder whether he had done right or what else he might have done to handle the situation better. Helping the sheep flocks of children across the intersection was one thing. Dealing with a subtle old man was quite another. He began to feel more and more that he had been tricked, but he did not know precisely what the trick was.

Riding past the house again just after his lunch, he saw Mr. Hardt sitting on the side porch in the big rocker. The old man smiled and waved his hand, and Officer Fergerson felt the twinge of discomfort. He had not gotten the candy bar. He did not care for candy, but that was not exactly the reason. After his lunch he had hesitated at the cash register where the display of candy and gum lay open to his selection, but he did not want candy. The dime in his watch pocket and his reluctance to use it pulled at him till he left the drugstore, neither having willed not to buy the candy nor having willed to buy it. And now, riding past the old man smiling at him from the tall rocker, he was conscious that he had been tricked into a trivial situation which nevertheless left him vaguely uneasy. Before he went to the intersection he stopped at the drugstore and bought a bar of candy, but even then he used his own dime, and Mr. Hardt's was heavy in his watch pocket all afternoon. He nibbled at the bar, but he did not eat it. As he helped a friendly little blond girl across the street, he offered her part of it.

"You remember what Mama said," her brother warned, hurt because he had been offered none. So Officer Fergerson put the half-finished bar back in his pocket, irritated that it could cause him so much trouble. Finally, angry at the whole silly affair, he ate it quickly, hardly chewing it. But he was still aware of a silver gong that kept reminding him of itself.

When Officer Jackson relieved him at four-thirty the first thing he did was go by the drugstore and buy a second bar with the dime. He ate it as he walked toward Mr. Hardt's, conscious only of the bar of candy which seemed somehow larger than he would have expected. When he got to the old house, Mr. Hardt was still sitting as he had been two hours earlier, and he smiled at Officer Fergerson with the same smile. Officer Fergerson felt a stir of resentment, but it passed.

"Well, Mr. Fergerson, come in." The old man motioned him to a second high-backed rocker. He sat down and rested his arms on the rocker arms, wide enough to use as a desk. He wondered whether this one had been dragged out in anticipation, whether Mr. Hardt had been sure of his coming.

"You've just missed Mrs. Johnson. I believe you know her."

He nodded.

"She comes most every afternoon. Brings flowers. Cheers up the invalid."

"Yes, sir, I've met her."

"Well, tell me now, Mr. Fergerson, how was the candy bar?"

"I ate it."

"Now, Mr. Fergerson, that is not what I asked."

"The truth is, Mr. Hardt, that I just don't care much for candy. I used to when I was a boy. I ate it, but . . ."

"But only because it was part of a bargain."

"Well, yes, sir."

"Mr. Fergerson, tell me. I'm just curious to know what you think — I mean really think — do you or do you not think a man is entitled to die a natural death, barring accidents of course. What I mean is, do you or don't you think a man has a right to die naturally without the interference of his friends?"

"Well, sir, I'm not a doctor." He felt more uneasy, as if he were at the revelation of the trick played on him.

"Nonsense. It is not a question of being a doctor. It is a question of a conviction about life."

"Well, I've never thought that much about it, sir."

"Exactly. That is because you are too attached to life. But what if you were, say, my age?"

"I don't know. That is a long way to go yet."

"Then do you think perhaps I might be better able to determine the answer to that question for myself, having passed my appointed span?"

"Well, I suppose so, Mr. Hardt." He felt he was getting into something beyond him and would rather be back directing five o'clock traffic than visiting Mr. Hardt, who was full of talk about death and death only, who somehow could confuse and upset one simply by having him eat a candy bar.

"Well, the question is, what is a natural death, don't you think?" Mr. Hardt went on without waiting for his answer. "A natural death, I should say, is the appropriate end of a natural life, wouldn't you? Now the next question is, have I or have I not lived a natural life, and if I have not, then at what point did I abandon a natural life? And if I am now living an unnatural life, then am I not justified in dying an unnatural death?" He smiled at Officer Fergerson, who began to rock to hide his confusion and discomfort.

"Now, Mr. Fergerson, since I have been a young man, I have lived with the joy of living. Do you know what that is? It is living so freely that one is not aware that he is living. Tell me, do you think you will ever forget that candy bar you ate this afternoon?"

Officer Fergerson smiled sheepishly, shaking his head.

"And now tell me quickly — don't you think too hard — do you remember eating another candy bar? I know you said you ate candy as a boy, liked it. What I want to know is, do you remember eating a particular candy bar at a particular time?" Then before he could answer, "You don't. But if you think very hard you will remember, because you will begin to look at the natural unnaturally — that is what memory is. That is why old people remember so much and so many trivial things. They are in an unnatural state looking back upon pure instances of natural living."

Officer Fergerson felt certain now that the old man was losing control of himself, something frantic and feverish about the words, though he was speaking unhurriedly, as if he were explaining an equation to a slow student. He rocked on respectfully, listening.

"So," Mr. Hardt went on, "an unnatural life involves looking back, you see. But it may also involve looking ahead. That sounds strange no doubt. But when one becomes conscious of the past, he becomes conscious of the future, when one becomes conscious that one has been born, he becomes conscious of the fact that he will die. That's the curse you finally come to. You can remember what happened two years ago, I dare say, better than you can remember what happened before that — when you were a boy. And you can contemplate what you are going to be next year with far more vivid insight than you can contemplate what you will be when you are, say, my age. So there you are in the middle not looking very far either way yet. It is an uncomfortable place if you think about it. Do you know why? Because I see something that you don't see and because I'm, shall I say, diabolical? Perhaps not. Because, perhaps, you weren't very positive when you came to forbid me the car, I got to wondering what you were doing on the force in the first place, or in this town.

"Anyway, if you think about it now, which I don't advise you to do, then you're going to find yourself either a Mrs. Johnson or a Mr. Harrison or — you know Mr. Harrison at Smith's?" The old man paused. "So most of my life I lived with the joy of living. I wasn't concerned with remembering the past or future. I didn't do too well, you see. This isn't really a good, substantial house, you've noticed. I built it and lived in it every moment without much concern about how long it would last or how long I would last. I repaired whatever needed repairing when it needed it. The yards were different. They were Miss Lucy's — my wife's. Now I find myself wondering whether this place will last as long as I. That is unnatural to me. I built that house in the back thinking it would have to outlast me because I needed the money I could get renting it, and so I didn't build it with the joy of building. It won't last as long as this. Do you see?" He turned to Officer Fergerson. "Do you see, Mr. Fergerson, if we do things out of fear of the past or future, they will have little past because they will have such a limited future. Do you suppose the Parthenon was built with much concern for our appreciation of it or for that matter, the Roman temples in France either? They were built in the joy of the present, that is, they were built by men living naturally in the present. That road out there" — he indicated the paved street in front of his house — 'it was built to last ten or fifteen years. It was built with the builder's eye on the future. Doesn't matter whether on fifteen years or forever. It is already breaking down. And it doesn't matter that the man who built it calculated the future for profit. It would carry the same weakness built for any other reason so long as the builder had his mind on the future. The Appian Way was built because the road was needed at the instant to support and carry troops and carts. And people are still using it."

Officer Fergerson, uncomfortable, looked at his watch. "Well, sir," he said, "you may be right. I hadn't thought about it."

"The point is," said Mr. Hardt. "The point is that I am living unnaturally and I will die unnaturally if you and Dr. Thompson and my son and Selima and Mrs. Johnson have your way. Was it more natural not to eat the candy, Mr. Fergerson, or to eat it? That is, assuming that what I have described as natural is so. Did you enjoy the candy bar, or did you know you were eating it?"

"Well, I certainly knew I was eating it."

"And do you think that tomorrow when you look at a candy wrapper or see candy in a window, you will be able to ignore it with the same unconscious pleasure you knew yesterday?"

"Mr. Hardt, you're getting me confused. I never supposed there was so much to eating a candy bar or not eating it. I don't think there is. I think you've been making a . . . a mountain out of a molehill, so to speak."

Mr. Hardt chuckled. "So you see, Mr. Fergerson, I want chocolate because I want this old natural joy of life back. It's the tree in my Eden. But I know that even if I have chocolate, it will not be the same again. I am trapped. We can't live forever — because of memory. That is what I want you to remember." He chuckled again, as mischievously as a boy. "You can't escape, you see. Tomorrow you'll remember today's candy bar. Today the chief remembers the accident I had. Mrs. Johnson remembers when Lucy was alive and all the flowers cared for in the back yard — she brought me chrysanthemums this afternoon. Dr. Thompson has to remember my attacks and what he has prescribed. It is a trap, you see. We kill ourselves and each other because we won't live naturally all our lives. Then we try to live unnatural lives till we force ourselves to die an unnatural death."

Selima came out onto the porch with a small tray. "You remember what Dr. Thompson said about forgetting your shot, Mr. Hardt," she said with patronizing concern.

"You see," said Mr. Hardt, chuckling again.

"I'd better go," Officer Fergerson said. "I have some errands to do downtown and I have to make my report."

Mr. Hardt stood up to see him off the porch. "I'm sorry I rattled on, Mr. Fergerson. But sometimes one can't just talk to himself. Don't be disturbed by my mischief. I'm just an old man, amusing myself the only way I can now." His tone of apology somehow stirred and reassured Officer Fergerson. He stopped on the walk, looking back at the old man.

"Mr. Hardt, suppose I come around and take you for a ride some afternoon. Maybe you'd like that."

"Perhaps."

"Well, good afternoon," he said, and walked toward Star Center not looking back. There was still a vague fog over his thinking, an impression that he had somehow witnessed a profound error, but whether or not it was his own or the old man's he couldn't determine. Mr. Hardt's talk had been confusing, but it carried an impression of sense even when Officer Fergerson was aware that the old man's mind was ready to give way. Nor could he feel certain of their relationship, his and Mr. Hardt's, of whether Mr. Hardt was playing some trick upon him of which he was only vaguely aware or whether the old man, worn out with lonely thinking, needed someone to talk with and had chosen the first person who would listen and appear interested. Certainly there was something fascinating and appealing about the old man, and he felt anxious for him. He remembered that Mr. Hardt had linked Mrs. Johnson with Mr. Harrison, who, through a strange species of logic, Officer Fergerson would have linked with the manager of the High-V. But Mr. Hardt was outside the conflict now, the slow change, and so he was a concern of Mrs. Johnson's and of the police department, as if each one of these disparate forces were trying to recruit him in their struggle.

As he walked along in front of the drugstore toward the corner to catch a town bus, he noticed the artificial fronts of the new business shops as he had not noticed them before, the gift shop and drugstore. The second story above each was the same old dirty brick and plain front that the entire buildings had been before the metamorphosis had begun. He noticed the older grade-school students had taken over the drugstore now. At the corner while he waited, Officer Jackson came by swiftly on the Harley-Davidson, its exhaust popping. A boy pushing a bicycle along the sidewalk stared at the man and motorcycle with a faraway look, conscious and unconscious of their presence. Officer Fergerson got on the bus and dropped his dime in the slot.

In the still, autumn afternoon, Officer Fergerson began to stop at Mr. Hardt's after he was relieved. Sitting on the side porch in the huge rockers, watching the dead pecan leaves slide down the air to the ground and drift along the hedges, watching the wisteria fade toward winter, he listened to the old man, fascinated by the strange music of his distraction, by the autumn color of his remembering. There were new paperback books which the old man would read the first pages of — *The Eye of the Painter, The Age of Reason, World's Great Economics,* the endless profusion of cultural medicine at 25 or 50 cents a copy which Officer Fergerson had begun buying and reading, though he hardly knew why. He was always mildly or, sometimes, radically disturbed by the ideas he discovered, but Mr. Hardt seldom read more than a chapter or the introduction, reading that much only to please Officer Fergerson. Sometimes Mr. Hardt listened while he muddled out his thoughts, trying to free his mind of the vapors that always accompanied his attempt. But most often in late-afternoon sun, the pedestrians, of whom there were few, and those motorists whose attention was caught by the decaying house long enough for them to glance at it a moment, would see the young policeman and the old man sitting there, the old man with a heavier coat on as the weather cooled, and with a thick scarf around his head and the old felt hat perched on top. Always the old man sat still; nearly always the young one rocked slowly back and forth. When the old man talked, it was seldom in the vein of that confusing afternoon after Officer Fergerson had eaten the chocolate bar. The young man remembered the chocolate bar far more clearly now than he did that strange conversation. But it was the conversation which had drawn him to the old man. It was as if Mr. Hardt had revealed the secret of the fountain that afternoon to unreceptive ears, and

Officer Fergerson returned again and again out of a mixture of affection and curiosity and desire until the companionship of the two began to be remarked around Star Center, even by the nonchalant wives of the leisurely shopping. In the afternoons, dressed more elegantly than in the morning when they saw Officer Fergerson patrolling on his motorcycle or walking about the shopping center, or when the late ones saw him guiding the first flushes of noon traffic, the wives in station wagons and new sedans noticed him on the porch. Or they saw the young man and the old one cruising in the Ford, Officer Fergerson driving, the old man talking, talking, the young one looking at buildings and the people with his endless curiosity. They would drive out to the University's experiment station while the old man reminisced about his experiences. They would drive downtown while he recalled an endless flow of his own history and that of the town — houses, people, even the trees. And through it all Officer Fergerson came to see, or to think he saw, more distinctly the changes in the town and in the people, but particularly in Star Center. The buildings themselves were creatures from a mythology which was as yet too young to be formulated myth. The sleek gift shop with its statistically procured items ranging from the sublime to the hideous served to draw the past, present, and future together. It had been simply a hardware store, a place where the local residents could get nails or tools or seed or whatever they might need for house or yard without having to go all the way downtown. It had served as a convenience to the farmers, too, who lived within tractor or truck distance. For, as Mr. Hardt pointed out to Officer Fergerson, those lands where the new subdivisions were going up, the neat efficient two- and three-bedroom houses, their identical natures cleverly disguised with paint and roof and window variations, were not five years earlier cotton fields or corn fields, or in one instance a pecan orchard. But the container factory and clock-parts factory, the other dozen small and growing factories, were spreading Star Center out in a pregnancy, the issue of which aroused Officer Fergerson's curiosity but left Mr. Hardt unconcerned.

So the gift-shop building, with its range of gifts for the range of people of the Star Center area, which even carried still an assortment of nails and screws and glue and a few simple tools, was to the Star Center people, though they did not think of it as such, a griffinlike institution, and the building itself had something in common with the centaur, the dirty brick second story where assorted families and individuals roomed — itinerant workers, shop girls, retired spinsters — and the modern façade and bright and artful interior of the gift shop.

Mr. Hardt's unconcern about the future of Star Center was of no moment to Mr. Harrison of Smith's Grocery. He was assured, because Selima was both lazy and businesslike, of the old man's business, though it was slight. Every morning Selima called in an order. Before noon the boy brought what she wanted on his bicycle and had her sign the bill and then went wandering aimlessly back toward Smith's Grocery to take the next order out. And if Selima (or any maid or mistress) called for something which Smith's Grocery did not carry in stock, Mr. Harrison had only to send the boy directly across the street to the High-V to find it. Then he would rub off the efficiently stamped price from the can or resack or rewrap the vegetables or meat and reprice it and send bill, boy, and groceries on their leisurely way. So, assured both that Mr. Hardt would spend no more for his concern and that what little he spent already would continue constant, Mr. Harrison did not bother that Mr. Hardt was above or beyond or behind the life of Star Center. The manager of the High-V was unaware that Mr. Hardt even existed. The druggist behind an array of antique medicine jars — red, purple, milk white — knew Mr. Hardt only from the labels he typed for the medicine Dr. Thompson prescribed. Mr. Hardt, Diabetic. The girl at the soda fountain had never seen him, for since its renovation, he had not been in the new store. He did not, of course, send gifts, so the gift shop did not know about him. Even Officer Jackson remembered him only vaguely as the old diabetic who ran into a post, causing a few minutes of hard work near the intersection till traffic could be cleared. So no one at Star Center itself was much aware of Mr. Hardt as a particular person whom they could recognize and identify until Officer Fergerson began to drive him around. Sometimes the two would park at the shopping center to watch people go in and out of the stores, to watch the big semitrailer unload the weekend specials at the back of the High-V, to watch the descent of older children upon the magazine rack as seen through the big plate-glass window, the old man talking, talking, the young man, still in his uniform, watching intently, looking intently, as if he were trying to see through and behind the buildings and people and signs.

Mrs. Johnson, unlike most of the people of Star Center, was concerned for Mr. Hardt. She brought flowers and sugarless cookies. She kept him informed of the defection of pioneers, which ones had bought new cars or let maids go or had bought radios or television sets. Sometimes the three of them would sit on the side porch talking, probing the surface of Star Center under Mrs. Johnson's guidance. Selima would serve tea, would put Mrs. Johnson's flowers in water and listen in silent reproof as Mrs. Johnson remembered the lovely flowers in the back yard where Miss Lucy had kept them. It was Mrs. Johnson, who somehow had gotten word that the health department was concerned over the problem, who had persuaded Officer Fergerson to do something about the rats. For when Mr. Hardt had decided to rent the upstairs rooms, at his son's and daughter's insistence, he had stored a multitude of the past in the garage, making an ideal breeding place, and now the neighborhood was being overrun with huge wharf rats, whose base of operation, as two neighbors had complained, was the garage. So late one afternoon, Officer Fergerson put out the poison and refreshed it several times. The health department did not call.

And Mrs. Johnson it was who became concerned about fire. The yards had become so overgrown that, as the weeds died back and dried with the slow beginning of October, there was a constant threat of fire. Officer Fergerson found a man and equipment, and the man worked two days, chopping, dragging, raking, burning until the yards were cleared and there was a look of new life in the place to all except Officer Fergerson, who could see the contrast more sharply now between the house which Mr. Hardt had built and the yards which his wife had taken care of. He knew, without Mrs. Johnson's assurance, that in the spring a variety of plants not seen in years would suddenly appear. But, because Mr. Hardt showed an indifference which bordered on objection, he would not agree to help patch the gutter or the roof where it leaked in one place. Mrs. Johnson, recruiter of the old order, became more and more an afternoon companion to Mr. Hardt and an apostle to Officer Fergerson. So by the end of October, the wives in station wagons began to notice, not only that the overgrown yards were cleared, but that now there was Mrs. Johnson as well as the young policeman on the porch in the afternoons, sipping tea, rocking with Mr. Hardt. But not even Mrs. Johnson knew that Officer Fergerson, every afternoon now, brought Mr. Hardt a candy bar. It was Selima who discovered it.

She discovered it one afternoon standing behind the screen from which she could see without being seen. The young policeman handed the bar of candy to the old man, and he slipped it quietly, without looking at it and without commenting at all, into his coat pocket. Selima watched several afternoons after that, and twice more she saw the exchange. The old man continued to take his insulin shots, though she had to remind him constantly. But the candy was strictly forbidden, and her orders were positively to let both Dr. Thompson and Mr. Hardt's son in Atlanta know. She did.

After that Officer Fergerson did not call so often, and when he did, it was usually a matter of standing on the steps, one foot up on the porch, his hat in his hand. The old man would be sitting in his rocker ten yards off, inviting him to the other rocker, which he would decline reluctantly. At first he would bring the latest book he had read, but after a while, sensing Selima always behind the screen door or window, he no longer brought the books. There had been direct pressure from the chief, from Dr. Thompson, who had spoken to him personally. There had been indignant letters from son and daughter. Even Mrs. Johnson had called him aside to scold him severely. Officer Fergerson finally stopped going altogether, after which Star Center became a dead unity, as if Mr. Hardt had supplied the magic with which he was enabled to see a strange and throbbing diversity. Smith's Grocery facing the High-V no longer aroused his imagination, nor did the contrast of Mrs. Johnson's dangerous '37 Oldsmobile in the midst of the powerful, careful cars of the insurgents challenge him. As mechanically careful as he was with his tasks, he did not perform them well. Once he stopped Mrs. Johnson and spoke rather definitely about her bad driving habits, cautioning that he would be forced to take stronger action. But Mrs. Johnson, offended, reported him. There was continuing dissatisfaction among the younger wives who felt themselves endangered by Mrs. Johnson and her kind. Officer Fergerson's situation became critical.

And all that time he was himself unsettled, missing the old man's remembering which seemed such a key to the tangled life of Star Center, which indeed showed that there was life where before, and now, he could see only motion. City Hall employed several volunteer mothers for traffic direction at school hours, and the one assigned to the Star Center intersection proved more competent, the wives said, than Officer Fergerson himself. It was a matter of time, as the chief had at first predicted to himself, before Officer Fergerson would resign or be transferred to prepare for dismissal.

And then in mid-November, on an afternoon just as the first school children were crossing the intersection, the radio on the Harley-Davidson began to squawk for Officer Fergerson. It was Mr. Hardt, determined to drive, ill. Dr. Thompson was already on his way from downtown. Officer Fergerson was to go immediately. He left the woman to handle the traffic alone.

When he got there and knocked on the door, Selima came running, lumbering awkwardly through the hall.

"He in the car, say he's going to the High-V for chocolate. Near knocked me down when I tried . . ."

Officer Fergerson ran around the house and up the drive. Already, curious neighbors were on their porches watching. Under the pecan tree past the trimmed hedges he stopped. The car was facing him and Mr. Hardt was sitting hunched forward at the wheel. The motor was dead, if it had been running. Officer Fergerson walked forward, uneasy, wondering what to say, how to say it, wishing that it had happened on Jackson's tour. He opened the driver's door, but he didn't need to say anything. He could see that Mr. Hardt was dead.

There was not a very big funeral. The son came from Atlanta, the daughter from Carolina. Mrs. Johnson was there, as were several of the older people of the community, the early settlers, who remembered Miss Lucy and who now would remember Mr. Hardt. Since the funeral was to be in midmorning, Officer Fergerson was assigned to escort it. He could have asked for relief and gone as the old man's friend in mourning. But somehow, after the coldness of the son and daughter and Dr. Thompson, he felt closer to the old man in grief if he led the slow procession. Even after he knew about the chocolate bars — Mrs. Johnson and not the son had told him — the others were impersonal. Selima, getting out the burial suit, had found them, carefully collected in a shoe box, untouched. There was no doubt that the old man had saved every one. Once more Officer Fergerson had the feeling he had been tricked, that somehow he had misunderstood the old man, or had misunderstood himself. And it seemed that in the tragedy of the old man's last weeks there was something which should have drawn him closer to Mrs. Johnson and Selima, whom he had largely ignored, and to the son and daughter, for all of them had been touched by the strange and fascinating old man. But he felt only indifference.

Unconsciously, he set the speed at twenty miles an hour. Through Star Center intersection, along the oak-lined drive, past the University, across the river to the cemetery. At the turn-off he stopped his motorcycle beyond the cemetery entrance and held up the oncoming traffic while the half dozen cars swung into the gates behind the hearse. The son and the daughter rode in the black Packard furnished by the funeral home, and behind them came the old '37 Oldsmobile with Mrs. Johnson and a woman he had never seen. Mrs. Johnson swung out across the center line and turned without changing her speed. The other four cars were only vaguely familiar and they were no doubt people from the Star Center area. It was, after all, a big place, growing, even putting economic pressure on the downtown shopping center now, so he couldn't know them all. But they were, obviously, the pioneers, the early settlers.

Officer Fergerson resigned and took a job with his brother-in-law's company for a while. He disappeared as completely into the growing population as Mr. Hardt had disappeared into a larger and still growing population, missed by few, mourned by none. The counter girl at the drugstore missed him most, for his habit of buying a book every day or every other day had become so thoroughly established that she noticed when he stopped buying, and noticed when he finally stopped coming into the drugstore for his lunch at all. The new policeman could not give her any details; he knew only that Fergerson had resigned and understood, from Officer Jackson, his relief man, that it had been just in time. The new officer, whose name was Johnny Merrick, had a midmorning cup of coffee at the drugstore most mornings, while he leafed through the magazines. That was what he was doing the morning the big semitruck off the Macon Highway failed to slow up enough approaching the intersection and hit a '37 Oldsmobile squarely as it pulled into his lane to make a right-hand turn in front of Smith's Grocery.

WRIGHT MORRIS

Magic

(FROM THE SOUTHERN REVIEW)

ROBERT COULD SEE Father in the front seat, steering. He could see Mother and the lover in the back seat, sitting. They came around the lake past the Japanese lanterns and Mrs. Van Zant's idea of a birthday party. The car stopped and Father got out and opened the door for Mother. Mother got out and pulled her dress down. She leaned back in and said, "Here we are — here we are, lover!"

"I object to your sentimentality," said Father.

"Here we are, lover," Mother said, and pulled him out of the car. His arms stuck out of the sleeves of his coat. One pocket of his pants was pulled inside out. Robert wanted to see the bump on his head but he had on his hat. "Here we are," Mother said, and turned him to look at Robert.

"This is Mr. Brady, son," said Father.

"I told you," Mother said, "Callie's boyfriend."

"Where's Callie?" said Robert.

"Callie's got her lungs full of water, baby. She's where they'll dry her out."

"He's dried out?" asked Robert. He didn't look it. There was a line around his hat where the water had stopped. Under the hat, where he had the bump, Mother said his head was shaved. "Why'd she hit him?"

"She didn't hit him, baby. He fell on it. When they fell out of the boat he fell on it."

"A likely story," Father said. "Is that Emily?"

Robert's sister Emily stood in the door holding one of Robert's rabbits and wearing both of Callie's slippers.

"Go put your clothes on!" Father said.

"My God, why?" cried Mother. "She's cute as cotton. Why would anybody put some lousy clothes on it?"

"Don't shout!" shouted Father.

To the lover, Emily said, "Did you ever hug a rabbit?"

"He doesn't want to hug a rabbit," Father said, "or see little girls with all their clothes off."

"Why not?" Mother said.

"Mr. Brady is not well," said Father. "When he fell from the boat he bumped his head and was injured."

"Where does he hurt?" said Robert.

"In his heart, baby."

"Mr. Brady has lost his memory," said Father.

"What a wonderful way to be," said Mother.

"How does he do it?" asked Robert.

Father said, "You don't *do* it. It just happens. You forget to feed your rabbits. He has forgotten his name."

"Isn't he wonderful?" Mother said. She took his hand. "You must be starving!"

"They said he had just eaten," said Father. "Where you going to put him?"

"Did Callie lose her memory too?" asked Robert.

Mother said, "No such luck, baby — "

"She has some water in her lungs," said Father, "but she didn't lose her memory. She said she wanted you in bed."

To Emily, Mother said, "Is that the *same* rabbit? My God, if I'm not sick of rabbits."

"Can't they dress themselves without her?" Father said. "Put down that rabbit, will you? Go put some clothes on."

"Isn't she cute as cotton?" Mother said to Mr. Brady. Emily put down the rabbit and showed her funny belly button. Robert's button went in, but Emily's button went out.

"Are you going to speak to her about that?" said Father.

"Show lover your sleeping doll, pet," said Mother.

Emily rolled her eyes back so only the whites showed. Robert called it playing dead.

"I'll show him up," Father said. "Where you putting him?"

"Callie's room!" they both cried.

To Mr. Brady, Mother said, "You like a nap? You take a nap. You take a nice nap, then we have dinner."

Father whinnied. "If Callie's not here, who's going to prepare it?"

Mother hadn't thought about it. She stood thinking, fingering the pins in her golden hair.

"We could eat pizzas!" cried Robert. "Pisa's Pizzas!"

Emily clapped her hands.

"You don't seem to grasp the situation," said Father. "You have a man on your hands. You have a legal situation."

"I hope so," said Mother.

"It's your picnic — " began Father.

"Picnic! Picnic!" Emily cried.

Father rubbed his palms together. "I'll show him up. You dress the children. You like to use the washroom, Mr. Brady?" Father led him down the hall.

Their mother took off the green hat and felt for the pins in her golden hair. She took them out like clothespins, held them in her mouth, while she raised her arms and let the fan cool beneath them. Through the open French doors she could see across the lake to Mrs. Van Zant's lawn and all the Japanese lanterns. Mrs. Van Zant lay in the hammock on the porch with her beach hat on her face. Mother gave Emily her hairpins, then threw back her head so the hair hung down like Lady Godiva's. When she shook her head more hairpins dropped on the polar-bear rug. These pins were for Robert. He picked them up and made a tight fistful of them.

"What was I going to say, pet?" Mother said.

"Where's Callie," said Emily.

"In the hospital, baby. She's in Mr. Brady's head. That's why it hurts him."

"He's got no memory?" said Robert.

"Who needs it, baby? Give Mother her pins." His mother sat on the stool between the three mirrors with her long golden hair parted in the middle, fanned out on her front. "Your mother is Lady Godiva," she said.

"Lady Godiva my lawn mower!" said Father. He came through the French doors with a drink and took a seat on the bed.

"You like horses, baby?" Mother said to Robert. "She was the one on the horse."

"Can you picture your mother on a horse?" said Father. Ho-ho-ho, he laughed.

"Tell your father he's no lover," said Mother.

"Tell your mother you could all have done worse," said Father. "Her looks, my brains."

"I'm not sure he understands her," said Mother. "You think he thinks she meant to hit him?"

Father said, "Just so she didn't lose any more than he did."

"She won't like it," said Mother. "She likes to make her own bed and eat her own food. Did you see it? White fish, white sauce, white potatoes, white napkins. I thought I'd puke."

"In my opinion," said Father, "he jumped out of that boat. He tried to drown himself."

"That's love for you," Mother said. "Your father wouldn't understand."

"It's a miracle he *didn't* drown," said Father.

"See how your father sits and stares," said Mother.

"Ppp-shawww, I'm too old for that stuff," said Father.

"God kill me I should ever admit it!" said Mother.

"What I came in to say, was — " Father said, "I'm washing my hands of the whole business."

"You're always washing your hands," Mother said.

"It's no picnic," Father said. "You get a man in the house and the first thing you know you can't get him out."

"No such luck," Mother said.

"I'm warning you — " Father said.

"Tell your father he can go wash his hands!" Mother shouted.

"Eva — " Father said, "there is no need to shout."

"It's this damn house," Mother said. "Twenty-eight rooms and two babies. An old man, and two pretty babies."

"All right," said Father, "have your stroke."

"When I do — " Mother said, "I want someone here with me. I won't have a stroke and be cooped up here alone."

"Eva — " Father said, "that will be enough."

Mother let her long hair slip from her lap and stared at her front face in the mirror. Her mouth was open, and the new bridge was going up and down. She took the bridge out of her mouth and felt along the inside of her mouth with her finger. She spread her mouth wide with her fingers to see if she could see something.

"If you just keep it up," Father said, "you're going to have a little something — "

"Where's my baby?" Mother turned to look for Emily. She was sitting on the head of the polar bear feeding fern leaves to the rabbit. "If you do that he'll make beebees," Mother said. "You want him to go around the house making beebees?"

"It's not a him," said Robert, "it's a her."

"You have to shout?" shouted Father. "We're sitting right here."

"That's why *I* have to shout!" shouted Mother.

"Don't pick her up," Father said, "put her down. It's picking her up that makes the beebees. If you don't want beebees pick her up by the ears."

Emily picks her up by the ears, then puts her down.

"I swear to God you're all crazy," Mother said. "Who could ever like that?"

Father takes his drink from the floor and holds it out toward Robert. There is a fly in it. "You see that?" Robert saw it. "What is it?"

"A fly," said Robert.

"Don't let him fool you, baby."

"Son — " said Father, "what kind of fly is it?"

"Are you crazy?" said Mother.

"Not so fast," said Father, "what kind of fly is it?"

"A drowned fly," said Robert.

"A drowned fly," said Father.

"Why should he look at a drowned fly?" said Mother.

Father didn't answer. He held the glass close to his face and blew on the fly as if to cool it. It rocked on the water but nothing happened.

"You would agree the fly is drowned?" his father asked.

"Don't agree to anything, baby."

"I'm going to hold this fly under water," said Father, "while you go and bring your father a saucer and a saltcellar."

"Don't you do it," said Mother.

"Obey your father," said Father.

Robert put his mother's hairpins in her lap and went back through the club room, the dining room, the game room, through the swinging door into the kitchen. Callie's metal saltcellar sat on the stove, where the heat kept it dry. He sprinkled some on the floor, crunched on it, then carried it back through the house to his father.

"Where's the saucer?" Father said.

"They're not for flies," said Mother. She took the ashtray from her dresser and passed it to Robert. Father used his silver pencil to push the fly to the edge of the glass, then fish it out. A drowned fly. It lay on its back, its wings stuck to the ashtray.

"This fly has been in the water twenty minutes," said Father. "That's a lot longer than your Mr. Brady."

"What did you drown him for?" asked Robert.

"I got the urge," said Father. "Cost me a drink!"

"It's probably a *her*," Mother said. "If it drowns, it's a her."

Father took the blotter from Mother's writing table and used one corner of it to pick up the fly. The drowned fly made a dark wet spot on the blotter. "Mumbo-jumbo, abra-cadabra — " chanted Father. "Your father will now bring the fly to life!" He put the blotter with the fly on the ashtray, then sprinkled the fly all over with salt. He kept sprinkling until the salt covered the fly like snow.

"My God, what next?" said Mother.

"It is now twenty-one minutes past five," said Father, and held out his watch so Robert could read it.

"Twenty-two minutes," said Robert.

"It was twenty-one when I started," said Father. "It was twenty-two when we had him covered. It takes a while for the magic to work."

"What magic?"

"Bringing the dead to life," said Father. He took one of Mother's cork-tipped cigarettes, lit it with her lighter, then swallowed the smoke.

"It's not coming out your ears," Emily said.

"That's another trick," said Father, "not this one." He swallowed more smoke, then he held the glowing tip of the cigarette very close to the fly. From where she sat Mother threw her brush at him and it skidded on the floor. "What we need is some light on the subject," said Father, "but more light than that." He looked around the room to the lamp Mother used to make her face brown. "Here we are," said Father, and pulled the lamp over. He held it so the green blotter and the salt were right beneath it. Robert could not see the fly. The brightness of the light made the green look blue. "Feel that!" said Father, and put his face beneath it.

"My God, you look like a turkey gobbler," Mother said.

"When you get my age — " Father began.

"What makes you think I'm going to get your age?" said Mother.

"Well, well — " Father said, "did you see it?"

"What?" said Robert.

"At sixty-two years of age," said Father, "I find my eye is sharper than yours. You know why?"

"Tell him your mother knows why," said Mother.

"You know why?" Father said. "I have trained myself to look out the corner of my eye. Out of the corner we can detect the slightest movement. With the naked eye we can pick up the twitch of a fly."

"How your father's taste has changed!" cried Mother.

Up through the salt, like the limb of a snowman, appeared the leg of the fly. "Look! Look!" cried Robert.

"Four minutes and twenty seconds," said Father. "Brought him around in less time than it took to drown him." The fly used his long rear legs like poles to clean off the snow. Using his naked eyes just like Father, Robert could see the hairs on the legs, like brushes. He used them like dusting crumbs from the table. He began to wash off his face, like a cat. "Five minutes and forty seconds so far," said Father.

"Does he know who he is?" asked Robert.

"The salt soaked up the water," said Father, and used the silver pencil to tip the fly to his feet. The fly buzzed but didn't fly anywhere. He buzzed like he felt trapped.

"How many times can he do it?" said Robert.

"A good healthy fly," said Father, "can probably come back four or five times."

"Don't he get tired?" Robert said.

"You get tired of anything," Father said, picked up the fly, and dropped him back into the drink. He just lay there, floating on the top. He didn't buzz.

"He's pooped," said Emily.

"Pooped?" said Father. "Where did she hear that?' Mother was looking at her face close to the mirror. Father pushed the fly under the water but he didn't buzz. "No reaction," said Father. He put the glass and the ashtray on Mother's dresser. "He's probably an old fly," Father said, "it probably wasn't the first time somebody dunked him."

"What's that?" Mother said. There was a flapping around from the direction of the game room.

"You leave the screen up, son?" Father said. When Robert left the screens up bats flew into the house because it was dark. They had flown so close to Robert the wind of their wings had ruffled his hair. Her golden hair fanned out on her shoulders, Mother went to the hall door and threw it open. The flapping sound stopped.

"Callie!" Mother called. "Is that you, Callie?"

"You crazy?" said Father. "Her lungs are full of water. She almost drowned."

"What a lunch!" said Mother. "You ever see anything like it? If I know her she just won't stand it."

There was a wheezing sound, then suddenly music. Through the dark beyond his mother, across the tile-floored room, Robert could see the keys of the piano playing.

"My God, it's him!" said Mother. "It's the lover!"

Father got up from the bed and put the robe with the dragons around her shoulders. He used both hands to lift her hair from inside it. Mother crossed the hall, her robe tassels dragging, to where the cracked green blinds were drawn at the windows. "You poor darling!" she cried, jerking on the blind cords. "How can you see in the dark?" When the blind zipped up, Robert could see the lover sitting on the bench at the player piano. His legs pumped. He gripped the sides of the bench so he wouldn't slip off. He wore his hat but his laces were untied and slapped the floor when he pumped.

"Now how'd he get in *there?*" said Father. "How explain that?"

"Go right on pumping," Mother said, "play as long as you like."

She stooped to read the label on the empty roll box. " 'The Barcarolle'! Imagine!"

"It's not," said Robert.

"I'd like to have it explained," Father said. "The only closed-up room in the house."

"It's not 'The Barcarolle,' " said Robert.

"I know, baby," said Mother. She stood with the empty roll box at the verandah window looking at the lovers' statue in the bird bath. Kissing. One of her orioles splashed them. Across the pond there were cars parked in Mrs. Van Zant's driveway and some of the Japanese lanterns were glowing.

"If only she was here to hear it," Mother said.

Robert said, "She likes it better when you play it backward."

"If only she was here to see it!" Mother said.

"She's seen it every summer since the war," said Father.

"Oh no you don't," said Mother. "It's just once you see it."

"Now you see it, now you don't, eh?" said Father. He rubbed his palms together. "When do we eat? Guess I'll go wash my hands."

Mr. Brady, the lover, sat in the covered wicker chair with the paper napkin and the plate in his lap. He wore his hat. He sat looking at Mrs. Van Zant's Japanese lanterns. Out on the pond was a boy in a red inner tube, splashing. Mrs. Van Zant's husband walked around beneath the lanterns, screwing in bulbs.

"All right, all right," Mother said, "but I'm not going to sit on these iron chairs."

"They were your prescription," Father said.

"Not to sit on." Mother spread her napkin on the floor, sat on it. She spread her golden hair on the wicker-chair arm.

"Listen to this," Father said, "rain tonight and tomorrow morning. Turning cool late tonight with moderately cool westerly winds." Father wet his finger and put up his hand. "Southwesterly," he said.

"Tell your father how we need him," Mother said.

"What about his h-a-t?" Father said.

"Don't you think he can s-p-e-l-l?" said Robert.

"Your father never takes anything for granted," Mother said.

"I don't want him forming habits," Father said, "that he's going to find hard to break when he's better."

"I don't think he's hungry," Mother said. "He's thinking about her. I know it."

"Asked him if he'd like a drink. Said he doesn't drink. Asked him if he'd like to smoke. Said he doesn't smoke."

"What's your father mumbling now?"

"A man has to do something — " Father said.

"Which would you rather be — " said Robert, "a rabbit or a hare?"

The lover stood up and spilled his pizza on the floor.

"You can just go and get me another plate," Mother said, and gave the lover the one she was holding. He sat down in the chair and held it in his lap.

"Asked him if he played rummy. He shook his head. Asked him if he played bridge. He shook his head. Suppose you ask him if he can do anything."

"Tell your father how we love him," Mother said.

"I don't care what his field is," Father said, "whether it's stocks and bonds, insurance, or religion. It doesn't matter what it is, a man has to do something. Smoke, drink, play the ponies — he has to do *some*thing."

"I never heard a sorrier confession," Mother said.

Robert sang —

Star light, star bright
First star I seen tonight

"Wouldn't that be *saw?*" Father said.

"SSSShhhhhhh — " said Mother. Across the lake Mrs. Van Zant's loudspeaker was saying something. Mrs. Van Zant's voice came across the water, the people clapped, the drummer beat his drums. More of the Japanese lanterns came on.

"If I don't love the Orient," Mother said.

"You didn't when we were there," Father said. The drummer beat his drums, stopped, and the music played.

"How old is Sylvia now?" Mother said.

"You don't know?" said Father. "Or you don't want to know? She's your first one, right? That makes her fifteen this summer."

"I don't know as it matters," Mother said. "The right time is whenever it happens. Heaven knows I was just a little fool when it happened to me."

"I wasn't so smart myself," Father said.

"If my mother had been like some people," Mother said, "she would have locked me in the bedroom, or shipped me off to Boston, or some place like that to a boarding school. But she *knew* — she knew the right time is whenever it happens."

"You talking to me, by chance?" Father said.

"I can honestly say — " Mother said, "I knew what it was the minute I saw her. I knew what it was the minute she came in the house. I knew what it was — I felt the whole business all over again."

"Just what's going on here?" Father said.

Robert jumped up from the steps and ran into the trees. He ran up and down, back and forth, up and down. He ran around and around the lovers in the bird bath. He stopped running and sang —

Beans, beans, the musical fruit
The more you eat, the more you toot.

"You hear that?" said Father.

"Baby — " Mother said, "we don't sing songs like that."

"I feel it — " Robert said. "I feel it — I feel it!"

"I know, baby," Mother said, "but we don't sing it."

"WHY?" Robert shouted.

"It doesn't show your breeding," Mother said. Robert stopped jumping up and down and looked across the lake. The Japanese lanterns were waving and the colors were on the water. The music played.

"Time for Amos and Andy," Father said. The music stopped. A man sang —

The moon was all aglow
And the devil was in your eyes.

"Fifteen is fifteen — " Mother said.

"Robert is eight!" Robert said, and ran up and down, up and down, up and down. The man sang —

How deep is the o-shun
How high is the skyyyy
How great my de-voshun
I'll tell you no lie —

"You ever hear anything like that?" said Father.

"Let it happen when it happens," Mother said, "and whatever else, they can't take it from you." Mother laughed.

Father stood up and walked to the edge of the porch. "You want to make yourself sick? Stop that fool running. You've just had your supper." Robert ran into the woods and hid. He hid behind the lovers kissing and peeked at the house. "If you people will excuse me — " Father said, and went inside. He walked down the hardwood floor and turned the radio on, loud.

"You want to be foolish, too?" Mother said.

"No — " Emily said.

"Go be foolish anyhow," Mother said, so Emily ran from the porch and around the sprinkler on the lawn. She ran through the sprinkler and into the trees and splashed her hands in the bird bath, splashing the lovers, splashing Robert in the face. Robert chased her back and forth on the lawn. Robert chased her through the trees, through the garden weeds, and down the cinder path to the pier. He chased her out on the pier and caught her out on the diving board. "Let go of me, you beast!" she said. He let her go.

"What are they doing?" he said.

"They are kissing," she said.

"They are not kissing!" he said.

"They are lovers!" she said, and almost pushed him into the water. Then she ran down the pier and into the grove, around and around the lovers with him behind her, until he caught her and smeared the fresh green slime in her hair. Then they ran around and around the lovers, around the sprinkler, around the verandah, until he caught her and they wrestled in the weeds. They stopped wrestling and lay quiet, listening. The man sang —

I walked into an April shower
I stepped into an open door
I found a million-dollar baby
In the five-and-ten-cent stoooore

"Ba-by — " Mother said. "Oh ba-by, come and play us something."

"See — " she said, and Robert rolled over, spit in her hair. Then he got up and ran around the house.

The light was on in the music room. From the steps of the verandah he could see the gold-fish bowl, the fairy castle, the lamp with the marble base, and the golden braid tassels on the shade. Beyond the lamp he could see part of the lover in the wicker chair.

"You like it fast or you like it slow?" Robert said.

"We like it slow," Mother said, and Robert moved the lever. He held onto the bench and played "Isle of My Golden Dreams." He played it forward, slow, then he played it backward, fast.

"Don't get in your mother's hair, pet — " Mother said.

Robert played "Officer of the Day." He played it forward, fast, then he played it backward, very slow.

"They're playing your song, baby — " Mother said. "Listen to the man singing your song." The man sang —

You're the cream in my coffee
You're the salt in my stew
You will always be
My ne-cess-ity
I'd be lost without youuuuu

When the man stopped singing, Robert played *William Tell.* He played it backward, very, very slow.

"Oh Ralph — !" Mother said. "Will you speak to your son?" Robert played "It's a Long Way to Tipperary," forward and backward very fast. Mother came in from the verandah and knocked on the folding doors. She tried the folding doors but they wouldn't move.

"You said those doors didn't work," Father said. Father was sitting at his desk with his eyeshade on. He was looking through his magnifying glass at some of his stamps. Mother kicked on the doors. "Now there's no need to get excited — " Father said. Mother went around through the club room and tried the other door.

"Will you unlock this door?" Mother said. Robert played very loud. "Baby — " Mother said, "you know what your mother is going to do?" "Son — " Father said, "you hear what your mother said?"

"You know what Mother's going to do? All right — " she said, "we'll see who likes to be locked in. We'll see who's best at this business of being locked in." Mother went back through the club room, the dining room, and across the hall to her own bedroom door. She opened the door, went in, turned the key in the lock. They could hear her slam the doors to the garden, turn the keys in the locks.

"Now you see what you've done?" Father said. "You know what you are doing to your mother?" Father pounded on the door.

"Tell your father to please go away," Mother said.

"Go to your mother," Father said to Robert. "Your mother is not well. Go to your mother." So he went back through the club room, and the dining room, and knocked at Mother's door.

"It's me, Mother — " he said. Mother opened the door and let him in. She kicked her shoes off and went back and lay down on the bed. "You love your mother?"

"Yes, Mother — "

"Yes, Mother, yes Mother, yes Mother, yes Mother, yes Mother," his mother said.

"Oh Eva — ?" his father said.

"Your father has the brains of a fish," Mother said.

"I got him stopped," Father said. "You hear? I got him stopped."

"Jabber, jabber, jabber, jabber, jabber — " said Mother.

"He's stopped," Father said. "Why don't you just relax?"

"Why don't I have a stroke?" Mother said. "Why don't I have a stroke and let you spoon feed me?"

"You're distraught," Father said.

"It's a plain simple question," Mother said. "You're a great one for plain simple questions."

"I wash my hands — " Father said, rubbing his palms.

"For the love of mud," said Mother, "go away!"

Father went away. Mother got up from the bed and took a seat on the stool where she had three faces in the mirrors. She put on jar number one and rubbed it in with her fingers. She looked at what she had done and wiped it off with tissue. She put on jar number two, in big thick gobs, and just let it run.

As if he were outside and wanted in, Robert said, "Knock, knock, knock."

"Yes, love," said Mother.

Robert put out his fists and said, "Which hand do you take?"

Mother looked at him in one of her mirrors. "You wouldn't fool your mother, baby?"

"Go on, choose," said Robert.

Mother turned on the stool to look at his fists, one green with slime.

"Pollywogs again!"

"You got to choose," he said.

Mother closed her eyes and chose his clean fist. She opened her eyes and looked at what he held in his palm.

"Sugar? Ain't I sweet enough, baby?"

"Why don't you taste it," he said, "it's not sugar."

She held his palm close to her face, sniffed at it, then flicked her tongue at it.

"Salt!" she shouted. "What does your mother want with salt?"

Robert just stood there with the salt in his palm.

At the door Father said, "You two have to shout? I'm going to take him for a walk. Little walk to the village. He's got to do something. The only thing left for him to do is to walk."

Father went away. Through the French doors his mother looked across the pond at the Japanese lanterns and the people dancing. The music came in. Mother said, "That one. What's that?"

"It's not 'The Barcarolle,' " said Robert. Mother picked up her brush and stroked it slowly through her golden hair. The electricity crackled. It would lift from her shoulders to be near the brush.

"Do something for your mother, baby." He waited to see what it was. "Go sprinkle it on your father," she said, and turned to give him a hug.

PHILIP F. O'CONNOR

The Gift Bearer

(FROM THE SOUTHERN REVIEW)

UNCLE DAVE HAD a great knot of a nose, scarlet and bumpy, and he visited us about twice a year. On his last visit, the one I remember best, he brought, as was his habit, a gift for each of us: for my mother "a little thing for the house," a flat package wrapped in brown paper and twine which she sniffed at and hummed over (unappreciatively, I thought) and then put on the top shelf of the kitchen cupboard; for my father a heavy carton which he and my uncle removed carefully from the trunk of his Model A, carried to the basement and placed delicately under the little workbench; and for me a stack of comic books, mostly Walt Disney's, which were all wrinkled like the magazines and comic books at the town's barber shop.

After handing my mother and me our gifts, he rubbed his hands briskly together, looked from one of us to the other, said loudly, "I hope all present are happy and well," then sat down to supper, the meal for which he had arrived, as usual, just in time. Before we finished eating he reached across the table and scratched the top of my head with his rough fingers. "It's a short life, Jackie," he said, "and time we made the best of it."

The remark, which he always made sooner or later after entering the house, was like a signal for my mother to start the dishes and my father to say, "Shall we take a little spin around the neighborhood, Dave?" It was magic in a way, for it never failed to set my parents kind of invisibly apart, where they remained until his visit ended.

"Make the best of it," my mother repeated mockingly to my father after the two men had returned from their spin and Dave had gone to bed. "He's the last man on earth to be talking about making the best of anything."

My father, on a wooden chair in the narrow space between a cupboard and the kitchen window, only grunted uneasily and said, "Give the man a chance, will you? Give him a bit of a chance."

"A chance," she said derisively from the sink, where she picked up a wet dishcloth and began, fiercely, to wring it dry. "Isn't that a laugh? He's frittered away most of his sixty-two years doing you-know-what and now you talk about giving him a chance." She looked at me over her shoulder and clicked her tongue disgustedly. "Did you hear that, Jackie? Give the man a chance?"

I wasn't about to take sides. Taking sides might have meant a commitment for the duration of my uncle's stay, offering moral and other kinds of support to the parent with whom I allied myself, cutting myself off from the other. At nine years I still felt too unsteady to stand without the security of both pillars. I only nodded politely.

My father was gazing at the fading red design on the linoleum, his shoulders down, looking smaller and thinner than he really was. "I don't know," he said weakly. "If you ask me it's an awfully poor way to talk about your own flesh and blood."

She pulled the string on the small light above the sink and turned around, crossing her arms beneath her large breasts. "Where did you two go after supper?" she said coldly. The only light now in the kitchen shone from the hall, fell full on her, making her, a big woman to begin with, seem whitely enormous.

"We just drove out to the edge of town to get a look at those new houses that're going up."

"Did you?"

"We did."

"And that's all?"

"Ah, well. Nearly all." My father, who had been reduced to a shadow in the diminished light, twisted uncomfortably.

"You stopped at Henry's, I'll wager."

"For a drop is all."

"By the watery eyes of you it was more than a drop."

No sound issued from the corner.

"I will not have a repeat of what happened at the train station last year." She spoke severely. "Not that or anything approaching it."

"How," said my father in tremulous voice, "did you learn about that?"

"It isn't any of your business, but if you must know it was one of the ladies in the sodality. She was waiting for the four-twenty to San Francisco and witnessed the whole thing. I nearly fell down dead when she told me. Imagine! Singing in public with your arms up!" She gave me a guilty look, seeming to realize she'd said a little more than she wanted me to hear.

"It — it wasn't as bad as she made out."

"Hah! And how do you know, not having heard her?"

"I — I can imagine."

"I'm sure it takes little imagining."

"Well, it was only once. I never did anything like it before or since."

"Nor ever will again if I have anything to say about it." She turned to him, scowling. "If I get a whiff of that poison in the next few days, he's going out of here, bag and baggage." My father started to reply, but she cut him off — "Him, or me and Jackie!" — and rumbled off to bed.

My father shook his head as though it weighed a ton, pulled himself up and started slowly for the door. He let out a sigh and mumbled, "A fella'd have to be made of steel to put up with the likes of her." He shuffled into the hall, looking more like rubber than steel.

The next morning I was sitting on the edge of the bathtub watching, fascinated, as my uncle shaved with his thick-handled brush, straight razor, and black mug, which had D. O'G. (for David O'Gorman) in fancy gold letters painted on the front and contained soap that smelled like a mountain. I heard the door open and turned to see my father bend low, raise his hand to his mouth and whisper cautiously, "Mag's on the warpath. Don't touch a drop 'til I get home. Not a drop."

Dave, with brush poised at the tip of his chin, had raised his head like a person who's just heard a suspicious sound in his basement. He stood very still until after my father, giving him an apologetic look, had shut the door. Then he reached up slowly and with thumb and forefinger squeezed the remaining soap out of his brush, sending it — splat! — perfectly into the hole at the bottom of the sink. His sole comment.

I knew war was unavoidable. I knew it as well as I knew what was in the carton in the basement or why my father's eyes were glassy or why the neighborhood only interested him when Dave was present. I knew it because I knew the reason for my mother's ultimatum the night before. I had witnessed the incident at the train station. I had, in fact, borne the memory of it like a hidden sore for nearly a year.

I was returning along the railroad tracks from the town's baseball diamond one Saturday afternoon when I heard a voice up ahead of me, a voice I recognized, calling out, "C'mon now, every one of you join in with us. Sure, you only live once!" I looked up, stunned, to see Uncle Dave and my father standing on the station platform. It was Dave who had spoken, and now my father raised his hands and started waving them like a spastic orchestra leader. Before I could move or even think, the two of them started singing, in grating counterpoint, the first few verses of "Sweet Rose of Dublin." No one joined them. In fact, the onlookers seemed disgusted, except for one or two men, who were smiling. By the time I had run, humiliated, behind a tree not far from the tracks, the two had stopped their attempts to form a choral group and were on their way across the street to the place called Henry's, which, until then, I had thought was only a restaurant.

It was the first time I'd seen either Dave or my father behaving peculiarly, and it so horrified me that I got sick on the way home and threw up behind a neighbor's hedge. I went to bed soon after that and I wept into the night, into many nights in fact. I never said anything to my mother, for I was afraid her reaction would be as fierce as mine, or worse. I was relieved now to learn that she'd found out what had happened, though I knew it must have been terrible for her.

Dave and I sat on the front-porch swing late that afternoon, waiting for my father to come down the street from work. The brisk western breeze, cutting between mountains that separated our little valley from the Pacific, made the wisteria branches rattle against eaves and crept across the porch, cooling us after a very warm day. It was a nice afternoon for a conversation.

"Uncle Dave," I said, after we'd been going squeakily forward and back for several minutes, "is it all right if I ask you a question?"

He put the palm of his thick hand on my knee and said, very seriously, "Do you know what uncles were made for?"

I told him I didn't.

"Hah," he said, making the swing stop, "I thought you didn't. Well, I'll tell you." He inhaled noisily and let the air out by opening and closing his mouth with little popping sounds. "Uncles," he said, "were made to answer questions." He looked down at me, smiling. "You didn't know that, eh?"

"No," I said, shaking my head. "Nobody ever told me."

He made a clicking sound with his tongue. "I wonder what sort of things they teach in school these days, if it isn't what uncles are for?"

I started reeling off some of my school subjects, but he wasn't listening.

"It's a shame," he said, "an unforgiveable shame." He inhaled once more and once more popped the air out. "I've always thought it a crime you weren't born and raised in the old country. Everything is different, *ev*-verything. The weather, the schools, the people. *Ev*-verything."

I believed him. Listening to him and my father and even my mother when they spoke about Ireland, I longed to visit there. From what I'd gathered there were a lot of hills, and the children spent more time in the hills than in schools or churches, and they weren't always (as I increasingly was) told to excel in this or that; they just sort of made their own way at their own pace and spent the evenings around the kitchen fire listening to their parents and their relatives and the neighbors tell stories about saints appearing and about banshees and leprechauns, the kind of stories I only heard when Dave came to our house.

He sat quietly for a few minutes, then said, "Did I ever tell you the time we were caught in the rowboat out in St. George's Channel during a storm, my two friends and I?"

"Yes." (One of the friends clung to the overturned boat while Dave and the other swam two, four or six miles — depending on the telling — for help. Unfortunately, about halfway to land the other swimmer collapsed and Dave had to pull him along. As, weakened by the extra weight, Dave was about to go under with his load, he spotted a fishing boat in the distance. It was quite far away, and the storm was making an awful howl. Still he called, louder than he could have imagined the human voice being able to cry out. "The sound," he said, "seemed to flatten the swells." Again and again he called. Finally the little boat turned toward them. Eventually all three of them were picked up and saved. "You'll notice," he always said when he came to the end of the story, "that I have a very deep voice." I would nod, for it was true, deep and penetrating with a crack of finality to it. "Well, I got that by calling out to the fishing boat.") "You told me this story," I said, "but I would like to hear it again." I looked at his broad hands and hard round forearms and wondered if those, too, had resulted from his adventures at sea.

He told me the story again, but he hurried through it, leaving out several parts. When he finished, he glanced through the vines toward the corner of the street. "What time does your daddy usually get home?" he said with a touch of impatience.

"Quarter to six," I said.

He frowned. "I thought it was five-thirty."

"No." I was certain. "Quarter to six."

He started to push the swing forward and back. As he did so he slipped his hand into a front pants pocket and removed a large round watch, one I always liked seeing and holding because it had very black numbers on the face and ticked very loudly, so loudly you could hear it when it was in his pocket. "It's only fifteen apast five," he said disgustedly.

"Maybe you have time to tell me a story, then."

Pop pop. His mouth was at it. He wasn't listening to me. Pop pop. He took out his watch again, just to make sure.

"Uncle Dave?"

"Eh?"

"Do you have time for a story?"

The swing stiffened against my back. Uncle Dave let out a long dreary sigh. At last he said, "All right, all right," and he told a story.

He told it with a terrible rapidity but with a terrible intensity too. From the way he spoke I doubt if he left out even a phrase:

There was a farming man from the town of Ballyanne who had only one pleasure in his life, and that pleasure was spending a single evening out of every week at a well-known gathering place, one where the conversation was always marked with good cheer and happiness. The woman he lived with, however (She was said by some to be his wife, though the man himself was never known to admit it.), took a foul view of his one simple joy and sought to put a stop to it. She claimed to the parish priest and others bent on taking her side that the man was spending all their money and returning home in a hard and vicious mood to rebuke her at every opportunity. He denied the charges, of course, pointing out that the woman ("Look at the size of her," he said.) clearly ate well on the money he made. He added that all the little visits did was loosen the muscles in his tongue which had gone tight after six days of living with her do's and don'ts. It was quite an argument and there was little question in the minds of most of the townspeople as to who was right and who was wrong. After hearing both sides, the great majority of them spoke the cause of the man, many of them saying they'd never known him to open his mouth except in laughter and song. This blackguardly woman, however, was not to be stopped. She devised a scheme which she thought would once and for all put an end to his happy excursions. Recalling that he had a terrible fear of ghosts, she planned a little surprise for him and fixed the location for it in a small cemetery he had to pass on his way to and from the village. As he was coming home late one night he saw, rising up from one of the graves that had just been dug near the road, a ghastly figure as if from another world. It was dressed all in white and crying out in terrible anguish. "'I am so cold and lonely," said the headless creature in a mysterious voice. It was, of course, none other than the woman herself. In trying to scare him forever from his weekly pleasure, however, she had neglected to take into account one small but not widely known fact: among other things that his weekly trips loosened in the man was his fear of the unknown. As with speech and his woman, so did they liberate him from the terror of ghosts. It was, indeed, a bad miscalculation on the woman's part, for the man only looked calmly at the strange figure and said, "It's no wonder you're cold and lonely. You haven't been properly buried." With that he rushed over and picked up the gravedigger's shovel and furiously began to fill in the deep grave. As the dirt came down upon her the woman shouted, "Stop, Jerry! It's me! It's only me!" but the man kept shoveling. As the dirt began to cover up her legs she cried out, "Don't you hear me at all? Don't you hear me?" The man, giving no sign of hearing anything, moved like a fiend and did not stop until the noisy creature was all covered up. Some say it was because of the drink that he didn't hear and others say his ears had long since gone deaf to the sound of the woman's voice. No one knows for sure. What is known is that she was neither seen nor heard from since. And the man thereafter spent many a happy night in the village with his companions.

It was a wonderful story, and I was about to tell him so when he stirred, reaching into his pocket, pulling out his watch, looking. "Good," he said, "good. Twenty minutes to." He glanced down at me. "Where's your mother now?"

"In the bank yard, I think, taking down some wash." I had heard the screen door bang closed and then the clothesline begin squeaking.

"Ah, fine," he said. "Now you go in the kitchen and open the icebox." He flicked his fingers, signaling me to get up. "Take the chunk of ice I knocked off the big block after lunch today and carry it down to the basement. Put it in the pan I left on your father's tool bench." He pointed to the front door. "Hurry now, hurry!"

I did just what he said.

When I got back to the porch, he was looking up the street, where my father had just turned the corner and was walking toward us.

"God, it's a wonderful cool afternoon, isn't it?" Dave said, noticing me at his side.

The question, his happy tone, caught me by surprise.

"You did what I asked you to, didn't you?" he went on.

I told him I had.

He put his hand on the back of my neck as we stood watching my father, who seemed to be picking up speed. He said, "I seem to remember that our little conversation of a few minutes ago began with you about to ask me a question." He took his eyes from my father long enough to look down at me. "What was it?"

I thought for a few moments, recalled it had something to do with them singing at the train station last year but couldn't remember the details. "I don't know," I said.

"It must be a question that oughtn't be asked." He sounded like a bishop making an important pronouncement.

"Hey, John," he called as my father neared the front yard. "Go in the basement quiet as a mouse and we'll have a quick one before you take off your hat. It's been an awful long day."

My father looked down the driveway to the back yard, I guess to make sure my mother hadn't heard Dave's instructions, and then, taking no chances calling back, raised his hand with thumb and forefinger forming a circle, flicked it at Dave, and rushed toward the basement door.

"Atta boy," said Uncle Dave breathlessly, and he turned and hurried across the porch and down the front stairs.

They didn't make it upstairs to supper. My mother took their absence with surprising calm. As we waited in the kitchen, listening to them get louder and louder just below us, she only tapped the big wooden spoon she had been using to prepare the meal against the edge of the sink and made occasional hissing sounds. Finally she looked at me and said, "Where did he catch him, on the way down the street?"

I nodded, knowing how disappointed she must have felt at not intercepting my father before my uncle had. When she got to him first, there was a good chance he'd keep himself from the basement or the jaunt through "the neighborhood." Around Dave he seemed to have no will, or maybe it was only a different sort of will.

"I thought it wouldn't happen 'til tomorrow," she said, as much to herself as to me. "He usually holds off for a couple of days trying to get on the good side of me." She was, of course, speaking of Dave. She sounded as though she wasn't going to let their vanishing act disturb her at all.

She remained calm for only a short time, however. When supper was ready, she smacked the head of the spoon loudly against the sink and sputtered, "There'll be retribution for this. There'll be retribution." She turned off the burner under the pot of stew that had been simmering all day. "Sit down," she said to me, "and eat your supper."

Later that evening, on the pretext of going to the baseball diamond near our home to watch the older boys play ball, I circled to the back yard determined to get my first look at the clandestine undertaking that was causing so much trouble.

I crept along the wall at the back of the house until I came to a small window looking in on the brightly lit corner where they sat.

My father was on the stool before his workbench. (He had only a few tools — a hammer, a screwdriver, a hacksaw, and a pair of pliers — all nailed awkwardly to the wall behind the bench.) He gripped, on the workbench, a large green bottle, which was, it seemed to me, about two-thirds full. In the hand which rested on his lap was a small glass from which, as he spoke to Dave, there dropped — plunk plunk — little splashes of whisky.

Dave himself was a few feet away in a kitchen chair on the concrete floor, looking up at my father. Dave's glass was nearly full, but he held it straight without even looking at it and not a drop was spilling. Between his feet was the pan of ice I had taken from the kitchen, only now the ice was smaller and floating in its own water. I put my ear very close to the window so as to hear what my father, whose mouth was moving with unusual speed, was saying.

"If she were to open that door right now, do you know what I'd tell her, Dave?"

Uncle Dave gave an inquisitive grunt.

"I'd say, 'There are certain portions of a home that are to be the man's alone. And certain times of the day when he is to be left to do what he wants. And certain companions he's to enjoy by himself.' I'd also say, 'There's no one! Not you! Not the Pope! Not Jesus himself! No one who can ever change that!' I'd say, 'These are as much a part of being a man as, as the hair on his face!' " He raised his glass to his lips, took a sip and gave a confident little nod. "That's what I'd say."

"God," said Dave, shaking his white-capped head in unrestrained appreciation, "if I thought you had it in you, I'd be greatly encouraged. Greatly."

"Well, I do. As sure as your sitting there. As sure as that." He raised his forefinger generally toward the top of the basement stairs. "All she has to do is open that door."

I was troubled at hearing my father speak of my mother as though she were bent on taking from him all the things he cared about. It bothered me, too, that he had certain times and places and friends (not including me) he wanted only for himself. (I'd suspected as much but only now had had it confirmed.) It shocked me to see his eyes dancing about madly, and his hands moving strangely, and his voice with a roughness in it I'd never known. But more than all this, I was desperately curious. I peered through the window, as though, looking harder, I would find the key to the horrible scene I was witnessing

Dave was speaking. "They say the curse of the Irish is whisky." The mention of the word "whisky" seemed to remind him what was in his glass, for he paused, looked down and then, in one unbelievable gulp, swallowed the entire contents. "Boowahhh! But it's not whisky at all. Do you know what it really is?"

"I think I do."

"It's woman, that's what it is."

"Dead right on the money. Here." My father brought the bottle forward and refilled Dave's upraised glass. "From the womb to the tomb," he said. He then filled his own.

I noticed for the first time that my father still had his hat on. It was tilted back on his balding head like the hat of a college boy I'd seen in an advertisement for a movie about the twenties. Everything I now observed set him farther apart from me. It struck me that if I knelt at that window long enough he would, Jekyll and Hyde, soon become completely unrecognizable. College boy indeed! How ridiculous he began to seem. I wanted to crash through the window and put a stop to everything.

They sat quietly for quite a while before my father spoke again, this time with a new weariness. "But it's life and we have to accept it. If you know that, you're ahead of the game. Am I right or wrong?"

My uncle shrugged and took another long swallow.

"Ah, it's the truth, Dave, and we're all better with knowing it."

Dave did not reply. He seemed to be getting very uncomfortable, fidgeting, looking nervously about the basement, which was completely dark except for the small space around the workbench, fixing his eyes finally on the carton beneath the bench.

I saw now, as I looked at it along with Dave, that the cardboard flaps were pulled all the way back and that it was full of bottles. Rather, nearly full, for one bottle, the one they were drinking from, was missing. Whisky, as my mother had often reminded my father, was terribly expensive. Looking at that carton I thought Dave must be very rich. I really didn't know, however.

What I knew about Dave was that he had run away from his home in Ireland as a youth, had worked with his hands all his life, and had never married. He now lived alone in Bakersfield (or was it Santa Barbara?), sold used furniture (or was it cars?), came to visit us once or twice a year, brought gifts and got in trouble with my mother for leading my father astray. My own great uncle but still a very mysterious man.

"I can't agree at all," Dave said at last. "You go around accepting all the malarky they give you, and you aren't but a shred of a man anymore." He knocked off his last glassful — "Booowahhh!" — and looked steadily at my father.

"Ah, well," said my father even more wearily, "maybe you're right, maybe you're right. I've never had it completely figured out."

My uncle smiled and said, "I don't think either one of us is going to solve the problems of the world sitting here. Let's go down and see how business is holding up at Hen-e-ry's."

"Now there's something," said my father, straightening his hat, "over which there can be no debate."

They went out the side door laughing.

I walked slowly upstairs and found my mother in the living room. She was listening to a program of Irish music from San Francisco and sewing a patch on the elbow of one of my flannel shirts. "They're gone for the night," she said. "I just heard the two of them giggle their way through the door beneath me. Did you happen to pass them on the street?"

I said no and then kissed her good night, more tenderly than I had kissed her in months.

I had no idea when they returned from Henry's, but knew it must have been very late, for Uncle Dave didn't get up until nearly noon, and my father remained in his bedroom even later than that. Luckily it was Saturday, and my father did not have to go to work.

My first look at Dave convinced me that, for all the apparent joy in drinking, its aftermath was Hell itself. I found him in the kitchen when I came in for lunch. A trembling apparition, he was standing in the doorway, his nose virtually aflame, his eyes buried deep in his swelled-up face. He was looking at my mother, who was on a little stool at the sink peeling turnips, and ignoring him. As I closed the screen door and headed for the sandwich my mother had set out for me on the table, he clapped his hands together and his mouth cracked open in a brave attempt to smile. "Well," he said, looking from my mother to me, "it seems like another warm one. I don't see a trace of clouds."

I smiled back at him, but my mother didn't look up or speak a word. I saw that at his place at the table, as at my father's, nothing was laid out, not even a spoon or a napkin. A little guiltily I raised half of my sandwich and took a bite. I felt like offering Dave a bite, but it didn't seem the thing to do.

"Yes, sir," he said, taking a cautious step into the kitchen, "a good day for me to do a little work on my car." He took another step. "Just as soon as I get a little fuel — heh — to keep me going."

Now my mother spoke, still not looking up. "I'd've thought you'd put enough fuel in you last night to last the rest of the month. That is, if one is able to judge from the noises you and your friend made coming up the steps at half-past two."

"The light was off, Mag. You left the light off, and we couldn't see the stairs. That's all."

"There was more than the light off," she said, taking a heavy swipe at the turnip in her hand, knocking the top completely off.

"And as far as the time goes," Dave said, "I think you'll find it was closer to twelve than two."

"Two thirty-three," she said firmly.

"Is that a fact?" he said. "I wouldn't have guessed."

"What is it you want?" she said in an unfriendly voice. "Apple juice?"

"Tomato." He waved his hand. "Don't you get up now. I'll find it."

"I'm not getting up," she said. "It's at the bottom of the icebox."

"Good, good." He went quickly to the icebox, found the large can of juice, went to the silverware drawer, fumbled about until he found an opener, shakily fiddled with the top of the can until he got it open, looked frantically about — "It's in the cupboard above the icebox," she said — went to the cupboard, took down the bottle of Worchestershire sauce and shook great beads of it into one of the holes in the can. He then put down the bottle and raised the can to his mouth. As my mother watched in disgust, he poured the contents down his throat in a steady brownish-red stream. The gurgling noise was terrible. When he finished he said, "Gahhhd, Mag, that was a life saver!" put the can on top of the icebox, and guided himself shakily toward the hall.

My mother, still on her little chair beside the sink, still peeling, spoke before he reached the doorway. "When are you leaving, Dave?"

"Huh?"

She repeated her question, pausing between each word. "When. Are. You. Leaving?"

"Well, ah . . . I thought I'd stay 'til . . . was planning, that is, to hold on here 'til . . ." As he spoke he looked at her, and seemed to change his statement as he looked. "Maybe tomorrow . . . or Monday . . . eh?" He was still looking. "Or tonight, for that matter, though I . . . wouldn't want to . . ."

"That'll be fine," she said, overturning the collander with the turnip peelings in it. "Tonight."

He gave her a disbelieving look. "But . . . but, Mag," he said, "I just got here . . . after nearly a year." He looked at me. "Hardly a chance to visit with the fine growing boy here." He looked pleadingly back at her. "Or you either." He moved toward her. "Give us a few days more."

"Tonight. Or Jackie and I won't stay in the house." She turned on the tap to wash her peeled turnips. "And that's as final as anything I've ever said."

Though I hadn't expected my mother to be friendly, I was surprised at her iciness, as surprised as I was at Dave's timidity. How strange my world was becoming. Overnight, it seemed, people you thought you knew changed altogether. My father, a mouse in the kitchen, was a lion in the basement. My mother, powerless in the living room, was now in complete command. My uncle, immune to women, was now being stung by one. It was all topsy-turvy, crazy.

It became even crazier when, after lunch, I watched my uncle put a tarpaulin on the dirt driveway, remove his tool kit from the trunk of his car, and then take off several parts of his engine and clean them piece by piece, with a powerful smelling rag. He had cleaned his engine in our driveway on earlier trips but never so carefully, never when he was in such a shaky condition, and never while talking as much as he did that afternoon.

As I stood behind him watching the pieces of the engine fly onto the tarp, he asked me which of the comic books I liked most of all those he'd brought. I told him I hadn't yet had time to read them. He said that that was too bad, for they were a very rewarding batch. I asked him if he had read them. He said that, indeed, he had. It didn't seem right, a white-haired man reading comic books, and I asked him why.

He came from under the hood then, wiped his hands with a rag, changed the socket on his wrench, looked at me and said, "Because I'm a philosopher."

"You are?"

"I am."

"What," I asked, "is that?"

He went back under the hood. "A philosopher," he said, "is a person who speculates on the world. He tries to make sense of things. I'm not very good at it . . . (He grunted, trying to pull loose a stubborn piece of the engine.) . . . but (grunt grunt) I do my best." He sent his hand back. "Give me that hammer there, will you, Jackie?"

I handed him the hammer.

Again he mentioned the comic books. "Now you take Mickey Mouse . . . (bang bang bang) . . . and Donald Duck. The two of them (bang) can . . . (grunt) teach you a lot. For one thing (bang) they're different types. Mickey (bang bang) is a steadier fella than Donald (bang grunt bang). Donald (bang) is . . . (grunt) pretty jumpy, pretty unsteady. The type (grunt) who should never get (bang) married." He came from under the hood without the piece he'd been trying to get, cursed, and threw his hammer and wrench onto the tarp. "Mickey, on the other hand," he said as he wiped his hands, "would make a pretty good husband. He's a kind of dull steady fella. A lad like you might call him 'a good guy.' He'll get his work done, not forget to bring flowers to Minnie, if that's the one he marries, and is a pretty good example for those nephews of his, Morty and Ferdie. But Donald . . ." He bent down and picked up the wrench and hammer again. "Donald should never get married." He shook his head. "No, sirree. Do you know what I'd do if Donald married that Daisy Duck?"

I told him I didn't.

"I'd stop buying those comic books."

He started to go under the hood once more, but hesitated and looked at me. "Now I'm not saying either of them should or shouldn't get married, but it'd be worse for Donald. Understand?" Once more he started to bend, but paused. "Which of the two do you like, Donald or Mickey? I mean if you had to choose?"

I thought about it and said I guessed I liked Donald, which, for some reason, was true.

He slapped me on the shoulder and said, "Atta boy!"

Then he did go under the hood, pulling and banging for a long time and finally let out a string of curses. He came up without the illusive piece he was after and said, "To hell with it." He cleaned the pieces that were on the tarp, put them back in the engine and then returned his tools to the trunk. It took a long time, and he didn't say much, except to curse when a piece didn't go back easily.

On the way into the house he said, "You know, Jackie, talk is talk. It's only good up to a point." He put his hand on my shoulder and said, "It's the same with philosophy. Only good up to a point. Do you know what I mean?"

I didn't and told him so.

"Someday you will," he said. "Someday, God willing."

My father didn't come out of his room until Uncle Dave had nearly finished packing. He stood reeling as my uncle calmly told him my mother had ordered him to leave. The pupils of my father's eyes had gone to tiny dots like the holes in a soda cracker and, as he listened, they seemed to revolve like toy springs rapidly unwinding. I thought they might jump out of his head and pounce on Dave. When my uncle finished speaking he said, "You're going nowhere. She . . . she hasn't the right."

"Never mind," said Dave. "I know when I'm beaten."

"What about our talk last night? Have you forgotten that?"

"No," he said, "but when they're as determined as she is you don't have a chance."

My father ignored him, chugged to the kitchen, scraping the wall, tripping once, moving as if he wasn't sure he was even headed in the right direction. "What's this all about?" he said after shakily turning the corner at the doorway and coming to a quick halt.

She was at the table, elbows on top of it, looking fierce and immovable. Her eyes set themselves on him like clamps.

My father, looking ridiculous in pajamas which were too large and which he'd buttoned unevenly at the top, advanced a tenuous step. "You've no heart," he said. The statement seemed to have a hundred holes, any one of which he could jump out through in a pinch.

She remained a statue.

"Do . . . do you hear me?" he said, pulling up his pajama bottoms, which had begun to slip down.

It wasn't she but Dave's car which sounded in reply. It had started with a couple of backfires in the driveway.

"For God sake," said my father, and, with a panicky look, he grabbed the string of his pajamas, and scrambled through the hall.

In a minute or so, with me right beside him, he was at the window of the Model A. "What the hell are you doing?" he said. "I had her half won over. Stop the engine now and get out of there."

My uncle looked out the car window. "She has us beat." All the spirit I'd felt coming through from him during his talks to me on the porch seemed to have been drained away. He put the car in reverse and with a few clinks and clanks it took him slowly backward into the street.

The widow lady next door had been pruning some of her roses, and now, with the car out of the way, she could see my father in his pajamas. She made a disgusted noise, dropped her shears and ran up her front stairs, slamming the door behind her.

"The wrinkled witch," my father muttered before calling to

Dave, who had turned the car in the street and was about to set off. "Come back here and don't be a fool!"

"Never give up," said Dave enigmatically, waving his hand at us. "You'll see me again. As soon as the climate is better." With a prolonged asthmatic cough the car lurched forward and hippity-hopped toward the corner.

I once more followed my father to the kitchen, where, addressing my mother, who was just as we'd left her, he sounded more definite than he had in days. "I'm camping downstairs until further notice," he said. "No need for you to put my supper on the table either. I'll be eating at Henry's." He turned abruptly and left the kitchen, a lot more steadily than he had a few minutes earlier.

My mother remained right where she was, an open-eyed corpse.

Though my mother a little later returned to her kitchen functions and my father dressed and did a little slow work in the yard, the remainder of the afternoon, for all that passed between them, was as still as a scene in a photograph, and it stayed that way until just before suppertime.

I was in my bedroom catching the end of a San Francisco Seals baseball game on the radio, and my father, who had just taken a mattress and some blankets to the basement, was coming up the stairs to change from work clothes to street clothes for his trip to Henry's. We both must have heard her crying at the same time, for we both arrived in the kitchen together.

She was at the table, but not sitting erect as she had been when my father spoke to her earlier. Her head was down, buried in her arms, and she was sobbing like a little girl. Before her lay brown wrapping paper, open, and at the center of it was something framed.

"What's this about? What's this?" My father crossed the kitchen slowly, me at his heels, and stood beside my mother, not, it seems, knowing what else to say. Finally he looked down at what was on the table.

I looked, too, saw what was in the frame: something written, inscribed in the round handwriting I'd seen on cards and letters sent us by Uncle Dave from time to time, only the writing here was bigger and blacker and neater than the writing on the cards and letters:

There once was a man
alone like the sea
Who went to visit
his loved ones three.

They gave him food
and a place to sleep
And sought, as always
his love to keep.

He prayed in return
and offered thanks
That they'd held him close
within their ranks.

He gave little else,
a few small gifts,
His own way of saying,
"My loneliness lifts."

My mother, gripping the sides of the table, now contained her tears and the girth of her long enough to utter, as if in proclamation, "He's a good man! God knows down deep he's a good man!"

"Ah, well," said my father, putting his hand lightly on her shoulder and running his eyes up the wall as if in search of something. "Ah, well."

She began to sob.

Finally my father spoke. "Don't forget his drinking. You're right to see the danger in that."

"I know, I know," said my mother, "but I shouldn't haven't sent him off the way I did."

They went on speaking to each other in low tones, and I retreated to my room.

I lay down on my bed, sadly, expecting to cry. I lay there until the darkness came through the mountains and hammered itself into the town and the house and the room. I didn't cry. I waited but, for some reason, I didn't cry. Finally I closed my eyes and slept.

I remained asleep until my parents, calling me to supper, startled me out of a dream that, on awakening, I found frightful: Dave was alone at the wheel of his little coupe, on a highway that stretched before him like an endless black ribbon. The car was being rocked by a violent wet storm that lifted and spun it and tossed water against and into it with terrible force. His face, up against the windshield, was etched with horror. Suddenly the car began to shrink, quickly, and soon I could no longer see the figure of my uncle, could only hear him crying frantically out to me to help him. But there was nothing I could do.

Strangely, as I lay there reliving the dream, I began to smile, then laugh, mildly at first and then vigorously, joyfully. I did not understand my reaction, but I remember being struck, a little later, with a thought that, though as powerful and relentless as the storm of my dream, seemed to deny the dream's message. It was a complicated thought, but what it came to was this: In some way my uncle could never be changed, harmed or destroyed, never touched. Never. Though the whole world might turn on him there was this part of him that would hold, go on, with a bump here and a rattle there, but *would go on,* the same, until his death, maybe even afterward, the same, the very same as it had been since I'd known him, since even before that, since his birth and even beyond that, perhaps since time first laid hands on earth. What this part of him was, or whether it was good or bad, remained a mystery to me. I knew only that I had heard it in the rumble in his voice, had seen it in the glowing whiteness of his hair, had felt it in the sharp touch of his eyes. I sensed, too, that it had somehow communicated itself to me, was part of me. I might have remained in my room through the night and the next day considering it and the mystery of it had I not remembered what he'd said about being careful not to take words, or was it thoughts, too seriously.

I got up and went to the kitchen, where I joined my parents for a late supper of boiled beef and cabbage with turnips, a favorite of my father's. He let me sip the ale he and Dave had brought back from Henry's the night before. My mother said I wouldn't have to help her with the dishes. Throughout the meal they smiled at me often and then began to cluck and coo at each other like a couple of sated pigeons. I fell asleep at the table before I'd even finished my dessert, chocolate pudding my mother had fixed especially for me.

TILLIE OLSEN

Requa I

(FROM THE IOWA REVIEW)

IT SEEMED he had had to hold up his head forever. All he wanted was to lie down. Maybe his uncle would let him, there in that strip of pale sun by the redwoods, where he might get warm.

I got those sittin kinks, too, his uncle said, but you don't see *me* staggerin round like an old drunk . . . Here, shake a leg and let's get wood for a fire. Dry pieces if there is any such. I'll catch the fish.

But he had to heave. Again.

How can you have 'ary a shred left to bring up. Remind me not to take you noplace but by streetcar after this . . . Alright, stretch out; you'll see you're feeling better.

Everything slid, moved, as if he were still in the truck. He had been holding up his head forever. The spongy ground squished under him, and the wet of winter and spring rains felt through the tarp. He was lying on the ground, *the ground.* There might be snakes. The trees stretched up and up so you couldn't see if they had tops, and up there they leaned as if they were going to fall. There hadn't even been time to say good-bye to the lamppost that he could hug and swing himself round and round. Round and round like his head, having to hold it up forever. Being places he had never been. Waiting moving sliding trying. Staying up to take care of his mother, afraid to lie down even when she was quiet, 'cause he might fall asleep and not hear her if she needed him.

Even the sun was cold. Wes took off his mackinaw and threw it over to him. He squinched himself together to try and fit under it. Moving sliding The road was never straight, the pickup bumped and bumped and he had to hold up his head. Even when he threw up, his uncle wouldn't stop. Maybe it was the whiskey they'd had when they got back from that place, made him sick. Or the up all night, up-down sorting and packing, throwing away and loading. Then that wet hoohoo wind on the auto ferry, and the night so dark he didn't even get to see the new bridge they were building.

The trees *were* red, like blood that oozied out of old meat and nobody washed the plate. Under them waved — ferns? Baddream giant ones to the baby kind they put around flowers for too sick people.

He had been holding up his head forever. The creek was slipping and sliding too. His uncle came from nowhere and put three fishes too close to him on a rock. They flopped and moved their sides, trying hard to breathe like too sick people.

He pulled the tarp farther down to the next stripe of sun. A wind made the skinny fire cough gallons of smoke and him shiver even more. Curling and curling till he got all in a ball under the mackinaw and didn't have to see

or smell.

When he woke up, he was warm. Fog curled high between the trees, the light shone rosy soft like a bedroom lamp lit somewhere. By the fire, a harmonica in his hand, his uncle was sleeping. Across the creek, just like in the movie show or in a dream, a deer and two baby deers were drinking. When he lifted his head, they lifted theirs. For a long time he and the doe looked into each other's eyes. Then swift, beautiful, they were gone — but her eyes kept looking into his.

Wes was mad to have conked out like that. Six more hours to go — that's if this heap holds up and we don't get stuck 'hind a load going up a grade. I'll have to put out at work like always tomorrow, and it's sure not any restin we been doin these gone days.

Just like before, but colder. Moving sliding. Having to hold up his head. Bumproad twisty in a dark moving tunnel of trees. The lumber trucks screamed coming round the bends, and after it was dark their lights made the moving fog look scary. Sometimes he could sleep, sagged against his uncle who didn't move away. Cold or jolts would wake him. He didn't understand how it was that he was sitting up or why he didn't have a bed to lie down in or why or where he was going. All he wanted was to lie down

forever

•

A long bridge with standing stone bears. His uncle said: Klamath, almost there. (*Underneath in the night, yearling salmon slipped through their last fresh waters, making it easy to the salt ocean years.*) When the car stopped, there wasn't even a light to see by. A lady came out to help; the light from the open door made the dark stand taller than even the redwoods and *that* leaned like it might fall on him too. The wind or something blew away her words and his uncle's words. His feet were pins and needles too many boxes and bundles too many trips down and back a long hall like a cave. A feather cape or something hanging got knocked down. His head gasped back and forth like the sides of the fish on the rock Something about: we didn't throw away nothin well I'm sure not goin to miss where I've been hot milk or coffee? but he didn't answer, just lay down on a cot with the bundles stacked around him and went into a dream.

So he came to Requa March, 1932 13 years old.

•

He stands with his back clamped hard against the door Wes has left open, and he has jumped up from the cot to close.

Hey. Leave it open. My can's still draggin. A block behind.

(*No smile. Skinny little shrimp. Clutching at the door knob, knuckles white, nostrils flaring. Funny animal noises in his throat.*)

Sleeping — all day? Cmon, you had to at least take a leak and put something into that belly . . . Mrs. Ed or Yee didn't stick their nose in? You didn't see nobody? . . . Well (looking around), one thing, you sure weren't neating up the place.

(*Pale. Ol Ghostboy. Silent Cal.*) (*Natural — it's plenty raw yet.*)

I been sleepin too — on my feet AND gettin paid for it. That's talent. (*No smile*) I wasn't bawlin you out, we can get squared away tonight or tomorrow . . . Sure you have to come to eat. It'll only be them that stays here. We all get along. You don't bother them, they don't bother you.

•

They are taking away the boxes and bundles, his low little walls.

That one on top: left over groceries. Into the kitchen, Yee. Forget takin it off the week's board, Mrs. Ed, they didn't cost me nothin. Bedding stuff, Bo; up to the attic. Pots and kitchen things, High. Attic. . . . Well who'd I leave them for and I thought they might be worth a dime or two. Listen, you'd be surprised how many's been in tryin to sell Evans their pots and blankets and everywhich things. Even guns and fishin gear, and thats get-by when nobodys workin. (Lowered voice) Just her clothes, Mrs. Ed, you know anybody? Mrs. Ed's room. Lamps and little rugs, Stevie *said* they was theirs. Sure lay it down, save me a splinter. Looks good. . . . Anyone for a lamp? (Funny noises in the kid's throat.) Gear. *He'll* put 'em away, Mrs. Ed. The bottom drawer, kid, yours and room to spare. Just a mitt? no ball, no bat? . . . Oddsies, endsies. Yah, a radio. Even works: Kingfish and Madam Queen, here we is. Stevie, Mrs. Edler is talking at you: you got clean stuff for school or does Yee have to wash? No, we never talked is he goin to school or what. . . . I'll tell you this, though, he's not goin through what me and Sis did: kicked round one place after another, not havin nobody. Nobody. Right, Stevie? Can you use a clock, High? Attic. . . . Was you startin to say something, Stevie? (*Ghostboy!* Swallowing, snuffling.) Naw, that last box stays: our ketchall; it'll take time, goin through it.

Wait, Bo, maybe I'll chase along after all IF you got the do-re-mi. Sattiday night, isn't it? and I feel the week. (*What am I doing, what am I goin to do with this miserable kid?*) Stevie's for the shuteye anyway, aren't you, kid.

Are you for the shuteye, Stevie?

Scratch of a twig on the window. All he has to lull to, who has rocked his nights high on a tree of noise, his traffic city.

Blind thick dark, whose sleep came gentled in streetlamp glow.

And the head on his pillow bulging, though still he is having to hold it up somewhere And the round and round slipping sliding jolting moved to inside him, so he has to begin to rock his body; rock the cot gently, down and back.

Down and back. It makes a throb for the dark. A clock sound.

That man Highpockets who stuck his hand out at supper and said "Shake, meet the wife" and everybody laughed, he had their clock that stood by the bamboo lamp. A tiny lady in a long dress leaned on it and laughed and held up a tinier flower branch. It had been one of his jobs to wind it and it wheezed while he was winding it.

Jobs.

He couldn't remember, was it Bo had taken the lamp? Telling everybody at the table like it was a joke or important. Would you believe it? He's never been fishin never been huntin never held a gun never been in a boat.

Never Forever

Down and back. The army blanket itched. When he was a kid he'd really believed that story about they were that color and scratchy because of blood and mud and poo and powdered licy things from the war that never could get washed out

Down and back A clock sound It keeps away

What had happened with the bloody quilt? Soft quilt She hadn't even asked how he was when they let him in after all that waiting and waiting to see her Just: *did you soak my quilt?* Burning eyes

Gentle eyes that looked long at him blood dripping from where should be eyes Out in the hall swathed bodies floating like in bad movies never touching the ground at the window

down and back down and back

If he had the lamp the boxes

You promised and see I'm someplace else again dark and things that can get me and I don't know where anything is. Don't expect *me* to be 'sponsible

they should have put the clock and lamp in with her the boxes and bundles and wall and put them round her everything would be together he wouldn't have to try and remember or hold up his head that wouldn't lay down inside the one on the pillow so he could sleep

down and back down and back

•

All that week he would be lying on the cot in the half dark when Wes got home from work; jump up to re-close the door; lie down again until Wes made him wash up, go in to supper.

At the table he looked at no one, answered in monosyllables, or seemed not to hear at all, stared at the wall or at his wrist, messed the food on his plate into the form of one letter or another, hardly ate

Supper over, he would walk somnambule back to the gaunt room, take off his shoes, get under the covers and lie there, one hand over his eyes.

Bo, Hi, crowded in chattering alongside the radio or playing a quick round of cards; Wes oiling his boots for work, tinkering with fishing-hunting gear, playing the harmonica; or the room empty: lying there, his arm over his eyes snuffling scratching swallowing

One Monday (let him be a while, Mrs. Ed had said), Wes, on his way to work, left the boy at the Klamath crossroads to wait the school bus.

He stands motionless in the moist fog that is almost rain, in Bo's too big fishing slicker. Blurs of shapes loom up and pass. Once a bindle stiff plods by. The across-the-road is blotted out.

When the bus stops and the door snorts open, he still does not move. The driver tries three honks, pokes his head out and yells: c'mon New, whatever your name, I'm late. You can do your snoozing inside.

Laughter from in the bus. In hoots.

Slowly, as if returning from an infinite distance, the boy focusses his eyes on the driver, shaking his head and moving his lips as if speaking. He is still mutely shaking "No," as the faces at the grimy windows begin to slip by fast and faster contorted or vacant or staring.

On *his* face, lifted to the fog, is duplicated one by one, the expressions on the faces of his fellow young. Still he stands, his lips moving. When he has counted thirteen cars passing (a long while), he crosses and goes back down the road, the way his uncle had brought him.

•

Days.

This time when Wes got home, his neatly made bed was torn up, its blanket bunched round the boy stretched out in dimness near the window.

At the expected convulsive jumpup, Wes stepped back and

grabbed the doorknob himself. Alright, alright, I'm closin it. The law ain't chasin *me*. Are they chasin you?

(but the boy had not moved at all)

He felt like yelling: why do you do that or: look at me for once, say hello.

Instead he sat down heavily in the big chair, unlaced his boots. No, I won't ask what he's been doin. Nothin. He'll say it in nothin, too.

Night scratched at the window and seeped from the room corners. No other sound but rising river wind.

The work of the day (of the week, of years) slumped onto Wes. For a minute he let go, slept: snored, great sobbing snores. In a spasm of effort, jerked awake, regarded the shadows, the rumple on the floor by the window.

Something about the light, the radio, not being snapped on; the absence of the usual attempted pleasantries; some rhythm not right, roused the boy from the trancing secret tremble of leaves against the low glowing sky. Was that his mother or his uncle sagged there in the weight of weariness, and why were her feet on the floor?

Get back he said implacably Your footstool's gone too In a box or throwed away or somebody else resting their tootsies on it Serves you right How you going to put up your feet and rub on the varicose like you like to, now?

(*Blue swollen veining*) (*Are you tired, Ma? Tired to death, love.*)

What are you twitchin your muscles like a flybit horse for? asked Wes. And stop swallowin snot.

He slept again This man he hardly knew who came and took everything and him and put him in a place he did not know where he was. Slumped, sagged, like . . .

Wes, if you set your feet up on something. *WES*

If I what?

If you set your feet up on a box

A box. For Crizake

Or a chair and rub where your feet hurt

A box Say, did you do up that box today like I told you?

It rests them, Wes. You rub up, not down

Answer me. Did you? No. You leave the only thing I ask you to do, for me to do, on my day off My one day Just look at this place You didn't help High neither when I asked you You think the candlefish run is goin to last forever? Maybe you might of brung in a basket or two Mrs. Ed would've took it into consideration You cost boy ghostboy don't you know that? My Saturday night for one thing my one night to howl you're costin

(Shrimp!) (I'd better watch it; I'm really spoiling tonight.) A rancorous: What's goin to be with you, you dummy kid? raps out anyway.

Sounding a long plaintive mockcowboy howl, switching on the light, yanking him up (God, he's skinny) and with a shove that is half embrace, steers him in to dinner.

Where he'd pushed the boiled salt salmon and potatoes away, the crack on his plate said: *Y. You cost, boy, you cost.* In his wrist a little living ball pushed, as if trying to get out Where the visiting nurse put her pinky and counted too sick people

Sagged with weariness like Wes her stockings rolled down rubbing rubbing where the blue veins swoll

On the wall the bottom of the Indian bow made: *U.* No, a funny *V. Y. V.* Vaud-e-ville. He'd stay for it twice and the feature twice and maybe the serial too while the light the silvery light Face bigger and bigger on the screen Closer Vast glutinous face Sour breath *IS YOU DERE, CHARLIE?*

Bo. Only Bo. Everybody at the table laughing

And now the faces start up bigger than the room on the fast track Having to hold up Hurry

At the door, Wes heard it again, that faint rhythmic creak. The first time, nights ago, he had thought: is the little bastard jacking off? but it wasnt that kind of a sound. Switching the light on, he saw the boy — as usual — lying on the cot, arm over his face — yes, and rolled into *his* blanket. The sound had stopped.

Sit up. Don't you know enough to excuse yourself when you leave a table sudden? Mrs. Edler was askin me, could you go upriver with her tomorrow to the deer or jumpdance or some such Indian thing they're having up at Terwer. She must want white company bad.

Is you dere, Charlie? You jumped a mile when Bo yelled that into your mug. Serves you right, sitting there night after night like you're no place at all, hardly answerin if people talk to you. Why are you such a snot? *Why?* (*savagely*) IS YOU DERE?

> (*Somewhere.*
>
> *But the stupor, the lostness, the torpor*) (*the safety*)
>
> *Keep away you rememorings slippings slidings having to hold up my head Keep away you trying to get me's*
>
> *Become the line on a plate, on a wall The rocking and the making warm the movement of leaves against sky*
>
> *I work so hard for this safety Let me a while Let me*)

— C'mon. Set up like you belong. We're going to get shed of that box. Right now. But first you make up my bed. Just *keep* that blanket you dragged round the floor, and give me yours.

— C'mon, tuck those corners in. We keep things neat around here. Monday you're starting school. For sure this time. No more of this laying round.

— Neat, I said. Now, where's that goddamn box. And quit making those damn noises.

Scooping onto the bed:

> boy-sitting-on-a-chamber-pot ash tray Happy Joss
> Hollywood California painted fringed pillow cover
> kewpie doll green glass vase, cracked

Jesus, what junk

> tiny India brass slipper ash tray enamel cigarette case, Fujiyama scene (thrown too close to the edge of the bed, it slithers off, slips down behind) pencils, rubber banded

Junk is right. We sure throwed it in in a hurry

> Plush candy box: sewing stuff: patches buttons in jars stork scissors pincushion doll, taffeta bell skirt glistening with glass pinheads

Now you got a dolly to play with Ketch Can't you even ketch?

> Red plush valentine box: nestled in the compartments:
> brown baby hair, ribbon tied perfume bottle, empty

china deer miniature, the fawn headless heart locket,
stone missing sand dollar gull feather

close quick

Now why did we . . .

tarnished mesh purse: in it a bright penny lipstick
rouge-powder compact, slivered mirror powder sifts

close quick

Pictures:

palm size, heart shaped frame

onto the bureau

celluloid frame, tin laddered back stand

onto the bureau

stained oblong cardboard, smaller snapshots clipped
round the large center one (His hand falters, steadies)

onto the bureau

More boxes, slender, rubber banded: in the first: letters tied in a man's handkerchief tin collar button red garter band ribboned medal pinned to a yellow envelope In the second: (vicious the rubber band snaps)

DON'T

The boy rigid on the floor, eyes glazed, mouth open, fixed; face contorted. A fit?

Steve? Stevie?

Crawling now, a snake. Rising. With the pillow batting the box out of Wes's hands, flailing at him. *Put it back.* With the pillow shoving everything off the bed into the box. *Put it back. If you was dead you'd put it back* With the pillow pushing the box into the hall slamming the door *all of it dead bury buried* Runs to the chamberpot vomits jabs at Wes when he tries to help him Runs to the door to run out sees the box runs back takes the coverlet to him and rocks

Alright alright Easy Some other day where was my marbles? Phew Just a bad day, Stevie mine was a Lulu Alright, it's over It was too soon, I know All her things Alright Easy

Heaving again.

You through? I'll get it out of here. (Almost falling over the box on his way to empty the slop.) (No, nobody home I can bum a drink off of. Sattiday night . . .) (*What am I doing what am I going to do with this miserable kid?*)

Bawling now like a girl.

Alright! It's over, Stevie It got me too Easy You got to grab hold . . . It's no good for you, all this layin round never goin out like normal Monday you're going to start school Keep you busy You'll be with other kids, play ball, have somebody to fish with Not lay around all the time thinkin about her, feelin bad.

Stopping his rocking. I don't. I don't.

Easy. It's all right; it's natural. But now you got to take hold.

Shut up bastard. Jabbing at him. Shut up. I told you I don't think about her, I don't feel bad. She's dead. Don't you know she's dead, don't you know?

Fending him off nodding wordlessly (*don't I know?*) Edging him back to the cot Easy Do I have to paste you one? Forget it, try to sleep, fella There's just so much I can stand Easy I'm so tired I could drop I'll help you to catch hold, Steve, I promise I'll help Stop now Try to sleep Holding him down to the cot I'm tryin. Doing the best I can, even if it turns out worse like usual But tryin. You try too. You hear that, Stevie? You try too.

Having to hold up

The pictures stayed, untouched, face down on the dresser. Where-ever the box went, Wes assumed it was to the attic. Days later, making his bed, he found the cigarette case, slipped it into a drawer against that far time he might no longer have to roll his own, could afford tailor-mades.

The boy would not rouse. Shaken awake, would not come to breakfast, refused to go out with him and Bo. "We was goin to start you practice shootin today, try for some fish, maybe even let you take the wheel awhile. *You're* the loser." But Wes did not do much urg-ing, wanting to get away from the incomprehensible moil of with-that-boy.

Before he went, he left instructions: Don't lay down *once,* not once. Neat up this room. If there's going to be any hot water, get yourself scrubbed up for school tomorrow squeak clean. Find out has Yee got some work you can do; God, what in hell CAN you do. Get outside even if it's raining down to the river throw rocks or something. Keep yourself moving Hear? And don't try to con me.

Asleep in the big chair when Wes got back; no, not asleep (hair still wet and an almost phosphorescent shine on his face) (*ghostboy*) So *gone,* Wes's breath stops for a moment. Maybe I ought to get a doc, or ask Mrs. Ed to look in the doctor book. But what would she look for? laying around? throwin up? actin nuts?

Then the tranced, shocked eyes looked at him but the voice said, perfectly normal: I did everything like you told. Yee cooked him and me rice chow yuk so I don't have to go in for supper tonight, do I. How was your fishing, Wes?

•

He did not go to school.

Clean to his one white shirt with its streaks of blueing, clutching his and Wes's lunch pails, he sat silent in the pickup till Wes slowed for the crossroads stop where, three weeks before, he had been left for the school bus. Quickly he is over the side.

Hey, *I'm* takin you. You forget? WAIT! Where do you think you're heading?

Plodding back towards Requa.

Get back here. Listen, don't pull no girl tantrum. Get in.

Having to pull over to the shoulder, park, run after him. His violent grab missing, so that he tears the sleazy jacket, half yanking down the boy.

I'm not going, Wes.

Get up, you're going all right. If I have to drag you.

I'd leave soon as you were gone, Wes.

Starting down the road again.

Spinning him around, socking him a good one, steering him back into the car. (*What am I doing, what am I going to do*)

— What you got against school anyway?

— You're headed straight for the nuthouse, layin round like you've been doing. Just nuttier every day. I'm not goin to let you.

— I'll have the truant officer, see? Wait, is 14 or 16 the limit?

— You're goin, see. What the hell else you got to do? C'mon, dust yourself off. I can't be late.

Starting to climb out again.

Really hurting him; pinning him back, banging and banging his head against the wheel, against the seat. You *have* to go, see?

Wes (in a strangled voice) Wes you're hurting. If I find me a job?

A job! Releasing him in disgust. You ARE in a nutworld. Half the grown men in the county's not working, High's down to two days, and this dummy kid talks about a job.

In Frisco then, Wes? Maybe set up pins again. Or ship?

In Frisco, my God. It's worse there, you know that. And how you goin to make that 500 miles? And who you got in your corner there? Nobody. You NEED learnin.

Starting up the motor.

Wes, I'll jump.

Socking him again. Hard.

Wes, if I go with you? Ask Mr. Evans, can I help? A learn job, Wes. By you.

Something in the boys voice . . . This time Wes's hands on his shoulders are gentle. Steve, don't fight it no more. It's five, maybe six weeks to vacation . . . fishin You'll have buddies. Maybe you're even goin to like school. And even if you don't, sometimes in this life you got to do what you *don't* like. (*Sometimes!*) Evans ain't about to put anybody on — if he did, Ez would be first choose; every week Ez is in askin: can he have his job back . . . Evans don't have it, Stevie. Sometimes its slow even for me. And everythings credit or trade-in; when we get a nickel, he bites it, makes sure its real. I'm surprised he pays *me*.

Ask him, Wes. You said: I'll help you, Steve. You said it. He don't have to pay me. You hurt me, Wes. A learn job. By you. You promised.

Not school
Never
Forever

•

NEW USED

U NAME IT — WE GOT IT
U ASK IT — WE FIX IT

Gas Butane Sportsmens Goods
Auto Parts Fittings Tools
Lumber Rags Scrap iron
Electric/plumber/builder supply
Housefurnish things

Auto Repair Towing Wrecking
Machining Soddering Welding
Tool & Saw Sharping
Glass work Boat caulking/repair

(Leaky, appraising eyes) Sure, why not? Favor to you, Wes. Anything he gets done, we're that much ahead. But if he's in the way, or it don't work out, that's it. And he's *your* headache. Anybody stick their nose in, he's helping you, not working for me. Don't get him expecting anything for the piggy bank, either. Used stock sometime maybe, whatever I think it's worth   and he's worth. Catch?

Tumble of buildings and sheds, stockpiles and junk — a block from the bridge — sprawled in the crotch between 101 going north/south and the short crooked upriver road to game and Indian country.

Landscape of thinghillocks and mounds innumerable. Which shed is which? The wind blows so. Too close: scaly, rapid river; too close: dwarfing, encircling: dark massive forest rise.

Stumbling the mounds in his too thin jacket or Bo's too big slicker after Wes. (*got to figure out what's simple enough he can do. Keep him up. Moving. Paying attention.*) Helping haul drag break apart; find the right sized used tire   generator   lumbersash; hand the measure   the part   the tool

I said the red devil   Red devil glass cutter   Your ears need reaming?

Does that even *look* like a 16 x 120? Why the thing they throw peanuts at could figger it

What you breathin like that for? I showed you: if you lift it this way, she goes easy. Easy. A right way and a wrong way — easy is the right way.

Is that a shimmy or a shiver? I ought to take me a razor cut, see is it blood or icewater runs in your carcass

The mess heap. Your baby to red up when I'm not needin you. Stack everything, that's what's here, everything — with its own kind. If theys a pile or shed already for it, get it over there Whats too far gone or cant be burnt, leave. Get them rotten carpets mattresses out first. Then them batteries Pile 'em so.   Where I expect to spot you when you're not workin with me, see?

Into the toolshed when it rains. Sort outa the bins into these here washboilers: like, pipe fittins: brass here copper there: elbows flanges unions couplings bends tees. Check out the drawers, see just what belongs is in 'em; get acquainted: like this row: wing nuts castellated slotted quarter inch *Pay attention!*

Heaps piles glut accumulation
Sores cuts blisters on his hands
Don't look: scaly rapid river dark forest encircling

Cold hardly comprehending wearing out so quick

Didn't you hear me callin? Answer me. What you staring at? You paralyzed? (*ghostboy*) Drop that carpet and get out of sight till you can come to Do I have to paste you one?

(The stiff mouldy rug breaks like cardboard in his hands. Underneath maggot patterns writhe)

Can't you tell the difference between taper and spiral fluted? (lock or finish washer?) (adapter, extension?) can't you? can't you?

Who said you could come in here and lay down? You sure tire instant Get yourself back to the burn pile and throw that filthy ragquilt out of here. No wonder you're always scratching.

Is that all you got done and I let you alone all mornin for it? What's there goin to be to show Evans you're of use Yah, as much use as a tit on a bull O for Crizake, you're not here at all

More and more wrapped in the peacock quilt, rocking, scratching, snuffling. Rain on the toolshed roof; the little kerosene stove hissing warmth through its pierced crown. Wes looming in the doorway, the gray face of evening behind him. C'mon, useless. 6:30. You killed another day. I *knowed* this was never going to work.

And once, in the most mournful of voices: Can't you do no better? I can't stand it, Stevie. You're ending up in the dummy or loony house, for sure.

But the known is reaching to him, stealthily, secretly, reclaiming.

Sharp wind breath, fresh from the sea. Skies that are all seasons in one day. Fog rain. *Known weather of his former life.*

Disorder twining with order. The discarded, the broken, the torn from the whole: weathereaten weatherbeaten: mouldering, or waiting for use-need. *Broken existences that yet continue.*

Hasps switches screws plugs tubings drills
Valves pistons shears planes punchers sheaves
Clamps sprockets coils bits braces dies

How many shapes and sizes; how various, how cunning in application. Human mastery, human skill. Hard, defined, enduring, they pass through his hands — link to his city life of manmade marvel.

Wes: junking a towed-in car, one hundred pieces out of what had been one. Singing — unconscious, forceful — to match the motor hum as he machines a new edge, rethreads a pipe. Capable, fumbling; exasperated, patient; demanding, easy; uncomprehending, quick; harsh, gentle: *concerned* with him. *The recognizable human bond.*

The habitable known, stealthily, secretly, reclaiming.

The dead things, pulling him into attention, consciousness.

The tasks: coaxing him with trustworthiness, pliancy, doing as he bids

having to hold up

Rifts:

Wes sets the pitch, the feed, the slide rest to chase a thread.

"Wes, *let* me. We're learning it in shop. It's my turn again Monday."

(Monday! What Monday? A Monday cobweb weeks miles gone life ago) Hard, reassuring, the lathe burrs; spins under his hands. (Somewhere in cobweb mist, a school — speck size. Somewhere smaller specks that move speak have faces)

Watch it! O my God, you dummy. How'm I going to explain *this* one to Evans.

Wheat wreathes enamelled on a breadbox he is tipping to empty of rain Remembered pattern; forgotten hunger peanut butter, sour french bread Remembered face, hand, wavering through his face, reflected in the rusty agitated water.

He lifts the wrecking mallet, pounds. Long after the spurting water has dried from his face and the tin is shreds in great muddy earth gouges, he still mindlessly pounds.

Later, dragging a mattress to the burn pile, his face contorts, fixes rigid, mouth open. The rest of the day in the toolshed, to lie immobile, and will not get up even to Wes's kick of rage.

Rags stiff and damp Green slime braids with the rope coils, white grubs track his palm

Bottle fly colors lustre the rotting harness rusty tongueless bells fall

Only the rain saves him — otherwise, before lunch, he practices shooting. Buckets, cans, are spotted in a semicircle for targets, the rococo scroll of a carpet beater nailed to a post. Sight. Squeeze. Splat. Shuddering rock of the recoil.

Who barks more, Wes or the gun? If you'd been concetrating if you'd just been concetrating. I want you good as me, Stevie. See? 200 yards right on target everytime.

The bruise on his shoulder — from when? Wes's beating the day he would not go to school? — purples, spreads.

Maybe this is better'n school for you Stevie Keep you outdoors, build you up I got so much to learn you All your life you can use it.

He is warmer now. An old melton coat with anchor buttons that Evans let Wes take from the clothes shed. Faint salt of a seaman's many voyagings seems to nest in it, and deep in the pockets mysterious graininesses crumble. Afternoons, if the strong northwest winds of May have cleared the sky an hour or two, the coat distills, stores the sun about him as he moves through mound-sheltered warmth in and out of the blowing cold; or sits with Wes, poncho over the muddy ground, eating their baloney and bread lunch in the sun-hive the back of the scrapiron pile makes.

Weeds, the yellow wild mustard and rank cow parsnip, are already waist high, blow between him and the river. Blue jays shrill, swoop for crumbs; chipmunks hover. Wes gabs, plays his harmonica. The boy lies face down in his pool of warmth. In him something keeps trembling out in the wind with the torn whirled papers, the bending weeds, the high tossed gulls.

Helping at the gas pump, he keeps his head lowered so that he knows the grease spots on the ground and how they change from day to day, but not who is in the cars. Even when the speech comes glottal, incomprehensible, Indian, he will not look up on the faces, nor on those of the riggers and swampers checking the chains tight around the two-three giant logs that make up their load.

Grease spots, and how they change from day to day; loggers muddied boots, flowerets and pine needles embedded; pliant redwood hair strands loosened from the logs and blowing across the road; the cars of the regulars; Evans dry ghost cough from the store, and that a certain worn-to-bareness tire tread will bring him watchfully into hearing distance; these he comes to know — but never faces.

Once, checking tires (young swaggering voices in the car), a girl steps out on the running board, so close he can smell her, round his hand to her bared thigh, the curve of her butt.

Relentless, vehement: clamor congests engorges. Gas bite, the soaked rag held to his nostrils, will not help.

Wes, don't call me to the pumps any more.

You'll do as you're told, you snotty kid Snotty's right Everytime I look at you. Wipe that nose. You need a washer in there?

relentless
engorged
clamorous
stealthily secretly reclaiming

Terrible pumps:

Evans out more and more.

Davis does what *I* say, see? Pay on the line or no tow. You heard me, no dough, no go. I don't care *how* many kids you got stuck in your jalopy, or how far you had to hitch to get here. Sure we got a used transmission. We got a used everything. But for do-re-mi. Don't ask *me* how you're going to manage without a heap . . . Well, you can junk it.

No, not even for five gallons trade, I won't take that mattress. I got a shed full now. There's maybe four hundred families the fifty miles around; they're sleeping on something already; who's going to buy 'em off me? No. That spare hasn't got a thousand miles left. Well maybe the gun.

Ten gallons gets you up — say — Grants Pass. How do *I* know how you'll make it to your brothers in Chehalis. One thing we *don't* sell here is a crystal ball.

. . . You'd think it was me knocked up their old ladies and lost 'em their jobs.

Whisper: Over here, Wes. I don't want ol Skinflint to spot me. You think you might have some link chain like this? An/8th or maybe a quarter inch. I got this idea, see? Sports season coming, and you know how they like to bring back a souvenir. Well, Christmas we didn't know what to do, so I whittled the boys up little lumber trucks — load of logs, chain and all — they're still playing with 'em. I thought till the woods open up again, I might pick up some loose change makin 'em to sell. Esty's doing up dolls out of redwood hair. Real cute. Evans won't help me out, but you will, won't you Wes. I'm about out of my mind.

When I call you I don't mean tomorrow sometime next week If I catch you cuddlin up to that stove again, I'll turn you every which way but loose

•

The smell or the whiskey is making him sick is making him happy is making him sleepy The brights and the ragtime making him happy lights lights little lights over the fireplace going on and off and on and off and on if you wink your eyes in time in time I love you lights Are you howling Wes is that how you howl your night to howl? O Wes in the blue of smoke and breaths tapdancing with Bo and that lady Esty in the middle and that fatso man Stop you don't know how to tap, Wes The keys on the player piano nickel in the slot piano know how jigging and tapping and nobody's playing them because I'M playing them long distance knowing how tapping and dancing (luxurious round the table round the dollars his fingers tapping) round and round

What you going to do with those two big beautiful cartwheels honey? Tapdance my fingers round and round them what he didn't answer her and should have because because and here the breathblue smokeblue clouded into his head and on and off and round tiniest sparkle on the wall calendar snow scene, moose locking horns sparkly I love you O I like that ragtime kitten on the keys I *am* the keys What did you say that's so ha ha Wes? wave wave dance my hand (no nobody's looking) highstep o high-step and off and on and round I wanta go to a movie show and round Red light that squiggles to you in the fog and when you get closer says E A T but nobody's eating they're dancing they think its dancing chewing the rag and swiggling and off and on and sparkle and round and fire jumping and Wes howling

Stop that, Bo

sticky and cold, the whiskey doused over him. *Best hair tonic there is, I'm tellin you, kid, use it myself every celebratin night and it stinks so purty*

It doesn't it doesn't and it doesn't wipe off and the smell is on his sleeve now so when he has to wipe his nose or wave his arm is making him sick and off and on and round o put another nickel in reeling waltz I wanta go to a picture show a man crying (Fatso) *sobby sentimental stew* O ma, that's funny, a sobby sentimental stew

Liar You promised and see I'm another place again no movies and no stores and no Chinatown and cold water in the faucet you have to pump not even lights just tonight little prickle kind and one squiggle sign just tonight

and round and round and off and on push on the keys dance tap float on the sadness sleep pushing down clouding and Sure I'm listening Wes No thanks you just gave me another nip Yah *how you keep Evans from catching on that I'm not all there* Yah and round sparks like blows from a fist the fire? over the fireplace, branching antlers, sad deer eyes in the fire, branching antlers glowing eyes am going to be sick

aaagh
aaagh

•

A dream? The yard lithe Bo tapdancing the mounds Wes in the furnish shed handing out bottles gurgling from one himself bootleg he don't know I know he's peddlin hooch but I do, gettin in on it just when it's goin to get legal end hard times Turning round and round a musical saw wheel dry whispery papery sad sound *they have taken her to Georgia* Wes's harmonica growl papery sad *there to wear her life away* making his saddest trainwhistle sounds round and round

•

The damp rushing air slaps slaps the boys face: *wake up* the lurching in his belly, the pitching truck: *wake up.* Wes slapping too, jabbing him away with his elbow every lurch he is thrown against him; waves of drunk smell from Wes's breath or is it his own sleeve: *wake up.* Wes driving jolty, not like Wes at all: shouting singing mumbling beating on the dash. Crooning: poor ol shrimp cant sit up poor ol shrimp passin out Take him out to celebrate Evans shakin loose two smackers and he cant take it cant celebrate FOOderackysacky want some seafood momma shrimpers and rice are very nice poor old shrimp (pounding on the dash) YOU'RE A SHIT EVANS YOU HEAR ME he don't know though does he (elbow jab) he don't know you're not all there (jab) cause I cover up good don't I Stevie? We'll have a heaver on that, hey? Me, not you, shrimp. Am taking care of you like I promised. Right?

Vamp me honey kitchaleecoo anything you'll want we'll do Jab. Forever long to get to Mrs. Eds. Not the same way they came. Jolt, jolt. Is it even a road? Headless shadows in the carlights. Stumps. *Not all there* Sparks like blows Hurtled, falling falling Wet on his face fir needles leaves Blood?

C'mon, up, up. See if you're hurt. Well I did stop sudden. You're fine, kid, sound as a dollar. Go ahead, puke. I got to go to this place down here, see?

Thick oblivious laughing mumbling pawing the floor of the truck for something, throwing the poncho at him, hard *Cover up* Dont want you ketching cold. You're running out of snot as is. Counting, recounting his silver by the light of a flash. Expansively: Keep 'em, Stevie, keep 'em; don't need 'em.

Need what? Thick black His trembling body redoing the hurtling fall over and over all scraped places burning. His shoulder . . . Far down in trees a weak light whorled, spectral, veined Eyes

Wes, wait, wait for me. Tripping over the poncho. On the ground again, his nose bubbling blood.

Easier to just lie there roll into the poncho shrink into the coat Cry (In one soft pocket his fingers tap round and round the silver dollars; in the other, hold the tongueless bell.) Put another nickel Some celebrating! *Not all there*

Faint salt smell from drying blood? the coat? Warm. Round and round not even minding the dark

Sudden the knowledge where Wes has gone. *Annie Marines,* she sells it. Nausea. Swelling, swollen aching. Helpless, his hand starts to undo the coat layer (*meet the wife, meet the wife*).

Slap. On his face. Another slap. Great drops. *Rain.* Move, you dummy. Pushing himself up against a tree, giant umbrella in the mottled dark. Throb sound in and around him (his own excited blood beat?) Rain, hushing, lapping

City boy, he had only known rain striking hard on unyielding surface, walls, pavement; not this soft murmurous receiving: leaves, trees, earth. In wonder he lay and listened, the fir fragrance sharp through his caked nostrils. Warm. Dry.

Gently he began to rock. The hardness had gone down by itself.

Far down where Wes was, a branch shook silver into the light. Rain. *His mothers quick shiver as the rain traced her cheek. C'mon baby, we've got to run for it.*

Laughing. One of her laughing times. Running fast as her, the bundles bumping his legs. Running up the stairs too. Tickling him, keeping him laughing while she dried his face with the rough towel.

Twisting away from the pain: trying to become the cocoa steam, the cup ring marking the table, the wheat wreathed breadbox. *Her shiver.* How the earth received the rain, how keen its needles. Don't ask *me* where your umbrella got put, don't expect *me* to be sponsible, you in your leaky house.

Rain underneath, swelling to a river, floating her helpless away *Her shiver*

Twisting away from the pain: face contorted, mouth fallen open: fixed to the look on her dying, dead face.

When Wes lurched down the path, he still did not move. The helpless pain came again. For Wes this time, drunk, stumbling, whispering: O my God, I've had better imagines, O my God.

Stevie! Where the hell are you? You scared the hell out of me . . Let's get going. I feel lower than whale shit, and that's at the bottom of the ocean.

The light was still on. Wes must have carried or walked him in, been too drunk to make him wake up, undress. Wes hadn't undressed either, lay, shoes muddy on his bed, he, who was always the neat one.

The boy stared at the bulb staring at him; then, painfully, got up, pulled off his clothes, went over and knelt by Wes's bed to tug off the offending shoes and cover him.

One of Wes's fists trembled; a glisten of spit trickled out of the corner of his mouth. His fly was open. How rosy and budlike and quiet it sheathed there.

The blanket ends wouldn't lap to cover. He had to pile on his coat, Wes's mackinaw, and two towels, patting them carefully around the sleeping form. *There now you'll be warm,* he said aloud, *sleep sweet, sweet dreams* (though he did not know he had said it, nor in whose inflections.)

He was shivering with cold now. *Dummy or crazy house not all there* Though he put his hands out imploringly to protect himself, the blows struck at him again. His uncle moaned, whispered something; he leaned down to hear it, looked full on the sleeping face. Face of his mother. *His* face. Family face.

For once he was glad to turn off the light and have the shutting darkness: hugged the pillow over his face for more. At the window spectral shapes tapped; out in the hall, swathed forms floated, wrung their hands. Later he hurtled the fall over and over in a maggoty sieve where eyes glowed in rushing underground waters and fire branched antlers, fir needle after shining needle.

•

accurately threaded, reamed and chamfered

Shim Imperial flared

cutters benders grinders beaders
shapers notchers splicers reamers

how many shapes and sizes,
how various, how cunning in
application

What did Toots and Casper want? Did I hear them asking for two gallons of gas? *Two* gallons? Where they coming from anyway? I thought that kind were all riding 99.

Tentacle weeds pierce the dishpan he is trying to pry up. Orange rust flowerings flake, cling to the quivering stalks, embroider the gaping pan holes.
Beauty of rot rust mold

Wingding anchors bearing sheaves plated, crackle, mottle blue, satin finish

Are you dreamin or workin? That carbon should of been clean chipped off by now. I *promised* that motor. O for Crizake, you ain't here at all.

Something is different at Mrs. Eds. Is it the longer light? How clear everyone is around the table, though still he does not look into their faces. The lamps, once so bright and hung with shadows, are phantom pale; the windows, once black mirrors where apparitions swam, show green and clear to heads of trees, river glint, dark waver of hill against sunset sky.

Highpockets is gone. When had he gone, and why? The blurredness will not lift. A new man, thready, pale, sits in his place and has his room.

The talk eddies around him: ain't going to *be* no season, not in Alaska Vancouver or Pedro . . . like crabs feedin on a dead man, like a lot of gulls waitin for scraps . . . the Cascades the Olympics the Blues . . . nickel snatchin bastards

He sees that it is not shadows that hang on the wall around the bow, but Indian things: a feathered headdress, basket hats, shell necklace. Two faces dream in shell frames. One, for all the beard, Mrs. Ed's.

family face

•

sharping hauling sorting splicing
burring chipping grinding cutting
grooving drilling caulking sawing

the tasks, coaxing

rust gardens

Nippers. You bring nippers. Did you think I was going to *bite* the wire? Try it with *your* choppers.

Pilings on pilings. Rockers, victrolas, flyspecked mirrors, scroll trundle sew machines, bureaus, bedsteads, baby buggies.

Wes, I can't hardly open the door, it won't go in, there's no room.

No room, you make room, dummy. That's the job. You good for anything?

The wind blows the encircling forest to a roar. Papers fly up and blind; a tire is blown from his hand. He scrambles the scrap-iron pile to the shelter side, stands, coat flapping, blown riverspray wet on his face, hallooing and hallooing to the stone bears on the bridge, the bending trees.

Loony, loony, get down. You see that canvas needs tackin? Tack.

Miming Wes's face Sounding Evans dry ghost cough Gentling his bruised shoulder. Sometimes stopping whatever he is doing, his mouth opening: fixed to the look on her dying face

We'll be able to start burnin today or tomorrow if the wind stays down, says Wes. Don't this sun feel good? Just smell.

Brew of rose bay, forest, river, earth dryings, baked by the sun into a great fragrant steaminess. In it, every metal scrap, every piece of glass, glances, flashes, quivers, spangles, ripples light.

Wes stands in fountains of light: white sparkles as he moves the wheel for knife sharpening; blue jettings as he welds a radiator.

I didn't know you could sing, Stevie. You practicing for the Majors Amateur Hour?

It's for my head, Wes.

Outa your head, you mean.

The baking warmth, the vapor, the dazzle, the windlessness.

Toward noon the next day, they set the burn pile. Wes lets him douse on the gasoline, but the boys look is so unnatural — spasms of laughing and spastic body dance as the flames spurt — Wes cuffs him away.

You a firebug nut or something? Get away, loony.

The wordless ecstasy will not contain. Quiver and dazzle are magnified in the strange smoking air. Baking mud sucks at his shoes as he runs from flash to flash. Stench of burning rubber and smoldering wet rags layer in with the heady sweet spring vapors. How vast each breath. Wreathes of yellow and black smoke rise. A stately rain of ash begins. *And still the rippling, glancing, magnifying light.* It drives him down by the river, but the stench and dazzle are there too, and flashing rainbow crescents he does not know are salmon leaping.

There, where the blue water greens the edging forest, the climbing fir trees blue the sky, on a sandy spit, he lays himself down.

Only when they turn at Panther Creek for the Requa cutoff do they leave the smoke. They ride west into setting sun blare. The road is gold, black leaves shake out sungold, and from the low deer brush — outlined too in gilt — there reels a drunken wild-lilac smell.

Ten more days to huntin, Stevie. You don't know how much I want them few days . . . I shouldn't have got so mad; you're doin almost o.k. lately, sometimes as much help as trouble. Even your shootin

Four days in a half stupor, pumping for breath.

Why do you have to pull something like this for? Now I'll have to work Decoration Day, be far enough ahead so he'll give me them three days off . . .

Mrs. Ed, come here, isn't there anything you can do to help this poor kid catch his breath?

•

He stands beside her negligently, as if he is not there at all, stooping his newly tall, awkward body into itself while she introduces him to the preacher, families, other young.

Better go in, Stephen, you shouldn't be standing here in this strong wind. Betty'll show you where to sit, won't you, Betty?

his Dad . . . never knew him . . . before he was
born . . . AEF . . . a young woman, so sudden
. . . Wes Davis his uncle . . . all he has

His sleeves don't pull down to cover ugly scabs *That these dead shall not have* peely walls Mrs. Edler's arm light on his hurt shoulder *He breaketh the bow and snappeth the spear asunder* cobwebs under the backless benches spiders? his skin crawls Scratching the itch places he can reach scratching blood Somebody giggling whispering

There is a fountain filled with blood
dead fly in the hymn book sweet voice a girl or lady in back
and there may I, as vile as he wash all my sins away
somebody giggling whispering The sleeves don't pull down

•

At the first cemetery, he waits for her under the Requiescat in Pace gate. People come by, carrying wreaths and flowers and planting flags. If you were a dead soldier, you got a flag. The flags made crackle noises in the wind — like shooting practice — and kept getting blown down and having to be planted again.

A girl — that Betty maybe? — called his name, so he had to walk to a tangled part where nobody else was. His foot kicked over something — a glass canning jar — rust and dried things that might once have been flowers in it. Did it belong to the marble hand pointing to the sky, Leo Jordan, 1859–1911, He is Not Dead but Sleeping, or to the kneeling stone lamb, almost hidden by the tall blowing weeds?

He bent down and stood it by the lamb. Milena Willet was carved on it, 1 yr. old Budded on earth
Blooming in Heaven

He had to pull away the weeds and scratch out the sandy dirt to read the rest:

The mother strives in patient trust
Her bleeding heart to bow
For safe in God the Good the Just
Her babys sleeping now

That part was sunk in the ground.

How warm it felt down there in the weeds where nobody could see him and the wind didn't reach. The lamb was sun warm too. He put his arm around its stone neck and rested. Red ants threaded in and out; the smell was sweet like before they set the burn pile; even the crackling flags sounded far away.

The sleep stayed in him all the way to the second cemetery. Other people were in the car, they had stopped at back dirt roads to get them. You always get out and open the car door for ladies, Stephen, Mrs. Edler had said. But they weren't ladies, they were Indians.

The sun baked in through the car window and their trouble talk floated in haze He says the law on his side legal *but it's ours* the Sheriff bones don't prove it he says the law

This cemetery he didn't get out of the car. It trembled all the time, pushed and rattled by the wind. Trees, bent all their lives that one way, clawed toward the windows. There were firing sounds here too, but maybe they were ocean booms. He thought he could see ocean, lashing beyond the trees.

•

What did you do to him? Wes asked Mrs. Edler. When I heard where you went, I expected sure he'd get back near dead, bad as in the beginning. But he's been frisky as a puppy all day. Chased me round the junk heaps. Rassled went down to the river on his own throwed skimmers sharped a saw perfect Paid attention Curled up and fell asleep on the way home.

That's where he is — still sleeping. Lay down second we got home and I can't get him up. Blowing out the biggest bubble of snot you ever saw. Just try and figger that loony kid.

stealthily secretly reclaiming

IVAN PRASHKER

Shirt Talk

(FROM HARPER'S MAGAZINE)

WHEN HE HEARD his wife leave the apartment to go shopping in the afternoon, Moe Sohn, a retired shirt manufacturer in his late seventies, called his ex-partner, Sam Lipshitz, who'd bought him out and was running the business alone.

Moe hadn't spoken to Lipshitz for more than a year; they hadn't gotten along when they were partners, and they'd fought bitterly over price when the partnership broke up. Lipshitz, seventy years young but in good health save for slight prostate trouble, was surprised to hear from his ex.

"It's been so long we spoke I almost don't recognize you," Lipshitz couldn't resist.

"Big deal," Moe countered.

"What do you want?" Lipshitz asked tonelessly.

"I'm calling about business."

"What 'business' a rich, retired stud like you has to worry about?" Lipshitz needled.

"Did you ship the goods to Kuflik?"

"Goods? Kuflik?"

"I know he doesn't pay so fast, but he's proved to be a solid account over the years, so maybe you got to be a little lenient."

Lipshitz looked like a boss, sitting in his Thirty-fourth Street office opposite the Empire State Building. An oily black cigar rested amiably between his fat lips and his feet were propped comfortably on his desk. Now whether or not he shipped goods to a customer was simply no longer Moe's concern. Besides, six months ago, it became company policy to stop selling smalltimers. All of which meant that Lipshitz didn't owe Kuflik beans, let alone shirts.

"I'm not following you, Moe," Lipshitz said. "Maybe it's because today I'm thinking a little slow."

"Today is no different than any other day."

Lipshitz gritted his teeth. Moe always could get under his skin. "Look," he said impatiently, "I'm a busy man, and I don't quite get your train of thought. You're out of business, what's Kuflik got to do with you these days?"

"What do you mean I'm out of business?" Moe said indignantly. "I sold him six weeks ago for fall delivery. I want you to ship him even he does pay a little slow."

Lipshitz swung his feet off his desk. He put his cigar in the fancy copper ashtray on his desk, closed his eyes, and bit his lower lip. "Where's your wife, Moishe?" he asked. "Where's Ida?"

"I know Kuflik from the old country yet, seventy years I know him," Moe was saying. "How's it look, he buys and we don't ship cause he doesn't pay like a goddamn IBM machine."

"I want to talk to Ida," Lipshitz said.

"Ida's downstairs shopping. What's she got to do with shipping Kuflik? This is shirts I'm discussing."

"I'll tell you, Moe, let me think about it. I'll get back to you tomorrow about the Kuflik shipment."

But Lipshitz didn't wait until the following day to call back. He dialed Moe's number when he was reasonably sure he would catch Ida in the apartment later that same afternoon. She was preparing dinner.

"Ida, how's Moe feeling?" Lipshitz asked.

"I'll be right back," she said, wiping her hands on her apron. She went into the living room. Moe was taking a nap, sprawled in his favorite chair. His mouth was wide open.

Closing the kitchen door, Ida picked up the phone. "Why are you calling?" she asked Lipshitz. "Did something happen today?"

"Is Moe acting 'funny' lately?"

"Funny?" Ida stalled. But she had a good idea what Lipshitz meant. Not two days ago, looking Ida in the eye, Moe had asked, "Where's my wife?"

"Please," she said to Lipshitz, "why the questions?"

The ex-partner sighed. He hated to be the bearer of bad news but felt obliged to tell Ida she had to keep her husband from calling the office. Between the time Lipshitz had spoken to Moe and dialed Ida, he'd learned that for the last two weeks Moe had been discussing nonexistent business with the office personnel — the bookkeeper, two salesmen, an inside man, even the mailroom boy. And they'd all been afraid to tell him about Moe's calls, but once Lipshitz had broken the ice that afternoon, every other gossip with a contribution to make eagerly chimed in. And Lipshitz, who half enjoyed working himself up over shaky office morale, had decided to put a stop to the older man's foolishness before it got out of hand. "I'm sorry to have to add to your troubles, Ida," was how he began.

She listened patiently, as Lipshitz spelled out the telephone calls Moe had made to the office the past two weeks. Ida was not surprised. Moe had lived for his work. After his second heart attack a year and a half ago, she'd forced him to retire. It was a wifely duty she had had to perform for his own good. But sitting home with time on his hands after a lifetime of hard work, Moe suffered misery Ida became aware only even existed this last year; and now she hated herself for having laid down the retirement law to her husband.

"You know," she told Lipshitz, "I'm sorry I didn't send him back to the office with my blessing after the second heart attack. It would have been better for him to die on Thirty-fourth Street than be unhappy for a year counting the money other shirt people were raking in."

"But that's crazy talk," Lipshitz cut her short. Even just imagining Moe dropping dead in the office gave his ex-partner goose pimples. "About why I dialed you, Ida, dear," he said, bringing the conversation back to essentials. "Moe's calls got to stop."

Ida had an inspiration. "Is it really so terrible he telephones, talks business to you or someone else in the office once in a while?" she asked.

Somehow the question struck like a blade to the belly. Lipshitz squirmed. "Ida, I'm a manufacturer, not a psychiatrist."

"I know it's a big favor to ask, but couldn't you kid him along? Talk business to him as if he were still a partner?"

Lipshitz had always liked Ida and wished he could grant her request. Screw office morale! You pay your people good money, that's office morale. But Lipshitz couldn't forget that after selling to him, Moe had spread the word in the industry he'd been taken for a one-way ride by his former partner of twenty-five years.

"Ida, I wish I could go along with what you're asking, I really do," Lipshitz said. "But in the first place, I'm a busy man. Since Moe isn't here, I do two jobs. And in the second place, it's hard to forget Moe told everyone I took advantage he was sick and only offered a lousy price. I mean, my heart just isn't in the right place for him these days."

"What he said about you is nothing to what he says about me because I made him retire," Ida answered. "He can't work, and it's killing him, so he leaves it out. But if he could talk shirts to you, it might make it easier for him at home. He's got no friends. All his brothers and sisters are dead. Talk business to him. Do it. And if you can't do it for him, then do it for me."

Once, when everyone was younger, Lipshitz had gotten a woman buyer in trouble and needed money quickly. He was ashamed to ask Moe, a Sabbath observer, and in desperation turned to Ida. She gave him cold cash the following day, telling him explanations between friends were unnecessary. And now, twenty years later, she was asking this favor of him, and though Lipshitz hated getting involved he found he couldn't say no. "All right, Ida," he told her. "But remember, this is only for your sake."

Moe was still dozing when his wife went back into the living room. He looked shrunken. She knew he couldn't have weighed more than one hundred and ten pounds. Sometimes at night she would watch him put on his pajamas, and seeing he was all bone it was difficult for her to keep herself from gasping. He was almost seventy-nine years old, and she knew she was lucky he'd lived this long, and in relatively good health. But still, he was her husband, they'd been through a lot together, and she didn't want him to die.

Because he'd been having trouble sleeping during the nights the last two weeks, Ida gave him a sleeping pill that evening. The pill didn't do much good, however, for sometime after one o'clock she heard him getting out of bed. She thought he was going to the bathroom and said nothing. The next thing she knew she heard him opening the front door. She jumped out of bed. "Moe, what's the matter?" she exclaimed.

But he didn't answer her.

Snapping on the hall light, she said, "Moe, where are you going?"

He was standing near the front door, wearing only his pajamas, which no longer fit him. "I was looking for the paper," he said. A delivery boy dropped the *New York Times* opposite their apartment door each morning between seven and seven-thirty.

"But, Moe, it's only one-thirty in the morning."

He stared at her, squeezing the door's brass knob.

"It's still pitch-dark outside," she said.

"One-thirty," he said, closing the front door.

He went into the kitchen, where he studied the clock hanging over the kitchen table. "Are you sure this clock is working?"

"Come back to bed with me," Ida told her husband.

"I'm not sleepy."

"Would you like a cup of tea?"

"What's today?" he asked.

She forgot. "The day after yesterday," she said with more assurance than she felt.

He nodded. For some reason satisfied with her answer, he found his way back into their bedroom. He started to groan almost as soon as he fell asleep. And hearing him, Ida herself could only toss and turn. He mumbled a sentence; some words were in Yiddish, others in English. She caught his oldest brother's name.

Moe came of a family of four sons, two daughters, and when he was just past thirty he was supporting one of his sisters, paying the business debts of two brothers, shelling out rent money for his parents, sending his youngest brother through New York Law School, and maintaining his own family in an apartment near Central Park. He had carried them all, and whenever Ida rode a bus down Fifth Avenue and saw the statue of Atlas supporting the world on his shoulders, she couldn't help wondering, "But was Atlas as reliable as my Moe?" And it struck her as incredible that Moe now only weighed a little more than a hundred pounds. And still hearing his groans, she suddenly sat up in bed and prayed that Lipshitz would understand what forced retirement meant to a man whom everyone used to depend on; in a word, she prayed that Lipshitz would keep his promise and talk shirts.

And the next day, at the breakfast table, she purposely brought up the ex-partner's name. While she didn't expect miracles from a couple of phone conversations, she was prepared to be most grateful for any breaks that came her way, and for that reason she didn't want too much time to elapse between Lipshitz's promise and a call from Moe.

But Moe didn't need any prompting. The customer Kuflik was still on his mind, and when Ida went down shopping in the early part of the afternoon, Moe dialed the Thirty-fourth Street office and asked to speak to the boss.

"Moe, how are you?" Lipshitz greeted him as a long lost friend.

"Have you shipped the goods to Kuflik?"

Lipshitz, who would keep his promise to Ida, so help him, had decided not merely to talk to Moe but to sound convincing, in character.

"I've been thinking about what you said yesterday, Moe, and the truth is I don't like dealing with small potatoes," he uttered for openers. "Now I got mothing against this Kuflik personally, but when, in addition to only giving us peanut orders, he doesn't pay on time, then that's one kike who's more trouble than he's worth."

"But I sold him goods," Moe protested. "You can't let him keep expecting delivery and not ship. That's treating a man like a dog."

Lipshitz stayed in character. "He doesn't pay on time, he doesn't like our terms. Let the greaseball buy from some other house."

"I, Moe Sohn, personally promised him fall delivery!" Moe declared. "You dirty louse, ship him!"

Lipshitz's ears sprang to attention. He wasn't used to people calling him bad names; but remembering Moe's rotten ticker, he held his explosive temper in check. "The way you talk about Kuflik, one would think he was your brother, at least a relative," he temporized.

"I always argue with you, Lipshitz," Moe was saying. "We're partners, fifty-fifty, and we're always fighting. I guess the truth is I never liked you."

Suddenly Lipshitz forgot he was play-acting. "I'm not exactly crazy for you either."

"Your opinions couldn't make me care less." Moe shrugged.

"Goddamn it, we don't have to stay partners forever." Lipshitz was so angry he didn't know what he was saying. "Maybe I ought to buy you out, or vice versa."

"Don't threaten me," Moe said. "Make me an offer. A *fair* one."

Emphasis on the word "fair" brought the ex-partner back to his senses. The past was finished. If Moe was nuts, confused past with present, that didn't mean Lipshitz had to do likewise, could only talk to Moe by forgetting he was making believe they were still partners. Cooling off, yet remembering his promise to Ida, he took a deep breath.

"Look, Moe," he said after a while, "we don't have to agree on every single customer, but that doesn't mean we're still not good for each other. We've built a profitable business these last twenty-five years, and it wasn't by luck or accident either. There are things you know I don't, and there are tricks I can perform you're not so hot at. I mean, we do good as partners. But even in the best of families there are some disagreements, no?"

Moe, however, was implacable. He said one word: "Kuflik."

"All right, all right, we'll ship the *pisher*. But tell him, Moe, tell him from me, he doesn't pay on time this once, he should find himself another shirt firm to drive crazy."

"Ship him," Moe sighed.

"I said okay."

"Kuflik's a proud man, and he's ashamed for people to know, but he's blind in one eye and the other has a cataract; also, sometimes he doesn't remember, and he can't always make out the due date on his bills."

"But why didn't you tell me this before?" Lipshitz asked.

"I knew it before," Moe said. "It was enough I knew."

Lipshitz had a premonition, he shivered. "Moe," he whispered, "is there anything else I should know?"

Moe thought a moment. "Don't let them make you retire."

"Is that all?" Lipshitz asked, disappointed.

"Don't kid yourself, I'm telling you a lot."

Lipshitz squinted. Was Moe supposed to think he was still a partner or not? Sometimes he sounded like he did, sometimes not so. Lipshitz was confused. "I don't want to keep you," he said, hoping Moe would take the hint.

Moe complied. "I got to go now."

"Be okay," Lipshitz said, grateful the call had come to an end. And putting the phone down, he sighed. Talking to Moe, in character, had proved to be a bigger favor than even Lipshitz had bargained for. He lit up an oily cigar and, remembering his past prostate trouble, called his doctor and made an appointment for the following week.

Moe didn't mention the phone conversation he'd held with his ex-partner when Ida returned to the apartment that afternoon. He had a strange, faraway look in his eye, and she guessed that Lipshitz had said the wrong thing; everyone knew that the ex-partner wasn't exactly Mister Tactful. Besides, psychology was a tricky affair, you never could tell how it would work out.

Now she asked Moe if he'd like something to drink, maybe a glass of orange juice before supper.

But instead of answering her, he went to the hall closet and got out his coat and hat.

"Where are you going, Moe?" Ida asked. She didn't want to stop him, but it upset her when he went into the street alone, and the fact that it was getting close to dark now made her even more jumpy.

"I'm going home," he said, putting on his hat.

"You're going where?"

"Home. I'm going home."

The perfectly calm expression on his face alarmed her even more than what he said. She tried to smile; she tried to smile the way a mother does to reassure a bewildered child. "But this is your home. You live here, Moe."

"No, you're mistaken, I work here." Then he went over to the desk in the living room and withdrew from one of its drawers a small blue velvet bag containing his prayer shawl and phylacteries.

"What are you doing?" she asked.

"I'm taking these home with me," he said, stuffing the velvet bag into his coat pocket. "I need them for *shaharith* tomorrow morning."

"Come to the window with me," she said in the calmest voice she could manage. He let her lead him through the living room. They looked out the window together. "Don't you recognize this neighborhood? The apartment buildings? You've lived on this street for more than ten years."

"But why are you trying to fool me?" he asked angrily.

"I'm not trying to fool you," she said.

He pointed to a group of businessmen who were hurrying home

from work. "You see those men across the street? They've just left their offices. This is Thirty-fourth Street. I wouldn't mind sleeping here, but it's not safe; too many *goyim* around."

"Let's go out into the hall and ring Mrs. Feder's doorbell," Ida suggested. Mrs. Feder was their next-door neighbor. "She doesn't work downtown. If you see her, will you admit this is your home?"

He said nothing, and she took him by the hand. His fingers were cold to her touch, but she wouldn't let them go. And man and wife, they walked out of their apartment together.

Ida rang Mrs. Feder's doorbell, but there was no answer. She thought to try another neighbor's apartment, but frightened at the way fate seemed to be conspiring against her, she hurried back to the safety of her own living room, holding Moe tightly by the hand.

Stalling for time, she said, "Stay just tonight. If you still want to leave tomorrow, then okay, *gey shon*."

He seemed undecided.

"I work hard all day, I'm tired it comes five o'clock. Is that so terrible?" he asked.

"Of course not," she said, letting go of his hand.

"It may not sound hard, but today I had to tell Lipshitz how he should handle my friend Kuflik. Educating a dummy, that's not such easy work. And now I want to go home."

"How is Lipshitz?" she asked, trying to get his mind off leaving the apartment.

"I never hurt you. Why do you torture me like this?" Moe said bitterly.

"Shhh," she calmed him. "We'll eat supper soon, and you'll feel better."

She reached for his hand again. It was still cold, but she saw fat drops of sweat popping from his forehead.

"Take off your coat," Ida coaxed.

"I wish you wouldn't try to confuse me," he said. "It only makes it worse."

"I'm sorry I tried to confuse you," she apologized. "It was a mistake."

She took the bag containing the prayer shawl and phylacteries out of his coat and put it back in the desk drawer. Somehow it comforted her to know he wouldn't leave the apartment without his phylacteries.

NORMAN RUSH

In Late Youth

(FROM EPOCH)

1. Walter Palm stood resting at the top of the hill, watching the slow approach of his son up the steep sidewalk below. He motioned to him to hurry, calling out, "Come, Owen! Come up! Hurry!"

Owen was almost three, a frail, saturnine child with white hair so fair that in some light he appeared bald. He was ascending balkily. Walter thought, He hates this light: I would.

Walter had his back to Hession's house. He touched his shirt: he was sweating freely in one armpit. He saw himself as unmasked by the ascent, revealed as a sedentary, someone who would be spent by climbing a long but occasionally gradual incline which Hession and Hession's new regular visitors undoubtedly ran up and down easily every day of the week. He felt unequal to the heights, uncomfortable in the ceaseless irregular wind and the whiteness. He asked himself why he felt stupefied by a view of the Bay he had seen before (if not from that exact vantage), a view that by now meant nothing to Hession.

He felt his hair spring piecemeal from its combing, and he turned to align the grain of his combing with the grain of the wind, which brought his gaze around to Hession's house. He thought, The wealth alone would affect me in comparison to how he lived before. Under Hession's windows he was unwilling to recomb his hair.

He held his shirt collar open to let the wind play into his damp armpit. He had dressed neutrally, in demoded pleated dull black slacks, a shortsleeved white dress shirt. He thought, Thirty-two is *at best* late youth: you're in late youth then: your effort at literature is over with and not postponed.

2. His son had halted. Threateningly, Walter descended until Owen began to come up in earnest.

Walter thought, Fleshly Fathers Fail: so we hear in literature or in nine-tenths of first novels at any rate: Ah, also I'm thinking in titles again I see, due to what?: emanations?

Furtively he again looked around at Hession's house. He thought, Ah also once our fleshy father fails we think of the replacement we get as parentless or original, or at least I did when it comes to Hession: Or, if we fail to get our substitute in time we run the risk of becoming in some cases women rather than men, homo, out of disappointment: obviously men are meant to be progenitors but are they meant to be fathers really, continuing fathers?: Or, if we have elder brothers they can be used provided we have the right kind.

His son arrived.

"Owen, the *present!*, where is it? O Jesus look at it, halfway down the hill, Owen! Owen, go get it. See it? Look and see. I told you hold onto it, how many times do I have to say something to you, Owen, you baby? Now go get it, Owen; this time never let it go. Go get it now."

The boy turned obediently and started back to retrieve a small flat parcel visible where it had fallen on the sidewalk farther down.

Again waiting, Walter rehearsed what he wanted to say on seeing Hession again, but distracted himself enough to avoid hearing each word as he spoke it in his mind: This is my son Owen who's nearly three, Yes!, Yes!, his name is based on a remark you made, Yes! we just got back this week after how long is it now, eight years all told in the sodden East: O also my marriage, I'm married and my wife Joan is home painting our place: on Lombard.

He thought, Too bad you can't somehow imbed the history of eight years in one shot and be spared banalizing the first moments of the first meeting in nearly ten years: you can't, though.

Hession's voluminous mission-style house was set in an extensive raised lot. The house was finished in prodigally worked ivory stucco, and was roofed with terra-cotta tile; the windows were sunk in deep fluted frames matching the roof tile in color. The property appeared to take up the entire crown of the hill. Railed walks led through the grounds. The lower, lesser houses of the neighborhood had narrow lawns in their front plots; dense beds of pink flowering ice plant grew between Hession's walks.

Owen arrived with the parcel. The wind blew stiffly. Walter smoothed Owen's hair, beat at and straightened the boy's jacket.

"Owen, let me check. Stand up straight. Very good. Now. Owen: the man is a man I knew when I was a boy like Carl. I was young. Now today when we go in I want you *very much* to be a good boy, when we get inside. Will you be? Owen, will you be? I promise one thing if you will, I have a present for a good boy. Will you be good, my good guy? I hope so. I already have a present. Now carry this like this and when we go in give it to the man if he opens the door. This is for the man. I have your present too."

They went up the final stairs to the house. Walter felt the view widen with each upward step.

3. He placed himself at the door, pressed the doorbell, set his hands lightly on his son's shoulders. He heard movement in the hallway and involuntarily bent toward the wicket-grilled window in the door. A gross drop of sweat rode down the part in his hair, as far as his temple; he canted his head back, and found himself presenting his underjaw to the woman who opened the door. She was small, olive skinned, with dark long hair falling loosely around a short face. He saw that she was plain. Her eye whites seemed congested. He judged her to be about thirty. She was wearing several plain metal rings.

He asked, "Are you by any chance Ray's wife? You must be."

She nodded as she drew back to admit them.

He thought at first that she might be pregnant: she was wearing a homemade loosefitting khaki-and-yellow monk's-cloth tunic. But then remembered that Hession had occasionally dressed his first wife in brutally colored tie-dyed skirts and sheaths of his own making.

"Wait, don't let me forget my son," he said.

She proceeded rapidly through the hall. "Is Ray home?" he asked after her. He gathered that she was hurrying in order not to miss something underway in the living room. He let her precede him by a good distance, and decided against trying to give her his name. He stopped at the entrance to the living room while she continued ahead through the small scattered group there to her place. He stood unacknowledged at the side of the entry arch, making himself smile. Hession was there, and was speaking.

4. Hession's voice was unchanged, although his old trait of using a controlled nasality at times to suggest chest tones below his actual register seemed now more obtrusive to Walter than it had in the past.

The walls and ceiling of the room before him were white; the room was heavily daylit through broad windows in the two long walls. A smaller arch than the one he stood in divided the blind wall directly opposite; there were padded benches in recesses on either side of that arch, and Hession's wife was seated on one of them. Hession was at the middle of the long wall nearest the street, in an armchair, his back to Walter, his feet stretched out to an electric heater planted in the scoured fireplace. Another armchair, across the hearth, also faced the heater: it was occupied by a skeletal blond girl of eighteen or so. The other long wall was taken up by an oceanic parquet library table and a leather-covered sofa. On the sofa sat two young men, college students apparently, one a soft-looking light-complected Negro, the other a classic Nordic youth, very strongly built, self-possessed or insolent, handsome, wearing a narrow coppery jawline beard which made his face look as though it were held in a kind of sling. The girl and the two young men were dressed alike, in pastel jeans and starched and pressed chambray work shirts. The girl wore sandals, the young men wore Army-surplus paratroop boots black with neat's-foot oil. In the corner on his right, separated from the sofa by a reach of blank wall, Walter saw an empty armchair: he would take it, even though it meant a long tour in front of the sofa to get to the refreshments.

The artificial bareness of the room was oppressive. There were no shelves or decorations, the hardwood floor was bare and highly polished. Walter could detect shadows of former shelves and brackets under the fresh paint on the walls. The furniture was of the best quality. An ozone tinge, from the heater, hung in the air.

Hession half turned his head, gestured blindly to Walter to come in, and turned away again. Walter entered uncertainly. A final figure joined the group: a nondescript man in his sixties, in shirtsleeves, wearing a beret, emerged from the opposite arch and seated himself on the unoccupied bench. Walter knew his face.

"In," Hession said, waving Walter forward without looking at him, implying by his tone a familiarity so well established that there was no need to greet or introduce Walter or to interrupt the discussion in progress.

Ah no! Walter thought.

5. He had arrived during variations on a remark of Hession's to the effect that literary criticism would be corrupt until it could be placed in the hands of a special Order. Promising men would be trained from an early age in aesthetics and the classics; they would be maintained in isolation and opulence by the government; they would be forbidden to have friendships or connections outside their Order; each branch of art could have its own cloister; critics would be forbidden to produce any object competitive with those they criticized.

6. Walter thought, The perfect German military head, still!. He's physically German, which is why in person his radicalism carries so strongly to you when you're young especially: you see him despising and agitating against a system under which he could obviously be coldly leading and ruling and getting handsomely rewarded for it.

He felt that Hession had aged less than he himself had, comparatively. Hession's color was better than his; Hession's hair, still thick enough to be worn close-cropped without embarrassment, was only moderately grayer than it had been. At fifty he was no more than normally heavy through the chops and neck. He was unexpectedly well dressed, in a gray thin-wale corduroy suit and an oxblood silk shirt open at the throat. The wrists of his shirt puffed correctly out of his suit coat cuffs. Hession's dress seemed overformal for one o'clock on a Sunday afternoon, leading Walter to suppose Hession might be planning to go out, possibly for a reading.

The clearest change was in Hession's expression, which seemed to have lost a certain fixing or holding force. Obviously, very slight changes can alter the force of a face. Walter thought, He's reduced almost to staring, which is not the same thing as before.

On his lap Hession held a flask containing white wine: he languidly used it to fill a glass on the floor beside his chair. Then he rose, crossed to the table, put the flask down, and went back to his seat. Walter remembered him as being taller, as standing clearly over six feet.

7. Walter went to his chair, thinking, He doesn't know me. Or, it might be he might not want to show he knows me for some reason in front of his cult here, but there would be some plausible reason; of course in himself he knows me; I only thank God I dressed this way.

Hession said, "Sit down. The baby as well: we like babies. I don't think you had him before."

"No, not ten years ago, no."

Well then, Walter thought, but found no way to conclude.

The blond sitting near Hession smiled sociably at Walter, who thought, That girl is southern and her interminable worthless smile is the only amiable thing in the room toward us so far and unfortunately that only issues out of stupidity: good manners.

"O, my wife, by the way," Hession said, indicating the dark woman, "in the corner. Her name is Allegra for which I am in no way responsible and which was insisted on by her mother and which I understand stands for 'That was quick.' " His wife made no response.

He has an idea who I am, Walter thought, I'm dealing with shame now: he does know me, though.

Hession was up again, pacing. He stopped at the window by the table and put his forehead against the glass. He sighed deeply, producing wings of breath mist on the glass.

Walter thought, Even in the old days very few introductions were made, if you recall. He raised his son onto his lap. Owen folded his arms across the parcel.

8. The refreshments consisted of wheat crackers, two kinds of process cheese, wine, pastries, rolls, anise toast. There was hot water

in an electric urn. Cups, with a spoonful of instant coffee or a tea bag in each one, had been set out. Walter made tea for himself. He chose a pastry for Owen, tore the dry rim away from the custard center, held out the center to Owen, who accepted it. Walter collected the halves of the rim and kept them in his saucer.

Walter remembered the old man as a chain smoker: he was now smoking effortfully, four fingers and thumb forming a globe around the burning tip of his cigarette: white fore-smoke flowed liquidly through the spaces between his fingers.

Hession paced the axis of the room. While Hession was out of his seat, the others devised conversation or small personal make-work. Silence rose when Hession sat down. Walter felt himself yielding to the rhythm he observed. He gave lively but unnecessary attention to Owen.

9. Hession stopped at Walter's chair, and asked, "What're you up to these days?"

"Self-unemployed," Walter answered.

"What?"

"Self-unemployed. No, self-employed. I'm a small businessman. I'm in the book business, I sell out-of-print books. I think I once sent you some lists, my first list or so."

"O are you? At one point I thought of going into that myself as a last resort."

Yes I know!, Walter thought, but said, "Yes you were talking seriously about it. You had letterheads made. In fact you probably had something to do with why I went into it. You were serious. Now of course you don't need to."

"I'm well aware," Hession said, after a pause, with a mock-dumbfounded air.

Hession resumed his pacing. He continued, to Walter: "Of course out-of-print books, as a category — a commodity category — didn't exist until Hitler, in this part of the world. You only had the class 'secondhand books'; in print or out was beside the point. That only changed with the Frankfurt Jews coming over after Hitler got in. When they opened up over here they established for the first time that you pay more than the original list price when the book is out of print. We have them to thank. Before that everything used sold for less than it had new, in print or out. This isn't generally known, by the way."

Walter said, "Except that even before that you had some, a few, specialists, some I could name, who anticipated . . ."

"Ah, but only for the typically *rare* old book! Or art books. Incunables! But there was no intermediate zone of books two or five or six years old out of print where you had to pay fifty to five hundred per cent above the recent published price. This is a curse on scholarship."

"Well, but there were native specialists, nonemigrés . . . and also the change was coming by itself anyway sooner or later."

Hession said, "Without the Jews it would've been another forty years."

"O less than that."

"I think your knowledge of the particular rate at which your trade moves is slightly off. Your trade normally barely moves, left to itself. But this gets us into the Jewish question. Your knowledge of the Jews is off."

"No, all I'm saying is that forty years seems exaggerated."

"The Jew *everywhere* in every area has the same economic effect, in art or wherever you find him, he can't help it and this is not anti-Semitism, it's an appreciation more than anything. In literature the Jew writes more, or he edits more: he has velocity, he accelerates. One problem you'll never hear of in any branch of art is Jewish underproductivity, the problem of the lapidary Jew: Acton's Disease, if you know what that is. Acton could never finish anything to his satisfaction, he barely let himself finish the few articles that made him world famous. Acton's Disease is the disease of the Anglo-Saxon artistic temperament. Lord Acton represents a deformed or extreme form of a condition or tendency which is normally to the good, it leads to good art. Jews in some way have the power of intensifying the tendency of each . . . pursuit! to be what it is: so in some cases they can exhaust a pursuit, prematurely exhaust it; or they use up a genre for example before a natural master can appear, which is not to say that sometimes the natural master isn't Jewish, of course."

Walter thought, He has more than an idea who I am: I think he's ashamed he forgets my name, if that's it he'll try to show he remembers me, probably.

Hession went on, "Or in men's clothing, now you have seasonality. In book publishing you have the Jewish invention of remaindering. We never had it on any scale in this country until nineteen forty-six. Well in any case, how's business?"

"Well at first it was close. It's also different than what I once thought I'd be doing by now."

"You wanted to write, wasn't it?"

"I did, yes."

"O and you brought me some things to read . . . ?"

"*No.* Nono. Everyone did, though. You were taken up. So much so I remember I wondered how you got any writing done. But I never did, no." Simultaneously Hession had spoken, using the phrase "fairly good."

A silence followed.

Hession said, "I thought you had. No? All right."

After another pause, Hession asked, "What field are you?"

"General scholarly out-of-print books and modern first editions, mainly."

"Ah. Do you ever get any of my early stuff?"

"Well, so far I haven't. Very little. I think because people tend to hang onto them, Ray."

"What could you get for a copy of *Exactions,* if you had one?"

"O, well, a lot. A lot."

"About how much?"

"O a lot."

"But you don't know how much?"

"It would be a lot. Over fifteen dollars."

"That much," Hession said, with dull sarcasm.

"Over that. That was a minimum." Walter thought, I lied and it fell short.

Walter said, "Ray, what about all your books, your library, that enormous collection . . . ?"

In unison, the two young men on the sofa said, "Upstairs."

"Some I sold," Hession said.

"You had so many," Walter said.

"Too many. More than I needed. I sold only what I didn't need. As a dealer you wouldn't have any idea how few books you really need."

"No, as a dealer that's exactly, exactly what I, what I know. I do know that."

"Here, wipe his hands." Hession handed Walter a napkin for Owen.

In mind, Walter saw again the packed shelves in Hession's prior quarters, the mantelshelf solidly filled with the Loeb Classics, the *Poètes d'Aujourd'hui* lined up from #1 to #30, place marks in everything.

10. From his bench, the old man was gravely, at long range, offering cigarettes around: fixating someone, he held out his cigarette case, shook it, hunched his shoulders and squinted questioningly until he received a response. No one accepted. In refusing, the Negro playfully shook his own pack of cigarettes at the old man.

Walter thought, What did I want to say?: O yes, at forty he was one thing in the culture, at fifty he discovers he's considered an ancillary force or name or an associated force or force tributary to other names in his generation: so no matter what future work he looks forward to doing it has to fall into a secondary category: so: he divorces himself from everyone who expected something else, like Beryl: by accident someone like E. O. Arditi could write the greatest individual poem since "Dover Beach" but who would notice it?: you wouldn't like it: you wouldn't like that very well yourself.

The blond girl and the two young men were English majors at the Municipal College. Walter understood that there was some hope of Hession's appointment as resident poet at the college.

The girl student abruptly revived a compliment to Hession that she had offered earlier: "Anyway I loved it the way you read it this time."

"Which one again?" Hession asked.

"The one about, the same one you read the other way on television."

The handsome white student spoke out in a polished, manly, foisting voice, "She means 'Injurious Song.'" Walter had begun to refer mentally to the speaker as "Vandal."

The blond girl paged roughly through a book of Hession's verse.

Vandal observed generally, "Ray should do more light stuff."

Walter was overwhelmed by the need to manifest himself. He solicited himself for some vital idea. Hession asked Walter, "Did I get some letters from you from New York once?"

"What? I wasn't listening," Walter said.

"Never mind," Hession said.

"But what was it? I was thinking about something."

Hession dismissed the question. Walter glanced for help to the students, who smiled negatively, demonstrating their subjection to Hession's interest.

Walter thought, Then I have to go back before the question: I was on the verge of something to say. But he failed to descend usefully into himself, and finally thought, If I think well I can at least recover the question my mind heard: it's there: I order you.

11. The atmosphere had become oddly rancorous. Allegra began to play the overture to *Khovantchina* at low volume on the phonograph, and was ferociously overruled by Hession, who went so far as to instruct the old man (he was identified in Walter's mind as Compton, an illustrator of several of Hession's limited editions) to be sure that the phonograph was fully turned off before it was slid back into its cabinet. Then followed slow exchanges on the decline of reading. There was no longer a disinterested reading class, everyone now read for narrow utility or for what could be called venal reasons: if you were a serious vanguard writer you could expect your readership to consist of, One, other writers who read you for competitive reasons, and Two, critics who would get career points for being right ("being right" meant guessing which writers would become academic commodities ahead of others, become authors that people, the young, were compelled to read by force): the reason-for-being for a part of the prior or dead reading or culture-receiving class had been social guilt, guilt at having leisure: a considerable class had submitted itself to literature in an expiatory spirit and this had made them ideal readers: the object of vanguard writing was to advance human consciousness, but the size of the class accessible to true change was shrinking: vanguard writers ran the risk of writing directly for academic placement in an indirect competition for grants, preference, recommendation: the revival of

vanguard pornography was related to the whole development under discussion. Walter remained outside the discussion.

At points Compton had given an unvarying falsetto joke outcry which Walter finally interpreted as "Turn up the pornograph."

12. Owen had escaped to the fireplace. Walter called to him, then in dumb show signaled that he should give the parcel to Hession. Owen turned disobediently and faced the fireplace, studying the heater.

"He's ril cute," the blond said.

Walter said, "I made the mistake of calling that a present. At his age he thinks all presents are for him."

"O what is it?"

"O something for Ray. A book. More of a pamphlet."

"He's ril cute isn't he, how old is he?"

"He's two."

Walter thought, Men like to produce men, actively like to: women like to produce women: we love our own sex, each sex does.

"Turn around, Owen," Walter said.

Hession was noticing Owen. Walter thought, He had no children when I knew him: when he knew me, rather: now he has one, a son, but where is he, with Beryl?

"He thinks it's his, look at that," the blond girl said for Hession to overhear.

Again Walter said, "I made the mistake of calling that a present."

"What's in it?" Hession asked.

"O, only a copy of *The Ecliptic.* You once mentioned you couldn't get a copy when you needed one. So. I happened to have one. So. So I thought I'd bring it on the chance you still didn't have it. Probably by now you have."

Over his shoulder, Hession asked his wife, "Do we have that or not?"

"By Joseph Gordon MacLeod. No, we don't have a thing."

"O, then I would like it, yes. Apparently I never managed to get it. This is a very important thing, virtually unknown here in *outre-mer* in spite of my best efforts." For Vandal, Hession added: "You should read it if you haven't.

Flow full, Eurotas river, we hymn Castor dead.
Flow from your fond Borean watershed
Alone to wide ship-bare Laconian bight . . .

It's better than it sounds."

Hession's wife had come up. Diffidently she said to Hession, "He's beautiful, isn't he, his son? He's a beautiful boy."

"Owen better give that to me right now," Walter said.

Hession said, "Try again in a minute. Let him forget."

Walter thought, How much can I tell Joan about this?

"We'll all eat, we're all hungry," Vandal proclaimed, standing, directing the Negro and the blond girl to join him in diverting Owen's attention.

Discreetly the blond girl asked Walter, "Can he talk yet? He doesn't answer."

"Not much."

"Oh. But how old is he?"

"Two. But he doesn't yet, much."

The girl said to Hession's wife: "He doesn't talk."

Allegra answered, "He may not want to."

"No, he doesn't talk apparently," the blond girl said.

"O but he's still little," Allegra said.

"We are really *hungry,*" Vandal called. Playing at eating, noisily stirring the silverware, he beckoned Compton and Hession's wife to the table. They began praising the pastry.

Walter squatted next to Owen, who was flushed and frowning. His sweater! Walter thought, On all this time! I take off his jacket and leave this on, this is making me mad: I can't take it off now when I have to plan to leave: he has to bear it for my sake until we go, until we can go: it's my fault, he's so hot.

On impulse he whispered urgently, "Owen, you keep the present, you're good. You keep it. No, you keep this, keep it till we get home to Joan. When we get home you can open it, Owen. You keep it. You hold it, it's a toy inside. You keep the present."

O, and also my bald streak is showing: show it to them: here it is, boys! where the cold comes, Walter thought.

He remained squatting, in alarm and satisfaction, until silence at the table warned him to rise and proceed. He said, "He won't do it. He thinks it's his. It's my fault. I can't get it away. But I can easily mail it later. Sorry."

Hession approached Owen again, bent down, held out one and then both hands, and said, "Could I see that? Could I just look at it?"

"You can't ask to see it then keep it," Allegra said.

"Could I (what's his name?), could I see it a minute?"

Owen shrank from Hession.

"He won't, Ray. There's no use. It can be mailed," Walter said.

"O, he's too little to give it to anybody anyway. He's too little to come give it to me," the blond girl said.

"Yes, he is," Hession said. "He's too little to give it to us to let us see it, even."

Hession's wife said, "Ray, you can't do it, you can't take it to see it then keep it."

"He won't know the difference," Vandal said, unmistakably (to Walter) aping Hession's trait of skewing his gaze away from his respondents in conversation, when he wanted to provoke.

"What's up?" Walter asked.

"What?" Vandal asked in reply.

"You were looking over there as though you saw something outside. I thought you saw something I couldn't see," Walter said.

The Negro dropped to his knees, and then to hands and knees.

Owen retreated behind Walter's legs.

"Haven't we got that thing for Ray yet?" Vandal asked.

"We should all forget about it for now," Hession's wife said.

Vandal stretched and yawned tediously. He folded his shirt cuffs back once, exhibiting impressive wrists. He joined the circle around Walter and Owen.

"I guess that's that for us," Walter said.

"What's *in* that present, Owen? I could open it up for you. Why is Owen so mean? He's mean," the Negro said.

"O, he's *ril* mean. He should give it to the horse and get a ride from the horsie," the blond girl said.

Walter pressed and steered Owen out of the cluster and toward the hall. Owen's jacket lay folded across the arm of Walter's chair.

"His jacket, excuse me," Walter said, stepping away to get the jacket, momentarily abandoning Owen.

"Ah look, he *peed* himself!" the Negro said, then said more shrilly, "O let me out of here! Shame on you. You go in the bathroom, Owen. You give me that, you need to go to the bathroom. You go with Daddy."

"Get away from him! He can't help it! I'm sorry. I'm taking him home," Walter said, in a furious uneven voice.

Weakened by shame, Owen was about to surrender the parcel; but Walter returned, caught Owen's hand and clasped it shut on the parcel, concealing the act in the movement of lifting the boy. He carried him to the front door, maneuvering to keep the parcel between his body and Owen's.

Vandal followed them. Still holding Owen, Walter sought with one hand to work the two catches on the front door.

"Possibly we could trade with the child: Ray must have something we could trade, upstairs . . ." Vandal said.

"No."

"We could try it."

"No."

" (What's the book again?)"

"*The Ecliptic.* By Joseph Gordon MacLeod. You never heard of it."

He thanked Vandal for opening the door.

Hession had been coming forward as Walter left. On the stoop he imagined Hession staring after him. He forced himself onward. The door closed solidly.

13. Walter descended the porch steps, the walk, reached the walk steps at the edge of the property. He looked back. The porch and windows were empty.

Violently Walter seized the parcel and pried it away from Owen: he set the boy down and met his son's agonized cry of rage with a bestial and menacing grimace. He pushed the boy to a sitting position on the bottom step, left him, and ran stooping back to Hession's door. He leaned the parcel against the door, trying several angles. He ran back down to his son.

14. He stood with Owen in the shade of a high retaining wall near the foot of the hill. Owen's involved intractable weeping was drawing attention.

Walter thought, When he's older, when he can speak I can explain this.

But his own words, "when he can speak," released in him an abrupt and intolerable longing, an anticipation, which, swelling, drove all mental speech away.

DANNY SANTIAGO

The Somebody

(FROM REDBOOK)

THIS IS CHATO TALKING, Chato de Shamrock, from the Eastside in old L.A., and I want you to know this is a big day in my life because today I quit school and went to work as a writer. I write on fences or buildings or anything that comes along. I write my name, not the one I got from my father. I want no part of him. I write Chato, which means Catface, because I have a flat nose like a cat. It's a Mexican word because that's what I am, a Mexican, and I'm not ashamed of it. I like that language too, man. It's way better than English to say what you feel. But German is the best. It's got a real rugged sound, and I'm going to learn to talk it someday.

After Chato I write "de Shamrock." That's the street where I live, and it's the name of the gang I belong to, but the others are all gone now. Their families had to move away, except Gorilla is in jail and Blackie joined the navy because he liked swimming. But I still have our old arsenal. It's buried under the chickens, and I dig it up when I get bored. There's tire irons and chains and pick handles with spikes and two zip guns we made and they shoot real bullets but not very straight. In the good old days nobody cared to tangle with us. But now I'm the only one left.

Well, today started off like any other day. The toilet roars like a hot rod taking off. My father coughs and spits about nineteen times and hollers it's six-thirty. So I holler back I'm quitting school. Things hit me like that — sudden.

"Don't you want to be a lawyer no more," he says in Spanish, "and defend the Mexican people?"

My father thinks he is very funny, and next time I make any plans, he's sure not going to hear about it.

"Don't you want to be a doctor," he says, "and cut off my leg for nothing someday?"

"Due beast ine dumb cop," I tell him in German, but not very loud.

"How will you support me," he says, "when I retire? Or will you marry a rich old woman that owns a pool hall?"

"I'm checking out of this dump! You'll never see me again!"

I hollered it at him, but already he was in the kitchen making a big noise in his coffee. I could be dead and he wouldn't take me serious. So I laid there and waited for him to go off to work. When I woke up again, it was way past eleven. I can sleep forever these days. So I got out of bed and put on clean jeans and my windbreaker and combed myself very neat because already I had a feeling this was going to be a big day for me.

I had to wait for breakfast because the baby was sick and throwing up milk on everything. There is always a baby vomiting in my house. When they're born, everybody comes over and says: *"Qué* cute!" but nobody passes any comments on the dirty way babies act or the dirty way they were made either. Sometimes my mother asks me to hold one for her but it always cries, maybe because I squeeze it a little hard when nobody's looking.

When my mother finally served me, I had to hold my breath, she smelled so bad of babies. I don't care to look at her anymore. Her legs got those dark-blue rivers running all over them. I kept waiting for her to bawl me out about school, but I guess she forgot, or something. So I cut out.

Every time I go out my front door I have to cry for what they've done to old Shamrock Street. It used to be so fine, with solid homes on both sides. Maybe they needed a little paint here and there but they were cozy. Then the S.P. railroad bought up all the land except my father's place because he was stubborn. They came in with their wrecking bars and their bulldozers. You could hear those houses scream when they ripped them down. So now Shamrock Street is just front walks that lead to a hole in the ground, and piles of busted cement. And Pelón's house and Blackie's are just stacks of old boards waiting to get hauled away. I hope that never happens to your street, man.

My first stop was the front gate and there was that sign again, that big S wrapped around a cross like a snake with rays coming out, which is the mark of the Sierra Street gang, as everybody knows. I rubbed it off, but tonight they'll put it back again. In the old days they wouldn't dare to come on our street, but without your gang you're nobody. And one of these fine days they're going to catch up with me in person and that will be the end of Chato de Shamrock.

So I cruised on down to Main Street like a ghost in a graveyard. Just to prove I'm alive, I wrote my name on the fence at the corner. A lot of names you see in public places are written very sloppy. Not me. I take my time. Like my fifth-grade teacher used to say, if other people are going to see your work, you owe it to yourself to do it right. Mrs. Cully was her name and she was real nice, for an Anglo. My other teachers were all cops but Mrs. Cully drove me home one time when some guys were after me. I think she wanted to adopt me but she never said anything about it. I owe a lot to that lady, and especially my writing. You should see it, man — it's real smooth and mellow, and curvy like a blond in a bikini. Everybody says so. Except one time they had me in Juvenile by mistake and some doctor looked at it. He said it proved I had something wrong with me, some long word. That doctor was crazy, because I made him show me his writing and it was real ugly like a barb-wire fence with little chickens stuck on the points. You couldn't even read it.

Anyway, I signed myself very clean and neat on that corner. And then I thought, Why not look for a job someplace? But I was more in the mood to write my name, so I went into the dime store and helped myself to two boxes of crayons and some chalk and cruised on down Main, writing all the way. I wondered should I write more than my name. Should I write, "Chato is a fine guy," or, "Chato, is wanted by the police"? Things like that. News. But I decided against it. Better to keep them guessing. Then I crossed over to Forney Playground. It used to be our territory, but now the Sierra have taken over there like everyplace else Just to show them, I wrote on the tennis court and the swimming pool and the gym. I left a fine little trail of Chato de Shamrock in eight colors. Some places I used chalk, which works better on brick or plaster. But crayons are the thing for cement or anything smooth, like in the girls' rest room. On that wall I also drew a little picture the girls would be interested in and put down a phone number beside it. I bet a lot of them are going to call that number, but it isn't mine because we don't have a phone in the first place, and in the second place I'm probably never going home again.

I'm telling you, I was pretty famous at the Forney by the time I cut out, and from there I continued my travels till something hit me. You know how you put your name on something and that proves it belongs to you? Things like school books or gym shoes? So I thought, How about that, now? And I put my name on the Triple A Market and on Morrie's Liquor Store and on the Zócalo, which is a beer joint. And then I cruised on up Broadway, getting rich. I took over a barber shop and a furniture store and the Plymouth agency. And the firehouse for laughs, and the phone company so I could call all my girl friends and keep my dimes. And then there I was at Webster and Garcia's Funeral Home with the big white columns. At first I thought that might be bad luck, but then I said, Oh, well, we all got to die sometime. So I signed myself, and now I can eat good and live in style and have a big time all my life, and then kiss you all good-bye and give myself the best damn funeral in L.A. for free.

And speaking of funerals, along came the Sierra right then, eight or ten of them down the street with that stupid walk which is their trademark. I ducked into the garage and hid behind the hearse. Not that I'm a coward. Getting stomped doesn't bother me, or even shot. What I hate is those blades, man. They're like a piece of ice cutting into your belly. But the Sierra didn't see me and went on by. I couldn't hear what they were saying but I knew they had me on their mind. So I cut on over to the Boys' Club, where they don't let anybody get you, no matter who you are. To pass the time I shot some baskets and played a little pool and watched the television, but the story was boring, so it came to me, Why not write my name on the screen? Which I did with a squeaky pen. Those cowboys sure looked fine with Chato de Shamrock written all over them. Everybody got a kick out of it. But of course up comes Mr. Calderon and makes me wipe it off. They're always spying on you up there. And he takes me into his office and closes the door.

"Well," he says, "and how is the last of the dinosaurs?"

Meaning that the Shamrocks are as dead as giant lizards.

Then he goes into that voice with the church music in it and I look out of the window.

"I know it's hard to lose your gang, Chato," he says, "but this is your chance to make new friends and straighten yourself out. Why don't you start coming to Boys' Club more?"

"It's boring here," I tell him.

"What about school?"

"I can't go," I said. "They'll get me."

"The Sierra's forgotten you're alive," he tells me.

"Then how come they put their mark on my house every night?"

"Do they?"

He stares at me very hard. I hate those eyes of his. He thinks he knows everything. And what is he? Just a Mexican like everybody else.

"Maybe you put that mark there yourself," he says. "To make yourself big. Just like you wrote on the television."

"That was my name! I like to write my name!"

"So do dogs," he says. "On every lamppost they come to."

"You're a dog youself," I told him, but I don't think he heard me. He just went on talking. Brother, how they love to talk up there! But I didn't bother to listen, and when he ran out of gas I left. From now on I'm scratching that Boys' Club off my list.

Out on the street it was getting dark, but I could still follow my trail back toward Broadway. It felt good seeing Chato written everyplace, but at the Zócalo I stopped dead. Around my name there was a big red heart done in lipstick with some initials I didn't recognize. To tell the truth, I didn't know how to feel. In one way I was mad that anyone would fool with my name, especially if it was some guy doing it for laughs. But what guy carries lipstick? And if it was a girl, that could be kind of interesting.

A girl is what it turned out to be. I caught up with her at the telephone company. There she is, standing in the shadows, drawing her heart around my name. And she has a very pretty shape on her, too. I sneak up behind her very quiet, thinking all kinds of crazy things and my blood shooting around so fast it shakes me all over. And then she turns around and it's only Crusader Rabbit.

That's what we called her from the television show they had then, on account of her teeth in front.

When she sees me, she takes off down the alley, but in twenty feet I catch her. I grab for the lipstick, but she whips it behind her. I reach around and try to pull her fingers open, but her hand is sweaty and so is mine. And there we are, stuck together all the way down. I can feel everything she's got and her breath is on my cheek. She twists up against me, kind of giggling. To tell the truth, I don't like to wrestle with girls. They don't fight fair. And then we lost balance and fell against some garbage cans, so I woke up. After that I got the lipstick away from her very easy.

"What right you got to my name?" I tell her. "I never gave you permission."

"You sign yourself real fine," she says.

I knew that already.

"Let's go writing together," she says.

"The Sierra's after me."

"I don't care," she says. "Come on, Chato — you and me can have a lot of fun."

She came up close and giggled that way. She put her hand on my hand that had the lipstick in it. And you know what? I'm ashamed to say I almost told her yes. It would be a change to go writing with a girl. We could talk there in the dark. We could decide on the best places. And her handwriting wasn't too bad either. But then I remembered I had my reputation to think of. Somebody would be sure to see us, and they'd be laughing at me all over the Eastside. So I pulled my hand away and told her off.

"Run along, Crusader," I told her. "I don't want no partners, and especially not you."

"Who are you calling Crusader?" she screamed. "You ugly, squash-nose punk."

She called me everything. And spit at my face but missed. I didn't argue. I just cut out. And when I got to the first sewer I threw away her lipstick. Then I drifted over to the banks at Broadway and Bailey, which is a good spot for writing because a lot of people pass by there.

Well, I hate to brag, but that was the best work I've ever done in all my life. Under the street lamp my name shone like solid gold. I stood to one side and checked the people as they walked past and inspected it. With some you can't tell just how they feel, but with others it rings out like a cash register. There was one man. He got out of his Cadillac to buy a paper and when he saw my name he smiled. He was the age to be my father. I bet he'd give me a job if I asked him. I bet he'd take me to his home and to his office in the morning. Pretty soon I'd be sitting at my own desk and signing my name on letters and checks and things. But I would never buy a Cadillac, man. They burn too much gas.

Later a girl came by. She was around eighteen, I think, with green eyes. Her face was so pretty I didn't dare to look at her shape. Do you want me to go crazy? That girl stopped and really studied my name like she fell in love with it. She wanted to know me, I could tell. She wanted to take my hand and we'd go off together just holding hands and nothing dirty. We'd go to Beverly Hills and nobody would look at us the wrong way. I almost said "Hi" to that girl, and, "How do you like my writing?" But not quite.

So here I am, standing on this corner with my chalk all gone and only one crayon left and it's ugly brown. My fingers are too cold besides. But I don't care because I just had a vision, man. Did they ever turn on the lights for you so you could see the whole world and everything in it? That's how it came to me right now. I don't need to be a movie star or boxing champ to make my name in the world. All I need is plenty of chalk and crayons. And that's easy. L.A. is a big city, man, but give me a couple of months and I'll be famous all over town. Of course they'll try to stop me — the Sierra, the police and everybody. But I'll be like a ghost, man. I'll be real mysterious, and all they'll know is just my name, signed like I always sign it, CHATO DE SHAMROCK with rays shooting out like from the Holy Cross.

JONATHAN STRONG

Xavier Fereira's Unfinished Book: Chapter One

(FROM TRIQUARTERLY*)

JEFF KIMBERK AND I were both born on Groundhog Day 1945, and that coincidence was what first made us take note of each other seventeen and a half years later. It was the day of my arrival at Harvard College. Some fool was stopping everyone in the stairwell of the dormitory and asking him when he was born as a test of some esoteric theory of probability. Jeff was bounding down two steps at a time as I was strugging up with my steamer trunk which I rested on the banister when the fool asked his question. "February second," Jeff and I replied in the same breath and then looked at each other in amazement. Not that we became friends at that point. My impression then and throughout freshman year was that he did not wish to be publicly associated with me on any grounds in anyone's mind. Such paranoid impressions tormented me considerably in those days.

My birthday was the source of my college nickname, the Groundhog. That no one thought of applying it equally to Jeff bothered me, though I knew why well enough. He and all the others took to greeting me with, "How much ground would a groundhog hog if a groundhog could hog ground?" To which I was expected to reply, "A groundhog would hog all the ground he could hog if a groundhog could hog ground," not that I ever did. I would as soon forget those days and have no intention of referring to them

* Originally published in an earlier draft and as part of the novel *Ourselves*, published by the Atlantic Monthly Press in association with Little, Brown & Co. with Little, Brown & Co.

further except when it might add the proper shading to this story of more comradely times. I had a long and bad late-adolescence, but it is over. Jeff and I are now old friends.

We lived in the same house as sophomores, but in different entries, and Jeff took a year in Europe after his junior year. When he returned, our original class had graduated, and he was surprised to find himself assigned to room with me. I had fallen behind too, though somewhat less voluntarily.

I had changed considerably by then. Our old classmates were no longer there to perpetuate my groundhog image, and Jeff could approach the situation anew. For one thing I was no longer the baggy and drab sort I had been when I was known as the Groundhog. My curly black hair had been allowed to grow. I let my features and my hands express themselves — no more timid eyes, serious mouth, paws in pockets. I wore clothes which fit my shape, and instead of the old grays and browns, I wore whatever cheerful colors I felt like.

Jeff did not even recognize me at first. When he looked closer he said, "Oh, it's you," but there was an edge of pleasant surprise in his voice. He called me Xavy from the start and only referred to the groundhog business when the second of February came around. I suppose he did not want to feel he had a groundhog for a roommate and probably feared someone else might dig up the old nickname to embarrass him.

Jeff was considerably taller than I was and had much lighter and straighter hair which he, too, soon ceased to have cut. His eyes were blue, his features sharp. My Portuguese blood showed in my rounder features, my black eyes, and of course my almost African hair, once the curse of my life.

Jeff's body was naturally sure of itself in a way that mine, however I might liberate it, would never be. I never saw him drop anything or miss catching something, while I was as likely to drop a ball as catch it. He never tripped up or stubbed his toes, but I was always a stumbler, and my ankles sometimes simply buckled under me. I do not know why. It may have been a symptom of my timidity.

We graduated together, though there was some question whether I would make it. My year off had cured me of bookwormishness, and I only managed to finish three late term papers the day before graduation. Jeff and I had decided to continue rooming together after college, but in a share-and-share-alike fashion with whoever else might need a place to sleep. I was glad to have a circle of friends at last and particularly one good friend to depend on. The problem of the draft had been solved for both of us by Jeff's allergies and my psychiatric difficulties. I found a job at a bookstore, and Jeff had a trust fund.

Neither of us felt under any pressure to plan out a course of life. Our original classmates were in medical schools and law schools or in the army, but we were just doing a little more thinking, a little waiting. We rejected the idea that twenty-two-year-olds must at once begin their future careers, but I admit we were awfully uncontributory, unwilling to dedicate ourselves to anything, and quite presumptuous of our rights and privileges. I suppose I still am.

We rented the ground floor of one of those gray frame buildings which line up one after another in Somerville, a town with lower rents than the famous two-university town next to it. Somerville was much like the town I grew up in, and I felt at home there. Our furniture consisted of a card table, two dust-bag armchairs, and several bare mattresses. Needless to say it was a temporary arrangement, and we found a more civilized place in September. That was after Susannah Twombley had made her appearance; but before I bring in Susannah, let me establish Jeff and me by ourselves.

Scene: Beethoven piano sonatas dropping one by one on the automatic stereo, the ceiling globe surrounded by light green bugs, the windows open and the yellowed shades flapping in the light breeze; a very sticky summer evening. Jeff in a pair of madras bermudas, leftovers from his sharp collegiate wardrobe, reading The Good Soldier *in the maroon armchair; Xavy in torn-off Levi's on one of the mattresses reading* Victories in Defeats.

Jeff: We should buy a fan, you know.

Xavy: You buy it. You've got the cash.

Jeff: I think I will.

Xavy: Good.

Jeff: It goes in my room, though.

Xavy: Fair enough.

Jeff: Of course I know it'll end up out here most of the time.

Xavy: I won't touch it.

Jeff: I wonder if I should get an exhaust fan or a rotating one.

Xavy: Suit yourself.

Jeff: Exhaust fans never seem to do anything.

Xavy: It's all in your mind.

Jeff: (*After quite a pause*) I think I'll get a rotating fan.

Xavy: Good.

Jeff: Tomorrow. (*They return to their books.*)

Scene: Jeff's room, bright sunlight outside, a fan rotating on the windowsill blowing on Jeff asleep in his underwear on a sheetless mattress, the torn windowshade pulled down to the top of the fan. A very fluffy brown and white cat walks across Jeff's back and wakes him up.

Jeff: (*Yelling*) Xavy, get your fucking cat out of here.

Xavy: (*From the hall*) It's not *my* fucking cat.

Jeff: Get it out anyway.

Xavy: (*Enters, in jeans, T-shirt, sandals*) Come on, Aztec. Hey, Az! It's time to get up anyway. Come on, Aztec.

Jeff: No it isn't. What time is it?

Xavy: Eight thirty. I'm going to work.

Jeff: Good night. (*Xavy departs with the cat under his arm.*) Shut the door. I don't want that fucking cat in here again. (*Xavy slams the door; Jeff yawns.*) Oh boy.

Scene: a summer storm, late Saturday afternoon, Bruckner's Sixth at full volume, the windows wide open, shades up, water pouring straight down. Xavy and Aztec in the navy-blue armchair, the former reading Fathers and Sons; *Jeff and a girl named Elly in the kitchenette making fudge; four anonymous legs visible through the double door on a mattress in Xavy's room.*

Elly: Get your fingers out of the fudge!

Jeff: Yes, ma'am.

Elly: Hand me that spoon.

Jeff: Yes, ma'am! (*Pause, some giggling.*)

Elly: Cut it out, Jeff.

Xavy: (*To Aztec*) Like the rain, Az?

Jeff: (*Coming into the living room*) I'm not very cooperative. (*Pause*) Couldn't you put on something else, Xavy?

Xavy: What's wrong with this?

Jeff: You always overdo things. You've been playing Bruckner's Sixth at full volume all week. The neighbors must know it by heart.

Xavy: I just bought it.

Jeff: But you don't savor things, Fereira. You run them into the ground.

Xavy: Why is everyone so picky? Elly's picky, you're picky. (*Jeff sits in the maroon armchair, stretches, and stares out the window.*)

Jeff: Sure is coming down.

These scenes remind me of the way it was, not that anything particular happens in them. I really could not reconstruct the more important scenes of that summer, such as the huge fight we had after Jeff ran over Aztec (it had been my sister Susie's cat that I was keeping for the summer) or the long conversation in which Jeff told me all the details of his first true love affair in Europe during his year off. Those scenes would probably tell more about our friendship, but they have not stuck in my mind. I remember the reading of books, the listening to records, the dumb conversations. It was part of the thinking and waiting we were doing. And it surprised me that Jeff seemed at times as much at a loss as I.

I come from a large family. Besides my sister Susie two years younger, I have an older married brother Mike, a younger brother Tony, and a sister Lucy who is still in high school. I come from this part of the country, a mill town with a fair-sized Portuguese community. My parents are rather well off by local standards. I went to a second-string prep school on a partial scholarship and then amazed everyone by getting into Harvard. My parents had always suspected I had it in me but had never been quite sure and had not got their hopes up. Neither of them had ever gone to college.

Jeff is a midwesterner and as Anglo-Saxon as they come. He has one sister, Zada, now a sophomore at Radcliffe. Even every one of his grandparents had a college degree, and there are two colonial governors in his genealogy. However, he did not go to a prep school. The Kimberks lived in one of those self-sufficient suburbs with an unexcelled public school system.

The differences between Jeff and me did not affect our friendship, at least not in any profound way. The times he came up for dinner, Jeff tried to feel at home with my family and to admire it in its way, and I was careful not to seem intimidated by such things as the box at Orchestra Hall when I visited Chicago.

But back when we were freshmen, before we really knew each other, Jeff Kimberk produced two strong reactions in me. Publicly I considered him an unimaginative cool snot and disliked him, while in my private fantasies I forgave him the groundhog business and imagined wishfully that the things I did not like about him, the snotty things, were simply defensive reactions, that underneath he was as uncertain as anyone else and that we could somehow become friends.

By sophomore year that fantasy faded. I did not see much of Jeff anyway, and I tried to write him off as an unfriendly person to whom I had been attracted in an insecure adolescent way. But my freshman fantasy later proved close to the truth. Jeff had indeed been on the defensive. He never had anything against me at all and had simply been playing along with the power structure.

Consider the effect of finding I could be friends with him. If someone seems initially desirable to know there will always be a kind of prize waiting for you when you feel at last you have secured his friendship. What I wish to say is that rooming with Jeff did enough for my self-esteem to allow me to jump almost immediately into a new way of thinking about myself.

Susannah Twombley came from Huntington, West Virginia. She appeared in the midst of a crowd of six or seven peripheral acquaintances of ours who needed a place to stay over Labor Day weekend. She had been studying piano in New York City and was now looking for a job as a piano teacher in Boston.

She made quite an impression on each of us. She was quiet, unlike Jeff's Elly, simply sat amid the crowd, and was serenely beautiful. Her long red hair, her green eyes, her sunburn, her long pianist's fingers: it is hard to put them all into a portrait. Certainly the contrast of red hair and green eyes struck us most. I remember her leaning against the wall, elbow on knee Hindu style, her head tilted slightly, her bright green eyes looking up at the peeling ceiling. The orange and brown dress she wore, made from one of those Indian bedspreads, left only her hands and face uncovered. By Monday each of us knew her expressions and gestures very well because neither of us could stop watching her.

She thumbed through our records, scanned the titles of our books which stood about in piles, helped in the kitchen, and slept on the floor at the side of a fat girl named Betsy and Betsy's sweaty, bristly boy friend. Jeff was still sleeping with Elly though they were fast falling apart, and I was casually involved with an unattractive girl named Bonnie who needed no seducing to speak of. I was in my experimental stage, making up for lost time. I am sure that is why when the time came it was Jeff Susannah fell in love with and not me.

As Jeff has explained it since, one thought tormented him all weekend: that this Susannah was the most perfect girl he had yet encountered, but as fate had it he was still ridiculously messed up with Elly and would miss his only chance for her. He could not hope that Susannah would ever cross his path again. The memory of her would be all that would remain to torment him. I told him he was jumping to too many conclusions.

My own feelings were quite different and, frankly, acquisitive. Susannah was the most desirable person there. I had fallen back on Bonnie because she was so easy, but I was determined to make the effort of pursuing Susannah even though it was unlikely she would be interested in me.

The caravan of uninvited guests disbanded after Labor Day. Susannah moved in with a girl friend on Beacon Hill, and I got her phone number from Betsy who was the last to leave.

Jeff and I spent the week moving and arguing over what to buy for our new place, a fourth-floor flat overlooking a gas station. He wanted to get a lot of cheap, used things; I only wanted things I might want to keep. Consequently my bedroom ended up with one beautiful brass bed in it and that was all, while his had a mattress, a rickety dresser, an old office desk, a wicker chair, a frayed oriental rug, a grotesque standing lamp, and ratty curtains from Goodwill Industries. I compensated by painting the floor of my room black, the walls Chinese red, and the woodwork and ceiling gold. It took several weeks, and I was rather proud of the results.

I gave Jeff free rein in the living room because he got such a charge out of buying tacky things. The kitchen and bathroom were unredeemable, so we simply avoided spending time in them. Jeff got a job working as a research assistant to some sociologist and I stayed on at the bookstore and then quit and started doing nothing again. That was after he and Susannah had fallen in love.

When I first phoned Susannah she had just found a job as a music teacher at a special school in Roxbury. She was so pleased and excited that she did a lot of talking for the first time. I am ashamed to admit, but I must admit, that I paid little attention to what she had to say. The prime motivation in all my calls to attractive girls had always been the expectation that I might get something out of them. I would work up my nerve for the call by thinking of one thing only, and all the time I was talking it was the only thing I was really thinking of.

Dr. Lichty, my psychiatrist, is good at catching me on the use of words. For instance, when I talk about Jeff's sexual activity I use the phrase, "He was sleeping with," whereas when I speak of my own I say, "I had sex with." I would never have noticed it, but Lichty says I invariably make the distinction, giving Jeff's behavior a certain quality of sentiment but characterizing my own as mechanical. I have great doubts about my capacity for tenderness and the generosity of my approaches to people.

And yet something about Jeff strikes me as selfish too. I had better say more about it before I get to that unfortunate night in late September when I invited Susannah over for dinner. Jeff is selfish in a way I am not. I am selfish out of a lack of self-confidence, selfish in my attempt to pile up enough esteem to feel sufficiently safe giving back. This is a psychological problem, one I am honestly tackling in therapy, and, as unpleasant as my behavior may still be at times, I am ashamed of it and am desperately trying to do something about it. I am not the sort who at age twenty-four watches helplessly as his behavior patterns set into a mold. I truly do desire to learn greater humanity and find a satisfaction in my own spirit which will allow others to admire me.

But Jeff's selfishness is quite different and likely to increase with age. His cautiousness with new people and his possessiveness indicate a conservative nature. Even when limiting his possessions, as he has recently, he holds on tightly to what he chooses to keep. Jeff was never the casual sharing sort. He had been quite uncomfortable in our summer place (though he denied it) and was anxious to get entirely set up all at once in the new one. He determined how much he could spend, and before I had even found my brass bed he had everything he needed all in its proper place. He would not even begin to look for a job until everything was organized.

It was a natural nest-building instinct, and I should not criticize Jeff for wanting to be complete and cozy. But when Dr. Lichty asked me how I truly felt about it, I had to reply, "I felt it was silly to get so holed up, so sure of yourself, not to want to be freer. What sort of life will you lead at fifty if at twenty-two you set yourself down behind a little door with all your things about you?" And Lichty said, "Then that was how you felt about it. Don't apologize for it."

Dr. Lichty has been willing to extend his approval to things he knows I must grow out of because he knows it is the approval I am after and once I have it I am likely to say, "Hey, wait a minute, maybe I would like to settle down a little after all." It has taken some daring for him to do that. Jeff had the daring too. He always said, "If that's the way you feel about it, Xavy, then it's all right."

Jeff came home from work one night and found Susannah in the kitchen with me making dinner. He had not known she was coming. I had not even told him I had her number, and he was very surprised to see her. Immediately he dropped into a quiet mood and disappeared into his room.

Jeff's moods showed in his face rather obviously. When he was happy, his blue eyes brightened and his mouth got tense and ready to speak. When he was low, his eyes went dull, his lips drooped, and he got asthmatic. The awful noises Jeff would make having an attack truly frightened me. I had seen one of his worst ones after a game of soccer in the cold rain. His whole face swelled in awful puckers, and he threw himself around the locker room gasping for breath. It was called urticaria. He had been in the hospital with it three times already with oxygen tents and intravenous feedings, and the first time he actually might have died if the doctors had not got there in time to shoot him full of adrenalin. But it kept him out of the army, and otherwise he was in good shape. I always envied his athleticness.

Susannah looked at me as if to say, "What's wrong with him?" She was wearing one of her Indian dresses, but this one was not much more than hip length. Her sunburned arms were bare to the elbow, and she was longlegged and barefoot, in every way the kind of girl I most like to be with: quiet, soft, elongated, graceful.

I was wearing paint-stained jeans and a T-shirt. I would say that I am compactly built, but I am no outstanding specimen. My shoulders are rounder than Jeff's and not nearly as broad, and though I am basically firm I am not what you would call muscular. My skin is much darker than Jeff's, and my face, unlike his, does not reflect my moods. I am told I always look mild and calm.

We were cooking hamburg mixed with onions and mushrooms, sour cream, and soy sauce, improvising the proportions, doing a lot of tasting, and meanwhile setting the table in the living room. The kitchen was pale green, gray, or blue (I do not remember which). It had one filthy window high on a wall, cracks and peels everywhere, a grimy linoleum floor, and several sticky jelly jars in random places. The living room, on the other hand, had just been redone in Kimberk style, something between 1930 Goodwill Industries and 1967 Bargain Basement: sagging couch, wobbly table, various uncomfortable plastic chairs. A red barrel stood in one corner with a few scraggly cattails sticking out of it, and moldy junk-shop portraits of Shakespeare and Beethoven hung on the maroon-papered walls.

I do not recall what Susannah and I talked about. We probably filled each other in on our past lives or possibly talked politics, not a favorite subject of mine. At dinner with Jeff we talked about music. Jeff and I both loved music, and he loved it even more than books. It once surprised me that a sharp collegiate type could have such a feeling for it. He could hardly carry a tune himself.

We approached music in different ways. It was something relatively new for me, and so I used to get very excited when I discovered a new record and would play it and play it. But Jeff had been going to concerts since he was six and might decide he wanted to hear the *Waldstein* sonata, then some Vaughan Williams, then the Alto Rhapsody — some such mixed program, and never the same piece twice in a day.

Luckily our tastes coincided: beginning with Mozart, ending with Richard Strauss, allowing for Bach and Berg on each end — in general the great romantic tradition. But we used to have slight disagreements about performers. Jeff is an all-out romantic; I am more of a classicist. He loved Bruno Walter and Backhaus; I preferred Karl Böhm and Gieseking. Kathleen Ferrier was his favorite singer; Victoria De Los Angeles was mine.

That night Jeff chose Brazilian folk songs for dinner music. It was a record of mine left over from my prep-school days when I had spent much of my time alone in my room privately studying the Portuguese world. Jeff had never played the record before. Perhaps he was trying to please me and keep himself in the background. I knew he was still tormented over Susannah. It was a Jeff-like feeling I was well acquainted with, and it was mean of me not to have warned him she was coming over.

Jeff was the sort who always seemed on top of things, but there were certain things, particularly matters of romance, which had a mystical quality for him. I have tried to be, for the last three years at least, reasonably at ease about sex, but Jeff always felt there was an uncontrollable pattern which he would either fit into or not. He thought Susannah had not been designated for him and that was that, while I tended to see the whole thing as a free-for-all in which it was merely a question of working up my nerve.

As we ate our hamburg and drank our Mateus, Jeff found himself talking despite his low mood. He said he had not known Susannah was still in town. She told him about her new job in Roxbury and her apartment on Beacon Hill. She spoke quietly, in short phrases, and with a distinctly Appalachian accent which Jeff and I found very appealing. I do not think of her accent anymore (perhaps it has worn off a bit), but at the time we noticed it most of all and liked it. I myself had gone through a self-critical period when I upgraded my New England accent from the raspy flat A's of my hometown to the soft broad A's of my prep school. It had surprised my parents, half pleased, half annoyed them, but we never discussed it. Jeff, of course, had no regional accent at all.

Susannah talked about her roommate, Ida Lee Sims, who was from Huntington too and also taught in Roxbury. Jeff asked her how she liked Boston, and she simply said it was good to get away from New York. She had considered going back to Huntington, but she felt that would be giving up on her career. It seemed she had high hopes for her piano playing.

She asked what the record was, and we got into a discussion of the Portuguese language. I tried to teach them to say the nasal *ão* sound. Jeff acted as if I had just stepped off the boat (he liked the idea of being best friends with someone of exotic extraction), and I had to explain that only two of my grandparents had actually been born in Portugal, and they had died before I was old enough to know them. Susannah wanted to know if I spoke the language fluently, and I said I had studied it on my own in one of my lonely root-seeking periods at prep school but had forgotten most of it. My parents had not spoken it since they were children. Susannah had thought Xavier Fereira was a Spanish name. I explained there were a lot of Portuguese in New England, it being directly across the ocean from Portugal, and I suggested we take a drive up the coast some day to see one of the fishing fleets, if Jeff would loan me his car.

With the conversation back to me, Jeff was quiet again. I do not think Susannah felt the tension, but I knew a little contest was on and it was being judged by the topics we discussed. As long as we were on Portugal, Jeff felt peripheral. He let feelings of doom descend on him. But finally his natural friendliness and politeness got the better of his romantic mysticism, and he found a way back in.

"We never really talked," he said, "when you were here over Labor Day, about your piano playing, Susannah."

I remember her turning in her chair to face him. She had been looking across the table at me, but I saw her now in profile, the gentle line of her nose, her chin, and her neck pink with sunburn.

"I wish we had a piano here," said Jeff. "You know, Xavy, I almost picked one up for fifty bucks, but it would've cost as much to have it moved. What pieces are you working on now, Susannah?"

"I'm making an attempt on Schubert's B-flat Sonata," she said.

"Oh, I wish we had a piano!" Jeff was excited, and his low mood faded out quickly. It was one of the mystical moments he believed in because the Schubert sonata was one of his favorites. I should have sensed the whole thing was up for me then and there.

"Then a Brahms intermezzo," said Susannah, "Schumann's *Symphonic Etudes,* Beethoven's opus 90, the *Tombeau de Couperin.*"

"All my favorite things," said Jeff. "We should go somewhere tonight where there's a piano. Xavy, do you suppose the music building's open?"

"Oh, I'll play for you soon enough," said Susannah. "There's plenty of time. I'm out of practice this summer, you know? I worked most of that up for my juries in May."

"But Susannah," said Jeff with a delighted smile, "am I ever glad to know someone who can really play!"

Why did I not give it up right then? It was so obvious they suited each other. Jeff leaned back in his chair, and his lips stretched out across his face in a grin. I had seldom seen him so overjoyed. Susannah cautioned him to wait till he heard her play to make up his mind about her talents, but that did not deflate Jeff's enthusiasm a bit.

I announced the dessert, Royal Anne cherries. Jeff said he was going to have a Twinkie instead. That got us into a discussion of his tacky taste, and I must have taken the opportunity to tear him down a little. But I think Jeff's unpretentiousness appealed to Susannah. He never tried to impress a girl, though he easily could have. It was part of his feeling that a romance would begin or it would not. Still there were times I felt he ate Twinkies a little too self-consciously, as though he were trying to get my goat. At other times I honestly believed he preferred them to Royal Anne cherries.

As soon as we finished doing the dishes, Jeff took me aside and said he would go out and leave me with Susannah. He was acting according to form, but I am sure it was only the doomed side of him that made the offer while the mystical side expected me to say, "No, Jeff, stay here, we're having such a good time, all three of us — I'm not trying to put the make on her anyway." I said no such thing of course, despicable sort that I was.

What I did say was, "Okay, Jeff, but I don't want to screw up your schedule."

"You did the same for me with Elly," he said. "I've got some research I should do at the library anyway. Back at midnight."

He left before Susannah came out of the bathroom. She seemed disappointed when I said Jeff had gone out, but the romance I sensed beginning between them may have been entirely imagined, a sign of my old paranoia.

Can I go on with this? It is going to be painful. When I have told it all I am going to take a day off from this writing, this self-discipline, and see what I can scrounge up in the way of a female. And then I will come back and start Chapter Two. With that end in sight, I continue.

Susannah and I sat on the fuzzy gray couch in the living room and listened to Backhaus play the first Brahms concerto, her choice, and De Los Angeles and Fischer-Dieskau sing duets, mine. The duets did the trick. Her head was on my shoulder. A duet by Purcell:

Lost is my quiet forever,
lost is life's happiest part;
lost all my tender endeavours
to touch an insensible heart.

One by Johann Christian Bach:

Ah, lamenta, oh bella Irene,
che giurasti a me costanza?
Ah, ritorna, amato bene,
al primo amor.
Qual conforto, oh Dio, m'avanza,
chi sarà la mia speranza?
Per chi viver più degg'io
se più mio non è quel cor?

One of Beethoven's Irish songs:

He promised me at parting
to meet me at the springtime here;
yet see you roses blooming,
the blossoms how they disappear.
Return, my dearest Dermot!
or sure the spring will soon be o'er.
Fair long have blown the breezes,
oh, when shall I see thee more?

I got up to turn over the record. When I sat down again, closer to her, her hand crept around my waist and my hand fell on her thigh. Schubert:

Nur wer die Sehnsucht kennt,
weiss was ich leide.
Allein und abgetrennt
von aller Freude . . .

People have been making love to these songs for a century or two (a nice thought). Why was she so ready to let me? It makes me angry to think about it now. On the other hand, there is no sense laying the blame elsewhere, cowardly bastard that I am. "But how do you feel about it?" Dr. Lichty would say at this point. I happen to feel that part of the blames lies with me, but God dammit, part of the blame lies with her. I really had not expected her to respond at all and certainly not as readily as she did.

Susannah was a quiet girl, but she was also sensual. Just as I was excited by her body, she must have been excited by mine. I was not accustomed to such a quick response from a girl, and I still am not. It has always been a struggle for me, even with the least attractive ones, but this one time when I expected the greatest resistance I met none at all. It was quite a surprise, and I wondered how I had ever become so suddenly successful. At that time I still had many doubts about my attractiveness even though I was not as runty as I used to be and my curly hair had come into style.

We forgot the record and soon were tumbling around on the fuzzy couch. Susannah was limber and excitable, and we wrapped ourselves in various complicated positions. By the time side two was over and the automatic stereo had shut itself off, Susannah's Indian dress was all but removed, the left sleeve having got tangled. To ease matters we went into my room with its smell of fresh paint. We finished undressing, and we made love by the light of the gas station next door because there were no shades.

I have never felt quite so exuberant in bed. I remember looking around to see her flat-topped knees clasping me in the pale light and then down at her hair spread on the pillow. Those images stick with me. Her sunburn was hot and tender, but she did not hold back at all. We said nothing the whole time except each other's names. There were moments when I felt I might fall in love with her, and those moments were the finest, the most abandoned.

At midnight we heard Jeff's key in the front door, heard him pad quietly in, and heard his door shut. Somewhat later we heard his door open, heard the toilet flush and his door shut again.

Susannah and I lay peacefully propped up on pillows, she nestling on my chest, my arms around her. Her long fingers still stroked the inside of my thighs, and I played with her breasts. It was the last pleasant moment of the evening. The gas station lights had been turned off, and now the full moon was in the window.

"Xavy," said Susannah.

"What?"

"I do like you." She was being careful and truthful.

"I like you too, Susannah."

"You do," she said. It was not a question. She was repeating the fact.

I could not find anything to say in return.

"I liked your lovemaking very much," she said. "You're awfully . . ."

"I'm awfully what?"

"I think you're . . ." She was quiet. I was running a finger softly over her face. I touched just under her eyes, and it was wet.

"Are you crying, Susannah?"

"A little."

"What is it?"

She was quiet, and I thought it best to lie quietly beside her and let her gather up what she was upset over, but I should have said something. Several months later when the awkwardness had been forgotten, a more explicit Susannah and a more responsive Xavy drank tea on a winter afternoon and talked over the time they had tried to sleep together and thought they understood their reasons for doing what they had done.

In the silence I must have dozed. Suddenly I sensed Susannah getting up. Her hand brushed across my stomach, and then I saw her standing, a dark shape against the moonlit window.

"Do you suppose your roommate could drive me home?"

"What?"

"Do you suppose Jeff could drive me home?"

"Susannah, what is it? I don't understand what happened. What did you want to say? Why can't you sleep with me?"

"Xavy, I like you. I said I did."

"Why won't you stay?"

"I've thought something out," she said, "and it's a decision I've made."

"But what's wrong?"

"We'll have a chance to talk about it."

"But now," I said.

She was putting on her dress.

"Susannah?" I stood up and put my arms around her. Her dress felt strange against my skin. She stepped back.

"Would Jeff mind?" she said.

"I don't think he would, he's such an agreeable bloke."

At that point I had no sense of what had happened. I simply knew I wanted her in my bed all night. I decided she was probably a lot less serene than I had taken her for and she felt guilty about sex when it happened so easily, when she knew me so slightly.

"I'll just knock on his door," she said.

"Oh, I'll ask him," I said. "I'll get his keys. I'll take you back."

She was firm. "No, Xavy," she said. "I don't want you to."

I plunked down on the bed; she kissed my forehead, said goodnight, and went out. I had been feeling quite elated, but now I started to fall.

When I heard her tap on Jeff's door, I suddenly had one of my visions of the old supercool Jeff sweeping her into his arms. I am sure in reality he just stumbled into a pair of jeans, blinkily opened the door, and very politely, without asking any questions, took her home.

But I did not hear anything. The fact is, my head was buried in my pillow. It had hit me all of a sudden when I heard her tap on his door, the old paranoia, the whole horrible thing.

I have been left other times, before and since. This time was the worst, and even now I am not sure why it was. I cannot recall exactly what hopes I had put in Susannah in the earlier part of the evening, but, whatever they were, her leaving did away with them. I must have been hoping for a small break, an upturning—I was ready to raise my stunted expectations if someone would put up with me for a little while. But that is a poor excuse. If I had truly wanted to, I would have made my own break, my own upturning. I do not think I had seriously considered that I might actually *keep* Susannah. I had taken her to bed without thinking of that.

When Jeff came back I was sitting in his wicker chair in his room in a numbed state with a bright red towel wrapped around me.

"Do you have any idea what she was upset over?" I said, sounding very calm.

He sat on the edge of the desk and looked at me. His expression was strict and serious. With a tilt of his head he said, "You've got to be more careful, Xavy."

"What did she tell you?"

"Nothing. She didn't want to talk. But I know you, Xavier Fereira."

"You're a great help, Jeff," I said. I was too numb to argue with him. He would only make me feel more deserted and pointless, and there was no reason to defend myself.

Jeff did not realize till the morning that I had fallen into one of my worst depressions. I went into my room and looked at the white sheets crinkled on the bed in the moonlight. For some odd reason, perhaps as a punishment, I decided to sleep on the floor.

LEONARD TUSHNET

The Klausners

(FROM PRAIRIE SCHOONER)

EVERYBODY HAS ONE at some time or other. A Klausner, I mean. Only it should be spelled with a small k, like the r in robots. Not that klausners are robots, not at all. Klausners are independent thinkers, very independent, and far from submissive. That's what makes them klausners. They're domineering and aggressive in a politely offensive manner, one that gets under your skin and gives rise too late to cab-wit. They mean you no harm; rather, they mean you well. They point out your errors and try to help you overcome them. They go out of their way to do you good, whether or not you want to be the beneficiary of their philanthropy. They're constantly doing you favors that leave you feeling like a fool.

I didn't realize how pernicious klausners could be until after we moved to Great Neck and the family was exposed to their influence. Oh, in the city there were some but we instinctively avoided them, easy to do in the security of our own segment of the apartment-beehive. But in the suburbs, that's a different matter. There's more neighborliness, which means more personal unavoidable contact. For example, if you run out of gas for your power mower, the man next door will lend you a gallon out of his reserve. You thank him and reciprocate when he runs out of gas. Unless he's a klausner. Klausners *never* run out of gas. They're prepared for every contingency. *They* have big candles in the house, not ornamental ones, when the power fails. They see your darkened windows and send over a dozen candles without your asking for them. Of course, along with the candles comes advice. "Always keep a supply on hand. You never know when you'll need them. They're cheap. It's not a great expense."

My own klausners swam slowly into my ken. I'm busy all day in the city, so at the outset I heard about the Klausners only by dinner-table allusions. My wife mentioned Mrs. Klausner. My oldest son spoke about Gerald Klausner. My daughter (fourteen) told me about Emily Klausner, and Michael (seven) about Harvey. They told jokes and stories about the Klausners and it took a little while before I recognized that underneath the humor lay hostility and fear caused by my family's increasing sense of inferiority. Michael said, "Harvey's the first in the reading group." Berenice said, "Emily has a vinyl miniskirt." Joseph said, "Gerald made the football team." My wife, Estelle, said, "Mrs. Klausner has an automatic pineapple corer."

That last remark, thrown out in a discussion of what make of dishwasher we were going to buy, was so irrelevant that I laughed. "What has that to do with the price of eggs? You also have lots of gadgets. Like a garlic press you never use and an egg slicer."

Estelle laughed, too. "I just happened to think of it. That woman has every imaginable kitchen tool made and a few she thought up herself. By the way, we're invited to a party she's giving in two weeks. Just neighbors. The Wiglers will be there, and the Silvermans. You know them." After she passed the asparagus, she added, "I think it would be nice if you wore a turtleneck."

I looked at her in amazement. "What for? Isn't a clean white shirt good enough? Who are these Klausners, anyway?"

"They live at the end of the block," she answered. "The big red brick house with the curving driveway. I met her in the supermarket. She's very pleasant." A moment of silence. "Do you like the roast? It's a new cut she told me about. Tomorrow I'm making an Italian dinner. She took me to a little place on Northern Boulevard that has wonderful imported delicacies, and not expensive, either."

I looked forward to meeting the Klausners. It seemed to me that discussions about them took up more and more time as the days went on. I was amused by the interest they aroused in my family. The Klausners knew everything: where a knitting mill had a discount outlet, how to flatter the art teacher into making high school election posters, when to develop variations on the watusi and the frug, why dinosaurs became extinct.

The only one of the Klausners I had met before the party was Harvey Klausner, who had become Michael's best friend, or at least his constant companion. Harvey was a big boy, a little too fat in the behind and with the clumsy gait that goes with excess avoirdupois in that area. But he was a whole head taller than Michael and had apple-red cheeks, curly chestnut hair, and bright blue eyes that made him look like the models in the Sunday-magazine advertisements for boys' clothes. He was polite and never in the way; he went home well before our dinner hour and never came too early on Saturday mornings. The only problem we had with him was my own son. Often during his visits Michael would lose his temper and fling something at Harvey, and always after Harvey left Michael would misbehave and would have to be punished. Michael liked to ride his bike; he had just learned how to dispense with the training wheels. Harvey had been riding for more than a year and he kept showing Michael how to make sharp turns, how to carry a package in one hand and steer with the other, and how to go up and down curbs without falling off. On rainy days Michael played in the den with him, checkers or casino, at both of which Harvey was proficient. Michael's moods got worse and worse after Harvey became his friend, so that finally I had to give the warning, "Either you control yourself or I'll forbid Harvey to come here anymore." Michael burst into tears. Harvey had for him the fascination a snake has for a chicken. He wouldn't forgo the masochistic pleasure of being with him. My ultimatum couldn't be carried out.

The evening of the party Estelle wore a dress I hadn't seen before: a simple frock with an embroidered jacket. She looked very well in it. The gold and brown accentuated her hazel eyes and dark-brown hair; the jacket, in a Persian design, served to cut her height just enough. (Estelle is quite tall for a woman, as tall as I am.) "You look lovely," I said, kissing her. "When did you get that dress?"

Estelle reddened. "This week. I never spent so much on a dress before. It's an original from La Louise."

I whistled. La Louise is a boutique in Manhasset, an expensive chi-chi place I'd heard of in conversation. "You're really trying to make an impression, aren't you?" I asked with a twinge of jealousy. "Is Klausner so handsome?"

Estelle giggled. "Don't be silly. I've never met him. It's just that I need a new going-out dress and I liked this one. I think this is going to be a *very* fancy party. Yesterday I saw Myra Klausner coming out of the Gourmet Shop with two large shopping bags, and this morning Harvey asked Michael what we were going to bring."

The suburban custom of bringing a small *objet d'art* (known to my mother as a *chotchka*) or a bottle of wine was new to me but agreeable. In honor of the fanciness of the party, I took a bottle of aquavit I had bought for myself on my last trip to Denmark.

I didn't wear a turtleneck. Sweaters under jackets are too closely connected in my mind with the dice-playing, foul-mouthed young bloods who hung around the corner bar on the street where I grew up. I honored the occasion, however, by a new tie, one that Estelle had given me for my birthday.

We walked to the Klausners'. Even then, at the beginning of November, with the leaves from the trees steadily falling, their front lawn looked immaculate. I made a mental note to myself to help the boys clean up around our house next day. I had the picture before me of the drifts under our rhododendrons and the chewing-gum wrappers I'd seen entangled in the hedge.

Mrs. Klausner herself opened the door for us. I had expected to see a big woman but not someone like Myra Klausner She was no taller than Estelle but she was decidedly more imposing. Her very matronly bosom thrust forward barely in advance of her very large abdomen that was decorated by a broad red sash, the fringes of which reached to the knees of her lounging pajamas. She wore a white silk blouse straining at its buttons. Around her massive neck was a string of large red beads. Her face was red, too, its floridity incongruous with the obviously untinted pale blond hair loosely tied in a bun at the back. She didn't look ready for a gala party.

"I'm so glad you could come," she boomed, taking my topcoat and Estelle's wrap. "We had a disappointment. Two disappointments. The Wiglers couldn't get a babysitter and the Silvermans had a death in the family. But the others are here." She led us into the living room, patting Estelle's arm as she did so. "My, you look lovely, dear! So elaborate, though."

The remark, its double nature at once complimentary and disparaging, changed Estelle's expression. Her answering smile became artificially fixed and she reached out her hand for my support as though there were a high step before her.

"Herman will be in in a moment," Mrs. Klausner said. "He's getting more ice from the kitchen." She made the introductions to the other guests: a Mr. and Mrs. Antonius, a Dr. Leavitt and a Miss Gordon, the doctor's fiancée. Mr. Antonius, dark, slight, and nervous, wore a white turtleneck sans jacket; the doctor (of what I never learned during the course of the evening) wore an open-necked sport shirt and slacks; Mrs. Antonius had on a plain black dress adorned with a large gold brooch at the left shoulder; Miss Gordon, as befitted her presumed youth and single status, wore bell-bottom velvet pants and a dark cotton print blouse. I felt sorry for Estelle. My tie made me self-conscious; I knew how she was feeling. She was definitely overdressed for such an informal gathering as this was.

What made it worse was Mrs. Klausner's ("call me Myra") insistence that Estelle stand up to have her jacket admired. "The dress is nice. A little too plain for my taste, but the jacket is adorable! That intricate embroidery! It looks almost as though it were handmade. What wonderful machines they have nowadays!"

"It *is* handmade," Estelle said, tightening her lips ever so slightly. "I got it at La Louise."

Myra clapped her hand to her mouth. "I made a boo-boo!" Her cuteness was in such sharp contrast to her appearance that we all, including Estelle, laughed. Myra shrugged. "Excuse me, dear. Me, I never buy in small stores so I wouldn't know about their reliability." She showed me the bar set-up. "Help yourself." While I made our drinks, she explained to the assenting murmurs of the other women (again including Estelle) that one advantage of shopping in a department store was not being obligated to buy merely because a salesgirl spent time with you. "Besides, if you change your mind, you can always return the dress, and no hard feelings."

The discussion (or rather, disquisition) about the dress was terminated by the entrance of our host with a bucket of ice cubes. Myra was big but Herman Klausner was bigger. Bald, beefy, moon-faced, broad of shoulder and of girth, he loomed over us, a Gulliver among the Lilliputians. He had a hearty handshake and a deep chesty laugh. He was not as obvious a master of the put-down as his wife but he did well enough in his own way. He insisted on tasting our martinis, made a face, and said they were no good. He mixed another batch in substitution. They *were* better than those I had made.

Except for Estelle's discomfort, the evening passed pleasantly. Myra had potato chips and pretzels, cheese cubes and a dish of tiny pieces of herring, and finally a large tray of cocktail knishes. "Homemade," she announced. They were delicious. She offered to give Estelle the recipe.

Herman and Myra amazed me at the breadth of their interests and the skill with which they manipulated the conversational ball. The talk, while not brilliant, was above the level of the usual suburban affair. We agreed about the influence of the war on student politics. We discussed the effects of technologic changes on modern art. We laughed at the use of nudity as novelty in the theater. We argued about *Catch-22* being the best of the war novels.

The occupational status of the host and guests were soon identified. Mr. and Mrs. Antonius were real-estate brokers; Miss Gordon was a high school teacher; Dr. Leavitt worked for the state (in what capacity I couldn't discover); Herman Klausner owned a raincoat factory in Queens. I was the only one with an exotic background, being foreign buyer for a cutlery firm. Herman was immediately interested. He asked intelligent questions about my work and openly envied my frequent trips to Europe.

During our late snack (not at all what Estelle had envisaged — only lox, cream cheese, bagels, and a luscious chocolate cake), the talk turned to our community swimming pool. Herman had definite ideas about next year's program. "One of the reasons we all moved to the suburbs was to have a place for our children. Right? The swimming pool's fine but it's too loosely organized. Beginners get swimming lessons but once they've passed the test, they're on their own. We ought to have graded classes, not only by age but by skill, so that eventually the dog-paddlers could graduate to the butterfly. It would mean getting lifeguards who'll do more than loll around showing off their muscles and other possessions to the girls. They'd have to get paid more, of course, but the assessment for each member would be trivial."

"Why assess everyone?" I asked. "Why not only those who want to take the classes? I'm satisfied with my breast stroke for all the swimming I do."

"For the children's sake," Herman answered. "We eliminate the competitive spirit that way." He replied to my raised eyebrows with, "You don't follow me? And you think you're a liberal? I'll give you an example. At children's camps, you know, horseback riding is available but it costs extra. What happens? Those who didn't take horseback-riding lessons feel out of it, almost like a lower class, so to speak. But if riding lessons were optional, the same as archery or chorus, those who wanted to would take them and those who didn't wouldn't. No class distinction, strictly personal preference."

I nodded. His argument was persuasive. I promised to support him at the next meeting of the Pool Committee (of which all residents of our community are members).

On the way home, I noticed Estelle was unusually quiet. When we undressed for bed, she picked up the jacket from the chair where she had tossed it and examined it critically at the dressing table light.

"What's the problem, dear?" I asked her. "Did you get a food stain on it?"

"No," she muttered. "But I think I've been cheated. I hate to be made a fool of. See this?" She showed me a place where the stitching was loose. "Myra saw it and brought it to my attention while I was helping her clear away. This is an irregular." She stamped her foot. "I could cry! To spend so much money and then find out I could have bought the same thing at half price or less! The first thing tomorrow morning I'm bringing it back!" I reminded her that tomorrow was Sunday. "Then Monday morning, and I'll give that La Louise a piece of my mind. Myra told me of a place in New York that sells high-style merchandise of the same type La Louise has, but not at such terribly high prices."

Estelle never wore the jacket again. On Monday, Mrs. Lochman, of La Louise, offered to redo the separated stitching but would neither take back the ensemble nor give a discount. Estelle was furious and, as so often happens when the cause of one's fury cannot be touched, projected her anger onto Myra Klausner. From the time of the party she avoided her. She never extended the customary return invitation in spite of my rather weak protests that she was being childish, the dress affair being her own fault, not Myra's.

My protests were weak because right then we were having trouble with Berenice. Berenice was in the awkward stage, gawky, bony, budding, given to long telephone conversations with her girl friends and short giggly ones with boys. She refused Estelle's offer to drive her to school in bad weather. She preferred to walk with her friends, her lips blue, her legs goose-pimply through the net stockings she insisted on wearing. We bore with her. "It's only a phase," we said, and our neighbors with daughters of about the same age agreed with us and like us waited impatiently for the inevitable biologic and psychologic maturity. But they and we did not reckon with Emily Klausner. Emily's glands must have been different. She had ripened faster than her classmates. Emily had no acne, her well-filled bra showed clearly through her sweater, her movements were graceful. Emily was helpful to the girls who followed her like a queen's entourage. She arranged dates for them, she gave them advice on eyeliners and earrings, she showed them how to fold under the waistbands of their skirts in order to raise the hemlines well above the limits of maternal approval.

All that we could have tolerated but not the hair. Berenice was late for dinner one evening. When she appeared her curly hair had been ironed straight and lank, and starting from one temple was a glaring wide white strand. "I was at the beauty parlor," she explained. "This is a new style. It's sort of a club mark."

Estelle raged. So did I. "Next thing you'll be tatooing yourself!" I shouted. "Like the girls who hang around with gangsters!"

We could do nothing about the streak except forbid its being touched up. Berenice wept and carried on. "I look like a freak!" she screamed. She did, I must admit. As the hair grew and the natural color returned, the whiteness began to look ridiculous. Berenice developed a school phobia, the only cure for which, we decided, was a haircut, a procedure which further alienated Berenice, long straight hair being the current style.

Berenice's school work suffered during this period of Sturm und Drang. Before I left for Sweden I had a conference with her teacher. There I learned that Emily alone, of all the girls in the class, had not streaked her hair. Her explanation had been (not an excuse — klausners make no excuses) that being a natural blond, the white streak would mar her looks, besides being unnecessary to single her out amongst the brunettes of various shades who surrounded her.

I insisted on all relations with the Klausners being broken off when I returned from Europe to find Joseph's leg in a cast, the result of an ice-skating accident. Not that I could blame Gerald Klausner. The accident was entirely my own son's fault. Gerald was merely teaching him figure skating; the laces were badly tied by Joseph himself.

Enough was enough. I'm not superstitious. I don't believe in the evil eye but why take chances?

Of course, some inconveniences resulted. I had to say, "No, thanks. We need the exercise," when Herman Klausner brought over his snowblower to clean our driveway. We shoveled it at the risk of getting frostbite and sore muscles. I politely refused Herman's offer of a lift to the city in his car during the railwaymen's strike. Estelle changed butchers; the new one charged more for an inferior grade of meat. Berenice and Michael moped around the house, and Joseph had to buy his own magazines instead of borrowing Gerald's. But it was worth it. Serenity returned to our household.

Spring came, and summer. The pool was opened. Herman's idea was a great success, so much so that a demand arose for a grand and glorious finish on the Sunday after Labor Day. An open swimming tournament by age groups was arranged. Even I, who had not been around for much of the summer, participated. I am a good swimmer, I can say without false modesty. I had observed my neighbors in the pool and I knew that I should reach the finals without much difficulty.

So many entrants signed up that it was decided to start the tournament at eight in the morning, with the drawings for pairs at seven. Michael was the most excited in our family. The committee had decided that all semifinalists in his age bracket would be rewarded with silver pins, thus averting much chagrin on the part of the young ones. Berenice did not join us at the pool. She sneered, "Fat chance you're going to have against the Klausners. They'll win every prize." Estelle, who was of the same opinion, said she'd stay home to keep Berenice company.

The drawing started with subjuniors first. The little boys, their hearts visibly palpitating through their thin chests, crowded around the bowl. Harris, the chief swimming instructor, pulled the cards two at a time and called off the names to be paired for the first elimination round. It was comical to see the boys eye their competitors, compare muscles, and brag. Michael's name was called, and with it Harvey Klausner's. From where I sat, high up on the stand, I could see Michael bravely try to control his quivering under-lip while a solitary tear rolled slowly down his cheek. I quickly ran down to him but it was too late. He had flung himself on Harvey, punching and kicking with his bare feet.

Harvey easily held him off at arm's length. "I didn't do anything to him," he cried aggrievedly, turning his face to me. "I know you didn't," I replied, and to myself I thought, but you exist.

I took Michael away. He fell into my arms and wept. "Why did it have to be Harvey? I can beat everybody else!" The statement may not have been true but I knew how he felt. I calmed him down and persuaded him to withdraw and default to Harvey. That was better than having to go through the heartbreak of defeat and another tantrum. "All right," he said, "but you'll win in the fathers' group, won't you?" Joseph, who was not a good swimmer and who had not entered the tournament, tried to explain to Michael that playing the game was more important than winning. That sophistry was beyond Michael's comprehension (and mine too, I must admit). I promised Michael I'd try hard to win.

Adults were to compete last. The drawing took up so much time that the children were getting restless, and Harris decided to postpone the adult drawings until after the boys and girls had finished their races.

As was to be expected, Harvey Klausner won in his age group, but not without an argument. His competitor, an angry redhead, complained that Harvey had kicked him on the turn. The judges overruled the claim but then Harvey, in a gesture of magnanimity, offered the award, a little gold dolphin pin, to the redhead, "just so there'll be no hard feelings." The redhead lost all control then and rushed at Harvey. He butted him in the abdomen and threw him into the deep end of the pool. The redhead was led away, wailing.

I had no great interest in the tournament. By the time the adults were reached, it was after one o'clock and I was hungry. So were Joseph and Michael. Joseph went home to watch a football game on TV. I had to stay because of Michael's insistence. He reproached me for not being foresighted enough to bring a picnic lunch. He pointed to the Klausners sitting on the grass at the far end of the pool. They were eating sandwiches and pickles, and drinking soda. I sent Michael down to the refreshment stand to get a hot dog and cherry pop for himself. I lost my appetite looking at the Klausners.

Myra Klausner wore a tank bathing suit, her bulges unashamedly revealed. Emily was resplendent in a flowered bikini. Herman Klausner, his broad chest glistening with perspiration, wore very brief trunks. I saw his thick arms and legs and tried to console myself that he was better fitted for wrestling than for swimming. And there was always the possibility that I'd not be drawn to compete with him in the first or second rounds. It was only a possibility. I felt my doom hanging over me. I didn't need a Greek chorus to warn me of my fate. I didn't care for myself but I did for Michael. For a moment I thought of faking a heart attack but the thought was only fleeting. I would not only spoil the day for the other people, but I would be the unwilling recipient of the emergency care the Klausners would be sure to give me. I pictured Herman over me giving me closed-chest massage while his wife rubbed my hands and Emily waved spirits of ammonia under my nose.

I drew Klausner. We were the first pair drawn. He waved to me, "May the best man win!" and began anointing himself with a thick grease. "Here," he said, offering me the jar, "it cuts friction. Lets you glide through the water." I thanked him and said no, that I didn't like the feel on my skin. Herman shrugged and continued to smear himself. Then he clowned and danced around at the edge of the pool while the other pairs were being drawn. I stood morosely to one side. Poor Michael! I thought. He's going to be disappointed in his father.

Suddenly, just as the final two pairs came over to join us, Herman slipped. His feet slid from under him and he landed flat on his back. His head struck the tiling with a loud crack. He was knocked out.

I stood there, fixed, with my mouth open. It couldn't have been more than fifteen or twenty seconds but it seemed like forever before Herman opened his eyes, shook his head, felt it gingerly, and sat up. "What happened?" came the cries and a little knot clustered around him. Herman had a bump at the back of his head and said he felt woozy. Myra and Harris helped him into the lounge.

The competition was delayed until Dr. Meyers, who was present, came out after examining Herman and announced, "Nothing serious." Naturally, Herman was *hors de combat*. Atkins, who said the accident had made him too nervous to swim, withdrew. I was paired with Novgrad.

I won. Novgrad was very slow, my opposing semifinalist got a cramp, and the finalist was too winded. While I was swimming, above all the noise I could hear Michael's piping cheers and Herman's booming encouragement to me from the deck chair where he was sitting.

What good was winning? When we were dressed I handed Michael the gold pin to wear home. He slapped it from my hand to the floor and cried, "You didn't win against Mr. Klausner!" I knew what he meant.

Estelle and I talked things over during the following week. We rode around several developments in the area until we saw a house for sale, one that would be adequate for us, and placed a deposit on it. It wasn't as roomy as the one we were living in and the yard was neglected but it would do. The children would not have to change schools and yet it was far enough away from the Klausners for us to be safe — we thought.

Herman Klausner saved me money on the sale of our old house. He met me at the barber's. "The grapevine has it that you're selling your place. Does the agent have an exclusive on it?" When I said no, he nodded. "Good. I think I have a buyer for you. You won't have to pay any commission if it's a private deal between two principals. I have a friend of mine who wants to move out here from Brooklyn, and I'm sure he'll be interested." I was going to say, "Please, Herman, don't do me any favors," but, coward that I was, I merely smiled weakly at him.

His friend (poor man!) bought our house. We moved a month later and sighed with relief, all of us, when we stood in the empty hallway of the new house. The Klausners were done with.

I felt, however, that I owed Herman something for his unsolicited help. I sent him a little note of thanks with a present, a Danish silver punch-bowl set. Myra called Estelle and raved about its beauty. "It's a gorgeous showpiece," she said. "I wouldn't dare use it. And besides, when do I make punch?"

Showpiece or not, she liked it well enough to want first a matching tray, and then a tea service. "You get to Copenhagen so often, it's not really a bother, is it?" Then it was a carving set and last time it was a cruet stand. "I saw it in the same pattern at Georg Jensen's."

I figured it out. Between the nuisance and the duty, in the long run it would have been cheaper for me to have paid commission. Klausners are klausners.

W. D. VALGARDSON

Bloodflowers

(FROM TAMARACK REVIEW)

DANNY THORSEN saw Mrs. Poorwilly before he stepped off the freight boat onto Black Island. He couldn't have missed her. She was fat and had thick, heavy arms and legs. She stood at the front of the crowd with her hands on her hips.

"You the new teacher?" Mrs. Poorwilly said.

"Yes, I'm —"

Mrs. Poorwilly cut him off by waving her arm at him and saying, "Put your things on the wheelbarrow. Mr. Poorwilly will take them up to the house. Board and room is fifty a month. We're the only one's that give it. That's Mr. Poorwilly."

Mrs. Poorwilly waved her hand again, indicating a small man who was standing behind an orange wheelbarrow. He had a round, red face, and his hair was so thin and blond that from ten feet away he looked bald.

Danny piled his suitcases and boxes onto the wheelbarrow. He was tired and sore from the trip to the island. The bunk had been too short. The weather had been bad. For the first three days of the trip, he had not been able to hold anything down except coffee.

When the wheelbarrow was full, Mr. Poorwilly took his hands out of his pocket. They were twisted into two rigid pink hooks. He slipped them through two metal loops which had been nailed to the handles of the wheelbarrow, then lifted the barrow on his wrists.

At the top of the first rise, Mr. Poorwilly stopped. As if to reassure Danny, he said, "Mrs. Poorwilly's a good cook. We've got fresh eggs all winter, too."

Danny glanced back. Mrs. Poorwilly was swinging cases of tinned goods onto the dock. Her gray hair blew wildly about her face.

They started off again. As there were no paths on the bare granite, Danny followed Mr. Poorwilly. They walked along a ridge, dropped into a hollow. The slope they had to climb was steep so Danny bent down, caught the front of the wheelbarrow and pulled as Mr. Poorwilly pushed. They had just reached the top when they met an elderly, wasted man who was leaning heavily on the shoulder of a young girl as he shuffled along.

Danny was so surprised by the incongruity of the pair that he stared. The girl's black hair fell to her shoulders, making a frame for her face. She looked tired, but her face was tanned and her mouth was a warm red. Her cheeks were pink from the wind. She stopped when she saw Danny.

The man with her made no attempt to greet them. His breath came in ragged gasps. His dark yellow skin was pulled so tightly over his face that the bones seemed to be pushing through. His eyes protruded and the whites had turned yellow. He gave the girl's shoulder a tug. They started up again.

When they had passed, Danny said, "Who was that? The girl is beautiful."

"Sick Jack and his daughter. It's his liver. Mrs. Poorwilly helps Adel look after him. She says he won't see the spring. He'll be the second. How are you feeling after the trip? You look green."

"I feel green. It was nine days in hell. The boat never quit rolling."

"Good thing you're not going back with them, then." Mr. Poorwilly twisted his head toward the dock to indicate whom he meant. "Sunrise was red this morning. There'll be a storm before dawn tomorrow."

Mr. Poorwilly slipped his hands back into the metal loops. "Sorry to be so slow, but the arthritis causes me trouble. Used to be able to use my hands but not anymore. It's a good thing I've got a pension from the war. Getting shot was the best thing has ever happened to me."

Danny noticed a small, red flower growing from a crack in the rock. When he bent down to get a better look, he saw that the crack was filled with brown stems. He picked the flower and held it up. "What is it?"

"Bloodflower," Mr. Poorwilly replied. "Only thing that grows on the island except lichen. Shouldn't pick it. They say it brings bad luck. If you cut your finger or make your nose bleed, it'll be O.K."

Danny laughed. "You don't believe that, do you?"

"Mrs. Poorwilly says it. She knows quite a bit about these things."

When they reached the house, Danny unloaded his belongings and put them into his bedroom. Mr. Poorwilly left him and went back to the dock for the supplies Mrs. Poorwilly had been unloading.

While the Poorwillys spent the day sorting and putting away their winter supplies, Danny walked around the island. What Mr. Poorwilly said was true. Nothing grew on the island except lichen and bloodflowers. Despite the cold, patches of red filled the cracks which were sheltered from the wind.

The granite of the island had been weathered smooth, but there was nowhere that it was truly flat. Three quarters of the island's shoreline fell steeply into the sea. Only in scattered places did the shoreline slope gently enough to let Danny walk down to the water. To the west the thin blue line of the coast of Labrador was just barely visible. Two fishing boats were bobbing on the ocean. There were no birds except for some large gray gulls that rose as he approached and hovered in the air until he was well past them. He would have liked to have them come down beside him so that he could have touched them, but they rose on the updrafts. He reached toward them and shouted for them to come down, then laughed at himself and continued his exploring.

Except for the houses and the fish sheds, the only other buildings were the school and the chicken roost behind the Poorwillys'. All the buildings were made from wood siding. Because of the rock, there were no basements. Rock foundations had been put down so the floors would be level.

Most of the houses showed little more than traces of paint. The Poorwillys' and Mary Johnson's were the only ones that had been painted recently. Danny knew the other house belonged to Mary Johnson because it had a sign with her name on it. Below her name it said GENERAL STORE. POST OFFICE. TWO-WAY RADIO.

Danny explored until it started to get dark, then went back to the Poorwillys'.

"Heard you've been looking around," Mrs. Poorwilly said. "If you hadn't come back in another five minutes, I would have sent Mr. Poorwilly to bring you back."

"There's no danger of getting lost." Danny was amused at her concern.

"No," Mrs. Poorwilly agreed, "but you wouldn't want to slip and fall in the dark. You're not in a city now with a doctor down the street. You break a leg or crack your skull and you might have to wait two, three weeks for the weather to clear enough for a plane to come. You don't want to be one of the three."

Danny felt chastised, but Mrs. Poorwilly dropped the subject. She and Mr. Poorwilly spent all during supper asking him about the mainland. As they talked, Mrs. Poorwilly fed her husband from her plate. He sat with his hands in his lap. There were no directions given or taken about the feeding. Both Mr. and Mrs. Poorwilly were anxious to hear everything he had to tell them about the mainland.

When he got a chance, Danny said, "What'd you mean 'one of the three'?"

"Trouble always comes in threes. Maybe you didn't notice it on the mainland because things are so complicated. On the island you can see it because it's small and you know everybody. There's just thirty-five houses. Somebody gets hurt, everybody knows about it. They can keep track. Three, six, nine, but it never ends unless it's on something made up of threes.

"You'll see before the winter is out. Last month the radio said Emily died in the sanatorium. T.B. Now Sick Jack's been failing badly. He's got to be a hard yellow and he's lost all his flesh. He dies, then there'll be one more thing to end it. After that, everything will be O.K."

Mrs. Poorwilly made her pronouncement with all the assuredness of an oracle. Danny started on his dessert.

"Mr. Poorwilly says you think Adel's a nice bit of fluff."

Danny had started thinking about the book on mythology that he had been reading at summer school. The statement caught him off guard. He had to collect his thoughts, then he said, "The girl with the long dark hair? I only caught a glimpse of her, but she seemed to be very pretty."

"When her father goes, she'll be on her own," Mr. Poorwilly said. "She's a good girl. She works hard."

"Does she have any education?"

"Wives with too much education can cause a lot of trouble," Mrs. Poorwilly said. "They're never satisfied. The young fellows around here and on the coast have enough trouble without that."

Danny tried not to show his embarrassment. "I was thinking in terms of her getting a job on the mainland. If her spelling is good and she learned to type, she could get a government job."

"Might be that she will go right after her father. No use making plans until we see what the winter brings." Mr. Poorwilly turned to his wife for confirmation. "It's happened before."

Mrs. Poorwilly nodded as she scraped the last of the pudding from the dish and fed it to her husband.

"What you want is what those people had that I was reading about. They used to ward off evil by choosing a villager to be king for a year. Then, so the bad luck of the old year would be done with, they killed him in the spring."

"They weren't Christians," Mr. Poorwilly said.

"No," Danny replied. "They gave their king anything he wanted. A woman, food, gifts, everything since it was only for a year. Then when the first flowers bloomed, they killed him."

"Must have been them Chinese," Mr. Poorwilly said.

"No. Europeans. But it was a long time ago."

"Have you ever ridden on a train?" Mrs. Poorwilly asked. "Mr. Poorwilly and I rode on a train for our honeymoon. I remember it just like yesterday."

Mr. and Mrs. Poorwilly told him about their train ride until it was time to go to bed. After Danny was in bed, Mr. Poorwilly stuck his head through the curtain that covered the doorway. In a low voice, he said, "Don't go shouting at the seagulls when you're out walking. Most of the people here haven't been anywhere and they'll think you're sort of funny."

"O.K.," Danny said. Mr. Poorwilly's head disappeared.

The next day Mrs. Poorwilly had everyone in the village over to meet Danny. As fast as Danny met the women and children, he forgot their names. The men were still away fishing or working on the mainland. Mr. Poorwilly and Danny were the only men until Adel brought Sick Jack.

Sick Jack looked even thinner than he had the day before. The yellow of his skin seemed to have deepened. As soon as he had shaken Danny's hand, he sat down. After a few minutes, he fell into a doze and his daughter covered him with a blanket she had brought.

Mrs. Poorwilly waited until Sick Jack was covered, then brought Adel over to see Danny.

"This is Adel. She'll come for coffee soon, and you can tell her about the trains and the cities. She's never been off the island."

Adel blushed and looked at the floor. "Certainly," Danny said. "I've a whole set of slides I'm going to show Mr. and Mrs. Poorwilly. If you wanted, you could come and see them."

Adel mumbled her thanks and went to the side of the room. She stayed beside her father the rest of the evening, but Danny glanced at her whenever he felt no one was looking at him.

She was wearing blue jeans and a heavy blue sweater that had been mended at the elbows and cuffs with green wool. It was too large for her so Danny assumed that it had belonged to her father or one of the other men. From what Mrs. Poorwilly had said, Danny had learned that Adel and her father were given gifts of fish and secondhand clothing. When the men went fishing, they always ran an extra line for Sick Jack.

In spite of her clothing, Adel was attractive. Her hair was as black as he had remembered it and it hung in loose, natural waves. Her eyes were a dark blue. Underneath the too-large sweater, her breasts made soft, noticeable mounds.

She left before Danny had a chance to speak to her again, but he didn't mind as he knew that he would see her during the winter.

For the next two weeks, as busy as he was Danny could not help but notice the change in the village. The men returned at all hours, in all kinds of weather. Mostly they came two and three at a time, but now and again a man would come by himself, his open boat a lonely black dot on the horizon.

Most of the men brought little news that was cheerful. The fishing had been bad. Many of them were coming home with the absolute minimum of money that would carry them until spring. No one said much, but they all knew that winter fishing would be necessary to keep some of the families from going hungry. In a good year, the winter fishing provided a change in diet for people sick of canned food. This year the fishing would not be so casual.

By the end of September the weather had turned bitterly cold. The wind blew for days at a time. The houses rocked in the wind.

Danny walked the smallest children to their homes. The few days that the fishermen were able to leave the island, there were no fish. Some of the men tried to fish in spite of the weather, but most of the time they were able to do little more than clear the harbor before having to turn around.

The evening Sick Jack died, Danny had gone to bed early. The banging on the door woke him. Mr. Poorwilly got up and answered the door. Danny heard the muttered talk, then Mr. Poorwilly yelled the news to Mrs. Poorwilly. They both dressed and left right away. Danny would have offered to go with them, but he knew that he would just be in the way so he said nothing.

Mrs. Poorwilly was back for breakfast. As she stirred the porridge, she said, "She's alone now. We washed him and dressed him and laid him out on his bed. She's a good girl. She got all his clothes out and would have helped us dress him, but I wouldn't let her. Mr. Poorwilly is staying with her until some of the women come to sit by the body. If the weather holds, we'll have the funeral tomorrow."

"Why not have the funeral while the weather stays good? It could change tomorrow."

"Respect," Mrs. Poorwilly said. "But it's more than that, too. I wouldn't say it to her, but it helps make sure he's dead. Once just around when I married, Mrs. Milligan died. She was seventy. Maybe older. They rushed because the weather was turning. They were just pushing her over the side when she groaned. The cold did it. She died for good the next week, but since then we like to make sure."

Danny went to the funeral. The body was laid out on the bed with a shroud pulled to its shoulders. Mary Johnson sang "The Old Rugged Cross." Mrs. Poorwilly held the Bible so Mr. Poorwilly could read from it. Adel sat on a kitchen chair at the foot of the bed. She was pale and her eyes were red, but she did not cry.

When the service was over, one of the fishermen pulled the shroud over Sick Jack's head and tied it with a string. They lifted the body onto a stretcher they had made from a tarpaulin and a pair of oars. The villagers followed them to the harbor.

They lay the body on the bottom of the boat. Three men got in. As the boat swung through the spray at the harbor's mouth, Danny saw one of the men bend and tie an anchor to the shrouded figure.

Mrs. Poorwilly had coffee ready for everyone after the service. Adel sat in the middle of the kitchen. She still had a frozen look about her face, but she was willing to talk.

Sick Jack's death brought added tension to the village. One day in class while they were reading a story about a robin that had died, Mary Johnson's littlest boy said, "My mother says somebody else is going to die. Maybe Miss Adel now that her father's gone."

Danny had been sharp with him. "Be quiet. This is a Grade Three lesson. You're not even supposed to be listening. Have you done your alphabet yet?"

His older sister burst out, "That's what my mother said. She said — "

Danny cut her off. "That's enough. We're studying literature, not mythology. Things like that are nothing but superstition."

That night Danny asked about Adel. Mrs. Poorwilly said, "She's got a settlement coming from the mine where he used to work. It's not much. Maybe five or six hundred dollars. Everybody'll help all they can, but she's going to have to get a man to look after her."

During November, Danny managed to see Adel twice. The first time she came for coffee. The second time she came to see Danny's slides of the mainland. Danny walked her home the first time. The second time, Mrs. Poorwilly said, "That's all right, Mr. Thorson. I'll walk with her. There's something I want to get from Mary Johnson's."

Danny was annoyed. Mrs. Poorwilly had been pushing him in Adel's direction from the first day he had come. Then, when he made an effort to be alone with her, she had stepped between them.

Mrs. Poorwilly was back in half an hour with a package of powdered milk.

Danny said, "I would have got that for you, Mrs. Poorwilly."

"A man shouldn't squeeze fruit unless he's planning on buying," she replied.

Adel walked by the school a number of times when he was there. He got to talk to her, but she was skittish. He wished that she was with him in the city. There, at least, there were dark corners, alleyways, parks, even doorsteps. On the island, you could not do anything without being seen.

At Christmas the villagers held a party at the school. Danny showed his slides. Afterward they all danced while Wee Jimmy played his fiddle. Danny got to dance with Adel a good part of the night.

He knew that Mrs. Poorwilly was displeased and that everyone in the village would talk about his dancing for the rest of the year, but he didn't care. Adel had her hair tied back with a red ribbon. The curve of her neck was white and smooth. Her blouse clung to her breasts and was cut low enough for him to see the soft curves where they began. Each time he danced with one of the other women, Danny found himself turning to see what Adel was doing. When the party was over, he walked Adel home and kissed her good-night. He wanted her to stay with him in the doorway, but she pulled away and went inside.

Two days before New Year's, Mrs. Poorwilly's prediction came true. The fishing had remained poor, but Michael Fairweather had gone fishing in a heavy sea because he was one of those who had come back with little money. Two blocks from the island his boat capsized.

Danny had gone to school on the pretext of doing some work, but what he wanted was some privacy. He had been sitting at the window staring out to sea when the accident happened. He had seen the squall come up. A violent wind whipped across the waves and behind it a white, ragged line on the water raced toward the island. Michael Fairweather was only able to turn his boat halfway around before the wind and sleet struck.

Danny saw the boat rise to the crest of a wave, then disappear. The next time it appeared, it was bottom up, and Michael was hanging onto the keel. Danny bolted from the room, but by the time he reached the dock Michael had disappeared

The squall had disappeared as quickly as it had come. Within half an hour the sea was back to its normal rolling. The fishermen rowed out of the harbor and dropped metal bars lined with hooks. While one man rowed, another held the line at the back of the boat. As Danny watched, the boats crossed back and forth until it was nearly dark.

They came in without the body. Danny could not sleep that night. In the morning, when a group of men came to the Poorwillys', Danny answered the door before Mr. Poorwilly had time to get out of his bedroom. The men had come for the loan of the Poorwillys' rooster.

Mrs. Poorwilly nestled the rooster in her jacket on the way to the dock, then tied it to Mr. Poorwilly's wrist with a leather thong. Mr. Poorwilly stepped into the front of the skiff. The rooster hopped onto the bow. With that the other men climbed into their boats and followed Mr. Poorwilly and the rooster out of the harbor.

"What are they doing?" Danny asked.

Mrs. Poorwilly kept her eyes on the lead boat, but she said, "When they cross the body, the rooster will crow."

Danny turned and stared at the line of boats. In spite of the wind, the sun was warm. The rooster's feathers gleamed in the sun. Mr. Poorwilly stood as still as a wooden figurehead. The dark-green and gray boats rose and fell on the waves. Except for the hissing of the foam, there was no sound.

Danny looked away and searched the crowd for Adel. He had looked for a third time, when Mrs. Poorwilly, without turning, said, "She won't come for fear the current will have brought her father close to shore. They might bring him up."

All morning and into the afternoon the boats crossed and recrossed the area in front of the harbor in a ragged line. No one left the dock. The women with small babies did not come down from their houses, but Danny could see them in their doorways.

As the day wore on, Danny became caught up in the crossing and recrossing of the boats. None of the men dragged his hook. The only time that the men in the rear of the boats moved was to change positions with the men at the oars.

When the cock crew, the sound caught Danny by surprise. The constant, unchanging motion and the hissing of the spray had drawn him into a quiet trance. It had been as though the boats and he had been there forever.

The sound was so sharp that some of the women cried out. The men with the iron bars covered with hooks threw them into the sea, and shoved the coils of rope after them. They did not want to pass the spot where the cock crew until the hooks were on the bottom. The bars disappeared with little spurts of white foam.

The fifth boat has something, the woman's voice said. Danny turned away and could not look for fear that it would be a white shroud that would appear. Even with the sound of the foam, Danny could hear the rope rubbing against the side of the boat as it was pulled hand over hand.

"It's him," the same voice said. "God have mercy, they've got him."

Danny turned back. It was true. Instead of a white shroud, the men were pulling a black bundle into the boat.

The funeral was bad. Marj Fairweather cried constantly and tried to keep the men from taking the body. As they started to leave, she ran to the dresser for a heavy sweater, then sat in the middle of the floor, crying and saying, "He'll be so cold. He'll be so cold."

In spite of Marj, the tension in the community eased after the funeral was over. People began to visit more often, and when they came they talked more and stayed longer.

Adel came frequently to the Poorwillys'. When she came, she talked to the Poorwillys, but she watched Danny. She was not open about it, but when Danny looked at her, she let her eyes linger on him for a second before turning away. She had her color back and looked even better than before. Most of the time, Danny managed to walk her home. Kissing her was not satisfactory because of the cold and the bulky clothes between them, but she would not invite him in and there was no privacy at the Poorwillys'. In spite of the walks and the good-night kisses, she remained shy when anyone else was around.

The villagers had expected the weather and the fishing to improve. If anything, the weather became worse. Ice coated the boats. The wind blew night and day. Often, it only stopped in the hour before dawn.

Then, without warning, Marj Fairweather sent her children to the Poorwillys', emptied a propane lamp on herself and the kitchen floor, and lit a match.

This time there was no funeral. The entire village moved in a state of shock. While one of the sheds was fixed up for the children, Marj's remains were hurried to sea and dumped in the same area as her husband's.

The village drew into itself. The villagers stayed in their own houses. When they came to the door, they only stayed long enough to finish their business. The men quit going to the dock. Most of them pulled their boats onto the island and turned them over.

A week after the fire, Danny arrived to find his room stripped of his belongings. Mrs. Poorwilly waited until he had come into the kitchen. "Mr. Poorwilly and I decided to take two of the Fairweather children. We'll take the two youngest. A fourteen-year-old can't take care of six kids."

Danny was too stunned to say anything. Mrs. Poorwilly continued. "Some of us talked about it. We hope you don't mind, but there's nothing else to do. Besides, there's going to be no money from the mine. Adel needs your board and room worse than we do. We'll keep the Fairweather children for nothing."

When Danny didn't reply, Mrs. Poorwilly added, "We got help moving your things. We gave Adel the rest of this month's money."

Danny hesitated for a moment, but there was nothing to say. He went outside.

He knocked at Adel's door. She let him in. "Mrs. Poorwilly says you're to stay with me now."

"Yes, she told me," Danny said.

Adel showed him to his bedroom. All his clothes had been hung up and his books had been neatly piled in one corner. He sat on the edge of the bed and tried to decide what to do. He finally decided he could not sit in the bedroom for the next five months and went back into the kitchen.

The supper was good, but Danny was too interested in Adel to pay much attention. In the light from the oil lamp, her eyes looked darker than ever. She was wearing a sweater with a V-neck. He could see the soft hollow of her throat and the smooth skin below her breastbone. Throughout supper he told her about the mainland and tried to keep his eyes above her neck.

The next morning when he went to school, he expected to see a difference in the children's attitudes. Twice he turned around quickly. Each time the children had all been busy writing in their notebooks. There was no smirking or winking behind their hands. At noon, he said, "In case any of you need to ask me something, there's no use your going to the Poorwillys'. I'm staying at Miss Adel's now."

The children solemnly nodded their heads. He dismissed them and went home for lunch.

Adel was at home. She blushed and said, "The women at the sheds said I should come home early now that I've got you to look after. Since the men aren't fishing there isn't much to do."

"That's very good of them," Danny replied.

Danny and Adel were left completely alone. He had expected that some of the villagers would drop by, but no one came to visit. Danny and Adel settled into a routine that was disturbed only by Danny's irritation at being close to Adel. Adel shied away from him when he brushed against her. At the end of the second week, she accepted his offer to help with the dishes. They stood side by side as they worked. Danny was so distracted by Adel's warmth and the constant movement of her body that the dishes were only half dried.

Danny put his hand on Adel's shoulder and turned her toward him. She let him pull her close. There was no place to sit or lie in the kitchen so he picked her up and carried her to the bedroom. She did not resist when he undressed her. After he made love to her, he fell asleep. When he woke up, Adel had gone to her own bed.

Danny took Adel to bed with him every evening after that, but during the night she always slipped away to her own bedroom. At the beginning of the next week, they had their first visitor. Mrs. Poorwilly stopped by to see how they were doing. They had been eating supper when she arrived. Normally, they would have been finished eating, but Adel had been late in coming from the fish sheds. The weather had improved enough for the men to go fishing. Mrs. Poorwilly accepted a cup of coffee and sat and talked to them for an hour.

It was as though her coming had been a signal. After that, villagers dropped by in the evenings to talk for a little while. They nearly always brought something with them and left it on the table. Danny had wanted to protest, but he did not know what to say that would not embarrass their visitors so he said nothing.

Adel stopped going back to her own bed. Danny thought about getting married but dismissed the idea. He was comfortable with things the way they were.

The day Danny started to get sick he should have known something was wrong. He had yelled at the children for no particular reason. When Adel had come home, he had been grouchy with her. The next day his throat had been sore, but he had ignored it. By the end of the day, he was running a temperature and his knees felt like water.

Adel had been worried, but he told her not to call Mrs. Poorwilly. Their things had become so mixed together that it was obvious they were using the same bedroom.

For the next few days, he was too sick to protest about anything. Mrs. Poorwilly came frequently to take his temperature to see that Adel kept forcing whisky and warm broth into him. All during his sickness Danny was convinced that he was going to die. During one afternoon he was sure that he was dead and that the sheets were a shroud.

The crisis passed and he started to cough up phlegm, but he was so weak that it was an effort for him to lift up his head. The day he was strong enough to sit up and eat in the kitchen, Mrs. Poorwilly brought him a package of hand-rolled cigarettes.

"Nearly everyone is coming to see you tomorrow. They'll all bring something in the way of a present. It's a custom. Don't say they shouldn't or they'll think you feel their presents aren't good enough."

Danny said that he understood.

The school children came first with hand-carved pieces of driftwood. He admired the generally shapeless carvings, and after the first abortive attempt carefully avoided guessing at what they were supposed to be.

After the children left, the McFarlans came. Mr. McFarlan had made a shadow box from shingle. He had scraped the shingle with broken glass until the grain stood out. Inside the box he had made a floor of lichen and pebbles. Seagulls made from clam shells sat on the lichen.

His wife stretched a piece of black cloth over the end of a fish box. On it she had glued boiled fish bones to form a picture of a boat and a man.

Someone brought a tin of pears, another brought a chocolate bar. One of the men brought half a bottle of whisky.

Each visitor stayed just long enough to inquire how Danny felt, wish him well, and leave a present on the table. When the last visitor had gone, Danny was exhausted. Adel helped him to bed.

He felt much better by the end of the week, but when he tried to return to work, Mrs. Poorwilly said, "Mary Johnson's doing a fine job. Not as good as you, of course, but the kids aren't suffering. If you rush back before you're ready, everybody will take it that you think she's doing a poor job. If you get sick again, she won't take over."

Adel returned to work at the sheds, but the women sent her home. The weather had held and there were lots of fish, but they said she should be at home looking after Danny.

At first it was ideal. They had little to do except sit and talk or make love. Danny caught up on his reading. They both were happy, but by the end of March their confinement had made them both restless.

To get out of the house, Danny walked to Mrs. Poorwilly's. While they were having coffee, Danny said, "I guess everyone must have got the flu."

"No," Mrs. Poorwilly replied, "just some colds among the children. Adel and you making out all right?"

"Yes," Danny said.

"Her mother was a beauty, you know. I hope you didn't mind moving, but these things happen."

"No, I didn't mind moving."

They sat for five minutes before Danny said, "Could I ask you something? I wouldn't want anyone else to know."

Mrs. Poorwilly nodded her assent.

"Mary Johnson is doing such a good job that I thought I might ask her to radio for a plane. Maybe it would be a good idea for me to take Adel to the mainland for a week."

"Any particular reason?"

"Yes. If she wants, I'll marry her."

"Haven't you asked her?"

Danny shook his head. It had never occurred to him that she might say no.

"Wait until you ask her. The superintendent will want a reason. You'll have to tell him over the radio and everyone will know. You wouldn't want to tell him and then have her turn you down."

Adel was standing at the window when he returned. He put his arms around her. "You know, I think we should get married.'

Adel didn't answer.

"Don't you want to marry me?" he asked.

"Yes. I do. But I've never been off the island. You won't want to stay here always."

"We can stay for a couple of years. We'll go a little at a time. We can start with a week on the mainland for a honeymoon. We'll go somewhere on a train."

That evening he went to Mary Johnson's. Mary tried to raise the mainland operator, but the static was so bad that no contact could be made. Danny kept Mary at the radio for half an hour. He left when she promised to send one of the children with a message if the radio cleared.

Danny returned the next night, but the static was just as bad. Mary promised to send for him as soon as the call went through.

A week went by. The weather continued to improve. Danny checked the thermometer. The temperature was going up a degree every two days.

At the end of the week he returned to Mary's. The radio was not working at all. One of the tubes needed to be replaced. He left. Halfway home he decided to go back and leave a message for the plane. The radio might work just long enough for a message, but not long enough for him to be called to the set. When he came up to the house, he was sure that he heard the radio. He banged on the front door. Mary took her time coming. When she opened the door, he said, "I heard the radio. Can you send a message right away?"

Mary replied that he must have just heard the children talking. Danny insisted on her trying to make the call. She was annoyed, but she tried to get through. When she had tried for five minutes, Danny excused himself and left.

He walked partway home, then turned and crept back over the rock.

The windows were dark. He lay in the hollow of rock behind the house until the cold forced him to leave.

In the morning, he went to the dock to talk to the fishermen. He offered to pay any one of them triple the normal fare to take him down the coast. They laughed and said they would bring him some fresh fish for supper.

When he had continued insisting that he wanted to leave, they said that a trip at this time of year was impossible. Even planes found it difficult to land along the coast. A boat could be crushed in the pack ice which was shifting up and down the shore.

Danny told Adel about the radio and the boats. She sympathized with him, but agreed with the men that it was hopeless to try and make the trip in an open boat.

"Besides," she said, "the freight boats will be coming in a month or so."

True to their word, the fishermen sent a fresh fish. Danny tried to pay the boy who brought it, but he said that he had been told not to accept anything. Danny had put the money into the boy's hand. The boy had gone, but a few minutes later he returned and put the money in front of the door.

Late that afternoon, Danny walked to the dock. After looking around to see that no one was watching, he bent down and looked at the rope which held one of the boats. He untied it, then tied it again.

He returned to the house and started gathering his heavy clothing. When Adel came into the room, she said, "What are you going to do?"

"I'm leaving."

"Is the plane coming?"

"I'm taking myself. I've had enough. I'm not allowed to work. You're not allowed to work. Everyone showers us with things they won't let us pay for. I try to use the radio, but it never works." He turned to face her. "It always worked before."

"Sometimes it hasn't worked for weeks," Adel replied. "Once it was six weeks. It's the change in temperature."

"But it works. The other night I heard it working. Then when I asked Mary Johnson to call, she said it was just the children talking."

"Mary told me," Adel said. "You made her very upset. She thinks you're still not feeling well."

"I'm feeling fine. Just fine. And I'm leaving. I don't know what's going on here, but I'm getting out. I'm going to get a plane and then I'm coming back for you."

"You said we could leave a little at a time."

"That was before this happened. What if something goes wrong? Three people have died. One of them died right before my eyes and I couldn't do anything about it. What if we needed a doctor? Or a policeman? What if someone took some crazy notion into his head?"

Danny took Sick Jack's sou'westers off a peg. He laid out the clothes he wanted and packed two boxes with food. He lay awake until three o'clock, then slipped outside and down to the boats.

The boats were in their usual places. He reached for the rope of the first boat. His hand closed on a heavy chain. Danny could not believe it. He jumped onto the boat and ran his hand around the chain. He climbed out and ran from boat to boat. Every boat was the same. He tried to break the chains loose. When they would not break, he sat on the dock and beat his hands on the chains. When he had exhausted himself, he sat with his face pressed into his hands.

In the morning, Mary sent one of the boys to tell Danny that the radio had worked long enough for her to send a message. It hadn't been confirmed, but she thought it might have been heard. For the rest of the day, Danny was elated, but as the days passed and the plane did not appear, he became more and more depressed. Adel kept saying that the plane would come, but Danny doubted if it would ever come.

The weather became quite mild. Danny walked to the dock every day. The chains were still on the boats. He had spent an hour on the dock staring at the thin blue line that was the mainland and was walking back to Adel's when he noticed that the snow had melted away from some of the cracks in the granite. The cracks were crammed with closely packed leaves.

He paused to pick a leaf. *April the first,* he thought, *April the first will come and we'll be able to go.* Then, as he stared at the small green leaf in his hand, he realized that he was wrong. It was the bloodflowers which bloomed April the first. It wasn't until two weeks later that the first freight boat came.

The rest of the day he tried to make plans for Adel and himself, but he could not concentrate. The image of thousands and thousands of bloodflowers kept spilling into his mind.

L. WOIWODE

The Suitor

(FROM MCCALL'S MAGAZINE)

HE DREAMED he'd been sleeping in the catacombs, those cold tombs he'd heard of only from nuns' lips. The shuffling of a pair of slippers traced a series of paths and passageways through his sleep, the sound of a dropped object struck deep into his dream, and somebody in the kitchen (who?) whispering to somebody else in an insistent tone, rapidly, rapidly, like rain, had washed out a great cave, the hollow where he now lay. Moving toward the border of wakefulness, he became aware of the cold, a numbness in his nose, ears, and fingertips, and then conscious that his body was constricted, encased in something unnatural. And then he remembered that he was still fully dressed.

There was a sound of coals being shaken down at a cookstove. He opened his eyes and saw a pattern of cracks, intricate as a web, in the leather back of the horsehair sofa. January 1, 1939, registered in his mind. He closed his eyes. That date could mark the beginning, not just of a new year, but of a new life. Oh, let it He sighed and covered his head with the quilt. Until he knew Alpha was up and had come downstairs, he didn't want the Jensens to know he was awake. He'd never faced both her parents at the same time, alone, without Alpha present, and the prospect of that made him more uneasy than ever. The night before, sitting in front of the Jensens' fireplace, he had asked Alpha to be his wife. Now he lay in the front room of their house, *her* house, the house where she, at this moment, was deep asleep. A smile of pleasure appeared on his face.

Time and the elements themselves, as though they knew of his purpose, made the setting of the proposal a perfect one. First, the New Year. Then, the weather. When he had left home after lunch yesterday, the sky was clear, pale blue against the white line of the plain, and the air was still and brilliant; but soon small flakes started falling, a wind hit, and by the time he pulled into the Jensens' drive, a distance of just five miles, the white stuff was up to the axle hubs of his Model A.

The blizzard blew the rest of the afternoon, wrapping the house in blackness, and the windmill clattered and shrieked in the distance, because no one could go shut it off, for fear of getting lost. Kerosene lamps were lit, rags stuffed around doors, logs brought in from the back porch, along with two lumps of coal, precious coal, and blankets were hung over all the windows.

Except for telling God, in variations of His name, what He was doing to the livestock with the storm, Alpha's father maintained a strange silence. It was her mother who finally spoke the holy words; when there was no letup in the storm and it became obvious that he, the suitor, would have to spend the night, her mother, who was at the cookstove making supper, sighed, shrugged her shoulders, and without turning to him, said, "The couch will be yours," and Alpha, who was behind her mother, turned and winked at him.

Then the fire. In front of it on the hooked rug, their faces fevered with its heat. Popcorn and divinity in bowls between them. Their fingertips touching. The whine of the blizzard outside and the feeling it brought — that they were privileged beings, spared and put down on an island in the sea of it. Alone. On the O of the hooked rug. An oasis. The O of love, with them in its center. Lowering their voices when her parents, with several good-nights and a great deal of commotion, went into the bedroom. A long silence as they stared at the fire, and then the question, alive in him for two years, rising of its own accord.

"If you ever asked," she whispered, "I knew it would be tonight."

"How?"

"I knew."

"I've been afraid," he said.

"I know. *I've* been afraid."

"Of what?"

"Me. You." A glance toward her parents' bedroom. "What makes a man afraid?"

"I don't know. Everything. What you?"

"I'm not, really, now that you asked."

"Then will —" It was impossible for him to repeat it. The wind rose, and the flame swayed toward the left.

"Yes," she whispered.

Or did he imagine it? At that moment, her mother, wrapped in a robe, appeared in the doorway, saying, "Alpha, it's past time you were in bed." Then, "Here" — holding out bedclothes at arm's length, so he had to rise, go to her, and since she kept a firm grip on a quilt, look level into her eyes as she said, "*This* is to keep you warm."

Alpha's footsteps retreating up the stairs while her mother, ignoring his offers to help, saying, "Shoo! Shoo!" in a strange tone — was she being playful? — piled more logs on the fire and then stood with her back to the flames, facing him, her palms open at her sides to catch the heat. He couldn't see, from the couch, the expression of her face or know whether or not she had heard. "I sleep light," she said, and turned and left the room.

The floorboards groaned and creaked above him, and he tried to visualize Alpha upstairs, and when he did, so vividly, he realized it was a sin, and then tried not to. He said three Hail Marys. He said an Our Father. Out of habit, his boyhood bedtime prayers went through his head. He discovered that there were five buttons on his shirt, and pausing at each button, gripping it tight, he ran his fingers down his shirtfront — five Hail Marys — then ran them up it — a decade of the rosary — and touched his Adam's apple for an Our Father.

What did she do so long, moving around up there, before she went to bed? Then there was a sound of springs as she settled into bed, and that was worse. He lost track of the times he'd touched his Adam's apple and rolled on his side in agony and said an Act of Contrition.

Had she said yes, or was it the wind and fire? Her hand said yes, the angle of her head, bowed so that her dark hair concealed her features, showing only her high brow bronzed by fire; the fold of her legs beneath her dress, her bare feet, her tipped shoes lying beside them — all this said, *Yes, Yes,* but did she?

Yes.

Alpha Sommerfeld. Alpha and Martin Sommerfeld. The names belonged together. But if it were so, if she said yes, then it would be hard for them from this day on. The families lived on neighboring farms, but neither parents had ever been in the others' house, and that was not common in this part of the country, not a good sign.

His mother going to the mailbox, over three years ago, and seeing a stranger walking down the railroad tracks and then coming back into the house and describing him — "so little I thought it was a kid at first, and also because he wasn't wearing a hat, not even a cap, mind you, but his hair was gray on the sides, all mussed up like a madman's, flying in the wind, and his eyes were wild, and he was making a beeline for town like there was a train behind him!" — and wondering who it could be, a bum, or somebody she should know about?

"Oh, that's Ed Jensen," his father told her. "He just moved in at the old Hollingsworth place."

That same night, the household woke to the sound of someone singing and shouting obscene songs, and they looked out to see a figure weaving down the tracks in the moonlight; Ed Jensen on his way home.

Why did his mother have to be so pious and straitlaced and use her religion to measure everybody else? Why did she have to be that way? They were all adults; some of the songs were amusing. After a few weekends of the same kind of singing, she started calling Alpha's father "the Jensen devil" or "that insane atheist down the road," and she demanded that the men of the house, her son or her husband, one of them or both of them, go tell that drunk to use the roads like everybody else. He and his father going to the tracks and intercepting the man with the wild hair and wild blue eyes.

"I haven't got a car," Jensen said to them, "and I'll be damned if I'll waste the wear and tear on a good team just to go into town to get boozed, and that's where I'm bound. These tracks are the straightest shot I know from those two sections of quack grass back there, which some piker pawned off on me as a farm, to the front door of the closest gin mill. And after farming quack grass for a week straight with no help, no sons, I don't mind saying I like a snort or two. For the nerves. What do you folks do about quack grass? I've never seen it grow so thick. I beat it with a hoe, I keep the wife and daughter after it, I pull it up by hand — roots, runners, and all — and I even burn the stuff. That's right, you laugh, but I do, by Christ, I burn a hayrack of it every day, and the next morning it's up thick as ever, choking my wheat."

The Hollingsworth place was one of the last pieces of land in the area to see the plow, they told him; the sod was turned under just ten years ago, and only two or three crops were put in before the Depression.

"So that's it. It'll take me five years, then, or more, before all the buried stuff comes up where I can kill it. Damn! Well, I'll just keep at it till I win. It's part my fault I got took on the land. I left my old place for this Hollingsworth one because of the barn. Have you ever been in it? It's a beauty! It's built better than a brick — Well, it's the best barn I've seen in my life, and I've always said that if a man can't sleep in his own barn, it's not a fit place for any kind of livestock. We make use of the poor beasts their whole lives, we beat them — I do — we make money off them, we don't let them run wild the way they did, so the least we can do is not lock them up inside some drafty, stinking, dirt-floored, jerrybuilt shack that's never warm and you can't ever keep clean, isn't it?" They nodded.

The three of them talking a long time — rather, Jensen talking while the two of them, silent by nature, listened, blinking at the outpour, until they heard from the house: "Alfred! Martin! *Dinner!* Alfred!" Jensen saying good-bye, saying he hoped to see them soon, shaking their hands, and then the two of them going in to dinner, where his father said, "There's nothing the matter with that man. I like him, and he can walk where he wants."

So his mother quoted back at his father one of his father's favorite maxims: "You are judged not by who you are or what you are but by the company you keep," and from that time on, his father, though trying not to be unkind about it, shied away from Ed Jensen.

And Jensen sensed it from the first; nevertheless, he was always friendly to him — the neighbor boy, the suitor, "the big hulk," as Jensen called him — or was almost always friendly, anyway. Alpha's mother never was. All her mother ever said to him, it seemed, was hello and good-bye, and if he was in the same room with her, she managed to keep her back to him most of the time.

And when he finally finished college, working his way for five years, and took a job with the state, an accomplishment he thought would soften her mother, her mother instead became even more aloof and ironic. "It's the *ed*ucated one," she would call to Alpha, and walk out of the room.

Then, learning later, from Alpha, that her mother had been brought up a Missouri Synod Lutheran and could not believe that any Catholic was worth a grain of salt. Lord in heaven, angels and saints, pray for us all.

He listened for footsteps upstairs. Nothing. Silence.

Alpha's father liked him, though, or at least seemed to. Yes, liked him. Every time the Model A came into the yard, her father rushed out, so exuberant it was like a welcoming party in one, and was garrulous and personal, calling him "Martin" and "boy," clapping him on the shoulder — ha! — and speaking to him as an equal about Roosevelt and Landon, the repeal of Prohibition, horses (Jensen's passion) as opposed to mechanized farming, and, with a sly wink, subjects that caused the college graduate to blush.

Inside the house, however, Alpha's father was often as silent as his own father, remote and morose, and responded only with a nod, or else turned away to the radio. Why? So outspoken most of the time, on any topic, around anyone, even his daughter and wife, and then this silence in the house; why? The walls around him? The furniture — none of which, massive as it was, looked capable of containing the energy of his wiry body? Why no words?

Even Alpha couldn't explain. She knew very little of her father's past life, was uncertain about his behavior and person — "I don't know if he's mean. I don't know if he's kind" — and spoke of him as though he were an enigma to respect and beware of.

Then there had been the incidents. Two summers ago, in June, driving to the Jensens' and taking Alpha to a baseball game (five to three: home team lost) and on the way home, Alpha asking him to stop the noise of the car so they could talk. Pulling off the road, close to some tall weeds, and killing the engine. "What is it, Alpha?"

She leaned her head on his chest and didn't talk. He settled in the seat and put his arm over her shoulder. It was starting to turn dark, and a dove was mourning in the distance — yes, a dove, its three notes, the first two to proclaim the two of them together, *You* and *You,* the last one so stretched out and desolate it was like the plain around them, an *Oooo* that moved in a downward curve, solitary and final as a falling star. Heart, heart, does it have to end there? No. Yes. No. Holy Mary, sanctuary of — Fingertips under her chin, lifting her face close, her pupils enlarged and her eyes dark, and then, for the first time, kissing her on the lips.

Something hit the windshield, and they jumped back. Thirty feet away, high above them on the railway embankment, stood Alpha's father. The old man let some pebbles fall out of his fingers, put his fists on his hips, and stared at them for a long time. Finally, in humor or disgust — who could know? — Jensen turned away and kept on walking down the tracks toward town.

Alpha was terrified, in tears, and she held him by the arm all the way to her place, making him promise to stop by the next day to help her explain, to protect her if need be, to stand by her no matter what happened. Going to the Jensens' the next day, pale and afraid, and seeing the look of wonder on Alpha's face; nothing had happened.

The two of them lived in fear for a long time, thinking it would come out after one of Jensen's return trips from the tavern, but it never did. Apparently, Jensen told no one, not even his wife — certainly not his wife. Nothing ever came of it.

Unless that incident explained the other. Once, when Martin came for Alpha, Jensen was talking to a neighbor, Ray Peterson, in the front room, so he waited for Alpha in the kitchen, standing in the door next to the cookstove. Alpha's mother was at the kitchen table in a familiar attitude, her back to him, wetting her fingers and paging through the new Sears, Roebuck catalogue.

Suddenly he caught a phrase of conversation from the front room

—"those damn mackerel snappers"—in Peterson's voice, he thought, and he started to cough and clear his throat, to let them know he was inside the house.

Then the voice of Alpha's father was saying, "Show me a Catholic and I'll show you a hypocrite. They're the most lying, sanctimonious band of—" Were they drinking? Or drunk? He coughed and tried to make more noise, but there was a deliberate rise of volume in Jensen's voice: "They could maim or kill a man and call it okay, because they're the chosen, and there's no way around it. They know how to pray right, you see, and we don't. They use the *beads*. Then they got those little stalls where—"

Alpha's mother rose and went into the front room, to put a stop to it, he thought, but her footsteps carried through to the bedroom. "Like rabbits, the way they breed. You wonder when they got time to go to church! The daughter here is going with one, you know. Oh, he's all right by me, a fine boy, but someday if she doesn't watch it, I say"—more volume and a change in tone, as though he'd lifted his head toward her bedroom—"I say, 'Alpha! One of these days you're going to have a dozen kids running around in the same room, none of them over the age of ten, and the whole bunch swinging those beads like lassos. Whoop-ee, Ma! Whoooo-PEE!' "

On weak legs, he made it through the door, out the back porch, and into the fresh air. No doubt about it; Jensen had to be drunk. He went to the pump and wet his head and wiped his face and wrists with his handkerchief, then got into the car and waited for Alpha. When she finally came out, her face was flushed, her eyes cast down, and she was silent most of the afternoon, wadding and squeezing a kerchief in her lap, and later in the day, when he tried to bring up the subject, she said, "No. Don't. He didn't mean it. He's bitter because he has no sons."

That was more than a year ago, and neither of them had ever mentioned it since . . .

There was a sound of logs rumbling into the woodbox, and Martin rose out of the luxury of half-sleep, aware now of the morning coldness in the marrow of his bones, and a filmy sensation over his skin from sleeping in his clothes. He heard more whispering in the kitchen, a bang of the back door, and the sound of water starting to boil, the wet bottom of the kettle stuttering on the stove top. He strained to hear Alpha, but the floorboards above him were silent, the bedsprings were too. The back door opened, it closed, and footsteps started across the kitchen, cold snow screaking underneath them on the linoleum.

("Ed!") A piercing whisper.

("Yes?") *He* could whisper?

("What do you think you're *doing?*")

("Taking this in there.")

("No you're not.")

("He should be up by now.")

("I mean, not like that, not with those snowy boots.")

"Oh, that," he said coming out of the whisper. "It's clean snow. To hell with it."

The footsteps proceeded into the front room, passing so close Martin could smell the cold of outdoors on foreign clothes and then logs tumbled onto the hearth. There was a squeak of rubber, the crack of a knee joint, and some grunts and muttered curses as the wood was put in place.

Martin waited through a long silence, expecting the fire to start, anticipating its warmth, and then sensed Jensen's eyes on him.

"Hey, boy, aren't you up yet?"

Martin uncovered his head. "Yes."

Jensen stood in front of the fireplace in a sheepskin coat and fur cap, and when he saw Martin was awake, he started stomping his felt-booted feet as though dancing and slapping together his leather mittens. It was so cold in the room Martin could see his own breath. Wasn't he going to make a fire? Couldn't they afford one in here until night? Alpha must be freezing.

"Well!" Jensen said. "I finally got that windmill shut off before it rattled its damn brains out. The wind let up at four, and I ran out then. It's a good thing you're going into business and not farming, is all I can say. Do you know what time it is? It's almost eight o'clock."

"Oh."

"You're damn tootin'! And it's twenty below out."

"Oh."

"'Oh, oh.' Didn't you hear what I said?"

"Yes. I mean — *what's* that you said?"

"It's almost eight."

"Oh." So? He was baffled by this cheerful small talk from Jensen, here in the house, and then the old man moved closer, a scowl on his face, his black eyelashes fringed with big beads of ice that had begun to melt, his eyes questioning and fierce, and Martin, shivering at how cold it must be, was sure that something must be wrong.

"You're positive you're awake?" Jensen asked.

"Yes."

"Then you better get up and give me a hand."

"The stock?" Martin asked, and pushed off the quilt and sat.

"Stock, hell! That's done hours ago. We have to get your car out of the snow."

"Oh," Martin said. "Oh, my car." Puzzled by this, by Jensen's attitude, in a daze, Martin reached for a shoe with his curled toes, pulled it close, slipped his stockinged foot into its cold sheath, and bent to lace it. Ooooo. His bladder felt big as a pumpkin.

"Model A's!" Jensen exclaimed. "I tried cranking the son of a —"

"Ed!" From the kitchen. "Watch that tongue."

"I tried cranking it for a half-hour and couldn't even make it go poot. How do you adjust your spark?"

"A quarter down."

"No wonder!"

Then Martin felt weak and started trembling, and it wasn't from his physical condition or the cold. The Jensens were turning him out, on purpose, before he had a chance to see Alpha. He finished tying his shoes and looked up into Jensen's excited eyes, and tried to find calm and straightforward words to tell of the proposal. But had she said yes?

"Come on, come on, boy, what is it?" Jensen said, and clapped his mittens close to Martin's head. "I've never seen a man move so slow in my life!"

"I wanted —" Martin lowered his eyes.

"Are you sure you're still not asleep?"

"No."

"Then let's get going!"

Reluctant, Martin rose from the couch and followed the old man into the kitchen, where Alpha's mother was waiting. Her large gray eyes, usually as vague and glazed as those of a convalescent, were bright and understanding, Martin noticed. She gave him a brisk nod, and said, "Good morning. Sorry you can't have breakfast."

So that was it; she had heard him propose.

She took his overcoat from the shelf of the cookstove, shook it hard, and held it out for him by the shoulders. He looked at her, feeling his lips tremble, then at Jensen, a master study of impatience, then at the coat, then at her newly bright eyes. Please, God, couldn't Alpha appear now?

"Come on, come on," said Jensen, "you're acting like a sheep! Let's get a move on."

Martin turned, holding his hands out behind him, and the overcoat, its sleeves heated from the stove, slipped up his arms. He pulled it in place and buttoned it, and its warmth drew the chill from his bones. He turned to Alpha's mother. "Thank you," he murmured. "I — "

"No need for thanks." She handed him his cap. "And no time. Good-bye."

Martin tugged the cap over his ears, stalling for time, and was about to speak when the old man, muttering something, grabbed him by the elbow, opened the door, pulled him onto the porch, and kicked the kitchen door shut. The windows and door of the porch were covered with tar paper, and it was nearly dark as night inside it.

"My overshoes," Martin said.

"Right there, beside the separator. Better get them on and hurry it up."

The rubber overshoes were frozen stiff, difficult to bend, and they were icy against his ankles and shins. Oh, if he had to bend once more — His fingertip froze to a buckle. He jerked it loose, leaving a strip of skin, and felt anger and humiliation start rising in him. He took his gloves out of his pocket and drew them on while the old man clucked his tongue, and said, "What's the matter with you? You know you should have had those on first."

He finished buckling his overshoes and rose, standing tall above Jensen, and decided now was the time to speak; but the old man swung open the outside door, and it was as if two sharp objects, icicles, had been driven home above the tops of Martin's eyes, and his lids pinched shut against the brilliance of the snow. When he'd finished blinking and his vision adjusted, he saw his car standing in a drift that came up to the running board. A team of black Percherons, nodding against the traces, blowing frosty plumes from their nostrils, their broad backs steaming, was hitched up to the car's front bumper.

"I know it looks bad here," Jensen said, and took hold of his arm, leading him down the steps, dragging him through drifts, "but I've walked up to the main road, and it's already been traveled, so there won't be any trouble once we get there, or if there is, I'll pull you all the way in. Right there is the team that can do just that!" Jensen turned to him and gave a grin of pride, but it fell away, and his expression changed to consternation. "Damn it to hell," he said. "A tie. Do you need one?"

"Tie?"

Jensen stepped back a step, and his eyes narrowed, but not from snow glare. "What's the matter with you this morning, boy? Aren't you well, or didn't you sleep all last night, or what? I'm not up on all your rigamarole, but today is Sunday, for Christ's sake, *Sunday,* and I do know you've got to get to church. Now, do you need to borrow a tie or not?"

"Oh, no. No tie. I— "

"The wife, she was a regular churchgoer once, you know, so she's been on my tail for an hour to get you there. I guess she wants to keep you pure, now that you've proposed to the daughter. You don't have to look that way. It's all right. I know all about it, and I'm proud to say I was the first to know. The daughter — she finally gave out, or I suppose she'd be here helping us, that's how she is — she was so excited she couldn't sleep the whole night, so she came downstairs about five, right after I got the gag on that windmill, and told me the news, and I want you to know that both of us, the wife and I both, realize you've got a fine mind and body and everything will work out for the best. But do you want to know something?"

Martin felt that if he spoke, it would come out in a howl.

"Hold on, now," Jensen said. "Keep a hold of yourself. I'll tell you. With all the churchgoing and hymning and whatnot the wife has had — this is on her — and the praying for my soul and for this and for that — with all that, guess what? She forgot it was Sunday. *I* was the one that remembered. Now, what do you think of that?"

Jensen nudged Martin, winked an ice-fringed eye, and said, "You think I might be Christian?"

Biographical Notes

RUSSELL BANKS was born in 1940 and raised in New Hampshire and eastern Massachusetts. He attended Colgate and graduated from the University of North Carolina at Chapel Hill in 1967 with highest honors in English literature and creative writing. The co-founder and co-editor of the new *Lillabulero* magazine and press, he has recently completed a book of poems, *The Crossing Back,* and a pair of novels, *The Locus* and *After Beckmann: A Triptych.* His stories have appeared in many magazines, among them *The Partisan Review, New American Review, The Transatlantic Review,* and *The Minnesota Review.* At present he is teaching at Emerson College in Boston, working on a new novel, and continuing to edit *Lillabulero.* He lives in a farmhouse in New Hampshire with his wife and three daughters.

HAL BENNETT was born in Buckingham, Virginia, in 1930 and educated in the public schools of Orange, New Jersey. After a period in the air force, he attended Mexico City College until he withdrew in 1956 to devote his full time to writing. He has published three novels — *A Wilderness of Vines, The Black Wine,* and *Lord of Dark Places.* Although he has been writing short stories for many years, "Dotson Gerber Resurrected" is his first piece published in a magazine of national circulation. At present, he is working on his fourth novel and a collection of short stories.

JAMES BLAKE was born in 1920 in Edinburgh, Scotland, and grew up in Chicago. He studied to be a concert pianist during his childhood and adolescence, and attended the University of Illinois and Northwestern. He was evicted from both for the sin of sloth and became a jazz pianist. From 1950–1952 he served time on a county chain gang in Florida. Letters he wrote to Nelson Algren from there came to the attention of Simone de Beauvoir and were published in Jean Paul Sartre's *Les Temps Modernes.* George Plimpton published the letters as a prison chronicle in 1957 in the *Paris Review.* From 1955 to 1968, Mr. Blake served three sentences in the Florida State Prison, with brief periods of freedom. In 1967 George Plimpton suggested compiling a collection of Blake's letters from the penitentiary, and the book, *The Joint,* was published in 1971. He is now living in Woodbury, Connecticut, and working on a novel.

JACK CADY was born in 1932 and raised in the South and Midwest. He has worked as an over-the-road trucker, an auctioneer, a tree climber, and a sailor. He currently teaches English and short story writing at the University of Washington, Seattle, as an assistant professor. His publications include "The Burning," which won the *Atlantic Monthly* "First" Award in 1965. His work has also appeared in three of *The Best American Short Stories* volumes. He has published in *The Yale Review* and elsewhere and is currently working on a novel.

ROBERT CANZONERI's publications include a book of nonfiction, *"I Do So Politely": A Voice From the South,* a book of poems, *Watch Us Pass,* a novel, *Men With Little Hammers,* and *Barbed Wire and Other Stories,* which takes its title from the story in this collection. He is co-editor with Page Stegner of the textbook *Fiction and Analysis: Seven Major Themes.* Born in 1925, he grew up in Mississippi and has degrees from Mississippi College, the University of Mississippi, and Stanford University; currently he is Professor of English at Ohio State University. In addition to a short story coming along, he is working on a novel and a book on his Sicilian background. He and his wife Dottie have two children, Tony and Nina.

ALBERT DRAKE was born in Portland, Oregon, in 1935. Although he has lived for long periods of time in Europe, Greece, and Mexico, he feels his roots are in the Pacific Northwest. He has worked full time as a mechanic, gravedigger, warehouseman, laborer, and research assistant on a project to diagnose bone tumors by computer; more recently he has taught English at the University of

Oregon and at Michigan State University, where he is an associate professor. Over the past nine years he has published twenty-some stories, and has recently finished a novel. He edited an anthology of "experimental" short fiction entitled *The Extreme Story.* He is married and has three children just old enough to want to be held, all at once.

WILLIAM EASTLAKE was born in New York City and went to school in New Jersey. He was in the US Army from 1941–1945. His five novels are *Go In Beauty, The Bronc People, Portrait of an Artist with Twenty-Six Horses, Castle Keep,* and *The Bamboo Bed.* Recipient of a Ford Foundation grant and a Rockerfeller grant, he has also had a lectureship at the University of New Mexico. He has been writer-in-residence at the University of Southern California and the University of Arizona, and been Regents Lecturer at the University of California at Santa Barbara. The author of sixty short stories, ten anthologies, and represented in six textbooks, he is now working on a novel and living in Arizona on a small ranch with his wife, two dogs, and several horses.

BETH HARVOR was born in 1936 on the Canadian east coast and educated at rural schools there. When she graduated from high school she became a student nurse but dropped out in her final year. In the 1960's she twice won awards in the Canadian Broadcasting Corporation's New Canadian Writing Series and since that time has had work published in *The Canadian Forum, The Colorado Quarterly, The Fiddlehead, The Hudson Review,* and *Saturday Night.* At present she is writing a novel with the help of a grant from the Canada Council. Stories of hers will soon appear in *The Malahat Review* and *The Windsor Review.*

DAVID MADDEN was born in 1933 in Knoxville, Tennessee. His second novel, *Cassandra Singing,* was published in 1969; in the following year, the Louisiana University Press published a collection of his stories, *The Shadow Knows,* a National Council on the Arts selection. His stories, poems, and essays have appeared in a wide variety of publications, from *Playboy* to *The Southern Review* to scholarly journals. Many of his plays have been produced outside New York. Among his critical works are *Wright Morris, The Poetic Image in Six Genres* (informal essays in imaginative writing), and *James M. Cain.* He is also editor of *Tough Guy Writers of the Thirties* and *Proletarian Writers of the*

Thirties. Mr. Madden has received a Rockefeller Grant in Fiction. Presently writer-in-residence at Louisiana State University, he is working on a new novel, *Bijou.*

DON MITCHELL was born in 1947 and raised in the suburbs of Chicago and Philadelphia. He attended Swarthmore College and spent his vacations hitchhiking around the country, occasionally writing fiction. Upon graduating in philosophy in 1969, he moved to California and completed *Thumb Tripping,* a novel about a college couple on the road for a summer. "Diesel" is an episode from this novel. Later, the author adapted his novel to the screen for Joseph E. Levine. A conscientious objector, Mr. Mitchell presently lives near Philadelphia and is performing his alternate service to the draft at the American Baptist Board of Education and Publication. He is married and lives with his wife and several friends.

MARION MONTGOMERY, Professor of English at the University of Georgia, has published stories, poems, and essays in a number of periodicals. He has published two novels, *The Wandering of Desire* and *Darrell,* and three collections of poems: *Dry Lightning, Stones from the Rubble,* and *The Gull and Other Georgia Scenes.* Last year he produced *Ezra Pound: a Critical Essay* and *T. S. Eliot: an Essay on the American Magus.* Next year his *Father Eliot, Grandfather Wordsworth: Essays on Tradition and Individual Talents* is due to appear. He is currently at work on a new novel and a collection of his stories.

WRIGHT MORRIS was born in Central City, Nebraska. He is the author of *Man and Boy, The Huge Season, The Field of Vision* (National Book Award winner in 1957), *Ceremony at Lone Tree,* and other novels. Mr. Morris is now living in Mill Valley, California, and teaches at San Francisco State College.

PHILIP F. O'CONNOR was born in San Francisco, and raised both there and in San Anselmo, California. He holds degrees from the University of San Francisco, San Francisco State College, and the University of Iowa. His stories have appeared in *December, The Southern Review, Transatlantic Review, Western Humanities Review,* and numerous other literary magazines. Recently he won the second Iowa School of Letters Award for Short Fiction with a collection of stories, *Old Morals, Small Continents, Darker Times,* which the University of Iowa Press will publish this fall. He has been a lieutenant in the US Army, a reporter for the *San Francisco News,* a professional gambler, and a worker in the peace movement. An associate professor at Bowling Green University (Ohio), he recently developed the Bowling Green Writers, a writing and study program leading to the Master of Fine Arts degree. He is writing his first novel.

TILLIE OLSEN was born in Nebraska in 1931, and has lived in San Francisco since 1933. Self-educated, and having to work as well as raise a family, she did not begin actual writing until she was in her thirties. She is the author of *Tell Me A Riddle,* whose title piece received the O. Henry First Prize Award in 1961. This is her third appearance in *The Best American Short Stories.* She has been a recipient of a Ford Foundation and a National Endowment for the Arts grant, a member of the Radcliffe Institute, and has taught at Amherst College. She is now writing a work of fiction and a book on women.

IVAN PRASHKER was born in 1935 in New York City. He graduated from Queens College in 1956. Currently, he's an editor of a men's adventure magazine. His short stories have appeared in *Harper's, Playboy,* and *Redbook.*

NORMAN RUSH was born in San Francisco in 1933. He grew up in Oakland, California, attended the Los Angeles Branch School of the Telluride Association, was imprisoned as a war objector in 1951, and eventually completed his education at Swarthmore College. Since 1962 he has been self-employed as a dealer in antiquarian books. He lives in New City, Rockland County, New York, with his wife, the weaver Elsa Rush, and their two children. Recently he has published poetry and fiction in various literary magazines. His story, "Closing with Nature," published in *Massachusetts Review* in 1970, will appear in two anthologies. He is now at work on a novel.

DANNY SANTIAGO supplies no vital statistics. He has said of himself, "When it comes to biography, I am *'muy burro'* as we say in Spanish which means worse than mulish." "The Somebody" is his only published work, but several other stories of his have been mimeographed and are currently floating around in East Los Angeles.

JONATHAN STRONG was born in 1944 and raised in Winnetka, Illinois. He graduated from Harvard and now lives in Somerville, Massachusetts, and teaches at Tufts. A collection of his short fiction, *Tike and Five Stories,* won the Rosenthal Award of the

National Institute of Arts and letters in 1970. His stories, of which two have been chosen for the O. Henry Awards and one for the *American Literary Anthology,* have appeared in *The Partisan Review, The Atlantic Monthly, Esquire, Shenandoah,* and *TriQuarterly.* His first novel, *Ourselves,* begins with the chapter included here as "Xavier Fereira's Unfinished Book: Chapter One."

LEONARD TUSHNET was born in Newark, New Jersey. He worked throughout college and medical school as a soda fountain clerk. He received his B.S. from New York University in 1927 and his M.D. from New York University and Bellevue Hospital Medical College. After being a general practitioner for 35 years, he changed careers to devote his full time to writing. His published books are *To Die With Honor* and *The Uses of Adversity,* both about the Warsaw Ghetto, and *The Medicine Men,* a somewhat jaundiced view of medical practice in America today. In addition he has had published almost a hundred short stories, some of which have been anthologized.

WILLIAM DEMPSEY VALGARDSON was born in 1939 in Winnipeg, Manitoba, and raised in Gimli, Manitoba, the center for Icelandic settlement and for the freshwater fishing industry in Canada. He has a B.A. and B.Ed. from the University of Manitoba. An International Scholarship and a Canada Council writing grant allowed him to attend the University of Iowa Writer's Workshop where he earned an M.F.A. He currently is an instructor in creative writing at Cottey College, Nevada, Missouri.

L. WOIWODE was born in Sykeston, North Dakota, in 1941. He attended the University of Illinois and since 1964 has been writing full time. His short stories and poems appear with some frequency in *The New Yorker* and have also appeared in other mass-circulation and smaller magazines. Several stories have been reprinted in England, the Netherlands, Poland, and Russia; others are soon to be anthologized. His first novel, *What I'm Going To Do, I Think,* was the recipient of the William Faulkner Award for 1969. A new book, *Beyond The Bedroom Wall,* and a collection of poems, *Match Heads,* will be published soon. For the past three years Mr. Woiwode has been traveling around the U.S. with his wife and daughter. He is currently working on a third novel while on a grant from the Guggenheim Foundation.

THE YEARBOOK OF THE AMERICAN SHORT STORY

January 1 to December 31, 1970

Roll of Honor, 1970

I. *American Authors*

ALGREN, NELSON
Bet All the Money. Playboy, June.

AMFT, M. J.
More Like a Friend. Seventeen, October.

AUCHINCLOSS, LOUIS
The Sacrifice. Playboy, June.

BANKS, RUSSELL
With Ché in New Hampshire. New American Review, #10

BENNETT, HAL
Dotson Gerber Resurrected. Playboy, November.

BLAKE, JAMES
The Widow, Bereft. Esquire, January.

BRANDON, WILLIAM
The Life and White Horse of Ind. Joe. Massachusetts Review, Spring.

BRONER, E. M.
The Traveler and His Telling. Commentary, September.

C., E. H.
Watch the Running Wolf. Kenyon Review, Vol. XXXII, #1.

CADY, JACK
I Take Care of Things. Yale Review, Winter.

CANZONERI, ROBERT
Barbed Wire. Southern Review, Winter.

CHESTER, ALFRED
The Foot. New American Review, #9.

CLAYTON, JOHN
I Am Staying Where I Am. Antioch Review, Spring.

COATES, RUTH ALLISON
The Trunk. Phylon, Summer.

DEEMER, CHARLES
The Sextant. Northwest Review, Summer.

DEFOE, MARK
The Expiation of Dr. Ross. Western Humanities Review, Spring.

DIONNE, ROGER
Accidents of a Country Road. Playboy, November.

DOWNEY, DOROTHY
Of Butterflies, Pigeons and Eagles. Sewanee Review, Autumn.

DRAKE, ALBERT
The Chicken Which Became a Rat. Northwest Review, Summer.

DUNNING, LAWRENCE
The Test. Carolina Quarterly, Fall.

DURIE, ELSPETH
Nefertiti and Honest Abe. Tamarack Review, #50.

EASTLAKE, WILLIAM
The Dancing Boy. Evergreen Review, December.

ELKIN, STANLEY
The Dodo Bird. Iowa Review, Summer.

FEELEY, CONSTANCE
American Express. The New Yorker, November 14.

FIFIELD, WILLIAM
Care and Cure. Malahat Review, January.

FISHER, ELIZABETH
A Wall Around Her. Aphra, Autumn.

FRANCIS, H. E.
The Captain. Transatlantic Review, Summer.
Auction. Arlington Quarterly, Winter.

FREDERIKSEN, ALAN
Paradise. Sewanee Review, Summer.

GILL, BRENDA
Fat Girl. The New Yorker, September 26.

GOLDSTEIN, LAWRENCE
Revisiting. Sewanee Review, Summer.

GOODWIN, STEPHEN
Children and Cannibals. Sewanee Review, Spring.
Sole Surviving Son. Shenandoah, Autumn.

GREENBERG, JOANNE
Rites of Passage. Denver Quarterly, Spring.

HALLINGER, J. STURGIS
Blood Rights. Cimarron Review, October.

HARTER, EVELYN
The Stone Lovers. Southwest Review, Winter.

HARVOR, BETH
Pain Was My Portion. Hudson Review, Autumn.

HOPKINS, JOHN
Tangier Buzzless Flies. The New Yorker, October 10.

HOPPER, WILLIAM OTHA
Labyrinth. Arlington Quarterly, Winter.

HORNE, LEWIS B.
A Summer to Sing, A Summer to Cry. Prairie Schooner, Summer.

HUBBY, ERLENE
In Sherwood Forest. Western Humanities Review, Spring.

HUNT, HUGH ALLYN
When I Was Fifteen. Denver Quarterly, Summer.

IGO, JOHN
The Gesture. Epoch, Spring.

JOYCE, WILLIAM
Mrs. Bowle's Lover. Falcon, Summer.

KLEIN, NORMA
The Chess Game. Southwest Review, Winter.

LAYEFSKY, VIRGINIA
Jennifer. Virginia Quarterly Review, Winter.

LEEDS, CHARLIE
King of the Beasts. Prism International, Autumn.

LELCHUK, ALAN
Cambridge Talk. Modern Occasions, Fall.

MCHANEY, TOM
Three-Acre Plot. Georgia Review, Fall.

MCNAMARA, EUGENE
You Can't Get There From Here. West Coast Review, January.

MCNIECE, JAMES
The Relic of Mother Cabrini. Northwest Review, Summer.

MADDEN, DAVID
Frank Brown's Brother. South Dakota Review, Spring-Summer.
No Trace. Southern Review, Winter.

MALOON, JAMES
The Interlopers. Salmagundi, Summer.

MEEHAN, THOMAS
The Pied Piper. The New Yorker, July 4.

MERWIN, W. S.
We Have Nothing to Fear. The New Yorker. February 8.

MITCHELL, DON
Diesel. Shenandoah, Summer.
MONTGOMERY, MARION
The Decline and Fall of Officer Ferguson. Georgia Review, Summer.
MORRIS, WRIGHT
Magic. Southern Review, Winter.
MOSS, ROSE
Exile. Massachusetts Review, Spring.

NOWELL-SMITH, SIMON
The Case of Arthur Craven. Malahat Review, January.

OATES, JOYCE CAROL
Through the Looking-Glass. Malahat Review, July.
The Dark. Southwest Review, Autumn.
Where I Live and What I Lived For. Virginia Quarterly Review, Autumn.
The Demons. Southern Review, Winter.
O'CONNOR, FLANNERY
The Barber. Atlantic October.
O'CONNOR, PHILIP F.
The Gift Bearer. Southern Review, Summer.
OLSEN, TILLIE
Requa. Iowa Review, Summer.

PARA-FIGUEREDO, A.
The Estevez Holograph. Kansas Quarterly, Winter.
PRASHKER, IVAN
Shirt Talk. Harper's, January.
PRESCOTT, KATHERINE
Crazy Willie and the Choco-Bars. Redbook, November.
PROULX, E. A.
The Baroque Marble. Seventeen, September.

RANCK, HELEN
The Bush. Yale Review, Autumn.
RODEWALD, FRED
The Needle. Arlington Quarterly, Winter.
ROSE, CHARLES
The Buzzard. Sewanee Review, Autumn.
ROTH, PHILIP
Salad Days. Modern Occasions, Fall.
RUSH, NORMAN
In Late Youth. Epoch, Fall.

SANDBERG-DIMENT, ERIK
The Singing of Condors. South Dakota Review, Spring-Summer.
SANTIAGO, DANNY
The Somebody. Redbook, February.
SEGAL, LORE
Euphoria in the Root Cellar New American Review, #10.
SHAW, JOAN KATHERINE
At the Dressing Table, Brushing My Hair. Western Humanities Review, Summer.
SIKES, SHIRLEY
The Rose-Petal Necklace. Four Quarters, May.
SILVERTON, DORIS
The Mexican Maid. McCall's, October.
SINCLAIR, THOMAS
I've Loved Only You, I Think. Quartet, Fall.
SINGER, ISAAC BASHEVIS
Altele. TriQuarterly, Spring.
SMITH, WILLIAM
A Patchwork Hog in the Petunia World. New American Review, #8.
SORRELLS, ROBERT T.
A Mature and Civilized Relationship. Arlington Quarterly, Winter.
STRONG, JONATHAN
Xavier Fereira's unfinished book: chapter one. TriQuarterly, Spring.
STUART, JANE
This Business of Roses. Green River Review, Spring.
SULKIN, SIDNEY
In Place of Parent. Michigan Quarterly Review, Fall.
Miserable Catullus. Southwest Review, Winter.

TUSHNET, LEONARD
The Klausners. Prairie Schooner, Spring.

VALGARDSON, W. D.
Bloodflowers. Tamarack Review, Fall.

WEATHERS, WINSTON
St. Stephen's Green. Literary Review, Winter.

WEAVER, GORDON A.
Wouldn't I? South Dakota Review, Spring-Summer.

WEESNER, THEODORE
Irene, goodnight. Atlantic, January.
The Trainee. Esquire, January.

WEGNER, ROBERT E.
The Sentimentalist. Epoch, Winter.

WELBURN, RON
The Nightsong of Dashiki Henry. Intro, #3.

WOIWODE, L.
The Suitor. McCall's, January.
The Beginning of Grief. The New Yorker, October 17.
Burning the Couch. Atlantic, November.

WOODLEY, INEZ
Roses From My Father. Virginia Quarterly Review, Summer.

WOOLRICH, CORNELL
New York Blues. Ellery Queen's Mystery Magazine, December.

ZIMMERMAN, SETH
Autumn. Transatlantic Review, Summer.

II. *Foreign Authors*

ANONYMOUS
The Candidate. Massachusetts Review, Summer.

BECKETT, SAMUEL
Lessness. Evergreen Review, July.

BORGES, JORGE LUIS
The Meeting. The New Yorker, August 8.

CLARKE, AUSTIN C.
What Happened? Evergreen Review, December.

COLUM, PADRAIC
Another World From Mine. The New Yorker, October 10.

GARLAND, PATRICK
A Lull. Transatlantic Review, Summer.

JACOBSEN, DAN
The Rape of Tamar. Harper's, August.

O'FAOLAIN, SEAN
Of Sanctity and Whiskey. Playboy, September.

ROBINSON, BARBARA
Louisa May and the Facts of Life. Redbook, April.

WARNER, SYLVIA TOWNSEND
At the Stroke of Midnight. The New Yorker, September 12.
The Green Torso. The New Yorker, August 22.

YEHOSHUA, A. B.
Another Hot Day. Audience, Vol. 1, #1.

Distinctive Short Stories, 1970

I. *American Authors*

ADLER, RENATA
Collect Calls. The New Yorker, October 24.

ALT, ROBERT
Air Conditioning. South Carolina Review, May.

AMIDON, BILL
Cannonball Catchers. Evergreen Review, March.

ASTON, JOHN
Another Form of the Riddle. West Coast Review, January.

ATKINS, HARRY
We Could Go. Antaeus, Summer.

BANKS, RUSSELL
The Blizzard. Partisan Review, #4.

BAUMBACH, JONATHAN
Know Your Enemy. Epoch, Fall.

BEDARD, BRIAN
The Celebrated Return of Simon Laughing Owl. South Dakota Review, Autumn.

BENESCH, WALTER
The Double. Denver Quarterly, Spring.

BERGER, THOMAS
Son and Hair. Esquire February.

BERGSTEIN, ELEANOR
I'll Be Happy, Happy. Redbook, January.

BERKMAN, SYLVIA
Design Is All. Aphra, Winter.

BLISS, ALICE C.
The Trip "Home." Fiddlehead, October.

BOWLES, PAUL
Afternoon with Antaeus. Antaeus, Summer.

BREWSTER, ELIZABETH
Shivaree. Fiddlehead, May, June, July.

CAIN, EMILY
Mother Tiger. Redbook, September.

CARTER, ALBERT HOWARD
Cubs, Sox, and Maturation. Arizona Quarterly, Autumn.

CARVER, RAYMOND
Cartwheels. Western Humanities Review, Autumn.

CHAFFIN, LILLIE D.
The Scoring. Green River Review, Spring.

CHAY, MARIE
In Other People's Houses. Southwest Review, Winter.

CONNELL, EVAN S., JR.
The Caribbean Provedor. Southern Review, Summer.

CORRIGAN, MATTHEW
The Student Union. Windsor Review, Spring.

COWDIMAS, PETER
Dog-Burial. Massachusetts Review, Spring.

Cullinan, Elizabeth
Nora's Friends. The New Yorker, August 29.

Davis, George
Coming Home. Amistad, I.

de Gramont, Sanche
Boul' Mich. Harper's, October.

Devine, Richard
Parenthesis. Intro, #3.

Dixon, Kent
Hamlin Revisited. Iowa Review, Summer.

Dokey, Richard
St. Agnes' Day. Southwest Review, Winter.

Downey, Harris
Portrait of a Professor. Southern Review, Summer.

Drum, Charles S.
The Digger Indians. Southwest Review, Summer.

Dunn, Pat
The Beach. Intro, #3.

Eaton, Charles Edward
The Case of the Missing Photographs. Sewanee Review, Autumn.

Eldredge, Lawrence
Autumn Day. Falcon, Summer.

Engel, Marian
The Honeymoon Festival. Canadian Forum, Nov.-Dec.

Esslinger, Pat M.
The Life and Death of a Roustabout. Kansas Quarterly, Winter.

Feldman, Seth
The Famous Black Snow of New York. Prism International, Autumn.

Fernandez, Augustine
The Great Supper of Elentino Pombo. Southwest Review, Winter.

Fetler, Andrew
The Mandolin. Malahat Review, July.

Fine, Warren
The Mousechildren and the Famous Collector. New American Review, #9.

Finn, Seamus
And Still My Body Drank. Kansas Quarterly, Winter.

Fox, John P.
Torchy and My Old Man. Denver Quarterly, Fall.

Freitag, George
A Garden of Flowers. The New Yorker, February 7.

Fremlin, Celia
Don't Be Frightened. Ellery Queen's Mystery Magazine, October.

Ganz, Earl
Confabulation. Epoch, Winter.

Gold, Herbert
The Detroit Sons. Atlantic, February.

Goldberg, Victoria L.
Mrs. Washburn's Baby. Satire, Spring.

Goldknopf, David
Sky-View. University Review, June.

Goodwin, Janet
Soot. Colorado Quarterly, Autumn.

Greenberg, Alvin
A Brief Chronology of Death and Night. New American Review, #10.

Greene, George
The Last of the Listeners. Prairie Schooner, Spring.

Gusewelle, C. W.
Lagos Boy. Antioch Review, Spring.

Hacikyan, Agop
How Many Waves Can You Count in a Day? Ararat, Spring.

Hall, Martha Lacy
The Peaceful Eye. Southern Review, Autumn.

Halperin, Irving
One of the Boys. Kansas Quarterly, Winter.

Harter, Evelyn
A Congenial Duty. Northwest Review, Fall.
The Red Dot. Southwest Review, Autumn.

Hayden, Julie
Walking With Charlie. The New Yorker, November 7.

HERENDEEN, WARREN
Baby Horrid Among the Constubble and the Crows. Transatlantic Review, Summer.

HERMANN, JOHN
The Gold Watch. Northwest Review, Fall.

HIGGINS, GEORGE V.
Dillon Explained That He Was Frightened. North American Review, Fall.

HOBBS, JERRY R.
Flies, Flies, Flies. South Dakota Review, Spring-Summer.

HODGINS, JACK
A Matter of Necessity. Canadian Forum, January.

HOFFMAN, A. C.
A Winter's Tale. Western Humanities Review, Spring.

HORNE, LEWIS B.
Thor Thoorsen's Book of Days. Cimmarron Review, July.

HYDE, ELEANOR
In Name Only. Satire, Spring.

JACKMAN, OLIVER
A Poet of the People. Amistad, I.

KAHN, STEVEN
Connelly. Intro, #3.

KING, PAMELA
The Secret. Seventeen, January.

KITAIF, THEODORE
The Auricle. South Dakota Review, Spring.

KITTREDGE, WILLIAM
Native Cutthroat. Northwest Review, Winter.

KLEIN, NORMAN
The Betrayal. Prairie Schooner, Fall.

KOERTE, HELEN
The Chinese Music Box. Fiddlehead, July.

LAMB, MARGARET
Management. Aphra, Autumn.

LARSEN, RICHARD B.
La Tahitienne. New England Review, Jan.-Feb.

LEON, JOHN A.
The Closet Creature Reinterpreted. Fiddlehead, July.

LEVINE, GARY
Every Other Bar But This One. Intro, #3.

LEVOY, MYRON
Murillo's Eyes, But Blue. Massachusetts Review, Autumn.

L'HEUREUX, JOHN
Something Missing. Atlantic, August.

LITTIG, MARINA
Ambushed by the Naked Ones. Transatlantic Review, Summer.

LIVSEY, CHARLENE DEPEW
Blue Was His Color. Twigs, VI.

LYONS, EDWARD
The Deserted. New Renaissance Vol. I., #4.

MCCARTHY, MARY
A Small Death in the Rue de Pennes. Playboy, August.

MCNAMARA, EUGENE
The Drowned Girl. Western Humanities Review, Summer.
Down the Road. Malahat Review, October.

MACDOUGALL, RUTH DOAN
The Morning Man. Redbook, September.

MACEWEN, GWENDOLYN
The Day of the Twelve Princes. Tamarack Review.

MADDEN, DAVID
The House of Pearl. Twigs, VI.

MARSHALL, LENORE
Dialogue on a Cliff. Michigan Quarterly Review, Winter.

MASSA, RONALD
Estragon, My Brother. Prism International, Summer.

MATHESON, RICHARD
Button, Button. Playboy, June.

MAYR, WILLIAM
Coming-Out Night. Phylon, Fall.

MAZUR, JULIAN
Storm. Shenandoah, Autumn.

MERWIN, W. S.
The Death-Defying Tartonis. The New Yorker, January 10.
Four Pieces. New American Review, #9.
The Cliff Dance. Antaeus, Summer.

The Fountains. The New Yorker, July 11.

MIDDLETON, ED

Pipe Cleaner. Greensboro Review, Spring.

NEUBERG, PAUL

Drop Dead. Partisan Review, #2.

NISSENSON, HUGH

Lamentations. The New Yorker, September 19.

NOWLAN, ALDEN

Kevin and Stephanie. Tamarack Review, #54.

OATES, JOYCE CAROL

Wednesday. Esquire, August.

Dreams. Prairie Schooner, Winter.

O'DONNELL, TERENCE

The Pilgrimage. Atlantic, September.

OEHLER, MIKE

The Road. Southwest Review, Summer.

OLIVER, CHARLES

Down From the Sunland. Cimarron Review, January.

Wilder Than the White Rose. Epoch, Winter.

ORR, DANIEL

The Night Joy Nearly Died. Kansas Quarterly, Winter.

PANSING, NELLIE PELLETIER

The Dark Side. Twigs, VI.

PAPALEO, JOSEPH

The Word to Go. Harper's, November.

POUND, E. F.

The Girl in the Orange Fish. North American Review, Fall.

PRESLEY, JAMES

The Soldier. Kansas Quarterly, Winter.

RANCK, HELEN

An Hour in the Evening. Michigan Quarterly Review, Fall.

RANDALL, FLORENCE ENGEL

The Cat. Virginia Quarterly Review, Summer.

REED, ISHMAEL

D Herorcism of Noxon D. Awful. Amistad, I.

REID, BARBARA

The Old Lady. Sewanee Review, Autumn.

RICE, STAN

The Dogchain Gang. Evergreen Review, November.

ROBIN, MAX

Malki Was a Queen. National Jewish Monthly, December.

ROBIN, RALPH

Little Sister's Electric Finger. Western Humanities Review, Summer.

ROGIN, GILBERT

Taking Stock. The New Yorker, August 22.

ROSS, JAMES

Army Was Always Talking, See? Canadian Forum, June.

SALTER, JAMES

The Cinema. Paris Review, Summer.

SHAW, IRWIN

Thomas in Elysium. Playboy, January.

SCHRAM, IRENE

That Old Soft-Shoe. Prism International, Autumn.

SHATRAU, HARRIET B.

My Mother's Friend. DeKalb Literary Arts Journal, Spring.

SHELBY, KERMIT

Lonesome Johnny. North American Review, Fall.

SILBERT, LAYLE

The Double Hook. South Dakota Review, Spring-Summer.

SILVERMAN, ROSEMARY

The Best of Luck. Southern Humanities Review, Summer.

A Summer in the Country. Malahat Review, October.

SKILLINGS, R. D.

Deadwatch. Prairie Schooner, Winter.

SMYTH, GEORGE W.

Blue Butterflies and White Sacrifices. Southwest Review, Autumn.

SNYDER, RICHARD
Over the Fourth. North American Review, Fall.

STEEGMULLER, FRANCIS
The Griffe of the Master. Atlantic, October.

STERN, RICHARD
Veni, Vivi . . . Wendt. Paris Review, Summer.

STRONG, JONATHAN
Invoking Minerva. Shenandoah, Summer.

SUTTON, WILLIAM
A Hole Is A Place. Cimarron Review, January.

SWEAT, JOSEPH
Father Buh Buh Boo. Harper's, September.

TAYLOR, ELEANOR ROSS
About Love. Sewanee Review, Spring.

THAYER, DOUGLAS H.
The Turtle's Smile. Prairie Schooner, Fall.

THOMPSON, EARL
The Header, the Rigger, the Captain. Esquire, September.

THOMPSON, KENT
The Complicated Camera: Jeremy & Greta. Windsor Review, Spring.

THOMPSON, MARILYN
The Silence of Sad, Exotic Paranoia. Northwest Review, Fall.

TOLNAY, THOMAS
Pigeon Moon. Fiddlehead, October.

TRAYNOR, R. L.
A Sack of Muskmelons. South Dakota Review, Spring-Summer.

TRICON, BARBARA
Child of God. Carolina Quarterly, Fall.

TRIVELPIECE, LAUREL
Gentle Constancy. Denver Quarterly, Fall.

TUROW, SCOTT
The Carp Fish. Transatlantic Review, Summer.

ULLIAN, ROBERT
The Motherhood. Esquire, December.

WALTERS, THOMAS N.
Go Softly All My Years. Denver Quarterly, Summer.

WARNHOFF, S. M.
Center Street. Cimarron Review, January.

WEATHERS, WINSTON
The Man Who Was Tricked by God. Kansas Quarterly, Winter.

WEISS, MIRIAM
Mal did Denti. Colorado Quarterly, Autumn.

WILDMAN, JOHN HAZARD
The Do-It-Yourself-Trap. Southern Review, Autumn.

WILLIAMS, THOMAS
Paranoia. Esquire, November.

WILSON, WILLIAM E.
Spain Is A Fine Country. Colorado Quarterly, Summer.

WISER, WILLIAM
Where Sheep May Safely Graze. Redbook, October.

WOLITZER, HILMA
The Sex Maniac. Esquire, December.

II. *Foreign Authors*

ALFORD, NORMAN
To The Uncharted Land. Fiddlehead, May, June, July.
The Bungalow. Malahat Review, July.

HERNÁNDEZ, JUAN JOSE
The Farewell Party. Cimarron Review, October.

JOHNSON, B. S.
What Did You Say the Name of the Place Was? Transatlantic Review, Summer.

LITVINOV, IVY
Apartheid. The New Yorker, September 19.

The Boy Who Laughed. The New Yorker, October 31.
Holiday Home. The New Yorker, November 28.

SALAMA, HANNU
A Girl and a Bottle. Literary Review, Fall.

SWEET, WILLIAM T.
Boxcars. Northwest Review, Summer.

TOPOR, ROLAND
Four Tales. TriQuarterly, Spring.

WALKER, TED
Carnival. The New Yorker, December 5.

WARNER, SYLVIA TOWNSEND
Furnival's Hoopoe. The New Yorker, January 3.

Addresses of American and Canadian Magazines Publishing Short Stories

Amistad, Vintage Books, 33 West 60th Street, New York, New York 10023
Ann Arbor Review, 115 Allen Drive, Ann Arbor, Michigan 48104
Antaeus, % Villiers Publications, Ltd., London, N.W. 3, England
Antioch Review, 212 Xenia Avenue, Yellow Springs, Ohio 45387
Aphra, R.F.D. Box 355, Springtown, Pennsylvania 18081
Ararat, 109 East 40th Street, New York, New York 10016
Argosy, 205 East 42nd Street, New York, New York 10017
Arizona Quarterly, University of Arizona, Tucson, Arizona 85721
Arlington Quarterly, Box 366, University Station, Arlington, Texas 76010
Atlantic, 8 Arlington Street, Boston, Massachusetts 02116
Audience, 207 East 32nd Street, New York, New York 10016
Bennington Review, Box N, Bennington College, Bennington, Vermont 05201
California Review, 280 East Mountain Drive, Santa Barbara, California 91303
Canadian Forum, 30 Front Street West, Toronto, Ontario, Canada
Carleton Miscellany, Carleton College, Northfield, Minnesota 55057
Carolina Quarterly, P.O. Box 117, Chapel Hill, North Carolina 27514
Cavalier, 67 West 44th Street, New York, New York 10036
Charm, Glamour, 420 Lexington Avenue, New York, New York 10017
Chicago Review, Reynolds Club, University of Chicago, Chicago, Illinois 60637
Cimarron Review, 203B Morrill Hall, Oklahoma State University, Stillwater, Oklahoma 74074
Colorado Quarterly, University of Colorado, Boulder, Colorado 80303
Colorado State Review, 360 Liberal Arts, Colorado State University, Fort Collins, Colorado 80521
Commentary, 165 East 56th Street, New York, New York 10022
Cosmopolitan, 1775 Broadway, New York, New York 10019
Critic, 210 West Madison Street, Chicago, Illinois 60601
December, Box 274, Western Springs, Illinois 60558
Dekalb Literary Arts Journal, Dekalb College, 555 Indian Creek Drive, Clarkston, Georgia 30021

Denver Quarterly, University of Denver, Denver, Colorado 80210
Descant, Texas Christian University, Fort Worth, Texas 76129
Ellery Queen's Mystery Magazine, 219 Park Avenue South, New York, New York 10003
Epoch, 252 Goldwin Smith Hall, Cornell University, Ithaca, New York 14850
Esquire, 488 Madison Avenue, New York, New York 10022
Evergreen Review, 80 University Place, New York, New York 10003
Evidence, Box 245, Station F, Toronto, Ontario, Canada
Falcon, Mansfield State College, Mansfield, Pennsylvania 16933
Fantasy and Science Fiction, Box 271, Rockville Centre, New York 11571
Fiddlehead, Department of English, University of New Brunswick, Fredericton, New Brunswick, Canada
Florida Quarterly, University of Florida, 330 Reitz Union, Gainesville, Florida 32601
Forum, Ball State University, Muncie, Indiana 47302
Four Quarters, LaSalle College, Philadelphia, Pennsylvania 19143
Georgia Review, University of Georgia, Athens, Georgia 30601
Good Housekeeping, 959 Eighth Avenue, New York, New York 10019
Green River Review, Box 594, Owensboro, Kentucky 42301
Greensboro Review, University of North Carolina, Box 96, McIver Building, Greensboro, North Carolina 27401
Harper's Bazaar, 572 Madison Avenue, New York, New York 10022
Harper's Magazine, 49 East 33rd Street, New York, New York 10016
Holiday, 641 Lexington Avenue, New York, New York 10022
Hudson Review, 65 East 55th Street, New York, New York 10022
Husk, Cornell College, Mount Vernon, Iowa 52314
Infinity, Route 3, Box 104, South Point, Ohio 45680
Inland, Box 685, Salt Lake City, Utah 84101
Intro, Associated Writing Program, Brown University, Providence, Rhode Island 02912
Iowa Review, University of Iowa, Iowa City, Iowa 52240
Kansas Quarterly, Kansas State University, Manhattan, Kansas 66502
Ladies' Home Journal, 1270 Avenue of the Americas, New York, New York 10022
Laurel Review, West Virginia Wesleyan College, Buckhannon, West Virginia 26201
Literary Review, Fairleigh Dickinson University, Teaneck, New Jersey 07666
McCall's, 230 Park Avenue, New York, New York 10017
Mademoiselle, 420 Lexington Avenue, New York, New York 10022
Malahat Review, University of Victoria, Victoria, British Columbia, Canada
Manhattan Review, 229 East 12th Street, New York, New York 10003
Massachusetts Review, University of Massachusetts, Amherst, Massachusetts 01003

Michigan Quarterly Review, University of Michigan, Ann Arbor, Michigan 48104
Midstream, 515 Park Avenue, New York, New York 10022
Minnesota Review, Box 4086, University Station, Minneapolis, Minnesota 55414
Modern Occasions, 5A Bigelow Street, Cambridge, Massachusetts 02139
Motive, Box 871, Nashville, Tennessee 37202
National Jewish Monthly, 315 Lexington Avenue, New York, New York 10016
New American Review, 630 Fifth Avenue, New York, New York 10020
New Campus Review, Metropolitan State College, Room 608, 250 West 14th Street, Denver, Colorado 80201
New England Review, P.O. Box 5443, Hamden, Connecticut 06518
New Orleans Review, Loyola University, New Orleans, Louisiana 70118
New Renaissance, 9 Heath Road, Arlington, Massachusetts 02174
New Yorker, 24 West 43rd Street, New York, New York 10036
North American Review, University of Northern Iowa, Cedar Falls, Iowa 50613
Northern Minnesota Review, Bemidji State College, Bemidji, Minnesota 56601
Northwest Review, Erb Memorial Union, University of Oregon, Eugene, Oregon 97403
Occident, Eshelman Hall, University of California, Berkeley, California 94720
Ohio University Review, Athens, Ohio 45701
Orbit, Milford, Pennsylvania 18337
Panache, 153 East 84th Street, New York, New York 10028
Paris Review, 45-39 171 Place, Flushing, New York 11358
Partisan Review, 22 East 17th Street, New York, New York 10003
Pathway Magazine, P.O. Box 1483, Charleston, West Virginia 25325
Penthouse, 1560 Broadway, New York, New York 10036
Per Se, Box 2377, Stanford, California 94305
Perspective, Washington University Post Office, St. Louis, Missouri 63130
Phoenix, Ida Noyes Hall, 1212 East 59th Street, Chicago, Illinois 60637
Phylon, Atlanta University, Atlanta, Georgia 30314
Playboy, 232 East Ohio Street, Chicago, Illinois 60611
Prairie Schooner, Andrews Hall, University of Nebraska, Lincoln, Nebraska 68508
Prism International, University of British Columbia, Vancouver, Canada
Quarterly Review of Literature, 26 Haslet Avenue, Princeton, New Jersey 08540
Quartet, 1701 Puryear Drive (No. 232), College Station, Texas 77840
Queens Quarterly, Room 524, Humanities Building, Queens University, Kingston, Ontario, Canada
Quest, Box 207, Cathedral Station, New York, New York 10025

Redbook, 230 Park Avenue, New York, New York 10017
Red Cedar Review, 325 Morrill Hall, Michigan State University, East Lansing, Michigan 48823
Reflections, Box 109, Chapel Hill, North Carolina 27414
Roanoke Review, Box 268, Roanoke College, Salem, Virginia 24153
Salmagundi Magazine, Skidmore College, Saratoga Springs, New York 12866
Satire, State University College, Oneonta, New York 13820
Seneca Review, Box 115, Hobart and William Smith Colleges, Geneva, New York 14456
Seventeen, 320 Park Avenue, New York, New York 10022
Sewanee Review, University of the South, Sewanee, Tennessee 37375
Shenandoah, Box 722, Lexington, Virginia 24450
Sound, 15918 60th West, Edmonds, Washington 98020
South Carolina Review, Box 28661, Furman University, Greenville, South Carolina 29613
South Dakota Review, Box 11, University Exchange, University of South Dakota, Vermillion, South Dakota 57069
Southern Humanities Review, Auburn University, Auburn, Alabama 36830
Southern Review, Louisiana State University, Baton Rouge, Louisiana 70803
Southwest Review, Southern Methodist University, Dallas, Texas 75222
Tamarack Review, Box 157, Postal Station K, Toronto, Ontario, Canada
Texas Quarterly, Box 7527, University Station, Austin, Texas 78712
Transatlantic Review, Box 3348, Grand Central P.O., New York, New York 10017
Trans Pacific, Box 486, Lapotte, Colorado 80535
TriQuarterly, Northwestern University, Evanston, Illinois 60201
Twigs, Hilltop Editions, Pikeville College Press, Pikeville, Kentucky 41501
University Review, University of Missouri, 5100 Rockhill Road, Kansas City, Missouri 64110
Virginia Quarterly, 1 West Range, Charlottesville, Virginia 22903
Voyages, 2034 Allen Place, N. W., Washington, D.C. 20009
Wascana Review, Wascana Parkway, Regina, Saskatchewan, Canada
West Coast Review, Simon Fraser University, Burnaby 2, British Columbia, Canada
Western Humanities Review, University of Utah, Salt Lake City, Utah 84112
Western Review, Western New Mexico University, Silver City, New Mexico 88061
Windsor Review, University of Windsor, Windsor, Ontario, Canada
Wisconsin Review, Wisconsin State University, Oshkosh, Wisconsin 54901
Yale Review, Box 1729, New Haven, Connecticut 06520